RISING TIDES

Series

Irish Born Trilogy
BORN IN FIRE
BORN IN ICE
BORN IN SHAME

Dream Trilogy
DARING TO DREAM
HOLDING THE DREAM
FINDING THE DREAM

Chesapeake Bay Saga
SEA SWEPT
RISING TIDES
INNER HARBOR
CHESAPEAKE BLUE

Gallaghers of Ardmore Trilogy
JEWELS OF THE SUN
TEARS OF THE MOON
HEART OF THE SEA

Three Sisters Island Trilogy
DANCE UPON THE AIR
HEAVEN AND EARTH
FACE THE FIRE

Key Trilogy
KEY OF LIGHT
KEY OF KNOWLEDGE
KEY OF VALOR

In the Garden Trilogy
BLUE DAHLIA
BLACK ROSE
RED LILY

Circle Trilogy
MORRIGAN'S CROSS
DANCE OF THE GODS
VALLEY OF SILENCE

Sign of Seven Trilogy
BLOOD BROTHERS
THE HOLLOW
THE PAGAN STONE

Bride Quartet
VISION IN WHITE
BED OF ROSES
SAVOR THE MOMENT
HAPPY EVER AFTER

The Inn BoonsBoro Trilogy
THE NEXT ALWAYS
THE LAST BOYFRIEND
THE PERFECT HOPE

RISING TIDES

NORA ROBERTS

BERKLEY BOOKS, NEW YORK

THE BERKLEY PUBLISHING GROUP
Published by the Penguin Group
Penguin Group (USA) Inc.
375 Hudson Street, New York, New York 10014, USA

USA | Canada | UK | Ireland | Australia | New Zealand | India | South Africa | China

Penguin Books Ltd., Registered Offices: 80 Strand, London WC2R 0RL, England
For more information about the Penguin Group, visit penguin.com.

Library of Congress Cataloging-in-Publication Data

Roberts, Nora.
Rising tides / Nora Roberts.—Berkley trade paperback edition.
pages ; cm.
ISBN 978-0-425-26276-4
1. Brothers—Fiction.   2. Chesapeake Bay Region (Md. and Va.)—Fiction.   3. Eastern Shore
(Md. and Va.)—Fiction.   4. Domestic fiction.   I. Title.
PS3568.O243R57 2013
813'.54—dc23
2013001866

PUBLISHING HISTORY
Jove mass-market edition / August 1998
Berkley trade paperback edition / June 2013

PRINTED IN THE UNITED STATES OF AMERICA

10 9 8 7 6 5 4 3 2 1

Cover design by Rita Frangie.
Cover photographs: "Fishing Boat" by piotrwzk/Shutterstock; "Sand Dune" by
Nickolay Khoroshkov/Shutterstock; "Sea" by Mikhail Zahranichny/Shutterstock; "Wooden Panel" by
Dim Dimich/Shutterstock; "Chains" by Yezepchyk Oleksandr/Shutterstock; "Rough Wood" by
JoAnn Snover/Shutterstock.
Background photograph by simon@naffarts.co.uk/Shutterstock.
Photograph of author by Bruce Wilder.
Inside cover photographs: "Antique Fishing Rods" by Nick/Shutterstock;
"Fishing Boat Near Shore" by Chyrko Olena/Shutterstock.

For the witty and delightful Christine Dorsey
Yes, Chris, I mean you.

RISING TIDES

Prologue

ETHAN climbed out of his dreams and rolled out of bed. It was still dark, but he habitually started his day before night yielded to dawn. It suited him, the quiet, the simple routine, the hard work that would follow.

He'd never forgotten to be grateful that he'd been able to make this choice and have this life. Though the people responsible for giving him both the choice and the life were dead, for Ethan, the pretty house on the water still echoed with their voices. He would often find himself glancing up from his lone breakfast in the kitchen expecting to see his mother shuffle in, yawning, her red hair a wild tangle from sleep, her eyes half blind with it.

And though she'd been gone nearly seven years, there was a comfort in that homey morning image.

It was more painful to think of the man who had become his father. Raymond Quinn's death was still too fresh after a mere three months for there to be comfort. And the circumstances surrounding it were both ugly and unexplained. His death had come in a single-car accident in broad daylight on a dry road, on a March day that had only hinted of spring. The car was traveling fast, with its driver unable—or unwilling—to control it on a curve. Tests had proven that there had been no physical reason for Ray to crash into the telephone pole.

But there was evidence of an emotional reason, and that lay heavy on Ethan's heart.

Ethan thought of it as he readied himself for the day—giving his hair, still damp from the shower, a cursory swipe with his comb, which did nothing to tame the thick waves of sun-bleached brown. He shaved in the foggy mirror, his quiet blue eyes sober as he scraped lather and a night's worth of beard from a tanned, bony face that held secrets he rarely chose to share.

There was a scar that rode along the left side of his jawline— courtesy of his oldest brother and patiently stitched up by his mother. It had been fortunate, Ethan thought as he rubbed a thumb absently over the faded line, that their mother had been a doctor. One of her three sons was usually in need of first aid.

Ray and Stella had taken them in, three half-grown boys, all wild, all damaged, all strangers. And had made them a family.

Then months before his death, Ray had taken in another.

Seth DeLauter belonged to them now. Ethan never questioned it. Others did, he knew. There was talk buzzing through the little town of St. Christopher's that Seth was not just another of Ray Quinn's strays but his illegitimate son. A child conceived with another woman while his wife was still alive. A younger woman.

Ethan could ignore the talk, but it was impossible to ignore the fact that ten-year-old Seth looked at you with Ray Quinn's eyes.

There were shadows in those eyes that Ethan also recognized. The wounded recognized the wounded. He knew that Seth's life, before Ray had taken him on, had been a nightmare. He'd lived through one himself.

The kid was safe now, Ethan thought as he pulled on baggy cotton pants and a faded work shirt. He was a Quinn now, even if the legalities hadn't been completely worked out. They had Phillip to deal with that. Ethan figured his detail-mad brother would handle that end of things with the lawyer. And he knew that Cameron, the eldest of the Quinn boys, had managed to form a tenuous bond with Seth.

Fumbled his way to it, Ethan thought with a half smile. It had been like watching two angry tomcats spit and claw. Now that Cam had married the pretty social worker, things might just settle down some.

Ethan preferred a settled life.

They had battles yet, with the insurance company refusing to honor Ray's policy because there was suspicion of suicide. Ethan's stomach clutched, and he took a moment to will himself relaxed again. His father would never have killed himself. The Mighty Quinn had always faced his problems and had taught his sons to do the same.

But it was a cloud over the family that refused to blow away. There were others, too. The sudden appearance in St. Christopher's of Seth's mother and her accusations of sexual molestation, made to the dean of the college where Ray had taught English literature. That hadn't held—there'd been too many lies, too many shifts in her story. But there was no denying that his father had been shaken. There was no denying that shortly after Gloria DeLauter had left St. Chris again, Ray had gone away, too.

And he'd returned with the boy.

Then there was the letter found in the car after Ray's accident. An obvious blackmail threat from the DeLauter woman. There was the fact that Ray had given her money, a great deal of money.

Now she had disappeared again. Ethan wanted her to stay gone, but he knew the talk wouldn't stop until all the answers were clear.

Nothing he could do about it, Ethan reminded himself. He stepped out into the hall, gave a quick knock on the door opposite his. Seth's groan was followed by a sleepy mutter, then an annoyed curse. Ethan kept going, heading downstairs. He had no doubt that Seth would bitch again about getting up so early. But with Cam and Anna in Italy on their honeymoon, and Phillip in Baltimore until the weekend, it was Ethan's job to get the boy up, to get him headed over to a friend's house to stay until it was time to leave for school.

Crabbing season was in full swing, and a waterman's day started before the sun. So until Cam and Anna returned, so did Seth's.

The house was silent and dark, but he moved through it easily. He had a house of his own now, but part of the deal in gaining guardianship of Seth had been for the three brothers to live under the same roof and share the responsibilities.

Ethan didn't mind responsibilities, but he missed his little house, his privacy and the ease of what had been his life.

He flicked on the lights in the kitchen. It had been Seth's turn to clean it up after dinner the evening before, and Ethan noted that he'd done a half-assed job. Ignoring the cluttered and sticky surface of the table, he moved directly to the stove.

Simon, his dog, stretched lazily out of his curl. His tail thumped on the floor. Ethan set the coffee to brew, greeting the retriever with an absent scratch on the head.

The dream was coming back to him now, the one he'd been caught in just before waking. He and his father, out on the workboat checking crab pots. Just the two of them. The sun had been blinding bright and hot, the water mirror-clear and still. It had been so vivid, he thought now, even the smells of water and fish and sweat.

His father's voice, so well remembered, had carried over the sounds of engine and gulls.

"I knew you'd look after Seth, the three of you."

"You didn't have to die to test that out." There was resentment in Ethan's tone, an underlying anger he hadn't allowed himself to admit while awake.

"It wasn't what I had in mind, either," Ray said lightly, culling crabs from the pot under the float that Ethan had gaffed. His thick orange fisherman's gloves glowed in the sun. "You can trust me on that. You got some good steamers here and plenty of sooks."

Ethan glanced at the wire pot full of crabs, automatically noting size and number. But it wasn't the catch that mattered, not here, not now. "You want me to trust you, but you don't explain."

Ray glanced back, tipping up the bright red cap he wore over his dramatic silver mane. The wind tugged at his hair, teased the caricature of John Steinbeck gracing his loose T-shirt into rippling over his broad chest. The great American writer held a sign claiming he would work for food, but he didn't look too happy about it.

In contrast, Ray Quinn glowed with health and energy, ruddy cheeks where deep creases only seemed to celebrate a full and contented mood of a vigorous man in his sixties with years yet to live.

"You've got to find your own way, your own answers." Ray smiled at Ethan out of brilliantly blue eyes, and Ethan could see the creases deepen around them. "It means more that way. I'm proud of you."

Ethan felt his throat burn, his heart squeeze. Routinely he rebaited the pot, then watched the orange floats bob on the water. "For what?"

"For being. Just for being Ethan."

"I should've come around more. I shouldn't have left you alone so much."

"That's a crock." Now Ray's voice was both irritated and

impatient. "I wasn't some old invalid. It's going to piss me off if you think that way, blame yourself for not looking after me, for Christ's sake. Same way you wanted to blame Cam for going off to live in Europe—and even Phillip for going off to Baltimore. Healthy birds leave the nest. Your mother and I raised healthy birds."

Before Ethan could speak, Ray raised a hand. It was such a typical gesture, the professor making a point and refusing interruption, that Ethan had to smile. "You missed them. That's why you wanted to be mad at them. They left, you stayed, and you missed having them around. Well, you've got them back now, don't you?"

"Looks that way."

"And you've got yourself a pretty sister-in-law, the beginnings of a boatbuilding business, and this . . ." Ray gestured to take in the water, the bobbing floats, the tall, glossily wet eelgrass on the verge where a lone egret stood like a marble pillar. "And inside you, you've got something Seth needs. Patience. Maybe too much of it in some areas."

"What's that supposed to mean?"

Ray sighed gustily. "There's something you don't have, Ethan, that you need. You've been waiting around and making excuses to yourself and doing not a damn thing to get it. You don't make a move soon, you're going to lose it again."

"What?" Ethan shrugged and maneuvered the boat to the next float. "I've got everything I need, and what I want."

"Don't ask yourself what, ask yourself who." Ray clucked his tongue, then gave his son a quick shoulder shake. "Wake up, Ethan."

And he had awakened, with the odd sensation of that big, familiar hand on his shoulder.

But, he thought as he brooded over his first cup of coffee, he still didn't have the answers.

CHAPTER

1

GOT us some nice peelers here, Cap'n." Jim Bodine culled crabs from the pot, tossing the marketable catch in the tank. He didn't mind the snapping claws—and had the scars on his thick hands to prove it. He wore the traditional gloves of his profession, but as any waterman could tell you, they wore out quick. And if there was a hole in them, by God, a crab would find it.

He worked steadily, his legs braced wide for balance on the rocking boat, his dark eyes squinting in a face weathered with age and sun and living. He might have been taken for fifty or eighty, and Jim didn't much care which end you stuck him in.

He always called Ethan "Cap'n," and rarely said more than one declarative sentence at a time.

Ethan altered course toward the next pot, his right hand nudging the steering stick that most watermen used rather than a wheel. At the same time, he operated the throttle and gear levels with his left.

There were constant small adjustments to be made with every foot of progress up the line of traps.

The Chesapeake Bay could be generous when she chose, but she liked to be tricky and make you work for her bounty.

Ethan knew the Bay as well as he knew himself. Often he thought he knew it better—the fickle moods and movements of the continent's largest estuary. For two hundred miles it flowed from north to south, yet it measured only four miles across where it brushed by Annapolis and thirty at the mouth of the Potomac River. St. Christopher's sat snug on Maryland's southern Eastern Shore, depending on its generosity, cursing it for its caprices.

Ethan's waters, his home waters, were edged with marshland, strung with flatland rivers with sharp shoulders that shimmered through thickets of gum and oak.

It was a world of tidal creeks and sudden shallows, where wild celery and widgeongrass rooted.

It had become his world, with its changing seasons, sudden storms, and always, always, the sounds and scents of the water.

Timing it, he grabbed his gaffing pole and in a practiced motion as smooth as a dance hooked the pot line and drew it into the pot puller.

In seconds, the pot rose out of the water, streaming with weed and pieces of old bait and crowded with crabs.

He saw the bright-red pincers of the full-grown females, or sooks, and the scowling eyes of the jimmies.

"Right smart of crabs," was all Jim had to say as he went to work, heaving the pot aboard as if it weighed ounces rather than pounds.

The water was rough today, and Ethan could smell a storm coming in. He worked the controls with his knees when he needed his hands for other tasks. And eyed the clouds beginning to boil together in the far western sky.

Time enough, he judged, to move down the line of traps in the gut of the bay and see how many more crabs had crawled into the pots. He knew Jim was hurting some for cash—and he needed all he could come by himself to keep afloat the fledgling boatbuilding business he and his brothers had started.

Time enough, he thought again, as Jim rebaited a pot with thawing fish parts and tossed it overboard. In leapfrog fashion, Ethan gaffed the next buoy.

Ethan's sleek Chesapeake Bay retriever, Simon, stood, front paws on the gunwale, tongue lolling. Like his master, he was rarely happier than when out on the water.

They worked in tandem, and in near silence, communicating with grunts, shrugs, and the occasional oath. The work was a comfort, since the crabs were plentiful. There were years when they weren't, years when it seemed the winter had killed them off or the waters would never warm up enough to tempt them to swim.

In those years, the watermen suffered. Unless they had another source of income. Ethan intended to have one, building boats.

The first boat by Quinn was nearly finished. And a little beauty it was, Ethan thought. Cameron had a second client on the line—some rich guy from Cam's racing days—so they would start another before long. Ethan never doubted that his brother would reel the money in.

They'd do it, he told himself, however doubtful and full of complaints Phillip was.

He glanced up at the sun, gauged the time—and the clouds sailing slowly, steadily eastward.

"We'll take them in, Jim."

They'd been eight hours on the water, a short day. But Jim didn't complain. He knew it wasn't so much the oncoming storm that had Ethan piloting the boat back up the gut. "Boy's home from school by now," he said.

"Yeah." And though Seth was self-sufficient enough to stay home alone for a time in the afternoon, Ethan didn't like to tempt fate. A boy of ten, and one with Seth's temperament, was a magnet for trouble.

When Cam returned from Europe in a couple of weeks, they would juggle Seth between them. But for now the boy was Ethan's responsibility.

The water in the Bay kicked, turning gunmetal gray now to mirror the sky, but neither men nor dog worried about the rocky ride as the boat crept up the steep fronts of the waves, then slid back down into the troughs. Simon stood at the bow now, head lifted, his ears blowing back in the wind, grinning his doggie grin. Ethan had built the workboat himself, and he knew she would do. As confident as the dog, Jim moved to the protection of the awning and, cupping his hands, lit a cigarette.

The waterfront of St. Chris was alive with tourists. The early days of June lured them out of the city, tempted them to drive from the suburbs of D.C. and Baltimore. He imagined they thought of the little town of St. Christopher's as quaint, with its narrow streets and clapboard houses and tiny shops. They liked to watch the crab pickers' fingers fly, and eat the flaky crab cakes or tell their friends they'd had a bowl of she-crab soup. They stayed in the bed-and-breakfasts— St. Chris was the proud home of no less than four—and they spent their money in the restaurants and gift shops.

Ethan didn't mind them. During the times when the Bay was stingy, tourism kept the town alive. And he thought there would come a time when some of those same tourists might decide that having a hand-built wooden sailboat was their heart's desire.

The wind picked up as Ethan moored at the dock. Jim jumped nimbly out to secure lines, his short legs and squat body giving him the look of a leaping frog wearing white rubber boots and a grease-smeared gimme cap.

At Ethan's careless hand signal, Simon plopped his butt down and stayed in the boat while the men worked to unload the day's catch and the wind made the boat's sun-faded green awning dance. Ethan watched Pete Monroe walk toward them, his iron-gray hair crushed under a battered billed hat, his stocky body outfitted in baggy khakis and a red checked shirt.

"Good catch today, Ethan."

Ethan smiled. He liked Mr. Monroe well enough, though the man had a bone-deep stingy streak. He ran Monroe's Crab House with a tightly closed fist. But, as far as Ethan could tell, every man's son who ran a picking plant complained about profits.

Ethan pushed his own cap back, scratched the nape of his neck where sweat and damp hair tickled. "Good enough."

"You're in early today."

"Storm's coming."

Monroe nodded. Already his crab pickers who had been working under the shade of striped awnings were preparing to move inside. Rain would drive the tourists inside as well, he knew, to drink coffee or eat ice cream sundaes. Since he was half owner of the Bayside Eats, he didn't mind.

"Looks like you got about seventy bushels there."

Ethan let his smile widen. Some might have said there was a hint of the pirate in the look. Ethan wouldn't have been insulted, but he'd have been surprised. "Closer to ninety, I'd say." He knew the market price, to the penny, but understood they would, as always, negotiate. He took out his negotiating cigar, lit it, and got to work.

The first fat drops of rain began to fall as he motored toward home. He figured he'd gotten a fair price for his crabs—his eighty-seven bushels of crabs. If the rest of the summer was as good, he was going to consider dropping another hundred pots next year, maybe hiring on a part-time crew.

Oystering on the Bay wasn't what it had been, not since parasites had killed off so many. That made the winters hard. A few good crabbing seasons were what he needed to dump the lion's share of the profits into the new business—and to help pay the lawyer's fee. His mouth tightened at that thought as he rode out the swells toward home.

They shouldn't need a damn lawyer. They shouldn't have to pay some slick-suited talker to clear their father's good name. It wouldn't stop the whispers around town anyway. Those would only stop when people found something juicier to chew on than Ray Quinn's life and death.

And the boy, Ethan mused, staring out over the water that trembled under the steady pelting of rain. There were some who liked to whisper about the boy who looked back at them with Ray Quinn's dark-blue eyes.

He didn't mind for himself. As far as Ethan was concerned people could wag their tongues about him until they fell out of their flapping mouths. But he minded, deeply, that anyone would speak a dark word about the man he'd loved with every beat of his heart.

So he would work his fingers numb to pay the lawyer. And he would do whatever it took to guard the child.

Thunder shook the sky, booming off the water like cannon fire. The light went dim as dusk, and those dark clouds burst wide to pour out solid sheets of rain. Still he didn't hurry as he docked at his home pier. A little more wet, to his mind, wouldn't kill him.

As if in agreement with the sentiment, Simon leaped out to swim to shore while Ethan secured the lines. He gathered up his lunch pail, and with his waterman's boots thwacking wetly against the dock, headed for home.

He removed the boots on the back porch. His mother had scalded his skin often enough in his youth about tracking mud for the habit to stick to the man. Still, he didn't think anything of letting the wet dog nose in the door ahead of him.

Until he saw the gleaming floor and counters.

Shit, was all he could think as he studied the pawprints and heard Simon's happy bark of greeting. There was a squeal, more barking, then laughter.

"You're soaking wet!" The female voice was low and smooth and amused. It was also very firm and made Ethan wince with guilt. "Out, Simon! Out you go. You just dry off on the front porch."

There was another squeal, baby giggles, and the accompanying laughter of a young boy. The gang's all here, Ethan thought, rubbing rain from his hair. The minute he heard footsteps heading in his direction, he made a beeline for the broom closet and a mop.

He didn't often move fast, but he could when he had to.

"Oh, Ethan." Grace Monroe stood with her hands on her narrow hips, looking from him to the pawprints on her just-waxed floor.

"I'll get it. Sorry." He could see that the mop was still damp and decided it was best not to look at her directly. "Wasn't thinking," he muttered, filling a bucket at the sink. "Didn't know you were coming by today."

"Oh, so you let wet dogs run through the house and dirty up the floors when I'm not coming by?"

He jerked a shoulder. "Floor was dirty when I left this morning, didn't figure a little wet would hurt it any." Then he relaxed a little. It always seemed to take him a few minutes to relax around Grace these days. "But if I'd known you were here to skin me over it, I'd have left him on the porch."

He was grinning when he turned, and she let out a sigh.

"Oh, give me the mop. I'll do it."

"Nope. My dog, my mess. I heard Aubrey."

Absently Grace leaned on the doorjamb. She was tired, but that wasn't unusual. She had put in eight hours that day, too. And she would put in another four at Shiney's Pub that night serving drinks.

Some nights when she crawled into bed she would have sworn she heard her feet crying.

"Seth's minding her for me. I had to switch my days. Mrs. Lynley called this morning and asked if I'd shift doing her house till tomorrow because her mother-in-law called her from D.C. and invited herself down to dinner. Mrs. Lynley claims her mother-in-law is a woman who looks at a speck of dust like it's a sin against God and man. I didn't think you'd mind if I did y'all today instead of tomorrow."

"You fit us in whenever you can manage it, Grace, and we're grateful."

He was watching her from under his lashes as he mopped. He'd always thought she was a pretty thing. Like a palomino—all gold and long-legged. She chopped her hair off short as a boy's, but he liked the way it sat on her head, like a shiny cap with fringes.

She was as thin as one of those million-dollar models, but he knew Grace's long, lean form wasn't for fashion. She'd been a gangling, skinny kid, as he recalled. She'd have been about seven or eight when he'd first come to St. Chris and the Quinns. He supposed she was twenty-couple now—and "skinny" wasn't exactly the word for her anymore.

She was like a willow slip, he thought, very nearly flushing.

She smiled at him, and her mermaid-green eyes warmed, faint dimples flirting in her cheeks. For reasons she couldn't name, she found it entertaining to see such a healthy male specimen wielding a mop.

"Did you have a good day, Ethan?"

"Good enough." He did a thorough job with the floor. He was a thorough man. Then he went to the sink again to rinse bucket and mop. "Sold a mess of crabs to your daddy."

At the mention of her father, Grace's smile dimmed a little. There was distance between them, had been since she'd become pregnant with Aubrey and had married Jack Casey, the man her father had called "that no-account grease monkey from upstate."

Her father had turned out to be right about Jack. The man had left her high and dry a month before Aubrey was born. And he'd taken her savings, her car, and most of her self-respect with him.

But she'd gotten through it, Grace reminded herself. And she was doing just fine. She would keep right on doing fine, on her own, without a single penny from her family—if she had to work herself to death to do it.

She heard Aubrey laugh again, a long, rolling gut laugh, and her resentment vanished. She had everything that mattered. It was all tied up in a bright-eyed, curly-headed little angel just in the next room.

"I'll make you up some dinner before I go."

Ethan turned back, took another look at her. She was getting some sun, and it looked good on her. Warmed her skin. She had a long face that went with the long body—though the chin tended to be stubborn. A man could take a glance and he would see a long, cool blonde—a pretty body, a face that made you want to look just a little longer.

And if you did, you'd see shadows under the big green eyes and weariness around the soft mouth.

"You don't have to do that, Grace. You ought to go on home and relax a while. You're on at Shiney's tonight, aren't you?"

"I've got time—and I promised Seth sloppy joes. It won't take me long." She shifted as Ethan continued to stare at her. She'd long ago accepted that those long, thoughtful looks from him would stir her blood. Just another of life's little problems, she supposed. "What?" she demanded, and rubbed a hand over her cheek as if expecting to find a smudge.

"Nothing. Well, if you're going to cook, you ought to hang around and help us eat it."

"I'd like that." She relaxed again and moved forward to take the bucket and mop from him and put them away herself. "Aubrey loves being here with you and Seth. Why don't you go on in with them? I've got some laundry to finish up, then I'll start dinner."

"I'll give you a hand."

"No, you won't." It was another point of pride for her. They paid her, she did the work. All the work. "Go on in the front room—and be sure to ask Seth about the math test he got back today."

"How'd he do?"

"Another A." She winked and shooed Ethan away. Seth had such a sharp brain, she thought as she headed into the laundry room, off the kitchen. If she'd had a better head for figures, for practical matters when she'd been younger, she wouldn't have dreamed her way through school.

She'd have learned a skill, a real one, not just serving drinks and tending house or picking crabs. She'd have had a career to fall back on when she found herself alone and pregnant, with all her hopes of running off to New York to be a dancer dashed like glass on brick.

It had been a silly dream anyway, she told herself, unloading the dryer and shifting the wet clothes from the washer into it. Pie in the sky, her mama would say. But the fact was, growing up, there had only been two things she'd wanted. The dance, and Ethan Quinn.

She'd never gotten either.

She sighed a little, holding the warm, smooth sheet she took from the basket to her cheek. Ethan's sheet—she'd taken it off his bed that day. She'd been able to smell him on it then, and maybe, for just a minute or two, she'd let herself dream a little of what it might have been like if he'd wanted her, if she had slept with him on those sheets, in his house.

But dreaming didn't get the work done, or pay the rent, or buy the things her little girl needed.

Briskly she began to fold the sheets, laying them neatly on the rumbling dryer. There was no shame in earning her keep by cleaning houses or serving drinks. She was good at both, in any case. She was useful, and she was needed. That was good enough.

She certainly hadn't been useful or needed by the man she was married to so briefly. If they'd loved each other, really loved each other, it would have been different. For her it had been a desperate need to belong to someone, to be wanted and desired as a woman. For Jack . . . Grace shook her head. She honestly didn't know what she had been for Jack.

An attraction, she supposed, that had resulted in conception. She knew he believed he'd done the honorable thing by taking her to the courthouse and standing with her in front of the justice of the peace on that chilly fall day and exchanging vows.

He had never mistreated her. He had never gotten mean drunk and knocked her around the way she knew some men did wives they didn't want. He didn't go sniffing after other women—at least not that she knew about. But she'd seen, as Aubrey grew inside her and her belly rounded, she'd seen the look of panic come into his eyes.

Then one day he was simply gone without a word.

The worst of it was, Grace thought now, she'd been relieved.

If Jack had done anything for her, it was to force her to grow up, to take charge. And what he'd given her was worth more than the stars.

She put the folded laundry in a basket, hitched the basket on her hip, and walked into the front room.

There was her treasure, her curly blond hair bouncing, her pretty, rosy-cheeked face alight with joy as she sat on Ethan's lap and babbled at him.

At two, Aubrey Monroe resembled a Botticelli angel, all rose and gilt, with bright green eyes and dimples denting her cheeks. Little kitten teeth and long-fingered hands. Though he could decipher only half her chatter, Ethan nodded soberly.

"And what did Foolish do then?" he asked as he figured out she was telling him some story about Seth's puppy.

"Licked my face." Her eyes laughing, she took both hands and ran them up over her cheeks. "All over." Grinning, she cupped her hands on Ethan's face and fell into a game she liked to play with him. "Ouch!" She giggled, rubbed his face again. "Beard."

Obliging, he skimmed his knuckles over her smooth cheek, then jerked his hand back. "Ouch. You've got one, too."

"No! You."

"No." He pulled her close and planted noisy kisses on her cheeks while she wriggled in delight. "You."

Screaming with laughter now, she wiggled away and dived for the boy sprawled on the floor. "Seth beard." She covered his cheek with sloppy kisses. Manhood demanded that he wince.

"Jeez, Aub, give me a break." To distract her, he picked up one of her toy cars and ran it lightly down her arm. "You're a racetrack."

Her eyes beamed with the thrill of a new game. Snatching the car, she ran it, not quite so gently, over any part of Seth she could reach.

Ethan only grinned. "You started it, pal," he told Seth when Aubrey walked over Seth's thigh to reach his other shoulder.

"It's better than getting slobbered on," Seth claimed, but his arm came up to keep Aubrey from tumbling to the floor.

For a few moments, Grace simply stood and watched. The man, relaxed in the big wing chair and grinning down at the children. The children themselves, their heads close—one delicate and covered with gold curls, the other with a shaggy mop shades and shades deeper.

The little lost boy, she thought, and her heart went out to him as it had from the first day she'd seen him. He'd found his way home.

Her precious girl. When Aubrey had been only a fluttering in her womb, Grace had promised to cherish, to protect, and to enjoy her. She would always have a home.

And the man who had once been a lost boy, who had slipped into her girlish dreams years before and had never really slipped out again. He had made a home.

The rain drummed on the roof, the television was a low, unimportant murmur. Dogs slept on the front porch, and the moist wind blew through the screen door.

And she yearned where she knew she had no business yearning—to set down the basket of laundry, to go over and climb into Ethan's lap. To be welcomed there, even expected there. To close her eyes, for just a little while, and be part of it all.

Instead she retreated, finding herself unable to step into that quiet, lazy ease. She went back to the kitchen, where the overhead lights were bright and just a little hard. There, she set the basket on the table and began to gather what she needed to make dinner.

When Ethan came in a few moments later to hunt up a beer, she had meat browning, potatoes frying in peanut oil, and a salad under way.

"Smells great." He stood awkwardly for a minute. He wasn't used to having someone cook for him—not for years—and then not a woman. His father had been at home in the kitchen, but his mother . . . They'd always joked that whenever she cooked, they needed all her medical skills to survive the meal.

"It'll be ready in half an hour or so. I hope you don't mind eating early. I've got to get Aubrey home and bathed and then change for work."

"I never mind eating, especially when I'm not doing the cooking. And the fact is, I want to get to the boatyard for a couple hours tonight."

"Oh." She looked back, blowing at her bangs. "You should have told me. I'd have hurried things up."

"This pace works for me." He took a pull from the bottle. "You want a drink or something?"

"No, I'm fine. I was going to use that salad dressing Phillip made up. It looks so much prettier than the store-bought."

The rain was letting up, petering out into slow, drizzling drops with watery sunlight struggling to break through. Grace glanced toward the window. She was always hoping to see a rainbow. "Anna's flowers are doing well," she commented. "The rain's good for them."

"Saves me from dragging out the hose. She'd have my head if they died on her while she's gone."

"Wouldn't blame her. She worked so hard getting them planted before the wedding." Grace worked quickly, competently as she spoke. Draining crisp potatoes, adding more to the sizzling oil. "It was such a beautiful wedding," she went on as she mixed sauce for the meat in a bowl.

"Came off all right. We got lucky with the weather."

"Oh, it couldn't have rained that day. It would have been a sin." She could see it all again, so clearly. The green of the grass in the backyard, the sparkling of water. The flowers Anna had planted glowing with color—and the ones she'd bought spilling out of pots and bowls alongside the white runner that the bride had walked down to meet her groom.

A white dress billowing, the thin veil only accentuating the dark, deliriously happy eyes. Chairs had been filled with friends and family. Anna's grandparents had both wept. And Cam—rough-and-tumble Cameron Quinn—had looked at his bride as if he'd just been given the keys to heaven.

A backyard wedding, Grace thought now. Sweet, simple, romantic. Perfect.

"She's the most beautiful woman I've ever seen." Grace said it with a sigh that was only lightly touched with envy. "So dark and exotic."

"She suits Cam."

"They looked like movie stars, all polished and glossy." She smiled to herself as she stirred spicy sauce into the meat. "When you and Phillip played that waltz for their first dance, it was the most romantic thing I've ever seen." She sighed again as she finished putting the salad together. "And now they're in Rome. I can hardly imagine it."

"They called yesterday morning to catch me before I left. They said they're having a good time."

She laughed at that, a rippling, smoky sound that seemed to cruise along his skin. "Honeymooning in Rome? It would be hard not to." She started to scoop out more potatoes and swore lightly as oil popped and splattered on the side of her hand. "Damn." Even as she was lifting the slight burn to her mouth to soothe it, Ethan leaped forward and grabbed her hand.

"Did it get you?" He saw the pinkening skin and pulled her to the sink. "Run some cold water on it."

"It's nothing. It's just a little burn. Happens all the time."

"It wouldn't if you were more careful." His brows were knitted, his hand gripping her fingers firmly to keep her hand under the stream of water. "Does it hurt?"

"No." She couldn't feel anything but his hand on her fingers and her own heart thundering in her chest. Knowing she'd make a fool of herself any moment, she tried to pull free. "It's nothing, Ethan. Don't fuss."

"You need some salve on it." He started to reach up into the cupboard to find some, and his head lifted. His eyes met hers. He stood there, the water running, both of their hands trapped under the chilly fall of it.

He tried never to stand quite so close to her, not so close that he could see those little gold dust flecks in her eyes. Because he would start to think about them, to wonder about them. Then he'd have to remind himself that this was Grace, the girl he'd watched grow up. The woman who was Aubrey's mother. A neighbor who considered him a trusted friend.

"You need to take better care of yourself." His voice was rough as the words worked their way through a throat that had gone dust-dry. She smelled of lemons.

"I'm fine." She was dying, somewhere between giddy pleasure and utter despair. He was holding her hand as if it were as fragile as spun glass. And he was frowning at her as if she were slightly less sensible than her two-year-old daughter. "The potatoes are going to burn, Ethan."

"Oh. Well." Mortified because he'd been thinking—just for a second—that her mouth might taste as soft as it looked, he jerked back, fumbling now for the tube of salve. His heart was jumping, and he hated the sensation. He preferred things calm and easy. "Put some of this on it anyway." He laid it on the counter and backed up. "I'll . . . get the kids washed up for dinner."

He scooped up the laundry basket on his way and was gone.

With deliberate movements, Grace shut the water off, then turned and rescued her fries. Satisfied with the progress of the meal, she picked up the salve and smoothed a little on the reddened splotch on her hand before tidily replacing the tube in the cupboard.

Then she leaned on the sink, looked out the window.

But she couldn't find a rainbow in the sky.

CHAPTER
2

THERE was nothing like a Saturday—unless it was the Saturday leading up to the last week of school and into summer vacation. That, of course, was all the Saturdays of your life rolled into one big shiny ball.

Saturday meant spending the day out on the workboat with Ethan and Jim instead of in a classroom. It meant hard work and hot sun and cold drinks. Man stuff. With his eyes shaded under the bill of his Orioles cap and the really cool sunglasses he'd bought on a trip to the mall, Seth shot out the gaff to drag in the next marker buoy. His young muscles bunched under his *X-Files* T-shirt, which assured him that the truth was out there.

He watched Jim work—tilt the pot and unhook the oyster-can-lid stopper to the bait box on the bottom of the pot. Shake out the old bait, Seth noted and see the seagulls dive and scream like maniacs. Cool. Now get a good solid hold on that pot, turn it over, and shake it like crazy so the crabs in the upstairs section fall out into the washtub waiting for them. Seth figured he could do all that—if he really wanted to. He wasn't afraid of a bunch of stupid crabs just because they looked like big mutant bugs from Venus and had claws that tended to snap and pinch.

Instead, his job was to rebait the pot with a couple handfuls of disgusting fish parts, do the stopper, check to make sure there were no snags in the line. Eyeball the distance between markers and if everything looked good, toss the pot overboard. Splash!

Then he got to toss out the gaff for the next buoy.

He knew how to tell the sooks from the jimmies now. Jim said the girl crabs painted their fingernails because their pincers were red. It was wild the way the patterns on the underbellies looked like sex parts. Anybody could see that the guy crabs had this long T shape there that looked just like a dick.

Jim had shown him a couple of crabs mating, too—he called them doublers—and that was just too much. The guy crab just climbed aboard the girl, tucked her under him, and swam around like that for days.

Seth figured they had to like it.

Ethan had said the crabs were married, and when Seth had snickered, he lifted a brow. Seth had found himself intrigued enough to go to the school library and read up on crabs. And he thought he understood, sort of, what Ethan meant. The guy protected the girl by keeping her under him because she could only mate when she was in her last molt and her shell was soft, so she was vulnerable. Even after they'd done it, he kept carrying her like that until her shell was hard again. And she was only going to mate once, so it was like getting married.

He thought of how Cam and Miss Spinelli—Anna, he reminded himself, he got to call her Anna now—had gotten married. Lots of the women got all leaky, and the guys laughed and joked. Everybody made such a big deal out of it with flowers and music and tons of food. He didn't get it. It seemed to him getting married just meant you got to have sex whenever you wanted and nobody got snotty about it.

But it had been cool. He'd never been to anything like it. Even though Cam had dragged him out to the mall and made him try on suits, it was mostly okay.

Maybe sometimes he worried about how it was going to change things, just when he was getting used to the way things were. There was going to be a woman in the house now. He liked Anna okay. She'd played square with him even though she was a social worker. But she was still a female.

Like his mother.

Seth clamped down on that thought. If he thought about his mother, if he thought about the life he'd had with her—the men, the drugs, the dirty little rooms—it would spoil the day.

He hadn't had enough sunny days in his ten years to risk ruining one.

"You taking a nap there, Seth?"

Ethan's mild voice snapped Seth back to the moment. He blinked, saw the sun glinting off the water, the orange floats bobbing. "Just thinking," Seth muttered and quickly pulled in another buoy.

"Me, I don't do much thinking." Jim set the trap on the gunwale and began culling crabs. His leathered face creased in grins. "Gives you brain fever."

"Shit," Seth said, leaning over to study the catch. "That one's starting to molt."

Jim grunted, held up a crab with a shell cracking along the back. "This buster'll be somebody's soft-shell sandwich by tomorrow." He winked at Seth as he tossed the crab into the tank. "Maybe mine."

Foolish, who was still young enough to deserve the name, sniffed at the trap, inciting a quick and ugly crab riot. As claws snapped, the pup leaped back with a yelp.

"That there dog." Jim shook with laughter. "He don't have to worry about no brain fever."

<hr>

EVEN WHEN THEY'D taken the day's catch to the waterfront, emptied the tank, and dropped Jim off, the day wasn't over. Ethan stepped back from the controls. "We've got to go into the boatyard. You want to take her in?"

Though Seth's eyes were shielded by the dark sunglasses, Ethan imagined that their expression matched the boy's dropped jaw. It only amused him when Seth jerked a shoulder as if such things were an everyday occurrence.

"Sure. No problem." With sweaty palms, Seth took the helm.

Ethan stood by, hands casually tucked in his back pockets, eyes alert. There was plenty of water traffic. A pretty weekend afternoon drew the recreational sailors to the Bay. But they didn't have far to go, and the kid had to learn sometime. You couldn't live in St. Chris and not know how to pilot a workboat.

"A little to starboard," he told Seth. "See that skiff there? Sunday sailor, and he's going to cut right across your bow if you keep this heading."

Seth narrowed his eyes, studied the boat and the people on deck. He snorted. "That's because he's paying more attention to that girl in the bikini than to the wind."

"Well, she looks fine in the bikini."

"I don't see what's the big deal about breasts."

To his credit, Ethan didn't laugh out loud, but nodded soberly. "I guess part of that's because we don't have them."

"I sure don't want any."

"Give it a couple of years," Ethan murmured under the cover of the engine noise. And the thought of that made him wince. What the hell were they going to do when the kid hit puberty? Somebody was going to have to talk to him about . . . things. He knew Seth already had too much sexual knowledge, but it was all the dark and sticky sort. The same sort he himself had known about at much too early an age.

One of them was going to have to explain how things should be, could be—and before too much more time passed.

He hoped to hell it wasn't going to have to be him.

He caught sight of the boatyard, the old brick building, the spanking new dock he and his brothers had built. Pride rippled through him. Maybe it didn't look like much with its pitted bricks and patched roof, but they were making something out of it. The windows were dusty, but they were new and unbroken.

"Cut back on the throttle. Take her in slow." Absently Ethan put a hand over Seth's on the controls. He felt the boy stiffen, then relax. He still had a problem with being touched unexpectedly, Ethan noted. But it was passing. "That's the way, just a bit more to starboard."

When the boat bumped gently against the pilings, Ethan jumped onto the pier to secure lines. "Nice job." At his nod, Simon, all but quivering with anticipation, leaped overboard. Yipping frantically, Foolish clambered onto the gunwale, hesitated, then followed.

"Hand me up the cooler, Seth."

Grunting only a little, Seth hefted it. "Maybe I could pilot the boat sometime when we're crabbing."

"Maybe." Ethan waited for the boy to scramble safely onto the pier before heading to the rear cargo doors of the building.

They were already open wide and the soul-stirring sound of Ray

Charles flowed out through them. Ethan set the cooler down just inside the doors and put his hands on his hips.

The hull was finished. Cam had put in dog's hours to get that much done before he left for his honeymoon. They'd planked it, rabbeting the edges so that they would lap, yet remain smooth at the seams.

The two of them had completed the steam-bent framing, using pencil lines as guides and "walking" each frame carefully into place with slow, steady pressure. The hull was solid. There would be no splits in a Quinn boat's planking.

The design was primarily Ethan's with a few adjustments here and there of Cam's. The hull was an arc-bottom, expensive to construct but with the virtues of stability and speed. Ethan knew his client.

He'd designed the shape of the bow with this in mind and had decided on a cruiser bow, attractive and, again, good for speed, buoyant. The stern was a counterdesign of moderate length, providing an overhang that would make the boat's length greater than her waterline length.

It was a sleek, appealing look. Ethan understood that his client was every bit as concerned with appearance as he was with basic seaworthiness.

He'd used Seth for grunt labor when it was time to coat the interior with the fifty-fifty mix of hot linseed oil and turpentine. It was sweaty work, guaranteed to cause a few burns despite caution and gloves. Still, the boy had held up fine.

From where he stood, Ethan could study the sheerline, the outline at the top edge of the hull. He'd gone with a flattened sheerline to ensure a roomier, drier craft with good headroom below. His client liked to take friends and family out for a sail.

The man had insisted on teak, though Ethan had told him pine or cedar would have done the job well enough for hull planking. The man had money to spend on his hobby, Ethan thought now—and money to spend on status. But he had to admit, the teak looked wonderful.

His brother Phillip was working on the decking. Stripped to the waist in defense against the heat and humidity, his dark bronze hair protected by a black cap without team name or emblem and worn bill to the back, he was screwing the deck planks into place. Every few seconds, the hard, high-pitched buzz of the electric driver competed with Ray Charles's creamy tenor.

"How's it going?" Ethan called over the din.

Phillip's head came up. His martyred-angel's face was damp with sweat, his golden-brown eyes annoyed. He'd just been reminding himself that he was an advertising executive, for God's sake, not a carpenter.

"It's hotter than a summer in hell in here and it's only June. We've got to get some fans in here. You got anything cold, or at least wet, in that cooler? I ran out of liquids an hour ago."

"Turn on the tap in the john and you get water," Ethan said mildly as he bent to take a cold soft drink from the cooler. "It's a new technology."

"Christ knows what's in that tap water." Phillip caught the can Ethan tossed him and grimaced at the label. "At least they tell you what chemicals they load in here."

"Sorry, we drank all the Evian. You know how Jim is about his designer water. Can't get enough of it."

"Screw you," Phillip said, but without heat. He glugged the chilly Pepsi, then raised a brow when Ethan came up to inspect his work.

"Nice job."

"Gee, thanks, boss. Can I have a raise?"

"Sure, double what you're getting now. Seth's the math whiz. What's zip times zip, Seth?"

"Double zip," Seth said with a quick grin. His fingers itched to try out the electric screwdriver. So far, nobody would let him touch it or any of the other power tools.

"Well, now I can afford that cruise to Tahiti."

"Why don't you grab a shower—unless you object to washing with tap water, too. I can take over here."

It was tempting. Phillip was grimy, sweaty, and miserably hot. He would cheerfully have killed three strangers for one cold glass of Pouilly-Fuisse. But he knew Ethan had been up since before dawn and had already put in what any normal person would consider a full day.

"I can handle a couple more hours."

"Fine." It was exactly the response Ethan had expected. Phillip tended to bitch, but he never let you down. "I think we can get this deck knocked out before we call it a day."

"Can I—"

"No," Ethan and Phillip said together, anticipating Seth's question.

"Why the hell not?" he demanded. "I'm not stupid. I won't shoot anybody with a stupid screw or anything."

"Because we like to play with it." Phillip smiled. "And we're bigger than you. Here." He reached into his back pocket, pulled out his wallet and found a five. "Go on down to Crawford's and get me some bottled water. If you don't whine about it, you can get some ice cream with the change."

Seth didn't whine, but he did mutter about being used like a slave as he called his dog and headed out.

"We ought to show him how to use the tools when we have more time," Ethan commented. "He's got good hands."

"Yeah, but I wanted him out. I didn't have the chance to tell you last night. The detective tracked Gloria DeLauter as far as Nags Head."

"She's heading south, then." He lifted his gaze to Phillip's. "He pin her yet?"

"No, she moves around a lot, and she's using cash. A lot of cash." His mouth tightened. "She's got plenty to toss around since Dad paid her a bundle for Seth."

"Doesn't look like she's interested in coming back here."

"I'd say she's got as much interest in that kid as a rabid alley cat has in a dead kitten." His own mother had been the same, Phillip remembered, when she'd been around at all. He had never met Gloria DeLauter, but he knew her. Despised her.

"If we don't find her," Phillip added, rolling the cold can over his forehead, "we're never going to get to the truth about Dad, or Seth."

Ethan nodded. He knew Phillip was on a mission here, and knew he was most likely right. But he wondered, much too often for comfort, what they would do when they had the truth.

⁂

ETHAN'S PLANS AFTER a fourteen-hour workday were to take an endless shower and drink a cold beer. He did both, simultaneously. They'd gotten take-out subs for dinner, and he had his on the back porch alone, in the soft quiet of early twilight. Inside, Seth and Phillip were arguing over which video to watch first. Arnold Schwarzenegger was doing battle with Kevin Costner.

Ethan had already placed his bets on Arnold.

They had an unspoken agreement that Phillip would take responsibility for Seth on Saturday nights. It gave Ethan a choice for the evening. He could go in and join them, as he sometimes did for these movie fests. He could go up and settle in with a book, as he often preferred to do. He could go out, as he rarely did.

Before his father had died so suddenly and life had changed for all of them, Ethan had lived in his own little house, with his own quiet routine. He still missed it, though he tried not to resent the young couple who were now renting it from him. They loved the coziness of it and told him so often. The small rooms with their tall windows, the little covered porch, the shady privacy of the trees that sheltered it, and the gentle lap of water against shore.

He loved it, too. With Cam married and Anna moving in, he might have been able to slip out again. But the rental money was needed now. And, more important, he'd given his word. He would live here until all the legal battles were waged and won and Seth was permanently theirs.

He rocked, listening to the night birds begin to call. And must have dozed because the dream came, and came clearly.

"You always were more of a loner than the others," Ray commented. He sat on the porch rail, turned slightly so he could look out to the water if he chose. His hair was shiny as a silver coin in the half light, blowing free in the steady breeze. "Always liked to go off by yourself to think your thoughts and work out your troubles."

"I knew I could always come to you or Mom. I just liked to have a handle on things first."

"How about now?" Ray shifted to face Ethan directly.

"I don't know. Maybe I haven't gotten a good handle on it yet. Seth's settling in. He's easier with us. The first few weeks, I kept expecting him to rabbit off. Losing you hurt him almost as much as it did us. Maybe just as much, because he'd just started to believe things were okay for him."

"It was bad, the way he had to live before I brought him here.

Still, it wasn't as bad as what you'd faced, Ethan, and you got through."

"Almost didn't." Ethan took out one of his cigars, took his time lighting it. "Sometimes it still comes back on me. Pain and shame. And the sweaty fear of knowing what's going to happen." He shrugged it off. "Seth's a little younger than I was. I think he's already shed some of it. As long as he doesn't have to deal with his mother again."

"He'll have to deal with her eventually, but he won't be alone. That's the difference. You'll all stand by him. You always stood by each other." Ray smiled, his big, wide face creasing everywhere at once. "What are you doing sitting out here alone on a Saturday night, Ethan? I swear, boy, you worry me."

"Had a long day."

"When I was your age, I put in long days and longer nights. You just turned thirty, for Christ's sake. Porch sitting on a warm Saturday night in June is for old men. Go on, take a drive. See where you end up." He winked. "I bet we both know where that's likely to be."

The sudden blare of automatic gunfire and screams made Ethan jerk in his chair. He blinked and stared hard at the porch rail. There was no one there. Of course there was no one there, he told himself with a quick shake. He'd nodded off for a minute, that was all, and the movie action in the living room had wakened him.

But when he glanced down, he saw the glowing cigar in his hand. Baffled, he simply stared at it. Had he actually taken it out of his pocket and lit it in his sleep? That was ridiculous, absurd. He must have done it before he'd drifted off, the habit so automatic that his mind just didn't register the moves.

Still, why had he fallen asleep when he didn't feel the least bit tired? In fact, he felt restless and edgy and too alert.

He rose, rubbing the back of his neck, stretching his legs on a pacing journey up and down the porch. He should just go in and settle down with the movie, some popcorn, and another beer. Even as he reached for the screen door, he swore.

He wasn't in the mood for Saturday night at the movies. He would just take a drive and see where he ended up.

⌇⌇⌇⌇⌇

GRACE'S FEET WERE numb all the way to the ankles. The cursed high heels that were part of her cocktail waitress uniform were killers. It wasn't so bad on a weekday evening when you had time now and then to step out of them or even sit for a few minutes. But Shiney's Pub always hopped on Saturday night—and so did she.

She carted her tray of empty glasses and full ashtrays to the bar, efficiently unloading as she called out her order to the bartender. "Two house whites, two drafts, a gin and tonic, and a club soda with lime."

She had to pitch her voice over the crowd noise and what was loosely called music from the three-piece band Shiney had hired. The music was always lousy at the pub, because Shiney wouldn't shell out the money for decent musicians.

But no one seemed to care.

The stingy dance floor was bumper to bumper with dancers, and the band took this as a sign to boost the volume.

Grace's head was ringing like steel bells, and her back was beginning to throb in time with the bass.

Her order complete, she carried the tray through the narrow spaces between tables and hoped that the group of young tourists in trendy clothes would be decent tippers.

She served them with a smile, nodded at the signal to run a tab, and followed the hail to the next table.

Her break was still ten minutes away. It might as well have been ten years.

"Hey, there, Gracie."

"How's it going, Curtis, Bobbie." She'd gone to school with them in the dim, distant past. Now they worked for her father, packing seafood. "Usual?"

"Yeah, a couple of drafts." Curtis gave Grace his usual—a quick pat on her bow-clad butt. She'd learned not to worry about it. From him it was a harmless enough gesture, even a show of affectionate support. Some of the outlanders who dropped in had hands a great deal less harmless. "How's that pretty girl of yours?"

Grace smiled, understanding that this was one of the reasons she tolerated his pats. He always asked about Aubrey. "Getting prettier every day." She saw another hand pop up from a nearby table. "I'll get you those beers in just a minute."

She was carting a tray full of mugs, bowls of beer nuts, and glasses when Ethan walked in. She nearly bobbled it. He never came into the pub on Saturday night. Sometimes he dropped in for a quiet beer midweek, but never when the place was crowded and noisy.

He should have looked the same as every second man in the place. His jeans were faded but clean, a plain white T-shirt tucked into them, his work boots ancient and scuffed. But he didn't look the same as other men—and never had to Grace.

Maybe it was the lean and rangy body that moved as easily as a dancer through the narrow spaces. Innate grace, she mused, the kind that can't be taught, and still so blatantly male. He always looked as though he were walking the deck of a ship.

It could have been his face, so bony and rugged and somewhere just at the edges of handsome. Or the eyes, always so clear and thoughtful, so serious that it seemed to take them a few seconds to catch up whenever his mouth curved.

She served her drinks, pocketed money, took more orders. And watched out of the corner of her eye as he squeezed into a standing spot at the bar directly beside the order station.

She forgot all about her much-desired break.

"Three drafts, bottle of Mich, Stoli rocks." Absently, she brushed at her bangs and smiled. "Hi, Ethan."

"Busy tonight."

"Summer Saturday. Do you want a table?"

"No, this is fine."

The bartender was busy with another order, which gave her some breathing room. "Steve's got his hands full, but he'll work his way down here."

"I'm not in any hurry." As a rule, he tried not to think about how she looked in the butt-skimming skirt, those endless legs in black fishnet, the narrow feet in skinny heels. But tonight he was in a mood, and so he let himself think.

Just at that moment, he could have explained to Seth just what the big deal was about breasts. Grace's were small and high, and a soft portion of the curve showed over the low-cut bodice of her blouse.

Suddenly, he desperately wanted a beer.

"You get a chance to sit down at all?"

She didn't answer for a moment. Her mind had gone glass-blank at the way those quiet, thoughtful eyes had skimmed over her. "I, ah . . . yes, it's nearly time for my break." Her hands felt clumsy as she gathered up her order. "I like to go outside, get away from the noise." Struggling to act normally, she rolled her eyes toward the band and was rewarded with Ethan's slow grin.

"Do they ever get worse than this?"

"Oh, yeah, these guys are a real step up." She was nearly relaxed again as she lifted the tray and headed off to serve.

He watched her, while he sipped the beer Steve had pulled for him. Watched the way her legs moved, the way the foolish and incredibly sexy bow swayed with her hips. And the way she bent her knees, balancing the tray, lifting drinks from it onto a table.

He watched, eyes narrowing, as Curtis once again gave her a friendly pat.

His eyes narrowed further when a stranger in a faded Jim Morrison T-shirt grabbed her hand, tugging her closer. He saw Grace flash a smile, give a shake of her head. Ethan was already pushing away from the bar, not entirely sure what he intended to do, when the man released her.

When Grace came back to set down her tray, it was Ethan who grabbed her hand. "Take your break."

"What? I—" To her shock he was pulling her steadily through the room. "Ethan, I really need to—"

"Take your break," he said again and shoved the door open.

The air outside was clean and fresh, the night warm and breezy. The minute the door closed behind them, the noise shut down to a muffled echoing roar and the stink of smoke, sweat, and beer became a memory.

"I don't think you should be working here."

She gaped at him. The statement itself was odd enough, but to hear him deliver it in a tone that was obviously annoyed was baffling. "Excuse me?"

"You heard me, Grace." He shoved his hands in his pockets because he didn't know what to do with them. Left free, they might have grabbed her again. "It's not right."

"It's not right?" she repeated, at sea.

"You're a mother, for God's sake. What are you doing serving drinks, wearing that outfit, getting hit on? That guy in there practically had his face down your blouse."

"Oh, he did not." Torn between amusement and exasperation, she shook her head. "For heaven's sake, Ethan, he was just being typical. And harmless."

"Curtis had his hand on your ass."

Amusement was veering toward annoyance. "I know where his hand was, and if it worried me, I'd have knocked it off."

Ethan took a breath. He'd started this, wisely or not, and he was going to finish it. "You shouldn't be working half naked in some bar or knocking anybody's hand off your ass. You should be home with Aubrey."

Her eyes went from mildly irritated to blazing fury. "Oh, is that right, is that your considered opinion? Well, thank you so much for sharing it with me. And for your information, if I wasn't working— and I'm damn well not half naked—I wouldn't have a home."

"You've got a job," he said stubbornly. "Cleaning houses."

"That's right. I clean houses, I serve drinks, and now and then I pick crabs. That's how amazingly skilled and versatile I am. I also pay rent, insurance, medical bills, utilities, and a babysitter. I buy food, I buy clothes, gas. I take care of myself and my daughter. I don't need you coming around here telling me it's not right."

"I'm just saying—"

"I hear what you're saying." Her heels were throbbing, and every ache in her overtaxed body was making itself known. Worse, much worse, was the hard prick of embarrassment that he would look down on her for what she did to survive. "I serve cocktails and let men look at my legs. Maybe they'll tip better if they like them. And if they tip better I can buy my little girl something that makes her smile. So they can look all they damn well please. And I wish to God I had the kind of body that filled out this stupid outfit, because then I'd earn more."

He had to pause before speaking, to gather his thoughts. Her face was flushed with anger, but her eyes were so tired it broke his heart. "You're selling yourself short, Grace," he said quietly.

"I know exactly how much I'm worth, Ethan." Her chin angled. "Right down to the last penny. Now, my break's over."

She spun on her miserably throbbing heels and stalked back into the noise and the smoke-clogged air.

CHAPTER

"NEED bunny, too."

"Okay, baby, we'll get your bunny." It was, Grace thought, always an expedition. They were only going as far as the sandbox in the backyard, but Aubrey never failed to demand that all her stuffed pals accompany her.

Grace had solved this logistical problem with an enormous shopping bag. Inside it were a bear, two dogs, a fish, and a very tattered cat. The bunny joined them. Though Grace's eyes were gritty from lack of sleep, she grinned broadly as Aubrey tried to heft the bag herself.

"I'll carry them, honey."

"No, me."

It was, Grace thought, Aubrey's favorite phrase. Her baby liked to do things herself, even when it would be simpler to let someone else do the job. Wonder where she gets that from, Grace mused, and laughed at both of them.

"Okay, let's get the crew outside." She opened the screen door—it

squeaked badly, reminding her that she needed to oil the hinges—
and waited while Aubrey dragged the bag over the threshold and
onto the tiny back porch.

Grace had livened up the porch by painting it a soft blue and
adding clay pots filled with pink and white geraniums. In her mind,
the little rental house was temporary, but she didn't want it to *feel*
temporary. She wanted it to feel like home. At least until she saved
enough money for a down payment on a place of their own.

Inside, the room sizes were on the stingy side, but she'd solved
that—and helped her bank balance—by keeping furniture to a
minimum. Most of what she had were yard sale bargains, but she'd
painted, refinished, re-covered, and turned each piece into her own.

It was vital to Grace to have her own.

The house had ancient plumbing, a roof that leaked water after
a hard rain, and windows that leaked air. But it had two bedrooms,
which had been essential. She'd wanted her daughter to have a room
of her own, a bright, cheerful room. She had seen to that, papering
the walls herself, painting the trim, adding fussy curtains.

It was already breaking her heart knowing that it was about time
to dismantle Aubrey's crib and replace it with a youth bed.

"Be careful on the steps," Grace warned, and Aubrey started
down, both tiny tennis shoes planting themselves firmly on each of
the steps on the descent. The minute she hit bottom, she began to
run, dragging her bag behind her and squealing in anticipation.

She loved the sandbox. It made Grace proud to watch Aubrey
make her traditional beeline for it. Grace had built it herself, using
scrap lumber that she meticulously sanded smooth and painted a
bright Crayola red. In it were the pails and shovels and big plastic
cars, but she knew Aubrey would touch none of them until she'd
set out her pets.

One day, Grace promised herself, Aubrey would have a real

puppy, and a playroom so that she could have friends visit and spend long, rainy afternoons.

Grace crouched down as Aubrey placed her toys carefully in the white sand. "You sit right in here and play while I mow the lawn. Promise?"

"Okay." Aubrey beamed up at her, dimples winking. "You play."

"In a little while." She stroked Aubrey's curls. She could never get enough of touching this miracle that had come from her. Before rising, she looked around, mother's eyes scanning for any danger.

The yard was fenced, and she had installed a childproof lock on the gate herself. Aubrey tended to be curious. A flowering vine rambled along the fence that bordered her house and the Cutters' and would have it buried in bloom by summer's end.

No one was stirring next door, she noted. Too early on a Sunday morning for her neighbors to be doing more than lazing about and thinking of breakfast. Julie Cutter, the eldest daughter of the house, was her much-treasured babysitter.

She noted that Julie's mother, Irene, had spent some time in her garden the day before. Not a single weed dared show its head in Irene Cutter's flowers or in her vegetable patch.

With some embarrassment, Grace glanced toward the rear of her yard, where she and Aubrey had planted some tomatoes and beans and carrots. Plenty of weeds there, she thought with a sigh. She'd have to deal with that after cutting the lawn. God only knew why she'd thought she would have time to tend a garden. But it had been such fun to dig the dirt and plant the seeds with her little girl.

Just as it would be such fun to step into the sandbox and build castles and make up games. No, you don't, Grace ordered herself and rose. The lawn was nearly ankle-high. It might have been rented grass, but it was hers now, and her responsibility. No one was going to say that Grace Monroe couldn't tend her own.

She kept the ancient secondhand lawn mower under an equally ancient drop cloth. As usual, she checked the gas level first, casting another glance over her shoulder to be certain Aubrey was still tucked in the sandbox. Gripping the starter cord with both hands, she yanked. And got a wheezing cough in response.

"Come on, don't mess with me this morning." She'd lost count of the times she'd fiddled and repaired and banged on the old machine. Rolling her protesting shoulders, she yanked again, then a third time, before letting the cord snap back and pressing her fingers to her eyes. "Wouldn't you just know it."

"Giving you trouble?"

Her head jerked around. After their argument the night before, Ethan was the last person Grace expected to see standing in her backyard. It didn't please her, particularly since she'd told herself she could and would stay mad at him. Worse, she knew how she looked—old gray shorts and a T-shirt that had seen too many washings, not a stitch of makeup and her hair uncombed.

Damn it, she'd dressed for yard work, not for company.

"I can handle it." She yanked again, her foot, clad in a sneaker with a hole in the toe, planted on the side of the machine. It nearly caught, very nearly.

"Let it rest a minute. You're just going to flood it."

This time the cord snapped back with a dangerous hiss. "I know how to start my own lawn mower."

"I imagine you do, when you're not mad." He walked over as he spoke, all lean and easy male in faded jeans and a work shirt rolled up to his elbows.

He had come around back when she didn't answer her door. And he knew he'd stood watching her a little longer than was strictly polite. She had such a pretty way of moving.

He had decided sometime during the restless night that he had better find a way to make amends. And he'd spent a good part of his morning trying to figure how to do so. Then he'd seen her, all those long, slim limbs the sun was turning pale gold, the sunny hair, the narrow hands. And he'd just wanted to watch for a bit.

"I'm not mad," she said in an impatient hiss that proved her statement a lie. He only looked into her eyes.

"Listen, Grace—"

"Eeee-than!" With a shriek of pure pleasure, Aubrey scrambled out of the sandbox and ran to him—full-out, arms extended, face lit up with joy.

He caught her, swung her up and around. "Hey, there, Aubrey."

"Come play."

"Well, I'm—"

"Kiss."

She puckered her little lips with such energy that he had to laugh and give them a friendly peck.

"Okay!" She wiggled down and ran back to her sandbox.

"Look, Grace, I'm sorry if I was out of line last night."

The fact that her heart had melted when he held her daughter only made her more determined to stand firm. "If?"

He shifted his feet, clearly uncomfortable. "I just meant that—"

His explanation was interrupted as Aubrey raced back with her beloved stuffed dogs. "Kiss," she stated, very firmly, and held them up to Ethan. He obliged, waiting until she raced away again.

"What I meant was—"

"I think you said what you meant, Ethan."

She was going to be stubborn, he thought with an inward sigh. Well, she always had been. "I didn't say it very well. I get tangled up with words most of the time. I hate to see you working so hard." He paused, patient, when Aubrey came back, demanding a kiss for her bear. "I worry about you some, that's all."

Grace angled her head. "Why?"

"Why?" The question threw him. He bent to kiss the stuffed bunny that Aubrey batted against his leg. "Well, I . . . Because."

"Because I'm a woman?" she suggested. "Because I'm a single parent? Because my father considers that I smeared the family name by not only having to get married but getting myself divorced?"

"No." He took a step closer to her, absently kissing the cat that Aubrey held up to him. "Because I've known you more than half my life, and that makes you part of it. And because maybe you're too stubborn or too proud to see when somebody just wants to see things go a little easier for you."

She started to tell him she appreciated that, felt herself begin to soften. Then he ruined it.

"And because I didn't like seeing men paw at you."

"Paw at me?" Her back went up; her chin went out. "Men were not pawing at me, Ethan. And if they do, I know what to do about it."

"Don't get all riled up again." He scratched his chin, struggled not to sigh. He didn't see the point in arguing with a woman—you could never win. "I came over here to tell you I was sorry, and so maybe I could—"

"Kiss!" Aubrey demanded and began to climb up his leg.

Instinctively, Ethan pulled her up into his arms and kissed her cheek. "I was going to say—"

"No, kiss Mama." Bouncing in his arms, Aubrey pushed at his lips to make them pucker. "Kiss Mama."

"Aubrey!" Mortified, Grace reached for her daughter, only to have Aubrey cling to Ethan's shirt like a small golden burr. "Leave Ethan be now."

Changing tactics, Aubrey laid her head on Ethan's shoulder and smiled sweetly—one arm clinging like a vine around his neck as

Grace tugged at her. "Kiss Mama," she crooned and batted her eyes at Ethan.

If Grace had laughed instead of looking so embarrassed—and just a little nervous—Ethan thought he could have brushed his lips over her brow and settled the matter. But her cheeks had gone pink—it was so endearing. She wouldn't meet his eyes, and her breath was unsteady.

He watched her bite her bottom lip and decided he might as well settle the matter another way entirely.

He laid a hand on Grace's shoulder with Aubrey caught between them. "This'll be easier," he murmured and touched his lips lightly to hers.

It wasn't easier. It rocked her heart. It could barely be considered a kiss, was over almost before it began. It was nothing more than a quiet brush of lips, an instant of taste and texture. And a whiff of promise that made her long, desperately, impossibly.

In all the years he'd known her, he had never touched his mouth to hers. Now, with just this fleeting sampling, he wondered why he'd waited so long. And worried that the wondering would change everything.

Aubrey clapped her hands in glee, but he barely heard it. Grace's eyes were on his now, that misty, swimming green, and their faces were close. Close enough that he only had to ease forward a fraction if he wanted to taste again. To linger this time, he thought, as her lips parted on a trembling breath.

"No, me!" Aubrey planted her small, soft mouth on her mother's cheek, then Ethan's. "Come play."

Grace jerked back like a puppet whose strings had been rudely yanked. The silky pink cloud that had begun to fog her brain evaporated. "Soon, honey." Moving quickly now, she plucked Aubrey out of Ethan's arms and set her on her feet. "Go on and build me a castle for us to live in." She gave Aubrey a gentle pat on the rump and sent her off at a run.

Then she cleared her throat. "You're awfully good to her, Ethan. I appreciate it."

He decided the best place for his hands, under the circumstances, was his pockets. He wasn't sure what to do about the itchy feeling in them. "She's a sweetheart." Deliberately, he turned to watch Aubrey in her red sandbox.

"And a handful." She needed to get her feet back under her, Grace told herself, and to do what needed to be done next. "Why don't we just forget last night, Ethan? I'm sure you meant it all for the best. Reality's just not always what we'd choose or what we'd like it to be."

He turned back slowly, and those quiet eyes of his focused on her face. "What do you want it to be, Grace?"

"What I want is for Aubrey to have a home, and a family. I think I'm pretty close to that."

He shook his head. "No, what do you want for Grace?"

"Besides her?" She looked over at her daughter and smiled. "I don't even remember anymore. Right now I want my lawn mowed and my vegetables weeded. I appreciate you coming by like this." She turned away and prepared to give the starter cord another yank. "I'll be by the house tomorrow."

She went very still when his hand closed over hers.

"I'll cut the grass."

"I can do it."

She couldn't even start the damn lawn mower, he thought, but was wise enough not to mention it. "I didn't say you couldn't. I said I'd do it."

She couldn't turn around, couldn't risk what it would do to her system to be that close again, face to face. "You have chores of your own."

"Grace, are we going to stand here all day arguing over who's going to cut this grass? I could have it done twice over by the time we finish, and you could be saving your string beans from being choked out by those weeds."

"I was going to get to them." Her voice was thin. They were both bent over, all but spooned together. The flash of sheer animal lust that streaked through the familiar yearning for him staggered her.

"Get to them now." He murmured it, willing her to move. If she didn't, and very quickly, he might not be able to hold himself back from putting his hands on her. And putting them on her in places they had no business being.

"All right." She shifted away, moving sideways while her heart knocked at her ribs in short rabbit punches. "I appreciate it. Thanks." She bit her lip hard because she was going to babble. Determined to be normal, she turned and smiled a little. "It's probably the carburetor again. I've got some tools."

Saying nothing, Ethan grabbed the cord with one hand and yanked it hard, twice. The engine caught with a dyspeptic roar. "It ought to do," he said mildly when he saw her mouth thin in frustration.

"Yeah, it ought to." Struggling not to be annoyed, she strode quickly to her vegetable patch.

And bent over, Ethan thought as he began to cut the first swath. Bent over in those thin cotton shorts in a way that forced him to take several long, careful breaths.

She didn't have a clue, he decided, what it had done to his usually well-disciplined hormones to have her trim little butt snugged back against him. What it did to the usually moderate temperature of his blood to have all that long, bare leg brushing against his.

She might be a mother—a fact that he reminded himself of often to keep dark and dangerous thoughts at bay—but as far as he was concerned, she was nearly as innocent and unaware as she'd been at fourteen.

When he'd first begun to have those dark and dangerous thoughts about her.

He'd stopped himself from acting on them. For God's sake, she'd just been a kid. And a man with his past had no right to touch anyone so unspoiled. Instead, he'd been her friend and had found contentment in that. He'd thought he could continue to be her friend, and only her friend. But just lately those thoughts had been striking him more often and with more force. They were becoming very tricky to control.

They both had enough complications in their lives, he reminded himself. He was just going to mow her lawn, maybe help her pull some weeds. If there was time he'd offer to take them into town for some ice cream cones. Aubrey was partial to strawberry.

Then he had to go down to the boatyard and get to work. And since it was his turn to cook, he had to figure out that little nuisance.

But mother or not, he thought, as Grace leaned over to tug out a stubborn dandelion, she had a pair of amazing legs.

GRACE KNEW SHE shouldn't have let herself be persuaded to go into town, even for a quick ice cream cone. It meant adjusting her day's schedule, changing into something less disreputable than her gardening clothes, and spending more time in Ethan's company when she was feeling a bit too aware of her needs.

But Aubrey loved these small trips and treats, so it was impossible to say no.

It was only a mile into St. Chris, but they went from quiet neighborhood to busy waterfront. The gift and souvenir shops would stay open seven days a week now to take advantage of the summer tourist season. Couples and families strolled by with shopping bags filled with memories to take home.

The sky was brilliantly blue, and the Bay reflected it, inviting boats to cruise along its surface. A couple of Sunday sailors had tangled the lines of their little Sunfish, letting the sails flop. But they appeared to be having the time of their lives despite that small mishap.

Grace could smell fish frying, candy melting, the coconut sweetness of sunblock, and always, always, the moist fragrance of the water.

She'd grown up on this waterfront, watching boats, sailing them. She ran free along the docks, in and out of the shops. She learned to pick crabs at her mother's knee, gaining the speed and skill needed to separate out the meat, that precious commodity that would be packaged and shipped all over the world.

Work hadn't been a stranger, but she'd always been free. Her family had lived well, if not luxuriously. Her father didn't believe in spoiling his women with too much pampering. Still, he'd been kind and loving even though set in his ways. And he'd never made her feel that he was disappointed that he had only a daughter instead of sons to carry his name.

In the end, she'd disappointed him anyway.

Grace swung Aubrey up on her hip and nuzzled her.

"Busy today," she commented.

"Seems to get more crowded every summer." But Ethan shrugged it off. They needed the summer crowds to survive the winters. "I heard Bingham's going to expand the restaurant, fancy it up, too, to bring more people in year-round."

"Well, he's got that chef from up north now, and got himself reviewed in the *Washington Post* magazine." She jiggled Aubrey on her hip. "The Egret Rest is the only linen-tablecloth restaurant around here. Spiffing it up should be good for the town. We always went there for dinner on special occasions."

She set Aubrey down, trying not to remember that she hadn't seen the inside of the restaurant in over three years. She held Aubrey's hand and let her daughter tug her relentlessly toward Crawford's.

This was another standard of St. Chris. Crawford's was for ice cream and cold drinks and take-out submarine sandwiches. Since it was noon, the shop was doing a brisk business. Grace ordered herself not to spoil things by mentioning that they should be eating sandwiches instead of ice cream.

"Hey, there, Grace, Ethan. Hello, pretty Aubrey." Liz Crawford beamed at them even as she skillfully built a cold-cut sub. She'd gone to school with Ethan and had dated him for a short, careless time that they both remembered with fondness.

Now she was the sturdy, freckle-faced mother of two, married to Junior Crawford, as he was known to distinguish him from his father, Senior.

Junior, skinny as a scarecrow, whistled between his teeth as he rang up sales, and sent them a quick salute.

"Busy day," Ethan said, dodging an elbow from a customer at the counter.

"Tell me." Liz rolled her eyes, deftly wrapped the sub in white paper and handed it, along with three others, over the counter. "Y'all want a sub?"

"Ice cream," Aubrey said definitely. "Berry."

"Well, you go on down and tell Mother Crawford what you have in mind. Oh, Ethan, Seth was in here shortly ago with Danny and Will. I swear, those kids grow like weeds in high summer. Loaded up on subs and soda pop. Said they were working down to your boatyard."

He felt a faint flicker of guilt, knowing that Phillip was not only working but riding herd on three young boys. "I'll be heading down there myself soon."

"Ethan, if you don't have time for this . . . " Grace began.

"I've got time to eat an ice cream cone with a pretty girl." So saying, he lifted Aubrey up and let her press her nose to the glass-fronted counter that held the buckets of hand-dipped choices.

Liz took the next order, and spared a wiggling-eyebrow glance toward her husband that spoke volumes. Ethan Quinn and Grace Monroe, it stated clearly. Well, well. What do you think of that?

They took their cones outside, where the breeze was warm off the water, and wandered away from the crowds to find one of the small iron benches the city fathers had campaigned for. Armed with a fistful of napkins, Grace set Aubrey on her lap.

"I remember when you'd come here and know the name of every face you'd see," Grace murmured. "Mother Crawford would be behind the counter, reading a paperback novel." She felt a wet drip from Aubrey's ice cream plop on her leg below the hem of her shorts and wiped it up. "Eat around the edges, honey, before it melts away."

"You'd always get strawberry ice cream, too."

"Hmm?"

"As I recall," Ethan said, surprised that the image was so clear in his mind, "you had a preference for strawberry. And grape Nehi."

"I guess I did." Grace's sunglasses slipped down her nose as she bent to mop up more drips. "Everything was simple if you had yourself a strawberry cone and a grape Nehi."

"Some things stay simple." Because her hands were full, Ethan nudged Grace's glasses back up—and thought he caught a flicker of something in her eyes behind the shaded lenses. "Some don't."

He looked out to the water as he applied himself to his own cone. A better idea, he decided, than watching Grace take those long, slow licks from hers. "We used to come down here on Sundays now and then," he remembered. "All of us piling into the car and riding into town for ice cream or a sub or just to see what was up. Mom and Dad liked to sit under one of the umbrella tables at the diner and drink lemonade."

"I still miss them," she said quietly. "I know you do. That winter I caught pneumonia—I remember my mother and yours. It seemed every time I woke up, one or the other of them was right there. Dr. Quinn was the kindest woman I ever knew. My mama—"

She broke off, shook her head.

"What?"

"I don't want to make you sad."

"You won't. Finish it."

"My mother goes to the cemetery every year in the spring and puts flowers on your mother's grave. I go with her. I didn't realize until the first time we went how much my mother loved her."

"I wondered who put them there. It's nice knowing. What's being said . . . what some people are saying about my father would have got her Irish up. She'd have scalded more than a few tongues by now."

"That's not your way, Ethan. You have to tend to that business your own way."

"They would both want us to do what's best for Seth. That would come first."

"You are doing what's best for him. Every time I see him he looks lighter. There was such a heaviness over him when he first came here. Professor Quinn was working his way through that, but he had such troubles of his own. You know how troubled he was, Ethan."

"Yeah." And the guilt weighed like a stone, dead center in his heart. "I know."

"Now I have made you sad." She shifted toward him so that their knees bumped. "Whatever troubled him, it was never you. You were one strong, steady light in his life. Anyone could see that."

"If I'd asked more questions . . . " he began.

"It's not your way," she said again and, forgetting her hand was sticky, touched it to his cheek. "You knew he would talk to you when he was ready, when he could."

"Then it was too late."

"No, it never is." Her fingers skimmed lightly over his cheek. "There's always a chance. I don't think I could get from one day to the next if I didn't believe there's always a chance. Don't worry," she said softly.

He felt something move inside him as he reached up to cover her hand with his. Something shifting and opening. Then Aubrey let out a wild squeal of joy.

"Grandpa!"

Grace's hand jerked, then dropped like a stone. All the warmth that had flowed out of her chilled. Her shoulders went straight and stiff as she turned forward again and watched her father walk toward them.

"There's my dollbaby. Come see Grandpa."

Grace let her daughter go, watched her race and be caught. Her father didn't wince or shy away from the sticky hands or smeared lips. He laughed and hugged and smacked his lips when kissed lavishly.

"Mmm, strawberry. Gimme more." He made munching noises on Aubrey's neck until she screamed with delight. Then he hitched her easily on his hip and crossed the slight distance to his daughter. And no longer smiled. "Grace, Ethan. Taking a Sunday stroll?"

Grace's throat was dry, and her eyes burned. "Ethan offered to buy us some ice cream."

"Well, that's nice."

"You're wearing some of it now," Ethan commented, hoping to ease some of the rippling tension that moved in the air.

Pete glanced down to his shirt, where Aubrey had transferred some of her favored strawberries. "Clothes wash. Don't often see you around the waterfront on a Sunday, Ethan, since you started building that boat."

"Taking an hour before I get started on it today. Hull's finished, deck's nearly."

"Good, that's good." He nodded, meaning it, then shifted his gaze to Grace. "Your mother's in the diner. She'll want to see her granddaughter."

"All right. I—"

"I'll take her over," he interrupted. "You can go on home when you're ready to, and your mother'll bring her on by your place in an hour or two."

She'd have preferred he slap her than speak to her in that polite and distant tone. But she nodded, as Aubrey was already babbling about Grandma.

"Bye! Bye, Mama. Bye, Ethan," Aubrey called over Pete's shoulder and blew noisy kisses.

"I'm sorry, Grace." Knowing it was inadequate, Ethan took her hand and found it stiff and cold.

"It doesn't matter. It can't matter. And he loves Aubrey. Just dotes on her. That's what counts."

"It's not fair to you. Your father's a good man, Grace, but he hasn't been fair to you."

"I let him down." She rose, quickly wiping her hands on the napkins she'd balled up. "And that's that."

"It's nothing more than his pride butting up against yours."

"Maybe. But my pride's important to me." She tossed the napkins into a trash container and told herself that was the end of it. "I've got to get back home, Ethan. There's a million things I should be doing, and if I've got a couple hours free, I'd better do them."

He didn't push, but was surprised how strongly he wanted to. He hated being nudged and nagged to talk about private matters himself. "I'll drive you home."

"No, I'd like to walk. Really like to walk. Thanks for the help." She managed a smile that looked almost natural. "And the ice cream. I'll be by the house tomorrow. Make sure you tell Seth his laundry goes in the hamper, not on the floor."

She walked away, her long legs eating up the ground. She made certain she was well away before she allowed her steps to slow. Before she rubbed a hand over the heart that ached no matter how firmly she ordered it not to.

There were only two men in her life she had ever really loved. It seemed neither of them could want her as she needed them to want her.

CHAPTER

ETHAN didn't mind music when he worked. The fact was, his taste in music was both broad and eclectic—another gift of the Quinns. The house had often been filled with it. His mother had played a fine piano with as much enthusiasm for the works of Chopin as for those of Scott Joplin. His father's musical talent had been the violin, and it was that instrument Ethan had gravitated to. He enjoyed the varying moods of it, and its portability.

Still, he found music a waste of sound whenever he was concentrating on a job, as he usually didn't hear it after ten minutes anyway. Silence suited him best during those times, but Seth liked the radio in the boatyard up, and up loud. So to keep peace, Ethan simply tuned out the head-punching rock and roll.

The hull of the boat had been caulked and filled, a labor-intensive and time-consuming task. Seth had been a lot of help there, Ethan admitted, giving him an extra pair of hands and feet when he needed them. Though Christ knew the boy could complain about the job as much as Phillip did.

Ethan tuned that out as well—to stay sane.

He hoped to finish leveling off the decking before Phillip arrived for the weekend, planing first on one diagonal, then across the next at a right angle.

With any luck, he could get some solid work done that week and the next on the cabin and cockpit.

Seth bitched about being on sanding detail, but he did a decent job of it. Ethan only had to tell him to go back and hit portions of the hull planking again a couple of times. He didn't mind the boy's questions, either. Though he had a million of them once he started.

"What's that piece over there for?"

"The bulkhead for the cockpit."

"Why'd you cut it out already?"

"Because we want to get rid of all the dust before we varnish and seal."

"What's all this other shit?"

Ethan paused in his own work, looking down from his position to where Seth frowned at a stack of precut lumber. "You got the sides and cabin ends, the toerail and drop-boards."

"It seems like an awful lot of pieces for one stupid boat."

"There's going to be a lot more."

"How come this guy doesn't just buy a boat that's already built?"

"Good thing for us he isn't." The client's deep pockets, Ethan mused, were giving Boats by Quinn its foundation. "Because he liked the other boat I built for him—and so he can tell all his big-shot friends he had a boat designed and hand-built for him."

Seth changed his sandpaper and applied himself again. He didn't mind the work, really. And he liked the smells of wood and varnish and that linseed oil, too. But he just didn't get it. "It's taking forever to put it together."

"Been at it less than three months. Lots of people spend a year—even longer—to build a wooden boat."

Seth's jaw dropped. "A year! Jesus, Ethan."

The loud, and very normal whine, made Ethan's mouth twitch. "Relax, this isn't going to take us that long. Once Cam gets back and can put in full days on it, we'll move along. And once school's out, you can pick up a lot of the grunt work."

"School is out."

"Hmm?"

"Today was it." Now Seth grinned, wide and bright. "Freedom. It's a done deal."

"Today?" Pausing in his work, Ethan frowned. "I thought you had a couple days yet."

"Nope."

He'd lost track of things somewhere, Ethan supposed. And it wasn't Seth's style—not yet, anyway—to volunteer information. "Did you get a report card?"

"Yeah—I passed."

"Let's see how." Ethan set his tools down, brushed his hands on his jeans. "Where is it?"

Seth shrugged his shoulders and kept sanding. "It's in my backpack over there. No big deal."

"Let's see it," Ethan repeated.

Seth did what Ethan considered his usual dance. Rolling his eyes, shrugging his shoulders, adding a long-suffering sigh. Oddly enough, he didn't end with an oath, as he was prone to. He walked over to where he'd dumped his backpack and riffled through it.

Ethan leaned down over the port side to take the paper Seth held up. Noting the mutinous expression on Seth's face, he expected the news would be grim. His stomach did a quick clench and roll. The required lecture, Ethan thought with an inner sigh, was going to be damned uncomfortable for both of them.

Ethan studied the thin, computer-generated sheet, pushing back his cap to scratch his head. "*All* A's?"

Seth jerked a shoulder again, stuffed his hands in his pockets. "Yeah, so?"

"I've never seen a report card with all A's before. Even Phillip used to have some B's, and maybe a C tossed in."

Embarrassment, and the fear of being called Egghead or something equally hideous, rose swiftly. "It's no big deal." He held up a hand for the report card, but Ethan shook his head.

"The hell it's not." But he saw Seth's scowl and thought he understood it. It was always hard to be different from the pack. "You got a good brain and you ought to be proud of it."

"It's just there. It's not like knowing how to pilot a boat or anything."

"You got a good brain and you use it, you'll figure out how to do most anything." Ethan folded the paper carefully and tucked it in his pocket. Damn if he wasn't going to show it off some. "Seems to me we ought to go get a pizza or something."

Puzzled, Seth narrowed his eyes. "You packed those lame sandwiches for dinner."

"Not good enough now. The first time a Quinn gets straight A's ought to rate at least a pizza." He saw Seth's mouth open and shut, watched the staggered delight leap into his eyes before he lowered them.

"Sure, that'd be cool."

"Can you hold off another hour?"

"No problem."

Seth grabbed his sandpaper and began to work furiously. And

blindly. His eyes were dazzled, his heart in his throat. It happened whenever one of them referred to him as a Quinn. He knew his name was DeLauter still. He had to put it at the top of every stupid paper he did for school, didn't he? But hearing Ethan call him a Quinn made that little beam of hope that Ray had first ignited in him months before shine just a little brighter.

He was going to stay. He was going to be one of them. He was never going back into hell again.

It made it worth being called down to Moorefield's office that day. The vice principal had reeled him in an hour before freedom. It had made his stomach jitter, as it always did. But she'd sat him down and told him she was proud of his progress.

Man, how mortifying.

Okay, so maybe he hadn't punched anybody in the face in the last couple months. And he'd been handing in his stupid homework assignments every dumb day because somebody was always nagging him about them. Phillip was the worst nag in that particular area. It was like the guy was a homework cop or something, Seth thought now. And yeah, he'd been raising his hand in class now and then, just for the hell of it.

But to have Moorefield single him out that way had been so . . . *blech*, he decided. He'd almost wished she'd hauled his butt in to give him another dose of In-School Suspension.

But if a bunch of dopey A's made a guy like Ethan happy, it was okay.

Ethan was absolutely cool in Seth's estimation. He worked outside all day, and his hands had scars and really thick calluses. Seth figured you could practically pound nails into Ethan's hands without him even feeling it, they were so hard and tough. He owned two boats—that he'd built himself—and he knew everything about the Bay and sailing. And didn't make a big deal about it.

A couple of months back Seth had watched *High Noon* on TV, even though it had been in lame black and white and there hadn't even been any blood or explosions. He'd thought then that Ethan was just like that Gary Cooper guy. He didn't say a lot, so you mostly listened when he did. And he just did what needed to be done without a lot of show.

Ethan would have faced down the bad guys, too. Because it was right. Seth had mulled it over for a while and had decided that's what a hero was. Somebody who just did what was right.

ETHAN WOULD HAVE been stunned and mortally embarrassed, if he'd been able to read Seth's thoughts. But the boy was an expert at keeping them to himself. On that level, he and Ethan were as close as twins.

It might have crossed Ethan's mind that Village Pizza was only a short block from Shiney's Pub, where Grace would be starting her shift, but he didn't mention it.

Couldn't take the boy into a bar anyway, Ethan mused as they headed into the bright lights and noise of the local restaurant. And Seth was bound to complain, loudly, if Ethan asked him to wait in the car for just a couple minutes while he poked his head in. Likely Grace would complain, too, if she caught on that he was checking on her.

It was best to let it go and concentrate on the matters at hand. He tucked his hands into his back pockets and studied the menu posted on the wall behind the counter. "What do you want on it?"

"You can forget the mushrooms. They're gross."

"We're of a mind there," Ethan murmured.

"Pepperoni and hot sausage." Seth sneered, but he spoiled it by bouncing a little in his sneakers. "If you can handle it."

"I can take it if you can. Hey, Justin," he said with a smile of greeting for the boy behind the counter. "We'll take a large, pepperoni and hot sausage, and a couple of jumbo Pepsis."

"You got it. Here or to go?"

Ethan scanned the dozen tables and booths offered and noted that he wasn't the only one who'd thought to celebrate the last day of school with pizza. "Go nab that last booth back there, Seth. We'll take it here, Justin."

"Have a seat. We'll bring the drinks out."

Seth had dumped his backpack on the bench and was tapping his hands on the table in time to the blast of Hootie and the Blowfish from the juke. "I'm going to go kick some video ass," he told Ethan. When Ethan reached back for his wallet, Seth shook his head. "I got money."

"Not tonight you don't," Ethan said mildly and pulled out some bills. "It's your party. Get some change."

"Cool." Seth snagged the bills and raced off to get quarters.

As Ethan slid into the booth, he wondered why so many people thought a couple hours in a noisy room was high entertainment. A huddle of kids was already trying to kick some video ass at the trio of machines along the back wall; the juke had switched to Clint Black—and that country boy was wailing. The toddler in the booth behind him was having a full-blown tantrum, and a group of teenage girls were giggling at a decibel level that would have made Simon's ears bleed.

What a way to spend a pretty summer night.

Then he saw Liz Crawford and Junior with their two little girls at a nearby booth. One of the girls—that must be Stacy, Ethan thought—was talking quickly, making wide gestures, while the rest of the family howled with laughter.

They made a unit, he mused, their own little island in the midst of the jittery lights and noise. He supposed that's what family was, an island. Knowing you could go there made all the difference.

Still the tug of envy surprised him, made him shift uncomfortably on the hard seat of the booth and scowl into space. He'd made his mind up about having a family years before, and he didn't care for this sharp pull of longing.

"Why, Ethan, you look fierce."

He glanced up as the drinks were set on the table in front of him, straight into the flirtatious eyes of Linda Brewster.

She was a looker, no question about it. The tight black jeans and scoop-necked black T-shirt hugged her well-developed body like a coat of fresh paint on a classic Chevy. After her divorce was final—one week ago Monday—she'd treated herself to a manicure and a new hairdo. Her coral-tipped nails skimmed through her newly bobbed, streaky blond hair as she smiled down at Ethan.

She'd had her eye on him for a time now—after all, she had separated from that useless Tom Brewster more than a year before and a woman had to look to the future. Ethan Quinn would be hot in bed, she decided. She had instincts about these things. Those big hands of his would be mighty thorough, she was sure. And attentive. Oh, yes.

She liked his looks, too. Just a little tough and weathered. And that slow, sexy smile of his . . . when you managed to drag one out of him, just made her want to lick her lips in anticipation.

He had that quiet way about him. Linda knew what they said about still waters. And she was dying to see just how deep Ethan Quinn's ran.

Ethan was well aware where her eye had wandered, and he was keeping his peeled as well. For running room. Women like Linda scared the hell out of him.

"Hi, Linda. Didn't know you were working here." Or he'd have avoided Village Pizza like the plague.

"Just helping my father out for a couple of weeks." She was flat broke, and her father—the owner of Village Pizza—had told her he'd be damned if she was going to sponge off him and her mother. She should get her sassy butt to work. "Haven't seen you around lately."

"I've been around." He wished she'd move along. Her perfume gave him the jitters.

"I heard you and your brothers rented that old barn of Claremont's and are building boats. I've been meaning to come down and take a look."

"Not much to see." Where the hell was Seth when he needed him? Ethan wondered a little desperately. How long could those damn quarters last?

"I'd like to see it anyway." She skimmed those slick-tipped nails down his arm, gave a low purr as she felt the ridge of muscle. "I can slip out of here for a while. Why don't you run me down there and show me what's what?"

His mind blanked for a moment. He was only human. And she was running her tongue over her top lip in a way designed to draw a man's eyes and tickle his glands. Not that he was interested, not a bit, but it had been a long time since he'd had a woman moaning under him. And he had a feeling Linda would be a champion moaner.

"Copped top score." Seth plopped into the booth, flushed with victory, and grabbed his Pepsi. He slurped some up. "Man, what's keeping that pizza? I'm starved."

Ethan felt his blood start to run again and nearly sighed with relief. "It'll be along."

"Well." Despite annoyance at the interruption, Linda smiled brilliantly at Seth. "This must be the new addition. What's your name, honey? I can't quite recollect."

"I'm Seth." And he sized her up quickly. Bimbo, was his first and last thought. He'd seen plenty of them in his short life. "Who're you?"

"I'm Linda, an old friend of Ethan's. My daddy owns the place."

"Cool, so maybe you could tell them to put a fire under that pizza before we die of old age here."

"Seth." The word and Ethan's quiet look were all it took for the boy to close his mouth. "Your daddy still makes the best pizza on the Shore," Ethan said with an easier smile. "You be sure to tell him."

"I will. And you give me a call, Ethan." She wiggled her left hand. "I'm a free woman these days." She wandered away, hips swinging like a well-oiled metronome.

"She smells like the place at the mall where they sell all that girl stuff." Seth wrinkled his nose. He hadn't liked her because he'd seen just a shadow of his mother in her eyes. "She just wants to get in your pants."

"Shut up, Seth."

"It's true," Seth said with a shrug, but happily let the subject drop when Linda came back bearing pizza.

"Y'all enjoy, now," she told them, leaning over the table just a little farther than necessary in case Ethan had missed the view the first time around.

Seth snagged a piece and bit in, knowing it was going to scorch the roof of his mouth. The flavors exploded, making the burn more than worth it. "Grace makes pizza from scratch," he said around a mouthful. "It's even better than this."

Ethan only grunted. The thought of Grace after he'd entertained—however unwillingly—a brief and sweaty fantasy about Linda Brewster made him twitchy.

"Yeah. We ought to see if she'd make it for us one of the days she comes to clean and stuff. She comes tomorrow, right?"

"Yeah." Ethan took a piece, annoyed that most of his appetite had deserted him. "I suppose."

"Maybe she'd make one up before she goes."

"You're having pizza tonight."

"So?" Seth polished off the first piece with the speed and precision of a jackal. "You could, like, compare. Grace ought to open a diner or something so she wouldn't have to work all those different jobs. She's always working. She wants to buy a house."

"She does?"

"Yeah." Seth licked the side of his hand where sauce dripped. "Just a little one, but it has to have a yard so Aubrey can run around and have a dog and stuff."

"She tell you all that?"

"Sure. I asked how come she was busting her butt cleaning all those houses and working down at the pub, and she said that was mostly why. And if she doesn't make enough, she and Aubrey won't have a place of their own by the time Aub starts kindergarten. I guess even a little house costs big bucks, right?"

"It costs," Ethan said quietly. He remembered how satisfied, how proud he'd been when he'd bought his own place on the water. What it had meant to him to know he'd succeeded at what he did. "It takes time to save up."

"Grace wants to have the house by the time Aubrey starts school. After that, she says how she has to start saving for college." He snorted and decided he could force down a third piece. "Hell, Aubrey's just a baby, it's a million years till college. Told her that, too," he added, because it pleased him for people to know he and Grace had *conversations.* "She just laughed and said five minutes ago Aubrey had gotten her first tooth. I didn't get it."

"She meant kids grow up fast." Since it didn't look as though his appetite would be coming back, Ethan closed the top on the pizza and took out bills to pay for it. "Let's take this back to the boatyard. Since you don't have school in the morning, we can put in a couple more hours."

⎯⎯

HE PUT IN more than a couple. Once he got started, he couldn't seem to stop. It cleared his mind, kept it from wandering, wondering, worrying.

The boat was definite, a tangible task with a foreseeable end. He knew what he was doing here, just as he knew what he was doing out on the Bay. There weren't so many shadowy areas of maybes or what-ifs.

Ethan continued to work even when Seth curled up on a drop cloth and fell asleep. The sound of tools running didn't appear to disturb him—though Ethan wondered how anyone could sleep with the best part of a large sausage-and-pepperoni pizza in his stomach.

He started work on the ends and corner posts for the cabin and cockpit coaming while the night wind blew lazily through the open cargo doors. He'd turned the radio off so that now the only music was the water, the gentle notes of it sliding against the shore.

He worked slowly, carefully, though he was well able to visualize the completed project. Cam, he decided, would handle most of the interior work. He was the most skilled of the three of them at finish carpentry. Phillip could handle the rough-ins; he was better at sheer manual labor than he liked to admit.

If they could keep up the pace, Ethan calculated that they could have the boat trimmed and under sail in another two months. He would leave figuring the profits and percentages to Phillip. The money would feed the lawyers, the boatyard, and their own bellies.

Why hadn't Grace ever told him she wanted to buy a house?

Ethan frowned thoughtfully as he chose a galvanized bolt. Wasn't that a pretty big step to be discussing with a ten-year-old boy? Then again, he admitted, Seth had asked. He himself had only told her she shouldn't be working herself so hard—he hadn't asked why she insisted on it.

She ought to make things up with her father, he thought again. If the two of them would just bend that stiff-necked Monroe pride for five minutes, they could come to terms. She'd gotten pregnant—and there was no doubt in Ethan's mind that Jack Casey had taken advantage of a young, naive girl and should be shot for it—but that was over and done.

His family had never held grudges, small or large. They'd fought, certainly—and he and his brothers had often fought physically. But when it was done, it was over.

It was true enough that he'd harbored some seeds of resentment because Cam had raced off to Europe and Phillip had moved to Baltimore. It had happened so fast after their mother died, and he'd still been raw. Everything had changed before he could blink, and he'd stewed over that.

But even with that, he would never have turned his back on either of them if they'd needed him. And he knew they wouldn't have turned their backs on him.

It seemed to him the most foolish and wasteful thing imaginable that Grace wouldn't ask for help, and her father wouldn't offer it.

He glanced at the big round clock nailed to the wall over the front doors. Phillip's idea, Ethan remembered with a half grin. He'd figured they'd need to know how much time they were putting in, but as far as Ethan knew, Phillip was the only one who bothered to mark down the time.

It was nearly one, which meant Grace would be finishing up at the pub in about an hour. It wouldn't hurt to load Seth in the truck and do a quick swing by Shiney's. Just to . . . check on things.

Even as he started to rise, he heard the boy whimper in his sleep.

Pizza's finally getting to him, Ethan thought with a shake of the head. But he supposed childhood wouldn't be complete without its quota of bellyaches. He climbed down, rolling his shoulders to work out the kinks as he approached the sleeping boy.

He crouched beside Seth, laid a hand on his shoulders, and gave a gentle shake.

And the boy came up swinging.

The bunched fist caught Ethan squarely on the mouth and knocked his head back. The shock, more than the quick and bright pain, had him swearing. He blocked the next blow, then took Seth's arm firmly. "Hold it."

"Get your hands off me." Wild, desperate, and still caught in the sticky grip of the dream, Seth flailed at the air. "Get your fucking hands off me."

Understanding came quickly. It was the look in Seth's eyes— stark terror and vicious fury. He'd once felt both himself, along with a shuddering helplessness. He let go, lifted both of his hands palms out. "You were dreaming." He said it quietly, without inflection, and listened to Seth's ragged breathing echo on the air. "You fell asleep."

Seth kept his fists bunched. He didn't remember falling asleep. He remembered curling up, listening to Ethan work. And the next thing he knew, he was back in one of those dark rooms, where the smells were sour and too human and the noises from the next room were too loud and too animal.

And one of the faceless men who used his mother's bed had crept out and put hands on him again.

But it was Ethan who was watching him, patiently, with too much knowledge in his serious eyes. Seth's stomach twisted not only at what had been, but that Ethan should now know.

Because he couldn't think of words or excuses, Seth simply closed his eyes.

It was that which tilted the scales for Ethan. The surrender to helplessness, the slide into shame. He'd left this wound alone, but now it seemed he would need to treat it after all.

"You don't have to be afraid of what was."

"I'm not afraid of anything." Seth's eyes snapped open. The anger in them was adult and bitter, but his voice jerked like the child he was. "I'm not afraid of some stupid dream."

"You don't have to be ashamed of it, either."

Because he was, hideously, Seth sprang to his feet. His fists were bunched again, ready. "I'm not ashamed of anything. And you don't know a damn thing about it."

"I know every damn thing about it." Because he did, he hated to speak of it. But despite the defiant stance, the boy was trembling, and Ethan knew just how alone he felt. Speaking of it was the only thing left for him to do. The right thing to do.

"I know what dreams did to me, how I had them for a long time after that part of things was over for me." And still had them now and again, he thought, but there was no need to tell the boy he might have to face a lifetime of flashing back and overcoming. "I know what it does to your guts."

"Bullshit." The tears were burning the backs of Seth's eyes, humiliating him all the more. "Nothing's wrong with me. I got the hell out, didn't I? I got away from her, didn't I? I'm not going back either, no matter what."

"No, you're not going back," Ethan agreed. No matter what.

"I don't care what you or anybody thinks about what went on

back then. And you're not tricking me into saying things about it by pretending you know."

"You don't have to say anything about it," Ethan told him. "And I don't have to pretend." He picked up the cap Seth's blow had knocked off his head, ran it absently through his hands before putting it back on. But the casual gesture did nothing to ease the tight, slick ball of tension in his gut.

"My mother was a whore—my biological mother. And she was a junkie with a taste for heroin." He kept his gaze on Seth's and his voice matter-of-fact. "I was younger than you when she sold me the first time, to a man who liked young boys."

Seth's breathing quickened as he took a step back. *No*, was all he could think. Ethan Quinn was everything strong and solid and . . . normal. "You're lying."

"People mostly lie to brag, or to get out of some stupid thing they've done. I don't see the point in either—and less in lying about this."

Ethan took his cap off again because it suddenly felt too tight on his head. Once, twice, he raked his hand through his hair as if to ease the weight. "She sold me to men to pay for her habit. The first time, I fought. It didn't stop it, but I fought. The second time, I fought, and a few times more after that. Then I didn't bother fighting because it just made it worse."

Ethan's gaze stayed level on the boy's. In the harsh overhead lights Seth's eyes were dark, and not as calm as they had been when Ethan had begun to speak. Seth's chest hurt until he remembered to breathe again. "How'd you stand it?"

"I stopped caring." Ethan shrugged his shoulders. "I stopped *being*, if you know what I mean. There wasn't anybody I could go to for help—or I didn't know there was. She moved around a lot to keep the social workers off her tail."

Seth's lips felt dry and tight. He rubbed the back of his hand over them violently. "You never knew where you're going to wake up in the morning."

"Yeah, you never knew." But all the places looked the same. They all smelled the same.

"But you got away. You got out."

"Yeah, I got out. One night after her john had finished with both of us, there was . . . some trouble." Screams, blood, curses. Pain. "I don't remember everything exactly, but the cops came. I must have been in a pretty bad way because they took me to the hospital and figured things out quick enough. I ended up in the system, might have stayed there. But the doctor who treated me was Stella Quinn."

"They took you."

"They took me." And saying that, just that, soothed the sickness in Ethan's gut. "They didn't just change my life, they saved it. I had the dreams for a long time after, the sweaty ones where you wake up trying to breathe, sure you're back in it. And even when you realize you're not, you're cold for a while."

Seth knuckled the tears away, but he didn't feel ashamed of them now. "I always got away. Sometimes they put their hands on me, but I got away. None of them ever . . . "

"Good for you."

"I still wanted to kill them, and her. I wanted to."

"I know."

"I didn't want to tell anybody. I think Ray knew, and Cam sort of knows. I didn't want anybody to think I . . . to look at me and think . . . " He couldn't express it, the shame of having anyone look at him and see what had happened, and what could have happened, in those dark, smelly rooms. "Why did you tell me?"

"Because you need to know it doesn't make you less of a man."

Ethan waited, knowing that Seth would decide whether he accepted the truth of that.

What Seth saw was a man, tall, strong, self-possessed, with big, callused hands and quiet eyes. One of the weights that hung on his heart lifted. "I guess I do." And he smiled a little. "Your mouth's bleeding."

Ethan dabbed at it with the back of his hand and knew they'd crossed a thin and shaky line. "You got a good right jab. I never saw it coming." He held out a hand, testing, and ruffled Seth's sleep-tumbled hair. The boy's smile stayed in place. "Let's clean up," Ethan said, "and go home."

CHAPTER
5

G RACE had a morning full of chores. The first load of laundry
went in at seven-fifteen while the coffee was brewing and her
eyes were still mostly shut. She watered her porch plants and the
little pots of herbs on her kitchen windowsill, and yawned hugely.

As the coffee began to scent the air and give her hope, she washed
the glasses and bowls Julie had used the night before while babysitting.
She closed the open bag of potato chips, tucked it into its place in the
cupboard, then wiped the crumbs from the counter where Julie had
had her snack while talking on the phone.

Julie Cutter wasn't known for her neatness, but she loved Aubrey.

At precisely seven-thirty—and after half a cup of coffee—Aubrey
woke.

Reliable as the sunrise, Grace thought, heading out of the tiny
galley kitchen toward the bedroom off the living room. Rain or
shine, weekday or weekend, Aubrey's internal clock buzzed away at
seven-thirty every morning.

Grace could have left her in the crib and finished her coffee, but she looked forward to this moment every day. Aubrey stood at the side of the crib, her sunbeam curls tangled from sleep, her cheeks still flushed with it. Grace could still remember the first time she'd come in and seen Aubrey standing, her wobbly legs rocking, her face glowing with success and surprise.

Now Aubrey's legs seemed so sturdy. She lifted one, then the other, in a kind of joyful march. She laughed out loud when Grace came into the room. "Mama, Mama, hi, my mama."

"Hello, my baby." Grace leaned over the side for the first nuzzle and sighed. She knew how lucky she was. There couldn't have been a child on the planet with a sunnier nature than her little girl. "How's my Aubrey?"

"Up! Out!"

"You bet. Gotta pee?"

"Gotta pee," Aubrey agreed and giggled when Grace lifted her out of the crib.

The toilet training was coming along, Grace decided, checking Aubrey's overnight diaper as they headed into the bathroom. It had its hits and its misses.

Aubrey hit it this time, and Grace launched into the lavish praise over bodily functions that only a parent with a toddler could understand. Teeth and hair were brushed in the closet-size bathroom Grace had brightened up with wallpaper and awning-striped curtains.

Then the breakfast routine began. Aubrey wanted cold cereal with bananas but no milk. She plopped her hand over the bowl when Grace started to pour it on, shaking her head vigorously. "No, Mama, no. Cup. Please."

"Okay, milk in a cup." Grace filled one, set it on the high-chair tray beside the bowl. "Eat up, now. We've got lots to do today."

"Do what?"

"Let's see." Grace made herself a piece of toast while she went through the projected day. "We have to finish the laundry, then we promised Mrs. West we'd wash her windows today."

A three-hour job, Grace estimated.

"Then we have to go to the market."

Aubrey gasped in pleasure. "Miss Lucy."

"Yes, you'll see Miss Lucy." Lucy Wilson was one of Aubrey's favorite people. The supermarket cashier always had a smile—and a lollipop—for Aubrey. "After we put the groceries away, we're going to the Quinns'."

"Seth!" Milk dribbled out of her grin.

"Well, honey, I don't know for certain that he'll be there today. He may be out on the boat with Ethan, or over at his friends' house."

"Seth," Aubrey said again, very definitely, and her mouth puckered up into a stubborn pout.

"We'll see." Grace mopped up the spills.

"Ethan."

"Maybe."

"Doggies."

"Foolish, for sure." She kissed the top of Aubrey's head and gave herself the luxury of a second cup of coffee.

⁂

AT EIGHT-FIFTEEN GRACE was armed with a stack of newspapers and a spray bottle that contained a mix of vinegar and ammonia. Aubrey was entertaining herself on the grass with her Mattel See 'n Say. Every few seconds a cow mooed or a pig oinked. And Aubrey never failed to echo the sound.

By the time Aubrey had switched her affections to her building blocks, Grace had finished cleaning and polishing the outside of the windows on the front and side of the cottage and was right on schedule. She would have stayed on schedule if Mrs. West hadn't come out with tall glasses of iced tea and a desire to chat.

"I don't know how to thank you for seeing to this for me, Grace." Mrs. West, the grandmother of many, had brought Aubrey her drink in a bright plastic cup with ducks on the side.

"I'm happy to do it, Mrs. West."

"Just can't do like I used to, with my arthritis. And I do like my windows to shine." She smiled, deepening the wrinkles on her weather-scored face. "And you do make them shine. My grand-daughter Layla said how she'd wash them for me. But I tell you the truth and shame the devil, Grace, that girl's a scatterbrain. She'd like as not start the job and end up sleeping in the vegetable patch. Don't know what's to become of that girl."

Grace laughed and scrubbed at the next window. "She's only fifteen. Her mind's on boys and clothes and music."

"Tell me." Mrs. West nodded so vigorously that her second chin wobbled with the movement. "Why, at her age I could pick a crab clean faster than you could blink. Earned my keep, and kept my mind on my work till the work was done." She winked. "Then I thought about boys."

She let out a hearty laugh before smiling at Aubrey. "That's one pretty little lamb you got yourself there, Gracie."

"The light of my life."

"Good as gold, too. Why, my Carly's youngest boy, Luke? He's not still for two minutes running and spends every waking hour looking for trouble. Just last week I caught him climbing up my parlor curtains like a house cat." Still, the memory made her chuckle. "He's a terror, that Luke is."

"Aubrey has her moments, too."

"Can't believe it. Not with that angel face. You're going to have to beat the boys off with a stick to keep them from sniffing around that sweetheart one of these days. Pretty as a picture. Already seen her holding hands with one."

Grace bobbled her spray bottle and looked around quickly to make certain her little girl hadn't grown up while she wasn't looking. "Aubrey?"

Mrs. West laughed again. "Walking on the waterfront with that Quinn boy—the new one."

"Oh, Seth." The sense of relief was so ridiculous, Grace set the bottle down and picked up her glass to drink. "Aubrey's got a crush on him."

"Good-looking boy. My young Matt goes to school with him—told me how Seth came to sock that little bully Robert a few weeks back. Couldn't help but feel it was about time somebody did. How they doing over at the Quinns?"

The question was her main purpose for coming out, but Mrs. West believed in leading up to matters.

"Just fine."

Mrs. West rolled her eyes. This pump needed more priming. "That girl Cam up and married sure is a beauty. She'll have to have quick hands, too, to keep that one in line. Always was wild."

"I think Anna can handle him."

"Went off to some foreign place to honeymoon, didn't they?"

"Rome. Seth showed me a postcard they sent. It's beautiful."

"Always puts me in mind of that movie with Audrey Hepburn and Gregory Peck—where she's a princess. Don't make movies like that anymore."

"*Roman Holiday.*" Grace smiled wistfully. She had a weakness for the classic and romantic.

"That's the one." Grace looked a bit like Audrey Hepburn, Mrs. West mused. Coloring was wrong, of course, with Grace being blond as a Viking, but she had the big eyes and the cool, pretty face. Lord knew, she was skinny enough.

"Never been anyplace foreign." Which included, in Mrs. West's mind, two-thirds of the United States. "They coming back soon?"

"A couple days."

"Hmm. Well, that house needs a woman, no question. Can't imagine what it's like over there, four males in one house. Must smell like a gym sock half the time. Don't know a man on this earth who can manage to pee and hit the toilet with the whole stream."

Grace laughed and went back to her windows. "They aren't so bad. The fact is, Cam was keeping the house pretty well before they hired me to take over. But the only one of them who remembers to empty the pockets before tossing his pants at the hamper is Phillip."

"If that's the worst of it, it's not bad. I expect Cam's wife'll take over the house once they get back."

Grace's hand tightened on her wad of newspaper as her heart did a quick hitch. "I . . . She works full-time in Princess Anne."

"Most likely she'll take over," Mrs. West said again. "A woman likes her house kept her way. Best thing for the boy, I expect, having a woman there full-time. Don't know what Ray was thinking of this time around, I swear. A good-hearted man he was, but once Stella passed . . . shifted his moorings, I'd say. A man his age taking on a boy thataway. No matter what was what. Not that I believe one word of the nasty gossip you hear now and then. Nancy Claremont is the worst, flapping her lips every chance she gets."

Mrs. West waited a beat, hoping that Grace would flap hers. But Grace was frowning intently at the window.

"You know if that insurance inspector's coming around again?"

"No," Grace said quietly, "I don't. I hope not."

"Don't see how it makes a matter where the boy came from as

far as the insurance company goes. Even if Ray did suicide himself—and I'm not saying it's so—they can't prove it, can they? Because . . ." She paused dramatically, as she did whenever she made the argument. "They weren't there!"

She said the last on a note of triumph, just as she had when she'd made the same statement to Nancy.

"Professor Quinn wouldn't have killed himself," Grace murmured.

"'Course not." But it did make for such interesting talk. "But the boy—" She broke off, her ears pricking up. "There goes my telephone. You just let yourself in when you want to do the inside, Grace," she said as she hurried off.

Grace said nothing, kept working steadily. But her mind was whirling. It shamed her that she couldn't concentrate on Professor Quinn. She could think only of herself and of what might happen.

Would Anna come back from Rome and want to take over the house? Would Grace lose her job there and the extra money that went with it? Worse—much worse—would she lose those opportunities to see Ethan once or twice a week? To share a meal now and then?

She'd gotten used to—even dependent on—being a part of his life, even a peripheral part, she realized. And as pathetic as it was, she loved folding his clothes, smoothing the sheets on his bed. She even allowed herself to believe that he would think of her when he found one of her little notes around the house. Or slipped between freshly laundered sheets at night.

Was she going to lose that, too—and lose the pleasure of seeing him coming in from his boat or scooping Aubrey up when she demanded a kiss, or glancing over at her and giving her that slow smile?

Was all of that going to be only pictures she tucked away in her mind now?

Her days would go on and on, without even that to look forward to. And her nights would go on and on, alone.

She squeezed her eyes tight, struggling with despair. Then opened them again when Aubrey tugged at the hem of her shorts.

"Mama. Miss Lucy?"

"Soon, honey." Because she needed to, Grace lifted Aubrey into her arms for a fierce hug.

※

IT WAS NEARLY one by the time Grace finished putting away the groceries and fixing Aubrey's lunch. She was only half an hour behind, and she thought she could make that up without too much trouble. It just meant moving a little quicker and keeping her mind on her work. No more projecting, she ordered herself as she strapped Aubrey into the car seat. No more foolishness.

"Seth, Seth, Seth," Aubrey chanted, bouncing madly.

"We'll see." Grace climbed behind the wheel, put the key in the ignition, and turned it. The response was a wheeze and a thump. "Oh, no, you don't. No, you don't. I don't have time for this." A little panicked, she turned the key again, pumped the gas pedal, and sighed with relief when the engine caught. "That's more like it," she muttered as she backed out of the short driveway. "Here we go, Aubrey."

"Here we go!"

Five minutes later, midway between her house and the Quinns', the old sedan coughed again, shuddered, then belched out steam from under the hood.

"Dammit!"

"Dammit!" Aubrey echoed joyfully.

Grace only pressed the heels of her hands to her eyes. It was the radiator, she was sure of it. Last month it had been the fan belt, and before that, the brake pads. Resigned, she eased to the side of the road and got out to open the hood.

Smoke billowed, made her cough and step away. Resolutely, she swallowed back the knot of despair in her throat. Maybe it wouldn't be anything major. It could just be some belt again. And if it wasn't—she sighed hugely—she would have to decide if it was better to pump more money into this wreck or to worry her beleaguered budget into buying another wreck.

Either way, there was nothing to be done about it now.

She opened the passenger-side door and unbuckled Aubrey. "The car's sick again, honey."

"Awww."

"Yeah, so we're going to leave it right here."

"Alone?"

Aubrey's concern over inanimate objects made Grace smile again. "Not for long. I'm going to call the car man to come take care of it."

"Make it feel all better."

"I hope so. Now we're going to walk to Seth's house."

"Okay!" Delighted by the change of routine, Aubrey set out at a scramble.

A quarter of a mile later, Grace was carrying her.

But it was a pretty day, she reminded herself. And walking gave her a chance to look and really see. Honeysuckle was tangling along the fence that bordered a tidy field of soybeans, and the scent was lovely. She picked off a blossom for Aubrey.

By the time they skirted the marsh that edged Quinn land, her arms were aching. They stopped to study a turtle sunning on the side of the road, to let Aubrey giggle over the way its head retreated into its shell when she reached out to touch.

"Can you walk for a while now, baby?"

"Tired." With her eyes pleading, Aubrey lifted her arms. "Up!"

"Okay, up you come. Nearly there." It was past nap time, Grace thought. Aubrey wanted her nap directly after lunch every day. She would sleep for two hours, almost to the minute, then wake up ready to roll.

Aubrey's head was already a snoozing weight on Grace's shoulder when she climbed the porch and slipped into the house.

Once she had her daughter tucked onto the couch, she hurried upstairs to strip beds, gather and sort laundry. With the first load in, she made a quick call to the mechanic who did his best to keep her ailing car alive.

She rushed upstairs again, remaking the beds with fresh sheets. To save herself steps, she kept cleaning supplies on each floor. Grace tackled the bathroom first, scrubbing and rinsing in a flurry until chrome and tile sparkled.

It would be, she realized, her last full hit on the Quinn place before Cam and Anna returned. But she'd already decided, sometime during the mile walk from her broken-down car, to carve out a couple of hours for a quick polish the day they were expected home.

She had pride in her work, didn't she? And certainly another woman would notice the tidiness, the clean corners, the few extra touches she tried to add. A professional woman like Anna, a woman with a demanding career, would see, wouldn't she, that Grace was needed here?

She raced downstairs again to check on Aubrey, to drag wet clothes out of the washer into a basket and put the second load in.

She would make sure there were fresh flowers in the master bedroom when the newlyweds returned. And she'd put out the good fingertip towels. She would leave a note for Phillip to pick up some fruit so she could arrange it prettily in the bowl on the kitchen table.

She'd make time to paste-wax the hardwood floors and wash and iron the curtains.

She hung clothes on the line quickly, without any of her usual enjoyment in the task. Still, the simple routine began to calm her. Everything would be all right, somehow.

She caught herself swaying and shook her head to clear it. Fatigue had come quickly, like a punch to the jaw. If she had bothered to calculate the time she'd been on her feet and moving that day, she would have counted seven hours, on a short five hours' sleep the night before. What she did calculate was that she had another twelve to go. And she needed a break.

Ten minutes, she promised herself, and as she sometimes did on long days, stretched out right in the grass by the clothes that waved on the line. A ten-minute nap would recharge her system and still give her time to scrub down the kitchen before Aubrey woke up.

ETHAN DROVE HOME from the waterfront. He'd cut his day on the water short, letting Jim and his son take the workboat out again to check the pots in the Pocomoke. Seth was off with Danny and Will, and Ethan figured on grabbing himself a quick, if delayed, lunch, then spending the next several hours at the boatyard. He wanted to finish the cockpit, maybe get the roof of the cabin started. The more he managed to do, the less time it would be before Cam could get into the finish and fancy work.

He slowed down when he saw Grace's car on the side of the road, then pulled over quickly. He only shook his head when he looked under the open hood. Damn thing was held together with spit and prayers, he decided. She shouldn't be driving something so unreliable. Just what if, he thought sourly, the goddamn thing had decided to break down when she'd been coming home from the pub in the middle of the night?

He took a closer look and hissed through his teeth. The radiator was a dead loss, and if she was entertaining the idea of replacing it, he'd just have to talk her out of it.

He would find her a decent secondhand car. Fix it up for her—or ask Cam, who knew engines like Midas knew gold, to tune it up. He wasn't having her driving around in a wreck like this, and with the baby, too.

He caught himself, took a couple steps back. It wasn't any of his business. The hell it wasn't, he thought, with an uncharacteristic flash of temper. She was a friend, wasn't she? He had a right to help out a friend, especially one who needed some looking after.

And God knew—whether or not Grace did—that she needed some looking after. He got back in his truck and drove home with a scowl on his face.

He'd nearly slammed the screen door before he saw Aubrey curled up on the couch. The scowl didn't have a chance. He eased the door shut and walked quietly over to her. Her hand was bunched into a fist on the cushion. Unable to resist, he took it gently and marveled at those tiny, perfect fingers. She had a bow around one of her curls, a little ribbon of blue lace that he imagined Grace had tied on that morning. It was lopsided now, and only sweeter for it.

He couldn't help hoping that she woke before he had to head out again.

But now, he needed to find Aubrey's mother and discuss reliable transportation.

He cocked his head, decided it was too quiet for her to be upstairs doing whatever it was she did up there. He walked into the kitchen and noted that the signs of a hurried breakfast were still in evidence.

She hadn't gotten to that yet. But the washing machine was humming, and he caught a glimpse of clothes flapping in the breeze on the line outside.

The minute he stepped to the door he saw her. And hit full panic. He didn't know what he thought, only that she was lying on the grass. Terrible images of illness and injury crowded into his head as he rushed outside. He was barely one full stride away from her when he realized she wasn't unconscious. She was sleeping.

Curled up much as her daugher was inside. One fist bunched near her cheek, her breathing slow and deep and even. He gave in to his weakened knees and sat down beside her, waited for his heartbeat to return to something approaching normal.

He sat, listening to the clothes flap on the line, to the water lick the eelgrass, and to the birds chatter while he wondered what the hell he was going to do with her.

In the end, he simply sighed, rose, then bending down gathered her up into his arms.

She stirred in them, snuggled, made his blood run a little too fast for comfort. "Ethan," she murmured, turning her face into the curve of his neck and inciting the bright fantasy of rolling over that sun-warmed grass with her.

"Ethan," she said again, skimming her fingers along his shoulder. And making him hard as iron. Then again, "Ethan," only this time in a squeak of shock as she jerked her head up and stared at him.

Her eyes were dazed with sleep and bright with surprise. Her mouth made a soft O that was gloriously tempting. Then color flooded her cheeks.

"What? What is it?" she managed over a stomach-churning combination of arousal and embarrassment.

"You're going to take a nap, you ought to have as much sense as Aubrey and take it inside out of the sun." He knew his voice was rough. He couldn't do anything about it. Desire had him by the throat with gleefully nipping claws.

"I was just—"

"Scared ten years off me when I saw you lying there. I thought you'd fainted or something."

"I only stretched out for a minute. Aubrey was sleeping, so— Aubrey! I need to check on Aubrey."

"I just did. She's fine. You'd have shown more sense if you'd stretched out on the couch with her."

"I don't come here to sleep."

"You were sleeping."

"Just for a minute."

"You need more than a minute."

"No, I don't. It's just that things got complicated today, and my brain got tired."

It almost amused him. He stopped in the kitchen, still holding her, and looked into her eyes. "Your brain got tired?"

"Yeah." It nearly shut off entirely now. "I needed to rest my mind a minute, that's all. Put me down, Ethan."

He wasn't ready to, not quite yet. "I saw your car about a mile down the road from here."

"I called Dave and told him. He's going to get to it as soon as he can."

"You walked from there to here, carting Aubrey?"

"No, my chauffeur drove us in. Put me down, Ethan." Before she exploded.

"Well, you can give your chauffeur the rest of the day off. I'll drive you home when Aubrey wakes up."

"I can get myself home. I've barely started on the house. Now I need to get back to it."

"You're not walking two and a half miles."

"I'll call Julie. She'll run down and pick us up. You must have work to do yourself. I'm . . . behind schedule," she said, desperately now. "I can't catch up if you don't put me down."

He considered her. "There's not much to you."

The shimmer of need wavered into annoyance. "If you're going to tell me I'm skinny—"

"I wouldn't say skinny. You've got fine bones, that's all." And smooth, soft flesh to cover them. He set her on her feet before he forgot he intended to look after her. "You don't have to worry with the house today."

"I do. I need to do my job." Her nerves were a jittery mess. The way he was looking at her made her want to take one flying leap back into his arms and also made her want to hightail it out the back door like a rabbit. She'd never experienced such a dramatic tug-of-war on her system, and could only stand her ground. "I can do it quicker if you aren't underfoot."

"I'll get out of your way as soon as you call Julie and see if she'll come by and get you." He reached up and brushed some dandelion fluff out of her hair.

"Okay." She turned, punched in numbers on the kitchen phone. Maybe it would be best, she thought wildly as the phone started to ring, if Anna didn't want her around after she got home. It seemed she couldn't be with Ethan for ten minutes anymore without getting jumpy. If it kept up, she was bound to do something to embarrass them both.

CHAPTER
6

ETHAN didn't mind putting in long hours on the boat at night. Especially when he could work alone. It hadn't taken much persuasion for him to agree to let Seth camp out with the other boys in their backyard. It gave Ethan an evening alone—a rarity now—and time to work without having to tune in to questions and comments.

Not that the boy wasn't entertaining, Ethan mused. The fact was, he was firmly attached to Seth. Accepting Seth into his life had been natural because Ray had asked it of him. But the affection, the appreciation, and the loyalty had grown and solidified until it simply was.

But that didn't mean the kid couldn't wear down his energies.

Ethan kept it to handwork tonight. Even if you *felt* awake and alert at midnight, the odds were you'd be a bit sluggish, and he didn't want to risk losing a finger to the power tools. In any case, it was soothing to work in the quiet, to hand-sand edges and planes until you felt them go smooth.

They would be ready to seal the hull before the week was out, and he could start Seth on sanding the rubrails. If Cam dived right in on dealing with belowdecks, and if Seth didn't bitch too much about working with putty and caulk and varnish over the next week or two, they'd do well enough.

He checked his watch, saw that time was getting away from him, and began to put away his tools. He swept up, since Seth wasn't there to wield the broom.

By quarter after one, he was parked outside the pub. He didn't intend to go inside any more than he intended to let Grace walk the mile and a half home when she clocked out. So he settled back, switched on his dome light, and passed the time reading his dog-eared copy of *Cannery Row*.

⌘

INSIDE, IT WAS last call. The only thing that would have made Grace happier would have been if Dave had told her that all she needed to get her car up and running was some used chewing gum and a rubber band.

Instead he'd told her it would cost the equivalent of three years' worth of both, and then she'd be lucky if the old bucket ran another five thousand miles.

It was something she would have to worry about later; at the moment, she had her hands full dealing with an overly insistent customer who was stopping off in St. Chris on his way down to Savannah and was sure Grace would like to be his form of entertainment for the night.

"I got me a hotel room." He winked at her when she stooped to serve his final drink of the night. "And it's got a big bed and twenty-four-hour room service. We could have us a hell of a party, honey pie."

"I don't do a lot of partying, but thanks."

He grabbed her hand, pulled it just enough to throw off her balance so she had to grip his shoulder or tumble into his lap. "Then now's your chance." He had dark eyes, and he aimed them leeringly at her breasts. "I got a real fondness for long-legged blondes. Always treat them special."

He was tiresome, Grace thought as he breathed one more beer into her face. But she had handled worse. "I appreciate that, but I'm going to finish up my shift and go home."

"Your place is fine with me."

"Mister—"

"Bob. You just call me Bob, baby."

She had to yank to get free. "Mister, I'm just not interested."

Of course she was, he thought, sending her a smile he knew was dazzling. He'd paid two grand to get his teeth bonded, hadn't he? "The hard-to-get routine always turns me on."

Grace decided he wasn't worth even a single disgusted sigh. "We're closing in fifteen; you're going to need to settle your tab."

"Okay, okay, don't get bitchy." He smiled widely and pulled out a money clip thick with bills. He always salted it with a couple of twenties on the outside, then filled it with singles. "You figure what I owe, then we'll . . . negotiate your tip."

Sometimes, Grace decided, it was best to keep your mouth firmly shut. What wanted to come out was vicious enough to get her fired. So she walked away and took her empties to the bar.

"He giving you trouble, Grace?"

She smiled weakly at Steve. It was just the two of them working now. The other waitress had clocked out at midnight, claiming a migraine. Since she'd been pale as a ghost, Grace had shooed her out and agreed to cover.

"He's just another of those gifts to womankind. Nothing to worry about."

"If he's not gone by closing, I'll wait until you're locked in your car and headed home."

She made a noncommittal humming noise. She hadn't mentioned her lack of transportation because she knew Steve would insist on driving her home. He lived twenty minutes away, in the opposite direction. And had a pregnant wife waiting for him.

She cashed out tables, cleared them, and noted with relief that her problem customer finally rose to leave. He paid his $18.83 bar bill with cash, leaving $20 on the table. Though he'd managed to monopolize most of her time and attention for the past three hours, Grace was too tired to be annoyed at the pitiful tip.

It didn't take long for the pub to empty. The crowd had been mostly college students, out for a couple of beers and conversation on a weekday night. By her calculations they'd turned about ten tables no more than twice since her shift had started at seven. Her tips for the evening weren't going to make much of a dent in the new car she would have to buy.

It was so quiet, they both jumped like rabbits when the phone rang. Even while Grace laughed at their reaction, the blood drained out of Steve's face. "Mollie," was all he said as he leaped on the phone. He answered it with a stuttering, "Is it time?"

Grace stepped forward, wondering if she was strong enough to catch him if he keeled over. When he began nodding rapidly, she felt her smile spread wide.

"Okay. You—you call the doctor, right? Everything's ready to go. How far apart . . . Oh, God, oh, God, I'm on my way. Don't move. Don't do anything. Don't worry."

He dropped the phone off the hook, then froze. "She's—Mollie—my wife—"

"Yes, I know who Mollie is—we went to school together from kindergarten on." Grace laughed. Then because he looked so dear, and so terrified, she cupped his face in her hands and kissed him. "Go. But you drive careful. Babies take their time coming. They'll wait for you."

"We're having a baby," he said slowly, as if testing each word. "Me and Mollie."

"I know. And it's just wonderful. You tell her I'm going to come see her, and the baby. Of course, if you just stand there like somebody glued your feet to the floor, I guess she'll have to drive herself to the hospital."

"God! I have to go." He knocked over a chair on his way to the door. "Keys, where are the keys?"

"Your car keys are in your pocket. Bar keys are behind the bar. I'll lock up, Daddy."

He stopped, tossed one huge, electrifying grin over his shoulder. "Wow!" And was gone.

Grace was still chuckling as she picked up the chair and replaced it upside down on the table.

She thought of the night when she had gone into labor with Aubrey. Oh, she'd been so afraid, so excited. She had indeed driven herself to the hospital. There'd been no husband there to panic with her. There'd been no one to sit with her, to tell her to breathe, to hold her hand.

When the pain and aloneness had been at its worst, she weakened and let the nurse call her mother. Of course her mother came, and stayed with her, and saw Aubrey into the world. They cried together, and laughed together, and it had made it all right again.

Her father hadn't come. Not then, not later. Her mother had made excuses, tried to smooth it over, but Grace had understood she was not to be forgiven. Others had come, Julie and her parents, friends and neighbors.

Ethan and Professor Quinn.

They'd brought her flowers, pink and white daisies and rosebuds. She had pressed one of each in Aubrey's baby book.

It made her smile to remember, so when the door behind her opened, she turned with a chuckle. "Steve, if you don't get going, she'll . . ." Grace trailed off, experiencing more annoyance than fear when she saw the man step inside. "We're closed," she said firmly.

"I know, honey pie. I figured you'd find a way to hang back and wait for me."

"I'm not waiting for you." Why the hell hadn't she locked the door behind Steve? "I said we're closed. You'll have to leave."

"You want to play it that way, fine." He sauntered over, leaned on the bar. He'd been working out regularly for months now and knew the stance showed off his well-toned muscles. "Why don't you fix us both a drink? And we'll talk about that tip."

Her patience dried up. "You already gave me a tip, now I'll give you one. If you're not out that door in ten seconds, I'm calling the cops. Instead of spending the night on your big hotel bed, you'll spend it in a cell."

"I got something else in mind." He grabbed her, shoved her back against the bar, and ground himself against her. "See? You had it in mind, too. I saw the way you've been eyeing me. I've been waiting all night for some action."

She couldn't get her knee up to ram it against what he was so proudly pushing against her. She couldn't get her hands free to shove or scratch. Panic started as a tickle in her throat, then spread like a hot flood when he shot a hand under her skirt.

She was preparing to bite, scream, and spit when he was suddenly airborne. All she could do was stay pressed against the bar and stare at Ethan.

"You all right?"

He said it so quietly that her head bobbed up and down in automatic response. But his eyes weren't quiet. There was rage in them, so primal and primitive that she shuddered.

"Go on out and wait in the truck."

"I— He—" Then she squealed. It would embarrass her to remember it later, but it was the only sound that came out of her tight throat when the man rushed at Ethan like a battering ram, head lowered, fists clenched.

She watched, staggered as Ethan simply pivoted, jabbed once, twice, and flicked the man off like a fly. Then he bent, grabbed the man by the shirtfront, and hauled him up on his rubbery legs.

"You don't want to be here." His voice was steel with dangerously sharp edges. "Because if I see you here after the next two minutes, I'm going to kill you. And unless you got family or close personal friends, nobody's going to give a damn."

He tossed him away, with what seemed to Grace no more than a twist of the wrist, and the man crashed into a table. Then Ethan turned his back as if the guy didn't exist. But none of the stony fury had faded from his face when he looked at Grace.

"I told you to go wait in the truck."

"I have to— I need to—" She pressed a hand between her breasts and pushed up as if to shove the words clear. Neither of them looked as the man scrambled up and stumbled out the door. "I have to lock up. Shiney—"

"Shiney can go to hell." Since it didn't appear that she was going to move, Ethan grabbed her hand and hauled her to the door. "He ought to be horsewhipped for letting a lone woman lock up this place at night."

"Steve— He—"

"I saw that sonofabitch go flying out of here like a bomb was ticking." Ethan intended to have a nice long talk with Steve as well. Soon, he promised himself grimly as he pushed Grace into the truck.

"Mollie—she called. She's in labor. I told him to go."

"You would. Damn idiot woman."

The statement, delivered with such bubbling fury, stopped the trembling that had just begun, cut off the babbling gratitude she'd been about to express. He'd saved her, was all she'd been able to think, like a knight in a fairy tale. But the thin, romantic mist that had been shimmering over her still-reeling brain evaporated.

"I'm certainly not an idiot."

"You sure as hell are." He whipped the truck out of the lot, spitting gravel and knocking Grace back against her seat. His rare but formidable temper was in full swing, and there was no stopping it until it had blown itself out.

"That man was the idiot," she shot back. "I was just doing my job."

"Doing your job damn near got you raped. The son of a bitch had his hand under your skirt."

She could still feel it, the way it had groped at her. Nausea bubbled up to her throat and was ruthlessly swallowed down. "I'm aware of that. Things like that don't happen at Shiney's."

"It just did happen at Shiney's."

"It doesn't draw that kind of clientele usually. He wasn't local. He was—"

"He was there." Ethan swung into her drive, hit the brakes, then shut the engine off with a hard flick of the wrist. "And so were you. Mopping up some bar in the middle of the goddamn night, by yourself. And what were you going to do when you were done? Walk almost two damn miles?"

"I could have gotten a ride, except—"

"Except you're too stiff-necked to ask for one," he finished. "You'd rather limp home in those mile-high heels than ask a favor."

She had sneakers in her bag, but decided it wouldn't help to mention it. Her bag, she remembered, which was back at the unlocked pub. Now she would have to go back first thing in the morning, get her things, and lock up before the boss checked.

"Well, thank you very much for your opinion of my failings, and the lecture. And the damn ride home." She shoved at the door, only to have Ethan grab her arm and yank her back.

"Where the hell do you think you're going?"

"I'm going home. I'm going to soak my stiff-neck and my idiot-brain and go to bed."

"I haven't finished."

"*I've* finished." She jerked free and jumped out. If it hadn't been for the blasted heels, she might have made it. But he was out the opposite door and blocking her way before she'd taken three strides. "I have nothing more to say." Her voice was cold and dismissive. Her chin was high.

"Good. You can just listen. If you won't quit at the pub—which is just what you should do—you're going to take some basic precautions. Reliable transportation comes first."

"Don't you tell me what I have to do."

"Shut up."

She did, but only because she was stunned speechless. She'd never, in all the years she'd known him, seen Ethan like this. In the moonlight she could see that the fury in his eyes hadn't dimmed a bit. His face was like stone, the shadows flittering over it making it seem harsh, even dangerous.

"We'll see that you get a car you can trust," he continued, in that same edgy tone. "And you won't be closing on your own again. When you finish your shift, I want somebody walking you out to your car and waiting until you lock it and drive off."

"That's just ridiculous."

He stepped forward. Though he didn't touch her, didn't lift a hand, she backed up a pace. Her heart began to pound too fast and too loud in her head.

"What's ridiculous is you thinking you can handle every damn thing by yourself. And I'm tired of it."

She sputtered, hating herself. "*You're* tired of it?"

"Yeah, and it's going to stop. I can't do much about your working yourself half to death, but I can do something about the rest. You don't make arrangements at the pub to see you're safe, I will. You're going to stop asking for trouble."

"Asking for it?" Outrage gushed through her in such a boiling wave, she was surprised that the top of her head didn't simply blow off. "I wasn't *asking* for anything. That bastard wouldn't take no for an answer, no matter how many times I said it."

"That's just what I'm talking about."

"You don't know what you're talking about," she said in a furious whisper. "I handled him, and I would have kept handling him if—"

"How?" There was red around the edges of his vision. He could still see the way she'd been pressed up against the bar, her eyes wide and frightened. Her face had been ghost-pale, her eyes huge and sheened like glass. If he hadn't come in . . .

And because the thought of what could have been scraped raw at the center of his brain, his already slippery control shattered.

"Just how?" he demanded, in one quick move yanking her hard against him. "Go ahead, show me."

She twisted, shoved. And her pulse began to race. "Stop it."

"You think telling him to stop once he's got your scent's going to make a difference?" Lemons and fear. "Once he feels the way you fit?" Subtle curves and long lines. "He knew there was no one to stop him, that he could do anything he wanted."

Everything inside her was in a mindless rush—her heart, her blood, her head. "I wouldn't— I would have stopped him."

"Stop me."

He meant it. A part of him wanted desperately for her to stop him, to do or say something that would hold the wildness in check. But his mouth was on hers, rough and needy, swallowing her gasps, inciting more and reveling in her fast, hard trembles.

When she moaned, when her lips yielded, parted, answered his, he lost his mind.

He dragged her onto the grass, rolled with her, atop her. The thick bolt he'd kept locked on his desires exploded open, and what poured out was reckless greed and primal lust. He ravaged her mouth with the single-minded hunger of a starving wolf.

Swamped with needs so long buried, she arched against him, straining center to center, core to core. Her system stuttered with shocked pleasure, then roared into full raging life. Pumping heat, strangled moans, quivering delights.

This was not the Ethan she knew, or the one she'd dreamed would finally touch her. There was no gentleness, no care, but she gave herself to him, thrilled at the sensation of being swept away.

She wrapped long limbs around him to bind him closer, let her fingers dive into his hair, grip there. And shivered with the dark delight of knowing he was stronger.

He feasted on her mouth, her throat, while he tugged at the low, snug bodice. He was desperate for flesh, the feel of it, the taste of it. Her flesh, her flavor.

Her breast was small and firm, the skin smooth as satin against his wide, hard palm. Her heart jackhammered under it.

She whimpered, stunned at the sensation of that rough hand cupping her, kneading her, churning an echoing tug between her legs, where muscles had gone liquid and lax.

And sighed his name.

She might have shot him. The sound of her voice, the hitch of her breath, the shivers on her skin, slapped him back cold and hard.

He rolled away, onto his back, and struggled to find his breath, his sanity. His decency. They were in her front yard, for God's sake. Her baby was sleeping inside the house. He'd nearly, very nearly done worse than the man in the pub. He'd very nearly betrayed trust, friendship, and vulnerability.

This beast inside him was precisely the reason he'd sworn never to touch her. Now by loosing it, he'd broken his vow and ruined everything.

"I'm sorry." A pitiful phrase, he thought, but he didn't have any other words. "God, Grace, I'm sorry."

Her blood was still flowing hot, and that wonderful, terrifying need aroused to screaming. She shifted, reached out to touch his face. "Ethan—"

"There's no excuse," he said quickly, sitting up so she wasn't touching him—tempting him. "I lost my temper and I stopped thinking straight."

"Lost your temper." She stayed where she was, sprawled on the grass that now seemed too cold, her face lifted to the moon that now shone too bright. "So you were just mad," she said dully.

"I was mad, but that's no excuse for hurting you."

"You didn't hurt me." She could still feel his hands on her, the rough, insistent press of them. But the sensation then, the sensation now, wasn't one of pain.

He thought he could handle it now—looking at her, touching her. She would need it, he imagined. He couldn't have lived with himself if she was afraid of him. "The last thing I want to do is hurt you." As gentle as a doting parent, he tidied her clothes. When she didn't cringe, he stroked a hand over her tousled hair. "I only want what's best for you."

She didn't cringe, but she did, suddenly and sharply, slap his hand aside. "Don't treat me like a child. A few minutes ago you were treating me like a woman easy enough."

There'd been nothing easy about it, he thought grimly. "And I was wrong."

"Then we were both wrong." She sat up, brushing briskly at her clothes. "It wasn't one-sided, Ethan. You know that. I didn't try to make you stop because I didn't want you to stop. That was your idea."

He was baffled, and abruptly nervous. "For Christ's sake, Grace, we were rolling around in your front yard."

"That's not what stopped you."

With a quiet sigh, she brought her knees up, wrapped her arms around them. The gesture, so purely innocent, contrasted sharply with the tiny skirt and fishnet stockings and made his stomach muscles tie themselves into hot, slippery knots again.

"You'd have stopped anyway, wherever it happened. Maybe because you remembered it was me, but it's harder for me to think that you don't want me now. So you're going to have to tell me you don't if you want things to go back to the way they were before."

"They belong back where they were before."

"That's not an answer, Ethan. I'm sorry to press you about it, but I think I deserve one." It was hard, brutal, for her to ask, but the taste of him still lingered on her lips. "If you don't think about me that way, and this was just temper pushing you to teach me a lesson, then you have to say so, straight out."

"It was temper."

Accepting the fresh bruise to her heart, she nodded. "Well, then, it worked."

"That doesn't make it right. What I just did makes me too close to that bastard in the bar tonight."

"I didn't want him to touch me." She drew in a long breath, held it, let it out slowly. But he didn't speak. Didn't speak, she thought, but moved back. He might not have shifted an inch, but he'd moved away from her in the way that counted most.

"I'm grateful to you for being there tonight." She started to rise, but he was on his feet ahead of her, offering a hand. She took it, determined not to embarrass either of them any further. "I was afraid, and I don't know if I could have handled it on my own. You're a good friend, Ethan, and I appreciate you wanting to help."

He slid his hands into his pockets, where they would be safe. "I talked to Dave about another car. He's got a line on a couple decent used ones."

Since screaming would accomplish nothing, she had to laugh. "You don't waste any time. All right, I'll talk to him about it tomorrow." She glanced toward the house where the front porch light gleamed. "Do you want to come in? I could put some ice on your knuckles."

"He had a jaw like a pillow. They're fine. You need to get to bed."

"Yeah." Alone, she thought, to toss and turn. And wish. "I'm going to come by on Saturday for a couple hours. Just to spruce things up before Cam and Anna get home."

"That'd be nice. We'd appreciate it."

"Well, good night." She turned, walked across the grass toward the house.

He waited. He told himself he just wanted to see her safely inside before he left. But he knew it was a lie, that it was cowardice. He'd needed the distance before he could finish asnwering her question.

"Grace?"

She closed her eyes briefly. All she wanted now was to get inside, crawl into bed, and indulge in a good, long cry. She hadn't let herself have a serious jag in years. But she turned back, made her lips curve. "Yes?"

"I think about you that way." He saw, even with the distance, the way her eyes widened, darkened, the way her pretty smile slid away so that she only stared. "I don't want to. I tell myself not to. But I think about you that way. Now go on inside," he told her gently.

"Ethan—"

"Go on. It's late."

She managed to turn the knob, to step inside, shut the door behind her. But she turned quickly to the window to watch him get back in his truck and drive away.

It was late, she thought with a shiver that she recognized as hope. But maybe it wasn't too late.

I appreciate you helping me out, Mama."

"Helping you out?" Carol Monroe tsk-tsked the thought away as she knelt to tie the laces on Aubrey's pink sneaker. "Taking this cube of sugar home with me for the afternoon is pure pleasure." She gave Aubrey a chuck under the chin. "We're going to have us a time, aren't we, honey?"

Aubrey grinned, knowing her ground. "Toys! We got toys, Gramma. Dollbabies."

"You bet we do. And I might just have a surprise for you when we get there."

Aubrey's eyes grew huge and bright. She sucked in her breath to let out a sharp squeal of delight as she jumped down from the chair to race through the house in her own version of a victory dance.

"Oh, Mama, not another doll. You spoil her."

"Can't," Carol said firmly, giving her knee a push to help herself straighten. "Besides, it's my privilege as a granny."

Since Aubrey was occupied running and shouting, Carol took a moment to study her daughter. Not sleeping enough, as usual, she decided, noting the shadows smudged under Grace's eyes. Not eating enough to feed a bird either, though she'd brought over Grace's favorite homemade peanut butter cookies to try to put some flesh on her girl's delicate bones.

A child not yet twenty-three ought to paint her face a little, put some curl in her hair, and go out kicking up her heels a night or two instead of working herself into the ground.

Since Carol had said as much a dozen times or more and had been ignored on the subject a dozen times or more, she tried a different tack. "You got to quit that night work, Gracie. It doesn't agree with you."

"I'm fine."

"Good hard work's necessary for living, and admirable, but a person's got to mix in some pleasure and fun or they dry right up."

Because she was weary of hearing the same song, however the notes might vary, Grace turned and scrubbed at her already spotless kitchen counter. "I like working at the pub. It gives me a chance to see people, talk to them." Even if it was just to ask them if they'd like another round. "The pay's good."

"If you're low on cash—"

"I'm fine." Grace set her teeth. She'd have suffered the torments of hell before she would admit that her budget was strained to breaking—and that solving her transportation problems was going to mean robbing Peter to pay Paul for the next several months. "The extra money comes in handy, and I'm good at waitressing."

"I know you are. You could work down at the cafe, have day hours."

Patiently, Grace rinsed out her dishcloth and hung it over the divider of the double sink to dry. "Mama, you know that isn't possible. Daddy doesn't want me working for him."

"He never said that. Besides, you help out with picking crabs when we're shorthanded."

"I help you out," Grace specified as she turned. "And I'm happy to do it when I can. But we both know I can't work at the cafe."

Her daughter was as stubborn as two mules pulling in opposite directions, Carol thought. It was what made her her father's daughter. "You know you could soften him up if you tried."

"I don't want to soften him up. He made it plain how he feels about me. Let it be, Mama," she murmured when she saw her mother preparing to protest. "I don't want to argue with you, and I don't want to put you in the position ever again of having to defend one of us against the other. It's not right."

Carol threw up her hands. She loved them both, husband and daughter. But she'd be damned if she could understand them. "No one can talk to either of you once you get that look on your face. Don't know why I waste breath trying."

Grace smiled. "Me, either." Grace stepped close, bent down and kissed her mother's cheek. Carol was six inches shorter than Grace's five feet eight. "Thanks, Mama."

Carol softened, as she always did, and combed a hand through her short, curly hair. It had once been as blond by nature as her daughter's and granddaughter's. But nature being what it was, she now gave it a quiet boost with Miss Clairol.

Her cheeks were round and rosy, her skin surprisingly smooth, given her love of the sun. But then, she didn't neglect it. There wasn't a single night she climbed into bed without carefully applying a layer of Oil of Olay.

Being female wasn't just an act of fate, in Carol Monroe's mind. It was a duty. She prided herself that though she was coming uncomfortably close to her forty-fifth birthday, she still managed to resemble the china doll her husband had once called her.

They'd been courting then, and he'd taken some trouble to be poetic.

He usually forgot such things these days.

But he was a good man, she thought. A good provider, a faithful husband, and a fair man in business. His problem, she knew, was a soft heart too easily bruised. Grace had bruised it badly simply by not being the perfect daughter he'd expected her to be.

These thoughts came and went as she helped Grace gather up what Aubrey would need for an afternoon visit. Seemed to her, children needed so much more these days. Time was, she would stick Grace on her hip, toss a few diapers into a bag, and off they'd go.

Now her baby was grown, with a baby of her own. Grace was a good mother, Carol thought, smiling a bit as Aubrey and Grace selected just which stuffed animal should have the privilege of a visit to Grandma's. The fact was, Carol had to admit, Grace was better at the job than she had been herself. The girl listened, weighed, considered. And maybe that was best. She herself had simply done, decided, demanded. Grace was so biddable as a child, she'd never thought twice about what unspoken needs had lived inside her.

And the guilt stayed with her because she had known of Grace's dream to study dance. Instead of taking it seriously, Carol passed it off as childish nonsense. She hadn't helped her baby there, hadn't encouraged, hadn't believed.

The ballet lessons had simply been a natural activity for a girl child as far as Carol had been concerned. If she'd had a son, she'd have seen to it that he played in the Little League. It was . . . just the way things were done, she thought now. Girls had tutus and boys had ball gloves. Why did it have to be more complicated than that?

But Grace had been more complicated, Carol admitted. And she hadn't seen it. Or hadn't wanted to see.

When Grace came to her at eighteen and told her she had her summer job money saved, that she wanted to go to New York to study dance, and begged for help with the expenses, she'd told her not to be foolish.

Young girls just out of high school didn't go haring off to New York City, of all places on God's Earth, on their own. Dreams of ballerinas were supposed to slide into dreams of brides and wedding gowns.

But Grace had been dead set on following her dream and had gone to her father and asked that the money they'd put aside for her college fund be used to pay tuition to a dance school in New York.

Pete had refused, of course. Maybe he'd been a little harsh about it, but he'd meant it for the best. He was just being sensible, just looking out for his little girl. And Carol had agreed wholeheartedly. At the time.

But then Carol watched as her daughter had worked tirelessly, saved every penny, month after month. She'd been bound and deter-mined to go, and seeing it, Carol had tried to nudge her husband into letting her.

He hadn't budged, and neither had Grace.

She was barely nineteen when that slick-talking Jack Casey came around. And that was that.

She couldn't regret it, not when Aubrey had come from it. But she could regret that the pregnancy, the hasty marriage and hastier divorce, had driven a thicker wedge between father and daughter.

But what was couldn't be changed, she told herself and took Aubrey's hand to lead her to the car. "You're sure this car Dave has for you runs all right?"

"Dave says it does."

"Well, he ought to know." He was a good mechanic, Carol thought, even if he had been the one to hire Jack Casey. "You know you could borrow mine for a while—give yourself more time to shop around."

"This one will be fine." She hadn't even laid eyes on the second-hand sedan Dave had picked out for her. "We're going to do the paperwork on Monday, then I'll have wheels again."

After securing Aubrey in the car seat, Grace slipped in while her mother took the wheel.

"Go, go, go! Go, fast, Gramma," Aubrey demanded. Carol flushed when Grace cocked a brow.

"You've been speeding again, haven't you?"

"I know these roads like the back of my hand, and I haven't had a single ticket in my life."

"Because the cops can't catch you." With a laugh, Grace strapped herself in.

"When do the newlyweds get home?" Not only did Carol want to know, she preferred to have the conversation veer away from her notoriously heavy foot.

"I think they're due in about eight tonight. I just want to give the house a buff, maybe put something on for dinner in case they're hungry when they get here."

"I imagine Cam's wife'll appreciate it. What a beautiful bride she was. I've never seen lovelier. Where she managed to get that dress when the boy gave her so little time to plan a wedding, I don't know."

"Seth said she went to D.C. for it, and the veil was her grandmother's."

"That's fine. I have my wedding veil put aside. I always imagined how pretty it would look on you on your wedding day." She stopped, and could cheerfully have bitten her tongue.

"It would have looked a little out of place in the county courthouse."

Carol sighed as she pulled into the Quinns' driveway. "Well, you'll wear it next time."

"I'll never get married again. I'm not good at it." While her mother gaped at the statement, Grace climbed quickly out of the car, then leaned in the window and kissed Aubrey soundly. "You be a good girl, you hear? And don't let Grandma feed you too much candy."

"Gramma has chocolate."

"Don't I know it! Bye, baby. Bye, Mama. Thanks."

"Grace . . ." What could she say? "You, ah, you just call when you're done here and I'll come by and pick you up."

"We'll see. Don't let her run you ragged," Grace added and hurried up the steps.

She knew she'd timed it well. Everyone would be at the boatyard working. She was determined not to feel awkward about what had happened the night before last. But she did—she felt miserably awkward and she wanted time to settle before she had to face Ethan again.

This was a home that always felt warm and welcoming. Caring for it soothed her. Because she knew that a large part of her motivation for working on it that afternoon was self-serving, she put more effort into the job. The results would be the same, wouldn't they, she thought guiltily as she ran the old buffer over the hardwood floors to make the wax gleam. Anna would come home to a spotless house, with the scents of fresh flowers, polish, and potpourri perfuming the air.

A woman shouldn't have to come home from her honeymoon to dust and clutter. And God knew the Quinn men generated plenty of both.

She was needed here, damn it. All she was doing was proving it.

She spent extra time in the master bedroom, fussing with the flowers she'd begged off Irene, then changing the position of the vase half a dozen times before she cursed herself. Anna would put them where she wanted them to be anyway, she reminded herself. And would probably change everything else while she was at it. More than likely, she would want new everything, Grace decided as she pressed the curtains she'd washed until not the tiniest wrinkle showed in the thin summer sheers.

Anna was city-bred and probably wouldn't care for the worn furniture and country touches. Before you knew it, she'd have things decked out in leather and glass, and all Dr. Quinn's pretty things would be packed up in some box in the attic and replaced with pieces of sculpture nobody could understand.

Her jaw tightened as she rehung the curtains, gave them a quick fluff.

Cover the lovely old floors with some fancy wall-to-wall carpet and paint the walls some hot color that made the eyes sting. Resentment bubbled as she marched into the bathroom to put a bunch of early rosebuds in a shallow bowl.

Anybody with any sense could see the place only needed a little care, a bit more color here and there. If she had any say in it . . .

She stopped herself, realizing that her fists were clenched, and her face, reflected in the mirror over the sink, was bright with fury. "Oh, Grace, what is *wrong* with you?" She shook her head, nearly laughed at herself. "In the first place you don't have any say, and in the second you don't know that she's going to change a single thing."

It was just that she could, Grace admitted. And once you changed one thing, nothing was quite the same again.

Isn't that what had happened between her and Ethan? Something had changed, and now she was both afraid and hopeful that things wouldn't be quite the same.

He thought of her, she mused and sighed at her own reflection.

And what did he think? She wasn't a beauty, and she'd never filled out enough to be sexy. Now and then, she knew, she caught a man's eye, but she never held it.

She wasn't smart or particularly clever, had neither stimulating conversation nor flirtatious ways. Jack had once told her she had stability. And he'd convinced them both, for a while, that that was what he wanted. But stability wasn't the sort of trait that attracted a man.

Maybe if her cheekbones were higher or her dimples deeper. Or if her lashes were thicker and darker. Maybe if that flirty curl hadn't skipped a generation and left her hair straight as a pin.

What did Ethan think when he looked at her? She wished she had the courage to ask him.

She looked—and saw the ordinary.

When she had danced she hadn't felt ordinary. She'd felt beautiful and special and deserving of her name. Dreamily, she dipped into a plié, settling crotch on heels, then lifting again. She'd have sworn her body sighed in pleasure. Indulging herself, she flowed into an old, well-remembered movement, ending on a slow pirouette.

"Ethan!" She squeaked it out, color flooding her cheeks when she saw him in the doorway.

"I didn't mean to startle you, but I didn't want to interrupt."

"Oh, well." Mortified, she snatched up her cleaning rag, twisted it in her hands. "I was just . . . finishing up in here."

"You always were a pretty dancer." He'd promised himself he would put things back the way they'd been between them, so he smiled at her as he would a friend. "You always dance around the bathroom after you clean it?"

"Doesn't everyone?" She did her best to answer his smile, but the heat continued to sting her cheeks. "I thought I'd be done before y'all got back. I guess the floors took longer than I figured on."

"They look nice. Foolish already had a slide. Surprised you didn't hear it."

"I was daydreaming. I thought I'd—" Then she managed to clear her brain and get a good look at him. He was filthy, covered with sweat and grime and God knew what. "You're not thinking of taking a shower in here?"

Ethan lifted a brow. "It crossed my mind."

"No, you can't."

He shifted back because she'd taken a step forward. He had a good idea just how he smelled at the moment. That was reason enough to keep his distance, but worse, she looked so fresh and pretty. He'd taken a solemn vow not to touch her again, and he meant to keep it.

"Why?"

"Because I don't have time to clean it up again after you, or the bath downstairs, either. I still have to fry the chicken. I thought I'd make that and a bowl of potato salad so you wouldn't have to worry about heating anything up when Cam and Anna get home. I have to deal with the kitchen after, so I just don't have time, Ethan."

"I've been known to mop up a bathroom after I've used one."

"It's not the same. You just can't use it."

Flustered, he took off his cap, dragged a hand through his hair. "Well, then, that's a problem because we've got three men here who need to scrape off a few layers of dirt."

"There's a bay right outside your door."

"But—"

"Here." She opened the cabinet under the sink for a fresh bar of soap. Damned if she'd have them use the pretty guest soaps she set out in a dish. "I'll get you towels and some fresh clothes."

"But—"

"Go on now, Ethan, and tell the others what I said." She shoved the soap into his hand. "You're already scattering dust everywhere."

He scowled at the soap, then at her. "You'd think the Royal Family was dropping by for a visit. Damn it, Grace, I'm not stripping down to my skin and jumping off the dock."

"Oh, like you've never done it before."

"Not with a female around."

"I've seen naked men a time or two, and I'm going to be too busy to take Polaroids of you and your brothers. Ethan, I've just spent the best part of my day getting this house to shine. You're not spreading your dirt around."

Disgusted, because in his experience arguing with a woman's made-up mind was as painful and fruitless as banging your head against a brick wall, he shoved the soap in his pocket. "I'll get the damn towels."

"No, you won't. Your hands are filthy. I'll bring them out."

Muttering to himself, he went downstairs. Phillip's reaction to the bathing arrangements was a shrug. Seth's was pure glee. He darted outside, calling for the dogs to follow, and sent shoes, socks, shirt, scattering as he raced for the dock.

"He'll probably never want to take a regular bath again," Phillip commented. He sat on the dock to remove his shoes.

Ethan remained standing. He wasn't taking off a blessed thing until Grace delivered the towels and clothes and was back in the house. "What are you doing?" he demanded when Phillip pulled his sweat-stained T-shirt over his head.

"I'm taking off my shirt."

"Well, put it back on. Grace is coming out."

Phillip glanced up, saw that his brother was perfectly serious, and laughed. "Get a grip, Ethan. Even the sight of my amazing and manly chest isn't likely to send her over the edge."

To prove it, he rose and shot Grace a grin as she crossed the lawn. "I heard something about fried chicken," he called out.

"I'm about to get to it." When she reached the dock, she set the towels and clean clothes in neat piles. Then she straightened, smiling out to where Seth and the dogs splashed. She imagined they'd scared every bird and fish away for two miles. "This arrangement suits them just fine."

"Why don't you take a dip with us?" Phillip suggested and swore he heard Ethan's jaw crack. "You can scrub my back."

She laughed and picked up the clothes that had already been discarded. "It's been a while since I've gone skinny-dipping, and as appealing as it sounds, I've got too much to do to play right now. You give me the rest of your clothes, I'll get them washed before I go."

"Appreciate it." But when Phillip reached for his belt buckle, Ethan jabbed an elbow into his ribs.

"You can wash them later if you're set on it. Go in the house."

"He's shy." Phillip wiggled his brows. "I'm not."

Grace only laughed again, but she headed back to the house to give them privacy.

"You shouldn't tease her that way," Ethan muttered.

"I've been teasing her that way for years." Phillip peeled himself out of his work-stained jeans, delighted to be rid of them.

"Now it's different."

"Why?" Phillip started to slip out of his silk boxers, then caught the look in Ethan's eye. "Oh. Well, well. Why didn't you say so?"

"I got nothing to say." Because Grace was in the house now and he couldn't imagine her pressing her nose to the window, he pulled off his shirt.

"It's her voice that always got me."

"Huh?"

"That throaty sound," Phillip continued, pleased to be able to rile Ethan about something. "Low and smooth and sexy."

Gritting his teeth, Ethan pried off his work boots. "Maybe you shouldn't listen so hard."

"What can I do? Can I help it if I have perfect hearing? Perfect eyesight, too," he added, judging the distance between them. "And as far as I can see, there's nothing wrong with the rest of her either. Her mouth's particularly attractive. Full, shapely, unpainted. Looks tasty to me."

Ethan took two slow breaths as he tugged off his jeans. "Are you trying to irritate me?"

"I'm giving it my best shot."

Ethan stood, gauged his man. "You want to go in head-first or feetfirst?"

Pleased, Phillip grinned. "I was going to ask you the same thing."

Both waited a beat, then charged, grappled. And with Seth's rousing cheers ringing, wrestled each other into the water.

Oh, my, Grace thought with her nose pressed up against the window. *Oh, my.* If she'd ever seen two more impressive examples of the male form, she couldn't say when. She'd only intended to sneak a quick glance. Really. Just one innocent little peek. But then Ethan had peeled off his shirt and . . .

Well, damn it, she wasn't a saint. And what harm did it do to anyone just to look?

He was just so beautiful, inside and out. And God, if she could get her hands on him again for just five minutes, she thought she could die a happy woman. Maybe she could, since he wasn't indifferent—the way she'd always assumed he was.

There'd been nothing indifferent in the way his mouth had crushed down on hers, or the way his hands had rushed over her.

Stop, she ordered herself and stepped back from the window.

The only thing she was going to accomplish this way was to get herself all worked up. She knew how to channel her more intimate needs, and that was to work until they passed away again.

But if her mind wasn't completely on her chicken, who could blame her?

⚬⚬⚬

SHE HAD THE potatoes cooling for the salad and the chicken frying when Phillip came back in. Gone was the image of the sweaty laborer. In its place was the smooth, the gilded, the casually sophisticated. He winked at her. "Smells like heaven in here."

"I made extra so you can have it for lunch tomorrow. You just put those clothes in the laundry room, and I'll see to them in a minute."

"I don't know what we'd do without you around here."

She bit her lip and hoped everyone felt the same. "Is Ethan still in the water?"

"No, he and Seth are doing something to the boat." Phillip went to the refrigerator and took out a bottle of wine. "Where's Aubrey today?"

"With my mother. In fact she just called and wants to keep her a little longer. I guess one of these days I'm going to have to give in and let her stay overnight." She glanced down blankly at the glass of cool golden wine he offered her. "Oh, thanks." What she knew about wine wouldn't fill a thimble, but she sipped because it was expected. Then her brows lifted. "This isn't anything like what they serve down at the pub."

"I wouldn't think so." He considered what they called the house white down at Shiney's one shaky step up from horse piss. "How are things going there?"

"Fine." She gave serious attention to her chicken, wondering if

Ethan had mentioned the incident. Unlikely, she decided when Phillip didn't press. She relaxed again and let Phillip entertain her while she worked.

He was always full of stories, she mused. Of easy, even careless conversation. She knew he was smart and successful and had slipped into city living like a duck in water. But he never made her feel inadequate or silly. And in a cozy way, he made her feel just a little more feminine than she had before he'd come into the room.

That was why Grace's eyes were laughing and her mouth prettily curved when Ethan came in. Phillip sat, sipping wine while she put the finishing touches on the meal.

"Oh, you're making that up."

"I swear." Phillip held up a hand in oath and grinned as Ethan came in. "The client wants the goose to be the spokesperson, so we're writing dialogue. Goose Creek Jeans, fine feathers for everyday living."

"That's the silliest thing I ever heard."

"Hey." Phillip toasted her. "Watch them sell. I've got a few phone calls to make." He rose, deliberately rounding the table to kiss her and make Ethan seethe. "Thanks for feeding us, darling."

He strolled out, whistling.

"Can you imagine, making a living writing words for a goose." Amused, Grace shook her head as she tucked the bowl of potato salad into the refrigerator. "Everything's done, so you can eat when you're hungry. Your clothes are in the dryer. You don't want to leave them sitting in there after it's done or they'll be wrinkled."

She moved around, tidying the kitchen as she spoke. "I'd wait and fold them for you, but I'm running a bit behind."

"I'll drive you home."

"I'd appreciate it. I'm dealing with the car on Monday, but until then . . ." She lifted her shoulders and saw with one last glance that she had nothing left to do. Still, she eyed every nook and corner as she walked through the house to the front door.

"How are you getting to work?" Ethan demanded when they were in his truck.

"Julie's taking me. Shiney's taking me home himself." She cleared her throat. "When I explained what happened the other night he was upset. Not mad at me, but really upset it had happened. He was set to skin Steve, but under the circumstances—they had a boy, by the way. Eight and a half pounds. They're calling him Jeremy."

"I heard" was Ethan's only comment.

Now she drew a bolstering breath. "About what happened, Ethan, I mean afterward—"

"I've got something to say about that." He'd worked it out carefully, word by word. "I shouldn't have been mad at you. You were scared and I spent more time yelling at you than making sure you were all right."

"I knew you weren't really mad at me. It was just—"

"I've got to finish this," he said, but waited until he'd turned into her driveway. "I had no business touching you that way. I'd promised myself I never would."

"I wanted you to."

Though the quiet words caused his stomach to clench, he shook his head. "It's not going to happen again. I've got reasons, Grace, good ones. You don't know, and you wouldn't understand."

"I can't understand if you don't tell me what they are."

He wasn't going to tell her what he'd done, or what had been done to him. And what he was afraid still lurked inside him ready to spring out if he didn't keep that cage locked. "They're my reasons." He shifted to look at her because it was only right to say what he had to say facing her. "I could have hurt you, and I nearly did. That's not going to happen again."

"I'm not afraid of you." She reached out to touch, to stroke his cheek, but he grabbed her hand and held her off.

"You're never going to have to be. You matter to me." He gave her hand a quick squeeze, then released it. "You always have."

"I'm not a child anymore, and I won't break if you touch me. I want you to touch me."

Full, shapely, unpainted lips. Phillip's words echoed in his head. And now Ethan knew, God help him, exactly how tasty they were. "I know you think you do, and that's why we're going to try to forget that the other night happened."

"I'm not going to forget it," she murmured, and the way she looked at him, her eyes soft and full of need, made his head swim.

"It's not going to happen again. So you stay clear of me for a while." Desperation tinged his voice as he leaned across and shoved open her door. "I mean it, Grace, you just stay clear of me for a while. I've got enough to worry about."

"All right, Ethan." She wouldn't beg. "If that's what you want."

"That's exactly what I want."

This time he didn't wait until she was in the house but backed out of the drive the minute she closed the truck's door.

For the first time in more years than he could count, he thought seriously about getting blind drunk.

CHAPTER

8

SETH kept watch for them. His excuse for being in the front yard as the shadows grew long was the dogs. Not that it was an excuse, exactly, he thought. He was trying to teach Foolish not just to chase the battered, well-chewed tennis ball but to bring it back the way Simon did. The trouble was that Foolish would race back to you with the ball, then expect you to play tug-of-war for it.

Not that Seth minded. He had a supply of balls and sticks and an old hunk of rope that Ethan had given him. He could toss and tug as long as the dogs were willing to run. Which was, as far as he could tell, just about forever.

But while he played with the dogs, he kept his ears tuned for the sound of an approaching car.

He knew they were on their way home because Cam had called from the plane. Which was just about the coolest thing Seth could think of. He couldn't wait to tell Danny and Will how he'd talked to Cam while Cam had been flying over the Atlantic Ocean.

He'd already looked up Italy in the atlas and found Rome. Had traced his finger back and forth, back and forth across that wide ocean from Rome to the Chesapeake Bay, to the little smudge on Maryland's Eastern Shore that was St. Christopher's.

For a little while he'd been afraid they wouldn't come back. He imagined Cam calling and saying they'd decided to stay over there so he could race again.

He knew Cam had lived all over the place, racing boats and cars and motorcycles. Ray had told him all about it, and there was a thick scrapbook in the den that was filled with all kinds of newspaper and magazine pictures and articles about how many races Cam had won. And how many women he'd fooled around with.

And he knew that Cam had won this big-deal race in his hydrofoil—which Seth wished he could ride in just once—right before Ray had run into the telephone pole and died.

Phillip had finally tracked him down in Monte Carlo. Seth had found that place in the atlas, too, and it didn't look all that much bigger than St. Chris. But they had a palace there and fancy casinos and even a prince.

Cam had come home in time to see Ray die. Seth knew he hadn't planned to stay very long. But he had stayed. After they'd had sort of a fight, he'd told Seth he wasn't going anywhere. That they were stuck with each other and he was staying put.

Still, that was before he'd gotten married and everything, before he'd gone back to Italy. Before Seth had started to worry that both Cam and Anna would forget about him and the promises they'd made.

But they hadn't. They were coming back.

He didn't want them to know he was waiting for them or that he was excited that they would be home any minute. But he was.

He couldn't understand why he was all pumped up about it. They'd only been gone a couple of weeks, and Cam was a pain in the ass most of the time anyway.

And once Anna was living there, everybody would say how he had to watch his language because there was a woman in the house.

A part of him worried that Anna would change things. Even though she was his caseworker, she might get tired of having a kid around. She had the power to send him away. More power now, he thought, because she was doing it with Cam all the time.

He reminded himself that she'd played it straight with him, from the minute she'd pulled him out of class and sat down with him in the school cafeteria to talk.

But working on a case and living in the same house with that case was different, wasn't it?

And maybe, just maybe, she'd played straight with him, she'd been nice to him, because she'd liked having Cam poke at her. She'd wanted to get married to him. Now that she was, she wouldn't have to be nice anymore. She could even write in one of her reports that he'd be better off somewhere else.

Well, he was going to watch, and he was going to see. He could still run if things got sticky. Though the idea of running made his stomach hurt in a way it had never done before.

He wanted to be here. He wanted to run in the yard, throwing sticks to the dogs. To crawl out of bed when it was still dark and eat breakfast with Ethan and go out on the water crabbing. To work in the boatyard or go down to Danny's and Will's.

To eat real food whenever he was hungry and sleep in a bed that didn't smell like somebody else's sweat.

Ray had promised him all of that, and though Seth had never trusted anyone, he'd trusted Ray. Maybe Ray had been his father, maybe he hadn't. But Seth knew he'd paid Gloria a lot of money. He thought of her as Gloria now and not as his mother. It helped to add more distance.

Now Ray was dead, but he'd made each of his sons promise to keep Seth in the house by the water. Seth figured they probably hadn't liked the idea, but they'd promised anyway. He'd discovered that the Quinns kept their word. It was a new and wonderful concept to him, a promise kept.

If they broke it now, he knew it would hurt more than anything had hurt him before.

So he waited, and when he heard the car—the not-quite-tamed roar of the Corvette—his stomach jittered with excitement and nerves.

Simon woofed twice in greeting, but Foolish set up a din of wild, half-terrified barking. When the sleek white car pulled into the drive, both dogs raced toward it, tails waving like flags. Seth stuck hands that had gone sweaty into his pockets and strolled over casually.

"Hi!" Anna shot him a brilliant smile.

Seth could see why Cam had gone for her, all right. He himself had sketched her face a number of times in secret. He liked to draw above all else. His fledgling artist's eye appreciated the sheer beauty of that face—the dark, almond-shaped eyes, the clear, pale-gold skin, the full mouth, and the exotic hint of cheekbones. Her hair was windblown, a dark, curling mass. Her wedding ring set glinted, diamonds and gold, as she stepped out of the car.

And caught him unprepared in a laughing, bone-crushing hug. "What a terrific welcome party!"

Though the embrace had surprised him into wanting to linger there, he wiggled free. "I was just out fooling with the dogs." He looked over at Cam, shrugged. "Hey."

"Hey, kid." Lean and dark, and just a little dangerous to the eye,

Cam unfolded his length from the low-riding car. His grin was quicker than Ethan's, sharper than Phillip's. "Just in time to help me unload."

"Yeah, sure." Seth glanced up, noted the small mountain of luggage strapped to the roof of the car. "You didn't take all that crap with you."

"We picked up some Italian crap while we were there."

"I couldn't stop myself," Anna said with a laugh. "We had to buy another suitcase."

"Two," Cam corrected.

"One's just a tote—it doesn't count."

"Okay." Cam popped the trunk, pulled out a generous dark green suitcase. "You carry the one that doesn't count."

"Putting your bride to work already?" Phillip crossed to the car, waded through the dogs. "I'll take that, Anna," he said and kissed her with an enthusiasm that had Seth rolling his eyes at Cam.

"Turn her loose, Phil," Ethan said mildly. "I'd hate for Cam to have to kill you before he even gets in the house. Welcome home," he added and smiled when Anna turned to give him as enthusiastic a kiss as Phillip had given her.

"It's good to be home."

THE TOTE, IT turned out, contained gifts, which Anna immediately began to dispense, along with stories of each one. Seth only stared down at the bright-blue-and-white soccer shirt she'd given him. No one had ever gone on a trip and brought him back a present. The fact was, if he thought about it, he could count the gifts he'd been given—something for nothing—on the fingers of one hand.

"Soccer's big over in Europe," Anna told him. "They call it football, but it's not like our football." She dug deeper, then pulled out an oversized book with a glossy cover. "And I thought you might like this. It's not as good as seeing the paintings. It really grabs you by the throat to see them in person, but you'll get the idea."

The book was filled with paintings, glorious colors and shapes that dazzled his eyes. An art book. She'd remembered that he liked to draw and had thought of him.

"It's cool." He muttered it because he couldn't trust his voice.

"She wanted to buy everyone shoes," Cam commented. "I had to stop her."

"So I only bought myself a half a dozen pair."

"I thought it was four."

She smiled. "Six. I snuck two by you. Phillip, I stumbled across Maglis. I could have wept."

"Armani?"

She sighed lustily. "Oh, yeah."

"Now I'm going to cry."

"You can sob over fashion later," Cam told them. "I'm starving."

"Grace was here." Seth wanted to try on his shirt right away but thought it would be too lame. "She cleaned everything—made us wash up in the Bay—and she fried chicken."

"Grace made fried chicken?"

"And potato salad."

"There's no place like home," Cam murmured and headed for the kitchen. Seth waited a few seconds, then followed.

"I guess I could eat another piece," he said casually.

"Get in line." Cam pulled the platter and bowl out of the fridge.

"Don't they give you stuff to eat on the plane?"

"That was then, this is now." Cam heaped a plate with food, then leaned back against the counter. The kid looked tanned and healthy, he noted. The eyes were still wary, but his face had lost that rabbit-about-to-run look. He wondered if it would surprise Seth as much as it had himself to know he'd missed the smart-mouthed brat. "So, how's it been going?"

"Okay. School's done, and I've been helping Ethan out on the boat a lot. Pays me slave's wages there and at the boatyard."

"Anna's going to want to know what you got on your report card."

"A's," Seth muttered around a mouthful of drumstick, and Cam choked.

"All?"

"Yeah—so what?"

"She's going to love that. Want to make more points with her?"

Seth jerked a shoulder again, narrowing his eyes as he considered what he would be asked to do to please the woman of the house. "Maybe."

"Put the soccer shirt on. It took her damn near half an hour to pick out the right one. Major points if you wear it the same night she gives it to you."

"Yeah?" As easy as that? Seth thought and relaxed into a grin. "I guess I can give her a thrill."

⚜

"HE REALLY LIKED his shirt," Anna said as she meticulously tucked away the contents of one suitcase. "And the book. I'm so glad we thought of the book."

"Yeah, he liked them." Cam figured the next day, even next year, was soon enough to unpack. Besides, he liked stretching out on the bed and watching her—watching his wife, he thought with an odd little thrill—fuss around the room.

"He didn't freeze up when I hugged him. That's a good sign. And his interaction with Ethan and Phillip is easier, more natural, than it was even a couple of weeks ago. He was anxious to see you again.

He's feeling a little threatened by me. I change the dynamics around here just at the point where he was getting used to how things worked. So he's waiting, and he's watching for what'll happen next. But that's good. It means he considers this his home. I'm the intruder."

"Miz Spinelli?"

She turned her head, arched a brow. "That's Mrs. Quinn to you, buster."

"Why don't you turn off the social worker until Monday?"

"Can't." She slipped one of her new shoes out of its bag and nearly cooed at it in delight. "The social worker is very pleased with the status of this particular case. And Mrs. Quinn, the brand-new sister-in-law, is determined to win Seth's trust, and maybe even his affection."

She slipped the shoe back into the bag and wondered how long she should wait before asking Cam to customize their closet. She knew just what she had in mind, and he was good with his hands. Considering, she studied him. Very, very good with his hands.

"I suppose I could finish unpacking tomorrow."

He smiled slowly. "I suppose you could."

"I feel guilty about it. Grace has this place so spotless."

"Why don't you come over here. We'll work on that guilt."

"Why don't I?" She tossed the shoe over her shoulder and, with a laugh, jumped him.

"SHE'S COMING ALONG." Cam studied the boat. It was barely seven in the morning, but his internal clock was still set to Rome. Since he'd awakened early, he hadn't seen the point in letting his brothers sleep the day away.

So the Quinns stood under the hard, bright lights of the boatyard, contemplating the job at hand. Seth mimicked their stance—hands in pockets, legs spread and braced, face sober.

It would be the first time the four of them had worked on the boat together. He was wildly thrilled.

"I figured you could start belowdecks," Ethan began. "Phillip estimates four hundred hours to finish the cabin."

Cam snorted. "I can do it in less."

"Doing it right," Phillip put in, "is more important than doing it fast."

"I can do it fast *and* right. The client'll have this baby under sail and the galley stocked with champagne and caviar in less than four hundred hours."

Ethan nodded. Since Cam had come through with another client, who wanted a sport fishing boat, he dearly hoped that was true. "Then let's get to work."

And work kept his mind off things his mind had no business being on. The brain had to be focused to use the lathe—if you were fond of your hands. Ethan turned the wood slowly, carefully, forming the mast. Ear protectors turned the hum of the motor and the hot rock blasting from the radio into a muffled echo.

He imagined there was conversation going on behind him, too. And the occasional ripe curse. He could smell the sweet scent of wood, the sting of epoxy, the stench of tar used to coat bolts.

Years ago, the three of them had built his workboat. She wasn't fancy, and he couldn't claim she had a pretty face, but she was sound and she was game. They'd built his skipjack as well because he'd been determined to dredge oysters in the traditional craft. Now the oysters were nearly gone, and his boat joined the other handful in the Bay, pulling in extra money during the summer by giving tours.

He rented it to Jim's brother during tourist season, because it helped them both and was the practical thing to do. But it bothered him some to see the fine old vessel used that way. Just as it bothered him some to know other people lived and slept in the house that was his.

But when push came to shove, money mattered. Seth's laugh snuck through his ear protectors and reminded him why it mattered now more than ever.

When his hands cramped from the work, he turned off the lathe to give them a rest. Noise filled his ears when he took off the protectors.

He could hear the pounding of Cam's hammer echoing from belowdecks. Seth was coating the centerboard with Rust-Oleum so the steel plate gleamed with wet. Phillip had the nastier job of soaking the inside of the centerboard case with creosote. It was good old-growth red cedar, which should discourage any marine borers, but they'd decided not to take chances.

A boat by Quinn was built to last.

He felt a stir of pride watching them and could almost imagine his father standing beside him, big hands fisted on his hips, a wide grin on his face.

"It makes a picture," Ray said. "The kind your mother and I loved to study. We had plenty of them put aside, to take out and look over again once you all grew up and went off your own ways. We never really had the chance because she left first."

"I still miss her."

"I know you do. She was the glue that kept us all together. But she did a good job of it, Ethan. You're still stuck."

"I guess I'd have died without her, without you. Without them."

"No." Ray laid a hand on Ethan's shoulder, shook his head. "You were always strong, heart and mind. You came out the other side of hell as much because of what's inside you as what we did. You should remember that more often. Just look at Seth. He handles things differently than you did, but he's got a lot of the same qualities inside him. He cares, deeper than he wants to. He thinks deeper than he lets on. And his wants go deeper than he'll admit even to himself."

"I see you in him." It was the first time Ethan had allowed himself to say it, even to himself. "I don't know how to feel about it."

"Funny, I see each one of you in him. The eye of the beholder, Ethan." Then he gave Ethan a quick slap on the back. "That's a damn fine boat coming along there. Your mother would have gotten a kick out of this."

"Quinns build to last," Ethan murmured.

"Who're you talking to?" Seth demanded.

Ethan blinked, felt his head go light, filled with thoughts thin as strands of cotton. "What?" He pushed a hand up his forehead, into his hair, knocking his cap back. "What?"

"Man, you look weird." Seth cocked his head, fascinated. "How come you're standing here talking to yourself?"

"I was . . ." Asleep on my feet? he wondered. "Thinking," he said. "Just thinking out loud." Suddenly the noise and smells seemed to roar into his dizzy brain. "I need some air," he muttered and hurried out through the cargo doors.

"Weird," Seth said again. He started to say something to Phillip, then was distracted as Anna came through the front door carrying an enormous hamper.

"Anybody interested in lunch?"

"Yeah!" Always interested, Seth made a beeline. "Did you bring the chicken?"

"What's left of it," she told him. "And ham sandwiches thick as bricks. There's a cooler of iced tea in the car. Why don't you go haul it in?"

"My hero," Phillip said, wiping his hands on his jeans before relieving her of the hamper. "Hey, Cam! There's a gorgeous woman out here with food."

The hammering stopped instantly. Seconds later, Cam's head popped up through the cabin roof. "My woman. I get first dibs on the food."

"There's plenty to go around. Grace isn't the only one who can put meals together for a bunch of hungry men. Though her fried chicken's a gift from the gods."

"She's got a way with it." Phillip agreed. He set the hamper down on a makeshift table fashioned of a sheet of plywood laid over two sawhorses. "She cooked for Ethan regularly when you two were away." He dug out a ham sandwich. "I get the feeling something's happening there."

"Happening where?" Cam wanted to know as he jumped down to explore the hamper.

"With Ethan and Grace."

"No shit?"

"Mmm." The first bite made Phillip close his eyes in pleasure. He might have preferred French cuisine served on fine china, but he could appreciate a well-built sandwich balanced on a paper plate. "My deathless observation skills have homed in on certain signs. He watches her when she's not looking. She watches him when he's not looking. And I got some interesting gossip from Marsha Tuttle. She works down at the pub with Grace," he explained to Anna. "Shiney's adding a security system and has a new policy that none of the waitresses are to close up alone."

"Did something happen?" Anna asked.

"Yeah." He looked over to be certain Seth hadn't come back in. "A few nights ago some bastard came in after closing. Grace was alone. He put his hands on her and, according to Marsha, would have done more. But it just so happened Ethan was outside. Interesting coincidence if you ask me, when we're talking of our early-to-bed, early-to-rise brother. Anyway, he put some dents in the guy." He took another healthy bite.

Cam thought of slender, fine-boned Grace. Thought of Anna. "I hope they were nice deep dents."

"I think we can assume the guy didn't walk off whistling. Of course, in typical Ethan style, he doesn't mention it, so I have to hear it from Marsha over the fresh produce at the market Friday night."

"Was Grace hurt?" Anna knew all too well what it was to be trapped, to be helpless, to be faced with what a certain kind of man would do to a woman. Or a child.

"No. Must have shaken her up, but she's like Ethan there. Never mentioned it. But there were several long, silent looks between them yesterday. And after Ethan ran her home, he came back sizzling." Remembering, Phillip chuckled to himself. "Which for Ethan is saying something. Got himself a couple of beers and went out in the sloop for an hour."

"Grace and Ethan." Cam considered it. "They'd fit." He saw Seth come in and decided to give the topic a rest. "Where is Ethan, anyway?"

"He went outside." With a grunt, Seth set the cooler down and nodded toward the cargo doors. "He said he needed some air, and I guess he did. He was standing there talking to himself." Thrilled with the bounty, Seth dived into the hamper. "He was, like, carrying on a conversation with someone who wasn't there. He looked weird."

The back of Cam's neck prickled. Still, he moved casually, dumping food on a plate. "I could use some air myself. I'll just take him a sandwich."

He saw Ethan standing out on the end of the pier, staring out at the water. The shore of St. Chris with all its pretty houses and yards was on either side, but Ethan looked straight out, over the light chop to the horizon.

"Anna brought some food out."

Ethan folded up his thoughts and glanced down at the plate. "Nice of her. You hit lucky with her, Cam."

"Don't I know it." What he was about to do made him a little nervous. But, after all, he was a man who lived for risks. "I still remember the first day I saw her. I was pissed off at the world. Dad was hardly buried, and everything I wanted seemed to be somewhere else. The kid had given me plenty of grief that morning, and it occurred to me that the next part of my life wasn't going to be racing, it wasn't going to be Europe. It was going to be right here."

"You gave up the most. Coming back here."

"It seemed like it at the time. Then Anna Spinelli walked across the yard while I was fixing the back steps. She gave me my second jolt of the day."

Since the food was there, and Cam seemed inclined to talk, Ethan took the plate and sat on the edge of the dock. An egret flew by, silent as a ghost. "A face like hers is bound to give a man a jolt."

"Yeah. And I was already feeling a little edgy. Not an hour before, I'd had this conversation with Dad. He was sitting in the back porch rocker."

Ethan nodded. "He always liked sitting there."

"I don't mean I remembered him sitting there. I mean I saw him there. Just like I'm seeing you now."

Slowly, Ethan turned his head, looked into Cam's eyes. "You saw him, sitting in the rocker on the porch."

"Talked to him, too. He talked to me." Cam shrugged, gazed out over the water. "So, I figure I'm hallucinating. It's the stress, the worry, maybe the anger. I've got things to say to him, questions I want answered, so my mind puts him there. Only that's not what it was."

Ethan stepped carefully onto boggy ground. "What do you figure it was?"

"He was there, that first time and the others."

"Other times?"

"Yeah, the last was the morning before the wedding. He said it would be the last because I'd figured out what I needed to figure out for now." Cam rubbed his hands over his face. "I had to let him go again. It was a little easier. I didn't get all the questions answered, but I guess the ones that mattered most were."

He sighed, feeling better, and helped himself to one of the chips on Ethan's plate. "Now you'll either tell me I'm crazy or that you know what I'm talking about."

Thoughtfully, Ethan tore one of the sandwiches in half, handed a share to Cam. "When you follow the water, you get to know there's more to things than you can see or touch. Mermaids and serpents." He smiled a little. "Sailors know about them, whether they've ever seen them or not. I don't think you're crazy."

"Are you going to tell me the rest?"

"I've had some dreams. I thought they were dreams," he corrected himself, "but lately I've had a couple when I was awake. I guess I have questions, too, but I have a hard time pushing somebody into answers. It's good to hear his voice, to see his face. We didn't have enough time to really say good-bye before he died."

"Maybe that's part of it. It's not all of it."

"No. But I don't know what he wants me to do that I'm not doing."

"I imagine he'll stick around until you figure it out." Cam bit into the sandwich and felt amazingly content. "So, what does he think of the boat?"

"He thinks it's a damn fine boat."

"He's right."

Ethan studied his sandwich. "Are we going to tell Phil about this?"

"Nope. But I can't wait until it happens to him. What do you bet he'll think about heading to some fancy shrink? He'll want one with lots of initials after his name and an office on the right side of town."

"Her name," Ethan corrected and began to smile. "He'll want a good-looking female if he's going to lie down on a couch. It's a pretty day," he added, suddenly appreciating the warm breeze and the flash of sun.

"You've got another ten minutes to enjoy it," Cam told him. "Then your ass goes back to work."

"Yeah. Your wife makes a damn good sandwich." He angled his head. "How do you think she'd do at sanding wood?"

Cam considered, liked the image. "Let's go talk her into letting us find out."

CHAPTER
9

ANNA was thrilled to have the afternoon off. She loved her job, had both affection and respect for the people she worked with. She believed absolutely in the function and the goals of social work. And she had the satisfaction of knowing she made a difference.

She helped people. The young single mother with nowhere to turn, the unwanted child, the displaced elderly person. Inside her burned a deep and bright desire to help them find their way. She knew what it was to be lost, to be desperate, and what one person who offered a hand, who refused to snatch that hand back even when it was slapped or snapped at, could change.

And because she had been determined to help Seth DeLauter, she'd found Cam. A new life, a new home. New beginnings.

Sometimes, she thought, rewards came back to you a hundred-fold.

Everything she'd ever wanted—even when she hadn't known she wanted it—was tied up in that lovely old house on the water. A white house with blue trim. Rockers on the porch, flowers in the yard. She remembered the first day she'd seen it. She'd traveled along this same road, with the radio blaring. Of course, the top had been up then, so the wind wouldn't tug her hair free of its pins.

That had been a business call, and Anna had been determined to be all business.

The house had charmed her, the simplicity of it, the stability. Then she walked around the pretty two-story house by the water and saw an angry, uncooperative, and sexy man repairing the back porch steps.

Nothing had been quite the same for her since.

Thank God.

It was her house now, she thought with a smug grin as she drove fast along the road flanked by wide, flat fields. Her house in the country, with the garden she'd imagined . . . and the angry, unco-operative, sexy man? He was hers, too, and so much more than she'd ever imagined.

She drove along that long, straight road with Warren Zevon howling about werewolves in London. But this time, she didn't care if the wind tugged at her once tidily pinned hair. She was going home, so the top was down and her mood was light.

She had work to do, but the reports she needed to complete could be done on her laptop at home. While her red sauce simmered on the stove, she decided. They'd have linguini—to remind Cam of their honeymoon.

Not that this particular event seemed to be over, even if they were back on the Shore rather than in Rome. She wondered if this wild and wicked passion they had for each other would ever ease.

And hoped not.

Laughing at herself, she zipped into the drive. And nearly

rammed her pretty little convertible into the rear of a dull gray sedan with a rusted bumper. Once her heart had bumped back down into its proper place, she puzzled over it.

It certainly wasn't Cam's kind of car, she decided. He might like to tinker with engines, but he preferred the fast and the sleek body to go around them. This aged and sturdy body looked anything but fast.

Phillip? She let out a snort. The fastidious Phillip Quinn wouldn't have placed his Italian-loafer-shod foot on the worn floorboard of such a vehicle.

Ethan, then. But she found herself frowning. Pickups and Jeeps were Ethan's style, not compact sedans that had fenders still painted with gray primer.

They were being robbed, she thought with a jolt that turned her heartbeat into a jackhammer. In broad daylight. No one ever thought to lock the doors around here, and the house was sheltered from its neighbors by trees and the marsh.

Someone was inside, picking through their things, right now. Eyes narrowed, she slammed out of the car. They weren't getting away with it. It was her house now, damn it, and her things, and if any half-baked burglar thought he could . . .

She trailed off as she looked into the sedan and saw the big pink rabbit. And the car seat. A house burglar with a toddler in tow?

Grace, she realized with a sigh. It was one of Grace Monroe's cleaning days.

City girl, she chided herself. Put the city instincts away. You're in another place now. Feeling monumentally foolish, she returned to her own car and hefted her briefcase and the bag of fresh produce she'd picked up on the way home.

As she stepped onto the porch, she heard the monotonous hum

of the vacuum, underscored by the bright tinkle of a commercial on TV. Good domestic sounds, Anna thought. And she was more than delighted that she wasn't the one running the vacuum.

Grace nearly dropped the wand when Anna came through the door. Obviously flustered, she stepped back, tripping the foot switch to turn the machine off. "I'm sorry. I thought I'd be finished before anyone got home."

"I'm early." Though her arms were full, Anna crouched in front of the chair where Aubrey sat manically scribbling purple crayon on a picture of an elephant in her coloring book. "That's beautiful."

"It's a phant."

"It's a terrific phant. Prettiest phant I've seen all day." Because Aubrey's nose just seemed to demand it, Anna gave it a quick kiss.

"I'm nearly done." Nerves danced down Grace's spine. Anna looked so professional in her business suit. The fact that her hair was tumbling out of its pins only made her seem . . . professionally sexy, Grace decided. "I finished upstairs, and in the kitchen. I didn't know . . . I wasn't sure what you'd like, but I made up a casserole— scalloped potatoes and ham. It's in the freezer."

"Sounds great. I'm cooking tonight." Anna rose and jiggled her bag cheerfully. She nearly stepped out of her shoes but then stopped herself. It didn't seem right to start cluttering things up when Grace was still in the middle of cleaning.

She'd wait until later.

"But I won't get off early tomorrow," she continued. "So it'll come in handy."

"Well, I . . ." Grace knew she was a little sweaty, a little grimy, and she felt miserably outclassed by Anna's crisp blouse and tailored suit. And oh, those shoes, she thought, doing her best not to make her survey obvious. They were so pretty, so classic, and the leather looked soft enough to sleep on.

Her toes curled in shame inside her frayed white sneakers. "The laundry's nearly done, too. There's a load of towels in the dryer. I didn't know where you wanted me to put your things, so I folded everything and left it on the bed in your room."

"I appreciate it. Catching up after a couple of weeks away takes forever." Anna caught herself before she squirmed. She'd never had a housekeeper in her life, and she wasn't quite sure of the proper procedure. "I should put these away. You want something cold to drink?"

"No, thanks. No. I should finish up and get out of your way."

Curious, Anna thought. Grace had never seemed cool or nervous before. Though they didn't know each other well, Anna had felt they were friendly. One way or the other, she decided, they had to come to terms. "I'd really like to talk to you if you have the time."

"Oh." Grace ran her hand up and down the metal wand of the vacuum. "Sure. Aubrey, I'm going in the kitchen with Mrs. Quinn."

"Me, too!" Aubrey scrambled up and raced ahead. By the time her mother caught up, she was sprawled on the floor, intently creating a purple giraffe.

"That's her color this week," Grace commented. Automatically she went to the refrigerator and took out the pitcher of lemonade she'd made. "She tends to settle on one until she wears the crayon down to a nub, then she picks another."

Her hand froze on the glass she'd been about to take from a cupboard. "I'm sorry," she said stiffly. "I wasn't thinking."

Anna set her bag down. "About what?"

"Making myself at home in your kitchen."

Aha, Anna thought, there was the problem. Two women, one house. They were both a little uneasy about the situation. She took a plump tomato from the bag, examined it, then set it on the counter. Next year she was going to try to grow her own.

"You know what I liked about this house from the first time I stepped into the kitchen? It's the kind of place where it's easy to make yourself at home. I wouldn't want that to change."

She continued to unload her bag, setting carefully chosen vegetables on the counter.

Grace had to bite her tongue to keep from mentioning that Ethan didn't care for mushrooms when Anna set a bag of them beside the peppers.

"It's your home now," Grace said slowly. "You'll want to tend to it your own way."

"That's true. And I am thinking of making some changes. Would you mind pouring that lemonade? It looks wonderful."

Here it comes, Grace thought. Changes. She poured two glasses, then took the plastic cup from the counter to fill for Aubrey. "Here, honey, now don't spill."

"Aren't you going to ask me what changes?" Anna wondered.

"It's not my place."

"When did we get to have places?" Anna demanded with just enough annoyance to put Grace's back up.

"I work for you—for the time being, anyway."

"If you're about to tell me you're quitting you're really going to spoil my day. I don't care how much progress women have made, if I'm alone in this house with four men, I'll end up doing ninety percent of the housework. Maybe not at first," she continued, pacing now, "but that's just how it'll end up. It won't matter that I have a full-time job on top of it, either. Cam hates housework, and he'll do anything he can to get out of it. Ethan's neat enough, but he has a habit of making himself scarce. And Seth, well, he's ten, so that says it all. Phillip only lives here on weekends, and he'll make the argument that he didn't make the mess in the first place."

She whirled back. "Are you telling me you're quitting?"

It was the first time Grace had seen Anna under full steam, and she was both impressed and baffled. "I thought you just said you were going to make some changes and you were going to let me go."

"I'm thinking about getting some new pillows and having the sofa re-covered," Anna said impatiently, "not losing the person I already realize I'm going to depend on for my sanity around here. Do you think I didn't know who made sure I didn't come home to a houseful of dishes and laundry and dust? Do I look like an idiot to you?"

"No, I . . ." The beginnings of a smile flirted at Grace's mouth. "I worked my tail off so you'd notice."

"Okay." Anna let out a breath. "Why don't we sit down and start over?"

"That'd be good. I'm sorry."

"For?"

"For all the nasty things I let myself think about you over the last few days." She smiled fully as she sat down. "I forgot how much I liked you."

"I'm outnumbered around here, Grace. I could sure use another woman. I don't know exactly how these things are done, and since I'm the outsider here—"

"You're not an outsider." Grace all but gaped in shock. "You're Cam's wife."

"And you've been a part of his life, of all their lives, a great deal longer." She turned her hands palms up, smiled. "Let's get this one thing out of the way so we can forget it. Whatever you've been doing around here works just fine for me. I appreciate knowing you're doing it so I can concentrate on my marriage, on Seth, and on my job. Are we clear there?"

"Yeah."

"And since my instincts tell me you're a kind, understanding person, I'm going to confess that I need you a lot more than you need me. And throw myself on your mercy."

The quick, easy laugh made shallow dimples flicker in Grace's cheeks. "I don't think there's anything you couldn't do."

"Maybe not, but I swear to God I don't want to be Wonder Woman. Don't leave me alone with all these men."

Grace nibbled on her lip for a moment. "If you're going to have the living room sofa redone, you'll need new curtains."

"I was thinking priscillas."

They beamed at each other, in perfect accord.

"Mama! Gotta pee!"

"Oh." Grace sprang up and scooped a frantically dancing Aubrey into her arms. "We'll be right back."

Anna had a good chuckle, then rose, stripped off her jacket, and prepared to start her sauce. This kind of cooking—the familiar, the dependable—relaxed her. And since she had no doubt that it would earn her points with the Quinn men when they got home, she intended to enjoy herself.

It pleased her as well that she'd cemented a basis of friendship with Grace. She wanted that benefit of small towns and country living—the neighbors. One of the reasons she'd been restless during her time in D.C. was the lack of connection with the people who lived and worked around her. When she'd moved to Princess Anne she'd found something of the old-neighborhood ease she'd grown up with in her grandparents' well-established section of Pittsburgh.

And now, she thought, she had the opportunity to become good friends with a woman she admired and believed she would enjoy.

When Grace and Aubrey came back into the room, she smiled. "You hear stories about toilet training being a nightmare for every-one involved."

"There are hits and misses." Grace gave Aubrey a quick squeeze before setting her down. "Aubrey's such a good girl, aren't you, sweetie?"

"I didn't wet my pants. I get a nickel for the piggy bank."

When Anna roared with laughter, Grace winced good-naturedly. "And bribery works."

"I'm all for it."

"I should finish up."

"Are you in a hurry?"

"Not really." Cautious, Grace glanced at the kitchen clock. By her judgment, Ethan shouldn't be back for at least an hour.

"Maybe you could keep me company while I put this sauce together."

"I suppose I could." It had been . . . she couldn't remember how long it had been since she'd just sat in the kitchen with another woman. The simplicity of it nearly made her sigh. "There's a show that Aubrey likes to watch that's just coming on. Is it all right if I settle her down with it? I can do the rest of the vacuuming when it's over."

"Great." Anna slid her tomatoes into the pot to let them simmer and soften.

"I've never made spaghetti sauce from scratch," Grace said when she came back in. "I mean, all the way from fresh tomatoes."

"Takes more time, but it's worth it. Grace, I hope you don't mind, but I heard what happened the other night at the bar where you work."

Surprise made Grace blink and forget to memorize the ingredients Anna had set out. "Ethan told you?"

"No. You have to pull on Ethan's tongue to get him to tell anything." Anna wiped her hands on the bib apron she'd put on. "I don't want to pry, but I have some experience with sexual assault. I want you to know you can talk to me if you need to."

"It wasn't as bad as it could have been. If Ethan hadn't been there . . ." She trailed off, discovered that thinking about it still made her cold inside. "Well, he was. I should have been more careful."

Anna had a quick flash of a dark road, the bite of gravel against her back as she was shoved to the ground. "It's a mistake to blame yourself."

"Oh, I don't—not that way. I didn't deserve what he tried to do. I didn't encourage him. The fact is, I made it clear I wasn't interested in him or his hotel bed. But I should have locked up after Steve left. I wasn't thinking, and that was careless."

"I'm glad you weren't hurt."

"I could have been. I can't afford to be careless." She glanced to the doorway where the bright music and Aubrey's brighter laughter came through. "I've got too much at stake."

"Single parenting's hard. I see the problems that can come out of it all the time. You're brilliant at it."

Now it wasn't surprise, but shock. No one had ever called her brilliant at anything. "I just . . . do."

"Yes." Anna smiled. "My mother died when I was eleven, but before that she was a single parent. When I look back and remember, I see that she was brilliant at it too. She just did. I hope I'm half as good at 'just doing' as both of you when I have a child."

"Are you and Cam planning on it?"

"I'm good at planning," Anna said with a laugh. "I want to give just being married a little time, but yes, I want children." She looked out the window to where the flowers she'd planted were blooming. "This is a wonderful place to raise kids. You knew Ray and Stella Quinn?"

"Oh, yes. They were wonderful people. I still miss them."

"I wish I'd known them."

"They'd have liked you."

"Do you think?"

"They'd have liked you for yourself," Grace told her. "And they'd have loved what you've done for the family. You helped bring them back together. I think they got a little lost for a while—after Dr. Quinn died. Maybe they all had to go their own way, just like they had to come back."

"Ethan stayed."

"He's rooted here—in the water, like eelgrass. But he drifted, too. And spent too much time alone. His house is around the bend that the river takes away from the waterfront."

"I've never seen it."

"It's tucked away," Grace murmured. "He likes his privacy. Sometimes on a quiet night if I went walking, when I was carrying Aubrey, I could hear him play his music. Just catch the notes on the air if the wind was right. It sounded lonely. Lovely and lonely."

Eyes that were dazzled by love saw some things with perfect clarity. "How long have you been in love with him?"

"Seems like all my life," Grace murmured, then caught herself. "I didn't mean to say that."

"Too late. You haven't told him?"

"No." At even the thought of it, Grace's heart clutched in panic. "I shouldn't be talking about this. He'd hate it. It'd embarrass him."

"Well, he's not here, is he?" Amused and delighted, Anna beamed. "I think it's terrific."

"It's not. It's awful. It's just awful." Horrified, she pressed a hand to her mouth to hold back a sudden and unexpected rush of tears. "I ruined it. Ruined everything, and now he doesn't even want to be around me."

"Oh, Grace." Flooded with sympathy, Anna abandoned her

chopping to wrap her arms tight around Grace's stiff form, then nudged her toward a chair. "I can't believe that."

"It's true. He told me to stay away." Her voice hitched, mortifying her. "I'm sorry. I don't know what's got into me. I never cry."

"Then it's time you broke tradition." Anna tore off a couple of sheets of paper towels and offered them. "Go ahead, you'll feel better."

"I feel so stupid." With the dam broken, Grace sobbed into the paper towels.

"There's nothing to feel stupid about."

"There is, there is. I made it so we can't even be friends anymore."

"How did you do that?" Anna asked gently.

"I was pushing myself at him. I guess I thought—after the night he kissed me . . ."

"He kissed you?" Anna repeated, and immediately began to feel better.

"He was mad." Grace pressed her face into the towel, breathing deep until she could regain some control. "It was after what happened at the pub. I've never seen him like that. I've known him most of my life and never knew he could be like that. I'd have been scared if I hadn't known him—the way he tossed that man aside like he was a bag of feathers. And he had this look in his eyes that made them hard and different, and . . ." She sighed and admitted the worst. "Exciting. Oh, it's horrible to think that."

"Are you kidding?" Anna reached over and squeezed her hand. "I wasn't even there and I'm excited."

With a watery laugh, Grace mopped at her face. "I don't know what came over me, but he was yelling at me. It got my back up, and we had a fight when he took me home. He was saying that I should quit my job and talking to me like I'd lost every working brain cell in my head."

"Typical male reaction."

"That's right." Abruptly angry all over again, Grace nodded. "It was just typical, and I never would have expected that from him. Then we were rolling around on the grass."

"You were?" Absolutely delighted, Anna grinned.

"He was kissing me, and I was kissing him back, and it was wonderful. All my life I'd wondered how it would be, and then there it was and it was better than anything I'd ever imagined. Then he stopped and said he was sorry."

Anna closed her eyes. "Oh, Ethan, you idiot."

"He told me to go inside, but just before I did he said he thought about me. That he didn't want to, but he did. So I hoped that things would start to change."

"I'd say they'd changed already."

"Yes, but not the way I'd hoped. The day you and Cam came back, I was here when he got home. And it seemed like, maybe . . . but he took me back to my house. He told me he'd thought it through and he wasn't going to touch me again and I was to steer clear of him for a while." She let out a long breath. "So I am."

Anna waited a moment, then shook her head. "Oh, Grace, you idiot." When Grace frowned, Anna leaned across the table. "Obviously the man wants you and it scares the hell out of him. You have the power here. Why aren't you using it?"

"The power? What power?"

"The power to get what you want if what you want is Ethan Quinn. You just need to get him alone and seduce him."

Grace snorted. "Seduce him? Me seduce Ethan? I couldn't do that."

"Why couldn't you?"

"Because I . . ." There had to be a simple and logical reason. "I don't know. I don't think I'd be good at it."

"I bet you'd be great at it. And I'm going to help you."

"You are?"

"Absolutely." Anna rose to fuss with her sauce and to think. "When's your next night off?"

"Tomorrow."

"Good, that's just enough time. I'd keep Aubrey for you overnight, but that might make it too obvious, and we'd better be subtle. Is there someone you'd trust with her?"

"My mother's been wanting to take her overnight, but I couldn't—"

"Perfect. You might feel inhibited with the baby in the house. I'll figure out how to get him over there."

She turned around, studied Grace. Cool, classic looks, she mused. Big, sad eyes. The man was already a goner. "You'll want to wear something simple but feminine." Considering, she tapped a fingertip against her teeth. "Pastel would be best, a fragile color, soft green or pink."

Because her head was starting to spin, Grace put a hand to it. "You're going too fast."

"Well, someone has to. At this rate, you and Ethan will still be circling each other when you're sixty. No jewelry," she added. "Just the bare minimum of makeup. Wear your usual scent, too. He's used to it, it'll say something to him."

"Anna, it doesn't matter what I wear if he doesn't want to be there."

"Of course it matters." As a woman who had a long-term love affair with clothes, she was very nearly shocked at the suggestion. "Men don't think they notice what a woman wears—unless it's next to nothing. But they do, subconsciously. And it helps click the mood or the image."

Lips pursed, she added fresh basil to the sauce and got out a skillet for sautéing onions and garlic. "I'm going to try to get him over there close to sunset. You should light some candles, put on music. The Quinns like their music."

"What would I say to him?"

"I can only take you so far here, Grace," Anna said dryly. "And I'm betting you'll figure it out when the time comes."

She was far from convinced of that. While new scents began to romance the air, Grace worried her lip. "It feels like I'd be tricking him."

"And your point would be?"

Grace chuckled. And gave up. "I have a pink dress. I bought it for Steve's wedding a couple years ago."

Anna glanced over her shoulder. "How does it look on you?"

"Well . . ." Grace's lips curved slowly. "Steve's best man hit on me before they cut the cake."

"Sounds like a deal."

"I still don't—" Grace stopped as her mother's ear caught the tinkling music from the living room. "That's the end of Aubrey's show. I have to finish up in there."

She rose quickly, panicked at the thought of Ethan coming home before she was gone. Surely everything she felt must show on her face. "Anna, I appreciate what you're trying to do, but I just don't think it's going to work. Ethan knows his own mind."

"Then it won't hurt him to come around to your house and see you in a pink dress, will it?"

Grace blew out a breath. "Does Cam ever win an argument with you?"

"On the rare occasion, but never when I'm at my best."

Grace edged toward the door, knowing that Aubrey's sit-and-behave time was nearly up. "I'm glad you came home early today."

Anna tapped her wooden spoon on the lip of her pot. "Me, too."

CHAPTER
10

T HE following day as sunset approached, Grace wasn't certain she was glad at all. Her nerves were stretched so tight she could feel them straining and bubbling under her skin. Her stomach continually jumped in quick little rabbit hops. And her head was beginning to throb in a sharp, insistent rhythm.

It would be just perfect, she thought in disgust, if Anna managed to get Ethan over, and she simply pitched forward, ill and babbling, at his feet.

That would be seductive.

She should never have agreed to this foolishness, she told herself as she paced through her little house yet again. Anna had thought so quickly, made up her mind so fast and put everything in motion so smoothly, that she'd been swept along before she could calculate the pitfalls.

What in the world would she *say* to him if he came? Which he probably wouldn't, she thought, caught between relief and despair.

He probably wouldn't even come and then she'd have sent her baby away for the night for nothing.

It was too quiet. There was nothing but the early-evening breeze rustling through the trees for company. If Aubrey had been there—where she belonged—they'd have been reading her bedtime story now. She would have been all scrubbed and powdered and curled up under Grace's arm in the rocker. Snuggly and sleepy.

When she heard her own sigh, Grace pressed her lips tightly together and marched to the small stereo system on the yellow pine shelves in the living room. She selected CDs from her collection—an indulgence that she refused to feel guilty over—and let the house fill with the weeping and romantic notes of Mozart.

She walked to the window to watch the sun drop lower in the sky. The light was going soft, slipping away shade by shade. In the ornamental plum that graced the Cutters' front yard a lone whippoorwill began to sing to the twilight. She wished she could laugh at herself, silly Grace Monroe standing by the window in her pink dress waiting for a star to wish on.

But she lowered her forehead to the glass, closed her eyes, and reminded herself that she was too old for wishes.

⌖

ANNA THOUGHT SHE would have done very well in the espionage game. She had kept her plans locked tight behind closed lips—no matter how desperately she'd wanted to spill out everything to Cam.

She had to remind herself that he was, after all, a man. And he was Ethan's brother, which was another strike against him. This was a woman thing. She thought she was very subtle about keeping her eye on Ethan as well. He wasn't going to escape somewhere directly after dinner, as was his habit, nor would he have a clue that his sister-in-law was keeping him on a short rein.

The ice cream idea had been a brainstorm. She'd picked up a gallon on the way home and now had all three of her men, as she liked to think of them, settled on the back porch downing bowls of Rocky Road.

Timing and execution, she told herself, and rubbed her hands together before she stepped out on the porch. "It's going to be a warm night. It's hard to believe it's nearly July already."

She wandered to the porch rail to lean over and scan her flower beds. Coming right along, she thought with a sense of righteous satisfaction. "I thought we could have a backyard picnic on the Fourth."

"They have fireworks on the waterfront," Ethan put in. "Every year, half hour after sunset. You can see them from right here on the porch."

"Really? That would be perfect. Wouldn't it be fun, Seth? You could have your friends over and we'd cook burgers and dogs."

"That'd be cool." He was already down to scraping his bowl and calculating how to finesse seconds.

"Have to dig out the horseshoes," Cam decided. "Do we still have them, Ethan?"

"Yeah, they're around."

"And music." Anna shifted just enough to rub her husband's knee. "The three of you could play. You don't play together nearly often enough to suit me. I'll have to make a list. You'll have to tell me who we should invite—and the food. Food." She thought she feigned flustered irritation very well as she pushed away from the porch rail. "How could I have forgotten? I promised Grace to trade her my recipe for tortellini for hers for fried chicken."

She dashed inside to retrieve the index card that she'd neatly written the recipe on—something she'd never done before in her life—then dashed back out again. All apologetic smiles.

"Ethan, would you run this over to her?"

He stared at the little white card. If he hadn't been sitting down, his hands would have jumped into his pockets. "What?"

"I promised I'd get her this today and it completely slipped my mind. I'd run it over myself, but I still have a report to finish. I'm just dying to try out that fried chicken," she went on quickly, pushing the recipe card into his hand, then all but dragging him to his feet.

"It's kind of late."

"Oh, it's not even nine o'clock." Don't give him time to think, she warned herself. Don't give him a chance to pick out the flaws. She pulled him into the house, used smiles and fluttering lashes to move him along. "I really appreciate it. I'm so scatterbrained these days. I feel like I'm chasing my own tail half the time. Tell her I'm sorry I didn't get it to her sooner and to be sure to let me know how it turns out once she tries it. Thanks so much, Ethan," she added, rising up to give him a quick, affectionate peck on the cheek. "I love having brothers."

"Well . . ." He was baffled, closing in on miserable, but the way she said that, the way she smiled when she did, left him helpless. "I'll be right back."

I don't think so, Anna thought with a wisely controlled chuckle as she cheerily waved him off. The second his truck was out of sight, she dusted her palms together. Mission accomplished.

"Just what the hell was that?" Cam demanded, making her jolt with surprise.

"I don't know what you mean." She would have sailed past him and into the house, but he stepped out, blocked her path.

"Oh, yeah, you know what I mean." Intrigued, he angled his head. She was trying to look innocent, he decided, but couldn't pull it off. Too much pure glee in her eyes. "Exchanging recipes, Anna?"

"So what?" She lifted a shoulder. "I'm a very good cook."

"No argument there, but you're not the recipe-emergency type, and if you'd been so hell-bent on giving one to Grace, you'd have picked up the phone. Which is something you didn't give Ethan a chance to point out, since you were so busy batting your lashes at him and cooing like some empty-headed twit."

"Twit?"

"Which you're not," he continued, slowly backing her up until she was trapped against the porch rail. "At all. Shrewd, savvy, sharp." He laid his hands on either side of her hips to cage her. "That's what you are."

It was, she supposed, a fine compliment. "Thank you, Cameron. Now I really should get to that report."

"Uh-uh. Why'd you con Ethan into going over to Grace's?"

She shook back her hair, aimed a bland look dead into his eyes. "I'd think a shrewd, savvy, sharp guy like you ought to be able to figure that out."

His brows drew together. "You're trying to get something going between them."

"Something *is* going between them, but your brother is slower than a lame turtle."

"He's slower than a lame turtle with bifocals, but that's Ethan. Don't you think they should muddle through this on their own?"

"All they need is five minutes alone, and that's all I did—work it out so they'd have a few minutes alone. Besides"—she slipped her arms up and around his neck—"we deliriously happy women want everyone else to be deliriously happy, too."

He cocked a brow. "Do you think I'm going to fall for that?"

She smiled, then leaned over to nip his bottom lip. "Yeah."

"You're right," he murmured and let her convince him.

⚜

ETHAN SAT IN his truck for a full five minutes. Recipes? That was the dumbest damn thing he'd ever heard of. He'd always thought Anna was a sensible woman, but here she was, sending him off to deliver recipes, for Christ's sake.

And he wasn't ready to see Grace just yet. Not that his mind wasn't made up about her, but . . . even a rational man had certain weaknesses.

Still, he didn't see how he was going to get out of it, as he was already here. He'd make it quick. She was probably putting the baby to bed, so he'd just get it done and get out of her way.

Like a man condemned, he dragged himself out of the truck and to her front door. Through the screen he could see the flickering lights of candles. He shifted his feet and noticed that music was playing, something with weeping strings and soaring piano.

He'd never felt more ridiculous in his life than he did standing there on Grace's front porch holding a recipe for a pasta dish while music slid around the warm summer night.

He knocked on the wood frame, not too loudly, as he worried about waking Aubrey. He gave serious thought to sticking the card in the door and hightailing it, but he knew that would be cowardice, plain and simple.

And Anna would want to know why he hadn't brought her the instructions for Grace's fried chicken.

When he saw her he wished to God Almighty he'd taken the coward's way.

She walked out from the kitchen, at the back of the house. It was a tiny place, had always made Ethan think of a dollhouse, so she didn't have far to travel. To him it seemed he watched her walk through that music, that light for hours.

She wore pale, fragile pink that skimmed down to her ankles, with a row of tiny pearl buttons from the hollow of her throat to the hem that flowed around her bare feet. He had rarely seen her in a dress, but now he was too thunderstruck by the sight of her to question why she was wearing it.

All he could think was she looked like a rose, long and slim and just ready to bloom. And his tongue tangled up in his mouth.

"Ethan." Her hand trembled lightly as she reached down, opened the screen. Maybe she hadn't needed a star to wish on after all. For here he was, standing close and watching her.

"I was . . ." Her scent, familiar as his own, seemed to wrap around his brain. "Anna sent you—she asked me to bring this by."

Mystified, Grace took the card he held out. At the sight of the recipe she had to bite the inside of her cheek to keep from laughing. Her nerves backed off just enough that her eyes smiled when she lifted them to his. "That was nice of her."

"You got hers?"

"Her what?"

"The one she wants. The chicken thing."

"Oh, yes. Back in the kitchen. Come on in while I get it." What chicken thing? she wondered, nearly giddy from suppressed laughter that she knew would come out well on the hysterical side. "The, um, casserole, right?"

"No." She had such a tiny waist, he thought. Such narrow feet. "Fried."

"Oh, that's right. I'm so scatterbrained lately."

"It's going around," he mumbled. He decided it was safer to look anywhere but at her. He noted the pair of fat white candles burning on the counter. "You blow a fuse?"

"Excuse me?"

"What's wrong with your lights?"

"Nothing." She could feel the heat rise into her cheeks. She didn't have a recipe for fried chicken written down anywhere. Why would she? You just did the same as you always did when it came time to make it. "I like candlelight sometimes. It goes with the music."

He only grunted, wishing she would hurry up so he could get the hell away. "You already put Aubrey to bed?"

"She's spending the night with my mother."

His eyes, which had been steadfastly studying her ceiling, shot down and met hers. "She's not here?"

"No. It's her first overnight. I've already called over there twice." She smiled a little, and her fingers reached up to fiddle with the top button of her dress in a way that made Ethan's mouth water. "I know she's only a few miles away, and as safe as she'd be in her own crib, but I couldn't help it. The house feels so different without her here."

"Dangerous" was the word he'd have used. The pretty little dollhouse was suddenly as deadly as a minefield. There wasn't any little girl innocently sleeping in the next room. They were alone, with music sobbing and candles flickering.

And Grace was wearing a pale-pink dress that just begged to have those little white buttons undone, one by one by one.

The tips of his fingers began to itch.

"I'm glad you stopped by." Holding tight to her courage, she took a step forward and tried to remember that she had the power. "I was feeling a little blue."

He took a step back. More than his fingertips was itching now. "I said I'd be back directly."

"You could stay for . . . coffee or whatever?"

Coffee? If his system got any more wired than it was at that moment, it would have jumped right through his skin to dance the hornpipe. "I don't think . . ."

"Ethan, I can't steer clear of you the way you asked me. St. Chris is too small, and our lives are too tangled up together." She could feel the pulse in her throat pounding against her skin in hard, insistent little knocks. "And I don't want to. I don't want to steer clear of you, Ethan."

"I said I had my reasons." And he could think of what they were if she'd just stop looking at him with those big green eyes. "I'm just watching out for you, Grace."

"I don't need you to watch out for me. We're all grown up, both of us. We're alone, both of us." She stepped closer. She could smell his after-work shower on him, but under it, as always, was the scent of the Bay. "I don't want to be alone tonight."

He edged back. If he hadn't known her better, he'd have sworn she was stalking him. "I've made up my mind on this." But damn it, it wasn't his mind working overtime, it was his loins. "Just stay back, Grace."

"It seems like I've been staying back forever. I want to move forward, Ethan, whatever that means. I'm tired of staying back or standing still. If you don't want me, I'll live with that. But if you do . . ." She moved closer, lifted a hand to lay it on his heart. And discovered that his heart was pounding. "If you do, then why won't you take me?"

He backed hard into the counter. "Stop it. You don't know what you're doing here."

"Of course I know what I'm doing." She snapped it out, suddenly furious with the pair of them. "I'm just not doing a good job of it, since you'd rather climb up my kitchen wall than lay a finger on me. What do you think I'd do, shatter into a million pieces? I'm a grown woman, Ethan. I've been married, I've had a child. I know what I'm asking you, and I know what I want."

"I know you're a grown woman. I've got eyes."

"Then use them, and look at me."

How could he do otherwise? Why had he ever believed he could? There, standing in shadow and light, was everything he yearned for. "I'm looking at you, Grace." With my back to the wall, he thought. And my heart in my throat.

"Here's a woman who wants you, Ethan. One who needs you." She saw his eyes change at that, sharpen, darken, focus. On an unsteady breath, she stepped back. "Maybe I'm what you want. What you need."

He was afraid she was, and that telling himself he could and would do without had been an exercise in futility. She was so lovely, all rose and gold in the candlelight, her eyes so clear and honest. "I know you are," he said at length. "But that wasn't supposed to change anything."

"Do you have to think all the time?"

"It's getting hard to," he murmured. "Right at the moment."

"Then don't. Let's both stop thinking." Even as the blood pounded in her brain, she kept her gaze locked on his. And lifted her hands, trembling hands, to the top button of her dress.

He watched her unfasten it, staggered at how that single, simple gesture, that tiny inch of exposed skin, could electrify him. He felt his lungs clog, his blood sizzle, and his needs, all the long-denied needs, beg for release.

"Stop, Grace." He said it gently. "Don't do that."

Her hands fell back to her sides in defeat, and she shut her eyes. "Let me do it."

Her eyes blinked open, stared stunned at his sober gaze as he stepped to her. She took in one shaky breath and held it.

"I've always wanted to," he murmured and slipped the next tiny button free.

"Oh." The breath she held came out in a hitch and a sob. "Ethan."

"You're so pretty." She was already trembling. He lowered his head to brush a kiss over her lips and soothe. "So soft. I've got rough hands." Watching her, he skimmed his knuckles down her cheek, over her throat. "But I won't hurt you."

"I know. I know you won't."

"You're shaking." He undid another button, then another.

"I can't help it."

"I don't mind." Patiently he eased the buttons free to her waist. "I guess I knew, deep down, if I walked in here tonight, I wouldn't be able to walk away again."

"I've been wishing you'd walk in here. I've been wishing it a long time."

"So have I." The buttons were so tiny, his fingers so big. Her skin, where the dress parted, where the edge of his thumb slid up, was so soft and warm. "You tell me if I do something you don't like. Or if I don't do something you want."

The sound she made was part moan, part laugh. "I'm not going to be able to talk in a minute. I can't get my breath. But I wish you'd kiss me."

"I was getting to it." He nibbled gently, teasingly, because he hadn't taken his time the first time he'd tasted her. Now he would linger, sample, find a rhythm that suited them both. When her sigh filled his mouth, it was sweet. He loosened more buttons and let the long, deepening kiss spin out.

Touched her nowhere else, not yet. Only mouth against mouth with flavors mixed. When she swayed, he lifted his head, looked into her eyes. Clouded now, heavy and aware.

"I want to see you." Slowly, inch by inch, he slipped the dress from her shoulders. They were sun-kissed, strong, gracefully curved. He'd always thought she had the prettiest shoulders, and now he indulged himself by tasting them.

The hum in her throat told him she was both surprised and pleased by the attention. He had a great deal more to give her.

She'd never been touched this way, as if she were something rare and precious. What that touch stirred in her was so new and warm. Her skin seemed to soften and sensitize under the brush of his lips, the blood beneath to go thick and lazy. She only sighed as her dress slid down to pool at her feet.

When he eased back again, she could only stare up at him in wonder. Her lashes fluttered, her pulse skipped when he stroked his fingers lightly over the swell of her breast above her simple cotton bra. She had to bite her lip to hold back the groan when he flicked open the hook, when he gently cupped her breast in his palms.

"Do you want me to stop?"

"Oh, God." Her head fell back, and this time the groan escaped. His workingman's thumbs were skimming slowly, rhythmically over her nipples. "No."

"Hold on to me, Grace." He spoke quietly, and when her hands came to his shoulders and gripped, he brought his mouth to hers again, drawing more this time, asking more until she went limp.

Then he lifted her into his arms. He waited until her eyes opened again. "I'm taking you, Grace."

"Thank God, Ethan."

He had to smile when she pressed her face into the curve of his shoulder. "I'll protect you."

For a moment as he carried her off, she thought of dragons and black knights. Then the more practical meaning got through. "I—take the Pill. It's all right. I haven't been with anybody since Jack."

He'd known that in his heart, but hearing it only added to his steadily rising need.

She'd lighted candles in the bedroom as well. Slim tapers there that lanced up out of tiny white shells. The white of her iron head-board glowed in the soft light. White daisies sprang out of a clear glass vase on the small table beside the bed.

She thought he would lay her down, but instead he sat, cradling her, holding her, drugging her with those slow, endless kisses until her pulse beat thickly, grew sluggish. Then his hands began to move.

Everywhere he touched a small fire fanned into flame.

Callused hands, slipping, sliding over her skin. Long, rough-edged fingers stroking, pressing. There, oh, yes, just there.

The day-long stubble of beard rubbed the sensitive curve of her breasts as his tongue circled, then flicked. And always, always, his mouth coming back to hers for one more, just one more endless, mind-reeling kiss.

She tugged at his shirt, hoping to give back some of the pleasure, some of the magic. Found the scars and the muscle and the man. His torso was lean, his shoulders broad, the flesh warm under her seeking fingers. The breeze whispered through the open window, the call of the whippoorwill chasing after it. And the sound no longer seemed so lonely.

He eased her back, settled her head on the pillow, then bent to pull off his boots. Pale-gold candlelight swayed against shadows the color of smoke. Both shades shimmered over her. He watched as her hand snuck up to cover her breast, and he paused long enough to take it and kiss the knuckles.

"I wish you wouldn't," he murmured. "You're such a pleasure to look at."

She hadn't thought she'd feel shy, knew it was foolish, but she had to order herself to let her hand fall onto the bed. When he slipped out of his jeans she had to struggle with her breathing all over again. No fairy-tale knight had ever been built more magnificently or borne scars more heroically.

Desperate with love, she held out her arms in welcome.

He slipped into them, careful not to press his full weight onto her. She was fragile, he reminded himself, so slim and so much more innocent than she believed.

As the rising moon slanted its first light through the window, he began to show her.

Sighs and murmurs, long, slow caresses, quiet sips and tastes. His hands aroused, devastated, but never hurried. Hers explored, admired, and forgot to hesitate. He found where she was most sensitive, the underside of her breast, the back of her knee, the sweet, shallow, seductive valley between her thigh and her center.

So focused on her was he that his own rising need took him by surprise, flashing once, hard and strong and dragging out his moan when he took her breast into his mouth.

She arched, shuddering at the edgier demand.

And the rhythm changed.

With his breath growing ragged, he lifted his head, his eyes intent on her face. His hand slid between her thighs, pressed there against the heat. Found her already wet.

"I want to see you go over." He played his fingers over her, in her, as her breath quickened. Pleasure, panic, excitement all raced over her face. He watched her climb, closer, closer, with her breath tearing, then releasing on a strangled cry as she peaked.

She tried to shake her head to clear it, but the delicious dizziness continued to spin. The familiar room revolved, hazed, so that only his face was clear, was real. She felt drunk and dazed and unspeakably aroused.

This, finally this, was love as she'd dreamed it would be.

Her skin quivered as he slid slowly up her body, his mouth laying a warm, damp trail.

"Please." It wasn't enough. Even this wasn't enough. She craved the mating, the union, the final intimacy. "Ethan." She opened for him, arched. "Now."

His hands cupped her face, his lips covered her lips. "Now," he murmured against them and filled her.

Their long, groaning sighs blended, that first endless shudder of pleasure as he buried himself inside her rocked them both. When they began to move, they moved together, smoothly, silkily as if they'd only been waiting.

Desire was fluid, its current steady. They rode it, thrilling to the pace, to the deep, resonant pleasure of each long, slow stroke. Grace swirled close to the edge, felt the orgasm build, slide through her system like velvet ribbon so that she rose up, farther up, wallowed in the glow, then floated down into weightless wonder.

He pressed his face into her hair, and let himself follow.

HE WAS SO quiet it worried her. He held her, but he would have known she'd need him to. Still he didn't speak, and the longer the silence stretched the more she feared what he would say when he broke it.

So she broke it first.

"Don't tell me you're sorry. I don't think I could stand it if you told me you were sorry."

"I wasn't going to. I promised myself I'd never touch you like this, but I'm not sorry I did."

She rested her head on his shoulder, just under his chin. "Will you touch me like this again?"

"Right this minute?"

Because she caught the lazy amusement in his voice, she relaxed and smiled. "I know better than to rush you on anything." She lifted her head because it was vital that she know. "Will you, Ethan? Will you be with me again?"

He traced a finger through her hair. "I don't see talking either one of us out of it after tonight."

"If you started to, I'd have to try to seduce you again."

"Yeah?" A smile crept over his face. "Then maybe I should start talking."

Thrilled, she rolled over him and hugged hard. "I'd be better at it the next time, too, because I wouldn't be so damned nervous."

"Nerves didn't seem to get in your way. I nearly swallowed my tongue when you walked to the door in that pink dress." He started to nuzzle her hair, stopped, narrowed his eyes. "What were you doing wearing a dress to sit around at home?"

"I don't know . . . I just was." She turned her head, ran kisses along his throat.

"Hold on." Knowing just how quickly she could distract him, he took her shoulders and lifted her up. "A pretty dress, candlelight . . . it's almost like you were expecting me to come along."

"I'm always hoping you will," she said and tried to kiss him again.

"Sending me off with a recipe, for Christ's sake." In a smooth and easy move he plopped her on her butt beside him, then sat up. "You and Anna got your heads together on this, didn't you? Set me up."

"What a ridiculous thing to say." She tried for indignant, but could only manage guilty. "I don't know where you get these ideas."

"You never could lie worth spit." Firmly, he took her chin in one hand, holding it until her eyes shifted to his. "It took me a while to figure it, but I've got it now, don't I?"

"She was only trying to help. She knew I was upset about the way things were between us. You've got a right to be mad, but don't take it out on her. She was only—"

"Did I say I was mad?" he interrupted.

"No, but . . ." She trailed off, drew in a careful breath. "You're not mad?"

"I'm grateful." His grin was slow and wicked. "But maybe you ought to try to seduce me again. Just in case."

CHAPTER
11

I N the dark, while an owl still hooted, Ethan shifted, easing out from under the arm Grace had wrapped around his chest. In response she snuggled closer. The gesture made him smile.

"Are you getting up?" she asked in a voice that was muffled against his shoulder.

"I've got to. It's after five already." He could smell rain on the air, hear it coming in the rising wind. "I'm going to get a shower. You go back to sleep."

She made a sound that he took for assent and burrowed into the pillow.

He moved lightly through the dark, though he had to check himself a couple of times on the way to the bathroom. He didn't know her house as well as his own. He waited until he was inside before turning on the light so the backwash of it wouldn't spill into the hall and disturb her.

The room was scaled to match the rest of the house, so small he could have stood in the center and touched each side wall with his hands. The tiles were white, the walls above them papered in a thin candy stripe. He knew she'd hung the paper herself. She rented from Stuart Claremont, and the man wasn't known for his generosity or his sense of decor.

He had to grin at the orange-billed rubber duck nested on the side of the tub. One sniff at the soap made him realize why Grace always smelled faintly of lemons. While he appreciated the fragrance on her, he hoped sincerely that Jim wouldn't notice the citrus scent on him.

He ducked his head under what he thought of as a piss-trickle of spray. She needed a new showerhead, he decided, and as he rubbed a hand over his face, noted that he needed a shave. Both would have to wait.

But it was likely that now that things had changed between them, she would let him take care of a few things around the house for her. She'd always been so blessed stubborn about accepting help. It seemed to him that even a proud woman like Grace would be less stiff about taking help from a lover than a friend.

That's what they were now, Ethan reflected. No matter how many promises he'd made to himself. It wouldn't end with one night. Neither one of them was built that way, and it had as much to do with heart as it did with loins. They'd taken the step and that step involved commitment.

That's what worried him most.

He would never be able to marry her, have children with her. She would want more children. She was too fine a mother, had too much love to give not to want them. Aubrey deserved brothers or sisters.

There wasn't any point in thinking about it, he reminded himself. Things were the way things were. And right now he had a right, and a need to live in the moment. They would love each other as much as they could for as long as they could. That would be enough.

It took him barely five minutes to discover that Grace's hot water heater was as small as the rest of the house. Even the miserly trickle of water turned cool, then cold, before he'd managed to rinse away all the lather.

"Cheap bastard," he muttered, thinking of Claremont. He switched off the spray and wrapped one of the bright-pink towels around his waist. He intended to go back and dress in the dark, but when he opened the door, he could see the light from the kitchen and hear Grace's still sleep-husky voice singing about finding love, just in the nick of time.

While the first drops of rain pattered against the windows, he stepped into the scent of bacon frying and coffee brewing. And the sight of Grace wrapped in a short cotton robe the color of spring leaves. His heart gave such a hard bounce of joy he was surprised it didn't simply leap out of his throat and land quivering in her hands.

He moved quick and quiet, so that when he wrapped his arms around her, pressed his lips to the top of her head, she jolted in surprise.

"I told you to go back to sleep."

She leaned back against him, closing her eyes and absorbing the lovely thrill of a kitchen embrace. "I wanted to fix you breakfast."

"You don't have to do things like that." He turned her around. "I don't expect things like that. You need your rest."

"I wanted to do it." His hair was dripping, his chest gleaming with wet. The sparkling gush of lust both delighted and shocked her. "Today's special."

"I appreciate it." He bent, intending to give her one soft morning kiss. But it deepened, lengthened until she was on her toes straining against him.

He had to pull himself back, block off the rushing need to tug off the robe and take her. "The bacon's going to burn," he murmured, and this time pressed his lips to her forehead. "I'd better get dressed."

She turned the bacon briskly to give him time to cross the room. Anna had been right, she thought, about having power. "Ethan?"

"Yeah?"

"I've got an awful lot of need for you stored up." She glanced over her shoulder, and her smile was smug. "I hope you don't mind."

The blood danced gleefully out of his head. She wasn't just flirting, she was challenging. He had a feeling she knew she'd already won. The only safe answer he could think of was a grunt before he retreated to the bedroom.

He wanted her. Grace did a quick dance and spin. They'd made love three times, three beautiful, glorious times during the night, had slept wrapped around each other. And he still wanted her.

It was the most beautiful morning of her life.

⁘

IT RAINED ALL day. The water was rough as the tongue of a shrew and just as likely to lash. Ethan fought to keep the boat on course and was glad he hadn't let the boy come with them. He and Jim had worked in worse, but he imagined Seth would have spent a good portion of the day hung over the rail.

But foul weather couldn't spoil his mood. He whistled even as rain slapped his face and the boat pitched under him like a rodeo bronc.

Jim eyed him sideways a few times. He'd worked with Ethan long enough to know the boy was the friendly, good-natured sort. But a whistling fool he wasn't. He smiled to himself as he hauled up another pot. Looked like the boy did something more energetic than reading in bed last night, if you asked him.

About time, too—if you asked him. By his reckoning Ethan Quinn was round about thirty years of age. A man should oughta be settled down with a wife and kids by that time of life. A waterman was better off going home to a hot meal and a warm bed. A good woman helped you through, gave you direction, cheered you up when the Bay got stingy. As God knew it could.

He wondered who this particular woman might be. Not that he stuck his nose in other people's business. He minded his own and expected his neighbors to do the same. But a man had a right to a little curiosity about things.

He pondered on how to bring the subject around when an under-the-limit she-crab found a tiny hole in his glove and snapped before he could toss her back.

"Little bitch," he said with a wince but without much heat.

"She get you?"

"Yeah." Jim watched her splash back into the waves. "I'll be back for you before the season's over."

"Looks like you need new gloves there, Jim."

"The wife's picking me up some today." He shoved the thawing alewives they used for bait into the trap. "Sure helps matters to know you got a woman to do for you some."

"Uh-huh." Ethan shoved the steering stick with one hand, picked up the gaff with the other, and timed the chop and the distance.

"A man spends the day working on the water, it's a comfort to know his woman's waiting for him."

A little surprised that they were having a conversation, Ethan nodded. "I suppose. We'll just finish up this line, Jim, then head in."

Jim culled the next pot, let the silence settle between them. A few gulls were having what Jim thought of as a pissing match overhead, screaming and diving and threatening each other over loose fish parts.

"You know, me and Bess, we'll be married thirty years come next spring."

"Is that so?"

"Steadies a man, a woman does. You wait too long to marry up, though, you get set in your ways."

"I guess."

"You'd be around thirty now, wouldn't you, Cap'n?"

"That's right."

"Don't want to get set in your ways."

"I'll keep that in mind," Ethan told him and shot out the gaff. Jim merely sighed and gave up.

WHEN ETHAN WANDERED into the boatyard, Cam was at the skill saw and three young boys were sanding the hull. Or pretending to.

"You hire a new crew?" Ethan asked as Simon trotted over to investigate.

Cam glanced to where Seth chattered away with Danny and Will Miller. "It keeps them out of my hair. You give up on crabs today?"

"Pulled in enough." He pulled out a cigar and lit it while he gazed thoughtfully out the open cargo doors. "Rain's coming down pretty hard."

"Tell me about it." Cam sent an accusing scowl toward the streaming windows. "That's why those three were in my hair. The little one'll talk your ears blue. And if you don't have the others doing something to keep them busy, they make trouble out of thin air."

"Well." Ethan puffed out smoke, watched the kids send Simon into ecstasy with rough rubs and scratches. "At the rate they're going, they'll have that hull sanded down in ten or twenty years."

"That's something we have to talk about."

"Hiring on those kids for the next two decades?"

"No, work." It was as good a time as any to take a break. Cam stooped and pumped iced tea out of the cooler. "I got a call from Tod Bardette this morning."

"The friend of yours who wants the fishing boat?"

"That's right. Now, Bardette and I go back a ways. He knows what I can do."

"He offer you another race?"

He had, Cam mused, cutting the dust in his throat with the sweet tea. Turning it down had stung, but the sting had eased more quickly this time around. "I made a promise here. I'm not breaking it."

Ethan tucked a hand in his back pocket and looked toward the boat. This place, this business, had been his dream, not Cam's, not Phillip's. "I didn't mean it that way. I guess I know what you put away to pull this off."

"We needed it."

"Yeah, but you're the only one who's given up anything to make it happen. I haven't bothered to thank you for it, and I'm sorry for that."

Every bit as uncomfortable as his brother, Cam stared at the boat. "I'm not exactly suffering here. The business is going to help us get permanent guardianship of Seth—and it's satisfying on its own account. Of course, Phil's bitching about our cash flow every time you turn around."

"That's his strength."

"Bitching?"

Ethan grinned around the cigar clamped in his teeth. "Yeah, and cash flows. You and me, we could never pull this off without him nagging us about the details."

"We may have more for him to nag about. That's what I started to tell you. Bardette has a friend who's interested in a custom catboat. He wants fast and he wants pretty, fitted out and sailing by March."

Ethan frowned and worked timetables in his head. "It's going to take us another seven or eight weeks to finish this one, and that puts us into end of August, beginning of September."

Calculating, he leaned back against the workbench, his eyes narrowed against the smoke. "Then we got the sport's fisher. I can't see us finishing her off before January, and that's pushing. That doesn't give us enough time to deliver."

"No, not the way things are. I can give it full-time and after crab season's over, I imagine you'll put in more hours here."

"Oystering isn't what it was, but—"

"You'll have to decide if you can juggle more time off the water, Ethan, and in here." He knew what he was asking. Ethan didn't just live on the water, he lived for it. "Phil's going to have to make some hard decisions before much longer, too. We're not going to have the cash to hire on laborers for a while yet." He blew out a breath. "Unless we count a couple of kids. This friend of Bardette's isn't ready to commit. He's going to come down and take a look at the place, and us, and what we've got here. I figure we make sure Phillip's around to sweet-talk him into a contract and a deposit."

Ethan hadn't expected it to happen so soon, to have one dream grow and steal from the other. He thought of the chill winter months spent dredging, the rise and fall of the skipjack over hard chop, the long, often frustrating search for oyster, for rockfish, for a living.

A nightmare for some, he supposed. But hope and glory for him.

He took the time to look around the building. The boat, nearly finished, waiting for willing and able hands under the hard overhead lights. Seth's drawings were framed on the wall and spoke of dreams and sweat. Tools, still shiny under a coating of dust, stood silent, waiting.

Boats by Quinn, he mused. If you wanted to grab ahold of one thing, you had to let go of another.

"I'm not the only one who can captain the workboat or the skipjack." He saw both the question and the understanding in Cam's eyes and jerked a shoulder. "It's just juggling time where it needs to be spent most."

"Yeah."

"I guess I could work up a design for a cat."

"And have Seth do the drawing," Cam added and laughed when Ethan grimaced. "We all have our strengths, pal. Art isn't yours."

"I'll think about it," Ethan decided. "And we'll see what happens next."

"Good enough. So . . ." Cam drained his cup. "How'd the recipe exchange go?"

Ethan ran his tongue around the inside of his cheek. "I'm going to have a talk with your wife about that."

"Be my guest." Smiling, Cam plucked the cigar from Ethan's fingers and took a trio of careless puffs. "You sure look . . . relaxed today, Ethan."

"I'm relaxed enough," he said evenly. "And I'd think you might have seen fit to mention to me that Anna had some plot to improve my sex life for me."

"I might have, if I'd known about it. Then again, since your sex life needed some improvement, I might not." On impulse, Cam grabbed Ethan in a headlock. "Because I love you, man." He only laughed when the elbow plowed into his stomach. "See? It even improved your reflexes."

Ethan shifted, angled his weight, and reversed their positions.

"You're right," he said and rubbed his knuckles hard on the top of Cam's head for good measure.

SINCE IT WAS his night to cook, Ethan added an egg to a bowl of ground beef. He didn't mind cooking. It was just one of those things you did to get through. He'd harbored a small, selfish, and purely chauvinistic hope that Anna would take over the kitchen duties as woman of the house.

She'd squashed that hope like a bug.

Of course, having her around did spread out the chore. But the worst of it, as far as he was concerned, was figuring out the menu. It was different from cooking for himself. He'd learned quickly enough that when you cooked for a family, everybody was a critic.

"What is that?" Seth demanded when Ethan shook oatmeal into the mix.

"Meat loaf."

"Looks like crap to me. Why can't we have pizza?"

"Because we're having meat loaf."

Seth made a gagging sound as Ethan dumped some tomato soup into the mix. "Gross. I'd rather eat dirt."

"There's plenty of it outside."

Seth shifted from foot to foot, rose up on his toes to get a closer look at the bowl. The rain was driving him crazy. There was nothing to *do*. He was starving to death, he had six million mosquito bites, and there was nothing but kid crud and news on TV.

When he listed this litany of complaints, Ethan merely shrugged. "Go bug Cam."

Cam had told him to go bug Ethan. Seth knew from hard experience that it took much longer to bug Ethan than Cam.

"How come you put all that crap in there if it's called meat loaf?"

"So it doesn't taste like crap when you eat it."

"I bet it does."

For a kid who only months before hadn't known where his next meal was coming from, Ethan thought darkly, Seth had gotten mighty particular. Instead of saying so, he aimed a single, sharp dart. "Cam's cooking tomorrow."

"Oh, man. Poison." Seth rolled his eyes dramatically, grabbed his throat, and staggered around the room. Ethan might have been mildly amused if the dogs hadn't gotten into the act by scrambling in and barking wildly.

By the time Anna walked in, Ethan had the meat loaf in the oven and was dumping aspirin into his palm.

"Hi. Miserable day. Traffic was filthy." She raised an eyebrow as Ethan downed the pills. "Headache, huh? All-day rain can sure give you one."

"This one's named Seth."

"Oh." Concerned, she poured herself a glass of wine and prepared to listen. "There's bound to be periods of stress and difficulties. He has a tremendous amount to overcome, and his belligerence is a defense."

"Did nothing but complain for the last hour. My ears are still ringing. Doesn't want meat loaf," Ethan muttered and snagged a beer from the fridge. " 'Why can't we have pizza?' He ought to be grateful somebody's putting food in his belly. Instead he's saying it looks like crap and will likely taste worse. Then he gets the dogs all fired up so I can't even work in peace for five damn minutes. And . . ."

He trailed off, steely-eyed, when he saw her grinning. "Easy for you to be amused by it."

"I am, I'm sorry. But I'm even more pleased. Oh, Ethan, it's so wonderfully normal. He's behaving just like an annoying ten-year-old after a rainy day. A couple of months ago he'd have spent that time sulking in his room instead of giving you a headache. It's such tremendous progress."

"He's progressing into being a pain in the ass."

"Yes." She felt tears of delight sting her eyes. "Isn't it marvelous? He must have been really annoying if it was enough to try your unflappable patience. At this rate he'll be a terror by Christmas."

"And that's a good thing?"

"Yes. Ethan, I've worked with children who haven't faced nearly the miseries Seth has, and it can take them so much longer to adjust, even with counseling. You and Cam and Phillip have done wonders for Seth."

Cooling off, Ethan sipped his beer. "You had a hand in it."

"Yes, I did, which makes me as happy on a professional level as I am on a personal one. And to prove it, I'll give you a hand with dinner." So saying, she shrugged out of her jacket and began to roll up her sleeves. "What did you have in mind to go with the meat loaf?"

He'd planned on sticking some potatoes in the microwave because they didn't require any fussing, and maybe digging some frozen peas out. But . . .

"I thought maybe some of those cheese noodles you make would go nice as a side dish."

"The alfredo? Cholesterol city, added to meat loaf, but what the hell. I'll fix them. Why don't you sit down until the headache passes?"

It already had, but it seemed smarter not to mention it.

He sat, prepared to enjoy his beer—and fix his sister-in-law's wagon. "Oh, Grace said I should thank you for the recipe. She'll let you know how it turns out for her."

"Oh?" Turning to hide her satisfied smile, Anna reached for an apron.

"Yeah, I got the fried chicken makings for you—stuck it in the cookbook." He hid his own smile with his beer when her head swiveled.

"You . . . oh, well . . ."

"I'd have given it to you last night, but it was late when I got back, and you were in bed. I ran into Jim when I left Grace's."

"Jim?" Puzzled annoyance showed clearly on her face.

"Went on over to his place to help him tune up this outboard that's been giving him trouble."

"You were at Jim's last night?"

"Stayed later than I meant to, but there was a ball game on. The O's were playing out in California."

She could have cheerfully smashed him over the head with his own beer bottle. "You spent last night working on an engine and watching a ball game?"

"Yeah." He sent her an innocent look. "Like I said, I got in kinda late, but it was a hell of a game."

She huffed out a breath, yanked open the refrigerator to get out cheese and milk. "Men," she muttered. "All of them idiots."

"What's that?"

"Nothing. Well, I hope you had a fine time watching your baseball game." While Grace was home alone, miserable.

"I can't remember enjoying myself more. Went into extra innings." He was grinning now, just couldn't help it. She looked so flustered and furious and was trying desperately to hide it.

"Well, hot damn." Fuming, she shifted to get the fettuccine out of the cupboard and saw his face. She turned slowly, holding the package of pasta. "You didn't go over to Jim's to watch a ball game last night."

"Didn't I?" He lifted a brow, glanced thoughtfully at his beer, then sipped. "You know, come to think of it, you're right. That was some other time."

"You were with Grace."

"Was I?"

"Oh, Ethan." With clenched teeth she slammed the jar down. "You're making me crazy! Where were you last night?"

"You know, I don't believe anyone's asked me that since my mother died."

"I'm not trying to pry—"

"You're not?"

"All right, all right, I am trying to pry and you make it impossible to be subtle about it."

He leaned back in his chair, studying her. He'd liked her, almost from the first—even when she made him uneasy. Wasn't it funny, he mused, to realize that sometime over the last few weeks, he had come to love her. Which meant that teasing her was, well, required.

"You're not asking me if I spent the night in Grace's bed, are you?"

"No. No, of course not." She snatched up the pasta, then set it down again. "Not exactly."

"Were the candles her idea, or yours?"

Anna decided it was a good time to get out a skillet. She just might need a weapon. "Did they work?"

"Yours, I imagine; probably the dress, too. Grace's mind doesn't work that way. She's not what you'd call . . . sneaky."

Anna hummed and prepared to make her cheese sauce.

"And it was sneaky, underhanded, meddling, to send me over there that way."

"I know it. But I'd do it again." More skillfully next time, she promised herself. "You can be annoyed with me all you want, Ethan, but I've never seen anyone more in need of some meddling."

"You're a pro at it. I mean, being a social worker, you make a living meddling in people's lives."

"I help people who need it," she said, firing up the skillet. "God knows you did." She yelped when his hand dropped on her shoulder. She half expected him to give her a quick shake, so when he kissed her cheek she could only blink at him.

"I appreciate it."

"You do?"

"Not that I'd care to have you do it again, but this once, I appreciate it."

"She makes you happy." Everything inside Anna softened. "I can see it."

"We'll see how long I can make her happy."

"Ethan—"

"Let it stand." He kissed her again, as much in warning as affection. "We'll take it a day at a time for a while."

"All right." But her smile bloomed. "Grace is working at the pub tonight, isn't she?"

"Yeah. And just so you don't have to bite your tongue in half to keep from asking, I'm thinking of going by for a while after dinner."

"Good." More than satisfied, Anna got to work. "Then we'll eat soon."

CHAPTER
12

IT was like walking wide awake into a dream, Grace thought, where you couldn't be sure what was going to happen next, but you just knew it would be wonderful. It was living inside a familiar world that had been polished into a constant state of anticipation and excitement.

Days and nights were still filled with work, responsibilities, small joys and petty annoyances. But for now, with this full rush of love, the joys seemed huge, the annoyances minute.

Everything she'd ever read about love was true, she discovered. The sun shined brighter, the air smelled fresher. Flowers were more colorful, the songs of birds more musical. Every cliché became her reality.

There were stolen moments—an embrace outside the pub during her break that left her jittery and delighted and unable to sleep long after she went home. A slow, intense look filled with awareness if she managed to linger long enough at the Quinn house to see him.

It seemed she was in a constant state of yearning, only more acute now that she knew what could be.

What would be.

She wanted to touch and be touched, to take that long, slow ride into pleasure and passion again. Side by side with the yearning was the endless frustration that life constantly intruded on dreams.

There was never enough time to be alone, to simply be.

She often wondered if Ethan felt the same edgy need dogging his heels throughout his day. She thought it must be something inside her, some long-hidden sexual greed—and she didn't know whether to be delighted by it or mortified.

She only knew that she wanted him constantly, and that with every day that want passed into another night alone, that want increased. She wondered if he would be shocked, worried that he would be.

She needn't have.

HE ONLY HOPED he'd timed it right, and that his excuses to Jim for taking in the catch before checking all the pots weren't as ridiculously transparent as they'd seemed. He wasn't going to let guilt eat at him either, Ethan promised himself as he secured his boat at his home dock.

He would work a couple extra hours that evening in the boatyard to make up for leaving Cam on his own that afternoon. If he didn't have one hour alone with Grace, if he didn't release some of this pressure that was building up, he'd go crazy. Then he'd be no good to anyone.

And if she'd already finished up at the house and left, well, he'd just have to hunt her down, that's all. He had enough control left not to scare her, or shock her, but he just couldn't get through another day without her.

His grin began to spread when he came through the back door and saw that the morning untidiness had yet to be cleared away. The washer was rumbling in the laundry room. She hadn't finished. He started into the living room, looking for signs of her.

The cushions were all smoothed and plumped, the furniture dust-free and shining. And as the floor above his head gave a quiet creak, he glanced up.

At that moment, he thought Fate was the most beautiful woman he'd ever known. Grace was in his bedroom, and what could be more perfect? It would be much easier to lure her into a daytime bed without jolting her sensibilities if she was already close by one.

He started up the stairs, delighted when he heard her humming.

Then his system suffered a sizzling lightning bolt of lust when he saw she wasn't just close by his bed, she was all but in it. She leaned over, smoothing and tucking fresh sheets, her long legs showcased in ragged cutoffs.

His blood raced, a roar of speed that left him breathless, that turned the low ache he'd learned to live with into a sharp and gnawing pain. He could see himself springing forward, dragging her onto the bed, pulling and tearing at her clothes until he could hammer himself inside her.

And because he could, because he wanted to, he made himself stand where he was until he was certain his control was firmly in place.

"Grace?"

She straightened, whirled, pressed a hand to her heart. "Oh. I . . . oh." She couldn't speak, could barely think coherently. What would *he* think, she wondered giddily, if he knew she'd been fantasizing about rolling naked and sweaty over those crisp clean sheets with him?

Her cheeks had gone pink, charming him. "Didn't mean to sneak up on you."

"That's all right." She let out a long breath, but it did nothing to calm her racing heart. "I didn't expect anyone to . . . What are you doing home so early in the day?" Quickly she clasped her hands together because they wanted to grab at him. "Are you sick?"

"No."

"It's not even three o'clock."

"I know." He stepped into the room, saw her press her lips together, moisten them. Take it slow, he reminded himself, don't spook her. "Aubrey's not with you?"

"No, Julie's minding her. Julie got a new kitten and Aubrey wanted to stay, so . . ." He smelled of the water, salt, and sun. It made her light-headed.

"Then we've got some time." He came a little closer. "I wanted to see you alone."

"You did?"

"I've been wanting to see you alone since we made love that night." He lifted his hand, gently encircled the nape of her neck. "I've been wanting you," he said quietly and lowered his mouth to hers.

So soft, so tender, her heart seemed to turn one long, loose somersault in her chest. Her knees went weak. They trembled even as she threw her arms around him, as she answered that tentative kiss with a flash of heat. His fingers dug into her skin, his mouth bruised hers. For one wild and wicked moment, she thought he would take her where they stood, fast and frantic and free.

Then his hands gentled, smoothed over her. His lips softened, cruising over hers now. "Come to bed with me," he murmured. "Come to bed with me," even as he lowered her, covered her.

She arched against him, wanting and willing, impatient with the clothes that separated her flesh from his. It seemed like years since she had last touched him, had last felt those hard planes, those iron muscles. Moaning his name, she tugged up his shirt, let her hands possess, and possessing, they aroused.

His breath came raggedly, burning his throat. Her movements under him urged him to hurry, hurry, but he was afraid he would bruise her if he didn't take time, didn't take care. So he fought to slow the pace, to taste rather than devour, to caress rather than demand.

But where as she had once seduced him, she now destroyed him.

He tugged off her shirt, found her naked beneath it. She saw his eyes flash, turn to a burning blue that all but scorched her skin. He was careful, so careful not to bruise, not to frighten. Slow, to slow the pace even while the brutal desire to take, take more, take swiftly, swarmed into him.

Then his mouth was on her, sucking her in with a desperate hunger that threatened to consume them both. She threw her arm back, reached, but there was nothing to hold on to except empty air. He dragged her up, his mouth streaking down her torso, teeth scraping, until, gasping for air, she folded herself around him.

He couldn't wait, knew it would kill him to wait. The only thought in his head was now, it had to be now, and even that was wrapped in the rusty edges of primal need. He tugged at her shorts, cursing, then plunged his fingers inside her.

She bucked, cried out, came. He watched her eyes go opaque, her head fall back so that the long line of her throat was there for him to feast on. Battling the violent urge to drive himself into her, he continued to taste until the sharp void was filled.

Then he freed himself from his jeans and slipped into her. She cried out again, her muscles clamping tight around him.

And he lost his mind.

Speed and heat and force. More. He shoved her knees up and

stroked deeper, harder, darkly thrilled when her nails bit into his shoulders. He plunged inside her, quivering with raw, blind greed.

Sensations swamped her, scraped at her, stripped her into one shuddering mass of need. She thought she might die from it. When the next orgasm slammed into her, a hard, hot fist, she thought she had.

And went limp, her hands sliding from Ethan's damp shoulders, the silver flash of energy draining to leave her exhausted. She heard his long, low groan, felt his body plunge, then stiffen. When he collapsed on her, panting, her lips curved in a smile of pure female satisfaction.

The sunlight dazzled her eyes as she stroked her hands down and over his hips. "Ethan." She turned her head to kiss his hair. "No, not yet," she murmured when he started to shift. "Not yet."

He'd been rough with her, and he cursed himself for allowing the knot on his control to slip. "Are you all right?"

"Mmmmmm. I could lie here all day, just like this."

"I didn't take the time I meant to."

"We don't have as much as most people."

"No." He lifted his head. "You wouldn't even tell me if I'd hurt you." So he looked for himself, carefully studying her face. And he saw in it the sleepy satisfaction of a woman well, if hurriedly, loved. "I guess I didn't."

"It was exciting. It was wonderful knowing you wanted me so much." Lazily, she twirled a lock of his sun-tipped hair around her finger and hugged the gorgeously wicked sensation of being naked in bed with him in the middle of the day. "I'd been worried that I wanted you more than you could ever want me."

"You couldn't." To prove it, he kissed her long and slow and deep. "This isn't the way I want it for you. Cramming minutes alone between chores. And using those minutes to jump into bed because it's all we've got."

"I've never made love in the middle of the day before." She smiled. "I liked it."

On a long breath, he lowered his brow to hers. If it had been possible, he would have spent the rest of the day right there, inside her. "We're going to have to figure out a way to find a little more time now and again."

"I've got tomorrow night off. You could come by for dinner . . . and stay."

"I ought to take you out somewhere."

"There's nowhere I want to go. I'd like it if we could have dinner in." Then her smile spread. "I'll make you some tortellini. I just got this new recipe."

When he laughed, she threw her arms around him and chalked up another of the happiest moments of her life. "Oh, I love you, Ethan." She was so giddy with it that it took her a moment to realize he was no longer laughing, had gone very still. Her wildly bounding heart slowed, and chilled.

"Maybe you don't want me to say that, but I can't help feeling it. I don't expect you to say it back, or feel obligated to—"

His fingers pressed lightly against her lips to silence her. "Give me a minute, Grace," he said quietly. His system had flooded, rising tides of joys, hopes, fears. He couldn't think past them, not clearly. But he knew her, knew that what he said now, and how he said it, would be vitally important.

"I've had feelings for you for so long," he began, "I can't remember when I didn't have them. I've spent just as long telling myself I shouldn't have them, so all of this is taking me some time to get used to."

When he shifted this time, she didn't try to stop him. She nodded, avoided his eyes and reached for her clothes. "It's enough that you want me, maybe even need me a little. It's enough for now, Ethan. This is all so new for both of us."

"They're strong feelings, Grace. You matter to me more than any woman ever has."

She looked at him now. If he said it, she knew he meant it. Hope began to beat in her heart again. "If you had feelings for me, strong feelings, why didn't you ever let me know?"

"First you weren't old enough." He pushed his hand through his hair, knowing that that was an evasion, an excuse, and not the core of it. He couldn't tell her the core of it. "And I wasn't real comfortable having the kind of thoughts and feelings for you I was having when you were still in high school."

She could have leaped up on the bed and danced. "Since I was in high school? All this time?"

"Yeah, all this time. Then you were in love with somebody else, so I didn't have any right to feel anything but friendship."

She let out a careful breath, because it would be a confession that shamed her. "I was never in love with anybody else. It was always you."

"Jack—"

"I never loved him, and everything that went wrong between us was more my fault than his. I let him be the first man to touch me because I never thought you would. And about the time I realized how foolish that was, I was pregnant."

"You can't say it was your fault."

"Yes, I can." To keep her hands busy, she began to tidy the bed. "I knew he wasn't in love with me, but I married him because I was afraid not to. And for a while I was ashamed, angry and ashamed." She lifted a pillow, tucked it into its case. "Until one night when I was lying in bed thinking my life was over, and I felt this fluttering inside me."

She closed her eyes, pressed the pillow against her. "I felt Aubrey, and it was so . . . so huge, that little flutter, that I wasn't ashamed or angry anymore. Jack gave me that." She opened her eyes again and carefully laid the pillow on the bed. "I'm grateful to him, and I don't blame him for leaving. He never felt that flutter. Aubrey was never real to him."

"He was a coward, and worse, for leaving you weeks before the baby was born."

"Maybe, but I was a coward, and worse, for being with him, for marrying him when I never had a fraction of the feeling for him that I did for you."

"You're the bravest woman I know, Grace."

"It's easy to be brave when you have a child depending on you. I guess what I'm trying to tell you is that if I made a mistake, it was in going so long without letting you know I loved you. Whatever feelings you have for me, Ethan, are more than I ever thought you would have. And that's enough."

"I've been in love with you for the best part of ten years, and it's still not enough."

She'd picked up the second pillow, and now it slipped out of her hands. When tears swam into her eyes, she closed them, squeezed tight. "I thought I could live without ever hearing you say that. Now I need to hear you say it again so I can get my breath back."

"I love you, Grace."

Her lips curved, her eyes opened. "You sound so serious, almost sad when you say it." Wanting to see him smile again, she held out a hand. "Maybe you should practice."

His fingers had just touched hers when the screen door slammed downstairs. Feet pounded on the stairs. Even as they jerked apart,

Seth raced down the hall. He skidded to a halt at the door to Ethan's room, then stood, stared.

He glanced at the bed, the sheets not quite smoothed out, the pillow on the floor. Then his gaze shifted, and filled with a bitter fury that was much too adult in his young face.

"You bastard." There was loathing in the tone as he snapped at Ethan, then disgust as his eyes locked on Grace. "I thought you were different."

"Seth." She took a step forward, but he turned on his heel and ran. "Oh, God, Ethan." When she started to rush after the boy, Ethan took her arm.

"No, I'll go after him. I know what he's feeling. Don't worry." He gave her arm a squeeze before walking out. Still, she followed him to the steps, worried sick. She'd never seen such dark hate in the eyes of a child.

"Damn it, Seth, I told you to hurry up." Cam slammed in the front door just as Ethan hit the bottom of the steps. Cam glanced up, saw Grace, and felt a grin tug at his mouth. "Oops."

"I don't have time for lame jokes," Ethan shot back. "Seth just took off."

"What? Why?" It struck him even before the word was out. "Oh, shit. He must have gone out the back."

"I'm going after him." He shook his head before Cam could protest. "It's me he's pissed off at right now. It's me he figures let him down. I have to fix it." He glanced up to where Grace sat on the steps. "Look after her," he murmured to Cam and headed for the back door.

Ethan knew Seth would have headed into the woods, and he had to trust that the boy wouldn't run too far into the marsh. He was a survivor, Ethan thought. But relief shimmered through him when he heard the rustle of brush and old leaves.

It was simple enough to spot where Seth had veered off the path. Ethan pushed through tangled vines, the prickle of briars, and followed. The leaves on the trees that arched overhead blocked the glare and the worst of the sun's heat. But the humidity was immense.

Sweat ran down Ethan's back, dripped into his eyes, as he patiently walked, and waited. He was well aware that Seth was evading him, keeping a few yards ahead. Finally he sat on a fallen log, deciding it would be easier to let the boy come to him.

It took ten long minutes, with gnats swarming in clouds and mosquitoes sniffing for blood, but finally Seth emerged from a thicket and faced him.

"I'm not going back with you." He all but spat it out. "If you try to make me, I'll just run again."

"I'm not going to make you do anything." From his seat on the log, Ethan studied him. Seth's face was filthy, streaked with dirt and sweat, flushed with heat and fury. His legs and arms were thoroughly scratched from pushing through briars.

They were going to sting like fury, Ethan knew, when Seth cooled off enough to notice.

"You want to sit down and talk this out?" he asked mildly.

"I don't believe anything you say. You're a liar. You're both fucking liars. You gonna try to tell me you weren't screwing each other?"

"No, that's not what we were doing."

Seth flew at him so fast, Ethan was thrown off guard enough to take the first fist solidly in the jaw. He would think later, much later, that the kid threw a fine punch. But at the moment it took all his concentration to wrestle Seth to the ground.

"I'll kill you! You bastard, I'll kill you as soon as I get a chance." He wiggled and struggled and fought and waited for the rain of blows.

"Just hold on." Frustrated as the slick, sweaty arms kept sliding out of his grip, Ethan gave Seth a quick shake. "You're not getting anywhere this way. I'm bigger than you are, and I'll just pin you down till you run out of steam."

"Take your hands off me." Seth set his teeth and snarled. "Son of a whore."

It was a blow harder, and more sharply aimed, than the fist had been. Ethan caught his breath and nodded slowly. "Yeah, that's what I am. That's why you and I know each other. You can run when I let you up, Seth. You can spill filth all over me. That's what people expect from sons of whores. I'm going to figure you want better for yourself than that."

Ethan eased back, sat on his heels and wiped the blood off his mouth. "That's the second damn time you've punched me in the face. You try it again, and I'm going to wallop your ass so you don't sit for a month."

"I hate your fucking guts."

"Fine. But you're going to have to hate them for the right reasons."

"All you wanted was to get between her legs, and she spread them for you."

"Watch it." In a lightning move, Ethan grabbed Seth by the shirt and hauled him up to his knees. "Don't you talk about her that way. You had sense enough to recognize right off what kind of person Grace was. That's why you trusted her, why you cared about her."

"I don't give a shit about her," Seth claimed and had to swallow hard before the hot tears poured out.

"If you didn't, you wouldn't be so mad at both of us. And wouldn't be feeling like we let you down."

He let Seth go, then rubbed his hands over his face. He knew how miserably inept he could be at explaining emotions. Especially his own. "I'm going to talk to you straight." He dropped his hands.

"You're right about what went on before you came home, you're just wrong about what it meant."

Seth's lips quivered into a snarl. "I know what fucking means."

"Yeah, the way you know it it's ugly sounds in the next room, fast gropes in the dark, sour smells, money changing hands."

"Just because you didn't pay her doesn't—"

"Be quiet," Ethan said patiently. "I used to think that's all it was, or the only kind there was. Hard and heartless, sometimes mean. All you want from the other is what you can get for yourself. So that makes it selfish, too. You get some release, pull your pants up and walk away. It's not always wrong. If it doesn't matter to either one of you, if it gets you through the night, it's not always wrong. But it's not the only way, and it sure as hell isn't the best way."

He remembered now thinking that he hoped someone else would explain such things to the boy when the time came. But it appeared that the time was now and he was in charge.

He couldn't say it all with a grin and a wink as Cam might, or smooth and fancy as Phillip surely would. He could only speak from the heart and hope it was right.

"Sex can be the same as eating. Just filling a hunger. Sometimes you pay for a meal, sometimes you trade something, and if it's fair you're giving as much as you're taking."

"Sex is just sex. They just pretty it up to sell books and movies."

"Do you figure that's all there is between Anna and Cam?"

Seth moved his shoulders, but he was thinking.

"They've got something that matters, and lasts, that lives get built on. It's not what you've grown up with, or what I spent the first part of my life with—that's why I can tell you straight."

Ethan pressed his fingers to his eyes and ignored the swarm of bugs and the sweat. "It's different when you care, when the other person isn't just a face or a body that's convenient and willing. I've had that. Most people do along the way. It's different when it's just that one person who matters, who makes it right. When it isn't all hunger pushing at you. When you want, more than anything, to give back more than you take. I never had with anyone what I have with Grace."

Seth shrugged and looked away, but not before Ethan saw the misery on his face. "I know you've got feelings for her, and that they're real and strong and important. Maybe part of you wanted her to be perfect, not to have the needs other women do. I think a bigger part of you wanted to protect her, to make sure nobody hurt her. So I'm telling you what I just finished finally telling her. I love her. I've never loved anybody else."

Seth stared off into the marsh. He hurt all over, but the worst of it was shame. "Does she love you back?"

"Yeah, she does. Damned if I can figure out why."

Seth thought he knew why. Ethan was strong, and he didn't put on a big show. He did what had to be done. What was right. "I was going to take care of her when I got older. I guess you think that's pretty lame."

"No." He suddenly, urgently, wanted to pull the boy against him, but he knew the timing was wrong. "No, I think that's pretty great. It makes me proud of you."

Seth's gaze flicked up, then quickly away again. "I kind of, you know, love her. Sort of. Not like I want to see her naked or anything," he added quickly. "Just—"

"I get it." Ethan clamped down on the tip of his tongue to stifle the chuckle. The quick surge of amused relief tasted finer than an icy beer on a hot day. "Kind of like she was a sister, like you wanted the best for her."

"Yeah." And Seth sighed. "Yeah, I guess that's it."

Thoughtfully, Ethan sucked air between his teeth. "It's got to be tough for a guy to walk in and see that his sister's been with some guy."

"I hurt her. I wanted to."

"Yeah, you did. You'll have to apologize if you want to put things right with her."

"She'll think I'm stupid. She won't want to talk to me."

"She wanted to come after you herself. By this time, I'd say she's pacing around the backyard, worried sick."

Seth sucked in a breath that was too close to a sob to suit either of them. "I razzed Cam until he brought me home for my ball glove. And when I . . . I saw you in there, it made me think of how I would come back to wherever Gloria was living, and she'd be doing it with some guy."

Where sex was a business, Ethan thought, both ugly and mean. "It's hard to put those things aside, or let yourself believe there's a different way." Since he was still working on it himself, Ethan spoke carefully. "That making love, when you care, when it matters, when things are right, it's clean."

Seth sniffled, wiped at his eyes. "Gnats," he muttered.

"Yeah, they're a bitch out here."

"You should've slugged me, for saying that shit."

"You're right," Ethan decided after a moment. "I'll slug you next time. Now, let's go home."

He rose, brushed off his pants, then held out a hand. Seth stared up at him, saw kindness, patience, compassion. Qualities in a man he might have sneered at once because he'd found so little of them in anyone who had touched his life.

He put his hand in Ethan's and, without realizing it, left it there as they walked down the path. "How come you didn't hit me back even once?"

Little boy, Ethan thought, you've had too many hands raised against you in your short life. "Maybe I was afraid you could take me."

Seth snorted, blinking furiously at tears that still wanted to come. "Shit."

"Well, you're small," Ethan said, taking the cap from Seth's back pocket and snugging it down on Seth's head. "But you're a wiry little bastard."

Seth had to take long breaths as they came close to where the sunlight struck the edge of the woods, slanting white light.

He saw Grace, as Ethan had predicted, in the yard, hugging her arms as if she were chilled. She dropped them, took a quick step forward, then stopped.

Ethan felt Seth's hand flex in his and gave it a quick encouraging squeeze. "It'd go a long way to making things up to her," Ethan murmured, "if you were to run up and hug her. Grace is big on hugs."

It was what he'd wanted to do, what he was afraid to risk. He looked up at Ethan, jerked a shoulder, cleared his throat. "I guess I could, if it'd make her feel better."

Ethan stood back, watched the boy race across the lawn, watched Grace's face light with a smile as she threw open her arms to take him in.

CHAPTER

13

IF you were going to have to work over a long holiday weekend, Phillip figured, it might as well be at something fun. He loved his job. What was advertising, anyway, but a knowledge of people and of which buttons to push to nudge them into opening their wallets?

It was, he often thought, an accepted, creative, even expected twist on picking those wallets. For a man who had spent the first half of his life as a thief, it was the perfect career.

On this day before the celebration of America's independence, he put his skills to use in the boatyard, schmoozing a potential client. He much preferred it to manual labor.

"You'll forgive the surroundings." Phillip waved a well-manicured hand, encompassing the enormous space, the exposed rafters and hanging lights, the yet-to-be-painted walls and scarred floors. "My brothers and I believe in putting our efforts into the product and keeping our overhead minimal. Those are benefits that we pass along to our clients."

At which time, Phillip thought, they had exactly one—with another in the box and this one nibbling at the line.

"Hmmm." Jonathan Kraft rubbed his chin. He was in his mid-thirties and fortunate enough to be a fourth-generation member of the pharmaceutical Krafts. Since his great-grandfather's humble beginnings as a storefront pharmacist in Boston, his family had built and expanded an empire on buffered aspirin and analgesics. It allowed Jonathan to indulge in his great love of sailing.

He was tall, fit, tanned. His hair was mink-brown and perfectly styled to showcase his square-jawed, handsome face. He wore buff-colored chinos, a navy cotton shirt, and well-broken-in Top-Siders. His watch was a Rolex, his belt hand-tooled Italian leather.

He looked exactly like what he was: a privileged, wealthy man with a love of the outdoors.

"You've only been in business a few months."

"Officially," Phillip said with a flashing smile. His hair was a rich, deep bronze, styled to make the most of a face that the angels had gifted with an extra kiss of pure male beauty. He wore fashionably faded Levi's, a green cotton shirt, and olive-drab Supergas. His eyes were shrewd, his smile charming.

He looked exactly like what he'd made himself into: a sophisticated urbanite with an affection for fashion and the sea.

"We've built or worked on teams that built a number of boats over the years." Smoothly, he guided Jonathan toward the framed sketches hanging on the wall. Seth's artwork was displayed rustically, as Phillip felt suited the ambience of a traditional boatyard.

"My brother Ethan's skipjack. One of the handful that still goes under sail every winter to dredge for oysters in the Chesapeake. She's had over ten years in service."

"She's a beauty." Jonathan's face turned dreamy, as Phillip had suspected it would. However a man chose to pick wallets, he had to gauge his marks. "I'd like to see her."

"I'm sure we can arrange that."

He let Jonathan linger before nudging him gently along. "Now, you may recognize this one." He indicated the drawing of a sleek racing skiff. "The Circe. My brother Cameron was involved with both her design and her construction."

"And she beat my *Lorilee* to the finish line two years running." Jonathan grimaced good-naturedly. "Of course, Cam was leading the team."

"He knows his boats." Phillip heard the buzz of a drill from where Cameron worked belowdecks. He intended to bring Cam into this shortly.

"The sloop currently under construction is primarily Ethan's design, though Cam added some points. We're dedicated to serving the client's needs and wishes." He led Jonathan over to where Seth continued his hull sanding. Ethan stood on deck, attaching the rubrails. "He wanted speed, stability, and some luxuries."

Phillip knew the hull was a brilliant show of smooth lap construction—he'd put in plenty of sweaty hours on it himself. "She's built for show as well as function. Teak from stem to stern, at the client's direction," he added, knocking his knuckles cheerfully against the hull.

Phillip wiggled his brows at Ethan. Recognizing the signal, Ethan bit back a sigh. He knew he was going to hate this part, but Phillip had pointed out that it was good business to bring the potential client into the fold.

"The joints are wedged and married, without glue." Ethan rolled his shoulders, feeling as though he were giving an oral school report. He'd always hated them. "We figured if the old-time boat builders could make a joint last a century or so without glue, so could we. And I've seen too many glued joints fail."

"Hmmm," Jonathan said again, and Ethan took a breath.

"The hull's caulked in the traditional way—stranded cotton. Planking's tight, wood to wood on the inside. We rolled two strands of cotton in most of the seams. Hardly needed the mallet. Then we payed them with standard seam components."

Jonathan hummed again. He had only a vague idea what Ethan was talking about. He sailed boats—boats that he'd bought fresh and clean and finished. But he liked the sound of it.

"She appears to be a fine, tight boat. A pretty pleasure craft. I'll be looking for speed and efficiency as well as aesthetics."

"We'll see that you get it." Phillip smiled broadly, waving a finger at Ethan behind Jonathan's head. It was time to pull out the next round.

Ethan headed belowdecks, where Cam was fitting out the framing for an under-the-bunk cabinet. "Your turn up there," he muttered.

"Phil got him on the string?"

"Couldn't tell by me. I gave my little speech, and the guy just nodded and made noises. You ask me, he didn't know what the hell I was talking about."

"Of course he doesn't. Jonathan hires people to worry about maintaining his boats. He's never scraped a hull or replanked a deck in his life." Cam rose from his crouch, worked the stiffness out of his knees. "He's the kind of guy who drives a Maserati without knowing dick about engines. But he'd have been impressed with your salty waterman's drawl and rugged good looks."

As Ethan gave a snorting laugh, Cam elbowed past him. "I'll go give him my push."

He climbed topside and managed to look credibly surprised to see Jonathan onboard, studying the gunwales. "Hey, Kraft, how's it going?"

"Fast and far." With genuine pleasure, Jonathan shook Cam's hand. "I was surprised when you didn't show at the San Diego regatta this summer."

"Got myself married."

"So I hear. Congratulations. And now you're building boats instead of racing them."

"I wouldn't count me out of racing entirely. I'm toying with building myself a cat over the winter if business slacks off any."

"Keeping busy?"

"Word gets out," Cam said easily. "A boat by Quinn means quality. Smart people want the best—when they can afford it." He grinned, fast and slick. "Can you afford it?"

"I'm thinking of a cat myself. Your brother must have mentioned it."

"Yeah, he ran it by me. You want light, fast, and tight. Ethan and I have been modifying a design for what I had in mind for me."

"That's bullshit," Seth murmured, only loud enough for Phillip to hear.

"Sure." Phillip winked at him. "But it's Class A bullshit." He leaned a little closer to Seth as Cam and Jonathan launched into the lure of racing a catboat. "Cam knows that while the guy likes him fine, he's competitive. Never beat Cam in a head-to-head race. So . . ."

"So he'd pay buckets of money to have Cam build him a boat that not even Cam could beat."

"There you go." Proud, Phillip gave Seth a light punch on the shoulder. "You got a quick brain there. Keep using it, and you won't be spending all your time sanding hulls. Now, kid, watch the master."

He straightened, beamed up. "I'd be happy to show you the drawings, Jonathan. Why don't we go into my office? I'll dig them out for you."

"Wouldn't mind taking a look." Jonathan climbed down. "The problem is, I need this boat seaworthy by March first. I'll need time to test her, work out the kinks, break her in before the summer races."

"March first." Phillip pursed his lips, then he shook his head. "That might be a problem. Quality comes first here. It takes time to build a champion. I'll look over our schedule," he added, dropping an arm over Jonathan's shoulder as they walked. "We'll see what we can work out—but the contract's already in place, and the work sheets tell me May is the soonest we can deliver the top-quality product you expect and deserve."

"That's not going to give me much time to get the feel of her," Jonathan complained.

"Believe me, Jonathan, a boat by Quinn is going to feel fine. Just fine," he added, glancing back at his brothers with a quick and wolfish grin before he nudged Jonathan inside the office.

"He'll buy us till May," Cam decided, and Ethan nodded.

"Or he'll make it April and skin the poor bastard for a bonus."

"Either way." Cam clamped a hand on Ethan's shoulder. "We're going to have ourselves another contract by end of day."

Below, Seth snorted. "Shit, he'll wrap it up by lunchtime. The guy's toast."

Cam tucked his tongue in his cheek. "Two o'clock, soonest."

"Noon," Seth said, peering up at him.

"Two bucks?"

"Sure. I can use the money."

❧

"YOU KNOW," CAM said as he dug out his wallet, "before you came along to ruin my life, I'd just won a bundle in Monte Carlo."

Seth sneered cheerfully. "This ain't Monte Carlo."

"You're telling me." He passed the bills over, then winced when he saw his wife come into the building. "Cool it. Social worker heading in. She's not going to approve of minors gambling."

"Hey, I won," Seth pointed out, but he stuffed the bills in his pocket. "You bring any food?" he asked Anna.

"Oh, no, I didn't. Sorry." Distracted, she dragged a hand through her hair. There was a sick ball in the pit of her stomach that she did her best to ignore. She smiled, a curve of lips that didn't quite manage to reach her eyes. "Didn't you all pack lunch?"

"Yeah, but you usually bring something better."

"This time I've been pretty tied up putting food together for the picnic tomorrow." She ran a hand over his head, then left it lying on his shoulder. She needed the contact. "I just . . . thought I'd take a break and see how things were going around here."

"Phil just nailed this rich guy for a ton of money."

"Good, that's good," she said absently. "Then we should celebrate. Why don't I spring for ice cream? You think you can handle picking up some hot fudge sundaes at Crawford's?"

"Yeah." His face split into a grin. "I can handle it."

She dragged money out of her purse, hoping he didn't notice that her hands weren't quite steady. "No nuts on mine, remember?"

"Sure. I got it. I'm gone." He raced out, and she watched him, heartsick.

"What is it, Anna?" Cam put his hands on her shoulders, turned her to face him. "What happened?"

"Give me a minute. I broke records getting here, and I need some time to settle." She blew out a breath, drew one in, and felt marginally steadier. "Go get your brothers, Cam."

"Okay." But he lingered, rubbing his hands over her shoulders. It was rare for her to look so shaken. "Whatever it is, we'll fix it."

He walked to the cargo doors, where Ethan and Phil stood outside arguing over baseball. "Something's up," he said briefly. "Anna's here. She sent Seth off. She's upset."

She was standing by a workbench, with one of Seth's drawing books open, when they came in. It made her eyes sting to see her own face, carefully, skillfully sketched by the young boy's hand.

He'd been more than a case file, almost from the start. And now he was hers, as much as Ethan and Phillip were hers. Family. She couldn't stand to think that anything or anyone would hurt her family.

But she was steadier when she turned, scanned the quiet and concerned faces of the men who'd become essential to her life. "This came in today's mail." Her hand no longer trembled as she reached into her purse and pulled out the letter.

"It's addressed to 'The Quinns.' Just 'The Quinns,' " she repeated. "From Gloria DeLauter. I opened it. I thought it best, and well, my name's Quinn now, too."

She offered it to Cam. Saying nothing, he took out the single sheet of lined paper and passed the envelope to Phillip.

"She mailed it from Virginia Beach," Phillip murmured. "We lost her in North Carolina. She's sticking with the beaches, but coming north."

"What does she want?" Ethan stuffed hands that had curled into fists into his pockets. A low, simmering rage was already pumping through his blood.

"What you'd expect," Cam answered shortly. "Money. 'Dear Quinns,' " Cam read. " 'I heard how Ray died. It's too bad. You might not know that Ray and me had an agreement. I think you'll want to make good on it since you're keeping Seth. I guess he's pretty settled in there in that nice house. I miss him. You don't know what a sacrifice it was for me to give him up to Ray, but I wanted what was best for my only son.'"

"You ought to have your violin," Phillip muttered to Ethan.

" 'I knew Ray would be good to him,' " Cam continued. " 'He did right by the three of you, and Seth's got his blood.' "

He stopped reading for a moment. There it was, in black and white. "Truth or lie?" He looked up at his brothers.

"That's to deal with later." Ethan felt the ache begin around his heart and move in to squeeze. But he shook his head. "Read the rest."

"Okay. 'Ray knew how much it hurt me to part with the boy, so he helped me out. But now that he's gone, I'm starting to worry that it might not be the best place for Seth there with you. I'm willing to be convinced. If you're set on keeping him, you'll keep up Ray's promise of helping me out. I'm going to need some money, like a sign that you've got good intentions. Five thousand. You can send it to me, care of General Delivery here in Virginia Beach. I'll give you two weeks, figuring the mail's kind of unreliable. If I don't hear back, I'll know you don't really want the kid. I'll come get him. He must be missing me something awful. Be sure to tell him his mom loves him, and might be seeing him real soon.' "

"Bitch," was Phillip's first comment. "She's testing us out, trying her hand at a little more blackmail to see if we'll fall for it the way Dad did."

"You can't." Anna put a hand on Cam's arm, felt the quiver of rage. "You have to let the system work. You have to trust me to see that she doesn't do this. In court—"

"Anna." Cam shoved the letter into the hand Ethan had held out. "We're not going to put that boy through a court case. Not if there's another way."

"You don't mean to pay her. Cam—"

"I don't mean for her to have one fucking cent." He prowled away, struggling to fight off fury. "She thinks she's got us by the balls, but she's wrong. We're not one lone old man." He whirled back, eyes blazing. "Let's see her try to get through us to lay hands on Seth."

"She was pretty careful how she worded things," Ethan commented as he scanned the letter again. "Doesn't make it less of a threat, but she's not stupid."

"She's greedy," Phillip put in. "If she's already angling for more after what Dad paid her, she's testing the depth of the well."

"She sees you as her source now," Anna agreed. "And there's no predicting what she'll do if she knows that source isn't easily tapped." Pausing, she pressed her fingers to her temples, ordered herself to think. "If she comes back into the county and attempts to make contact with Seth, I can have her detained, legally barred—at least temporarily—from direct contact with him. You have guardianship. And Seth is old enough to speak for himself. The question is, will he?"

She lifted her hands, frustrated, let them fall. "He's told me very little about his life before he came here. I'll need specifics in order to block any custody attempt on her part."

"He doesn't want her. And she doesn't want him." Ethan resisted, barely, crumpling the letter into a ball and heaving it. "Unless he's worth the price of another fix. She let her johns try for him."

Anna shifted to face him, kept her eyes calm and direct on his. "Did Seth tell you that? Did he tell you there had been sexual abuse and she'd been a party to it?"

"He told me enough." Ethan's mouth went hard and grim. "And it's up to him if he wants to tell anybody else and see it put in some goddamn county report."

"Ethan." Anna laid a hand on his rigid arm. "I love him, too. I only want to help him."

"I know." He stepped back because the anger was too fierce and too likely to spew on everyone. "I'm sorry, but there are times the system makes it worse. Makes you feel like you're being swallowed up." He struggled to block out the echo of pain. "He's going to know he's got us, with or without any system, to stand with him."

"The lawyer needs to know she made contact." Phillip took the letter from Ethan, folded it, and tucked it back into the envelope. "And we have to decide how we're going to handle it. My first impulse is to go down to Virginia Beach, dig her out of her hole, and tell her in a way she'd understand just what's going to happen to her if she comes within fifty miles of Seth."

"Threatening her won't help . . ." Anna began.

"But it would feel damn good." Cam bared his teeth. "Let me do it."

"On the other hand," Phillip continued, "I think it might be very effective—and look very good if it ever comes to a legal battle—if our pal Gloria got an official letter from Seth's caseworker. Outlining the status, the options, and the conclusions reached. Contacting or attempting to contact a birth mother who may be rethinking giving up custody of her child—a child who's in your files—would come within the parameters of your job, wouldn't it, Anna?"

She mulled it over, knowing it was a fine line and expert balance would be required to walk it. "I can't threaten her. But . . . I may be able to make her stop and think. But the big question is, do we tell Seth?"

"He's afraid of her," Cam murmured. "Damn it, the kid's just starting to relax, to believe he's safe. Why do we have to tell him she's poking her finger back into his life?"

"Because he's got a right to know." Ethan spoke quietly. His temper had leveled off, and he was able to think clearly again. "He's got a right to know what he might have to fight. If you know what's after you, you've got a better chance. And because," he added, "the letter was addressed to the Quinns. He's one of us."

"I'd rather burn it," Phillip muttered. "But you're right."

"We'll all tell him," Cam agreed.

"I'd like to do the talking."

Both Cam and Phillip stared at Ethan. "You would?"

"He might take it easier from me." He looked over as Seth came through the door. "So let's find out."

"Mother Crawford put on extra hot fudge. Man, she just poured it on. There's about a million tourists up on the waterfront, and . . ."

His excited chatter trailed off. His eyes went from gleeful to wary. Inside his chest, his heart began to drum. He recognized trouble, bad trouble. It had its own smell. "What's the deal?"

Anna took the large bag from him and turned to set the plastic-topped dishes of ice cream out. "Why don't you sit down, Seth?"

"I don't need to sit down." It was easier to get a head start running if you were already on your feet.

"There was a letter came today." It was best, Ethan knew, if hard news was delivered fast and clean. "From your mother."

"She's here?" The fear was back, sharp as a scalpel. Seth took one quick step in retreat, going stiff as a board when Cam laid a hand on his shoulder.

"No, she's not here. But we are. You remember that."

Seth shuddered once, then planted his feet. "What the hell did she want? Why's she sending letters? I don't want to see it."

"Then you don't have to," Anna assured him. "Why don't you let Ethan explain, then we'll talk about what we're going to do."

"She knows Ray's dead," Ethan began. "I gotta figure she's known right along, but she's taken her time getting to it."

"He gave her money." Seth swallowed hard to gulp down the fear. Quinns weren't afraid, he told himself. They weren't afraid of anything. "She took off. She doesn't care that he's dead."

"I don't suppose she does, but she's hoping for more money. That's what the letter's about."

"She wants me to pay her?" Fresh and bright fear exploded in Seth's brain. "I don't have any money. What's she writing to me for money for?"

"She wasn't writing to you."

Seth took a ragged breath and concentrated on Ethan's face. The eyes were clear and patient, the mouth firm and serious. Ethan knew, was all he could think. Ethan knew what it was like. He knew about the rooms, the smells, the fat hands in the dark.

"She wants you to pay her." Part of him wanted to beg them to do it. To pay her whatever she wanted. He would swear in blood that he would do anything they asked of him for the rest of his life to honor the debt.

But he couldn't. Not with Ethan watching him, and waiting. And knowing.

"If you do, she'll just come back for more. She'll keep coming back." Seth rubbed the back of a sweaty hand over his mouth. "As long as she knows where I am she'll keep coming back. I have to go someplace else, someplace where she can't find me."

"You're not going anywhere." Ethan crouched so they were closer to eye level. "And she's not going to get any more money. She's not going to win."

Slowly, mechanically, Seth shook his head back and forth. "You don't know her."

"I know pieces of her. She's smart enough to know we're set on keeping you with us. That we love you enough to pay." He saw the flash of emotion in Seth's eyes before the boy lowered them. "And we would pay if that would end it, if that would ease things. But it won't end or ease it. It's like you said. She'd just come back."

"What are you going to do?"

"It's what we're going to do now. All of us," he said and waited for Seth's gaze to settle on his face again. "We'll go on as we've been going on, mostly. Phil will talk to the lawyer so we got that end covered."

"You tell him I'm not going back with her," Seth said furiously, shooting a desperate look at Phillip. "No matter what, I'm not going back."

"I'll tell him."

"Anna's going to write her a letter," Ethan continued.

"What kind of letter?"

"A smart one," Ethan said with the hint of a smile. "With all those fifty-dollar words and that official-sounding stuff. She'll be doing it as your caseworker, to let Gloria know we've got the system and the law behind us. It might give her pause to think."

"She hates social workers," Seth put in.

"Good." For the first time in more than an hour, Anna smiled and meant it. "People who hate something are usually afraid of it, too."

"One thing that would help, Seth, if you can do it—"

He turned back to Ethan. "What do I have to do?"

"If you could talk to Anna, tell her how things were before—as close to exact as you can manage."

"I don't want to talk about it. It's over. I'm not going back."

"I know." Gently, Ethan put his hands on Seth's trembling shoulders. "And I know talking about it can be almost like being there again. It took me a long time to be able to tell my mother—to tell Stella. To say it all out loud, even though she already knew most of it. It started to get better after that. And it helped her and Ray get the legal crap handled."

Seth thought of *High Noon*, of heroes. Of Ethan. "It's the right thing to do?"

"Yeah, it's the right thing."

"Will you come with me?"

"Sure." Ethan rose, held out a hand. "We'll go home and talk it through."

CHAPTER
14

"READY? Mama? Time to go?"

"Almost, Aubrey." Grace put the finishing touches on her potato salad, sprinkling paprika on to give it zest and color.

Aubrey had been asking her the same question since seven-thirty that morning. Grace decided the only reason she hadn't run out of patience with her daughter was because she felt just as anxious and eager as a two-year-old herself.

"*Maaamaaa.*"

At the deep frustration in Aubrey's voice, Grace had to swallow a chuckle. "Let me see." Grace tucked the clear wrap tidily around the bowl before she turned and studied her little girl. "You look pretty."

"I have a bow." In a purely female gesture, Aubrey lifted a hand and patted the ribbon Grace had threaded through her curls.

"A pink bow."

"Pink." With a smile, Aubrey beamed up at her mother. "Pretty Mama."

"Thanks, baby." She hoped Ethan thought so. How would he look at her? she wondered. How should they behave? There would be so many people there, and no one—well, besides the Quinns—no one knew they were in love.

In love, she thought with a long, dreamy sigh. It was such a marvelous place to be. She blinked when little arms wrapped around her legs and squeezed.

"Mama! Ready?"

Laughing, Grace hauled her up for a big hug and kiss. "All right. Let's go."

NO GENERAL IN the hours before a decisive battle ever ordered his troops into action with more authority and determination than Anna Spinelli Quinn.

"Seth, you set those folding chairs up under the shade trees over there. Isn't Phillip back with the extra ice yet? He's been gone twenty minutes. Cam! You and Ethan are putting those picnic tables too close together."

"Minute ago," Cam said under his breath, "they were too far apart." But he walked backward, hauling the table another foot.

"That's good. That's fine." Armed with bright red, white, and blue striped cloths, Anna hurried across the lawn. "Now you can move the umbrella tables, nearer the water, I think."

Cam narrowed his eyes. "You said you wanted them over by the trees."

"I changed my mind." She scanned the yard as she spread the tablecloths.

Cam opened his mouth to protest, but caught Ethan's warning shake of the head in time. His brother was right, he decided. Arguing wasn't going to change a thing.

Anna had been on a tear all morning, and when he said as much to Ethan as they moved out of earshot, it was with the irritation of the baffled.

"We're talking about a practical-minded, organized woman here," Cam added. "I don't know what's gotten into her. It's just a damn picnic."

"I guess women get that way over things like this" was Ethan's opinion. He remembered the way Grace had refused to let him take a shower in his own bathroom just because Cam and Anna were coming home. Who knew what went on in a female mind?

"She wasn't this bad over the wedding reception."

"I expect she had her mind on other things then."

"Yeah." Cam grunted as he picked up one of the round umbrella tables—again—and began to cart it toward the sun-dazzled water. "Phil's the smart one. He got the hell out of the house."

"He's always had a knack for it," Ethan agreed.

He didn't mind moving tables, or setting up chairs, or any of the dozens of chores—small and large—that Anna came up with. It helped keep his mind off weightier matters.

If he let himself think too much, he started to get a picture of Gloria DeLauter in his head. Because he'd never seen her, the image his brain conjured up was a tall, fleshy woman with tangled straw-colored hair, hard eyes smeared with sooty makeup, a mouth lax from too many trips to the bottle, too many matings with the needle.

The eyes were blue, like his own. The mouth, despite its slick coat of lipstick, shaped like his own. And he knew it wasn't Seth's mother's face he was seeing. It was his own mother's.

The picture wasn't dim and fuzzy as it had become over time. It was sharp and clear as yesterday.

It still had the power to ice his blood, to churn a sick animal fear in his stomach that was kin to shame.

It still made him want to strike out with bruised and bloodied fists.

He turned slowly as he heard the squeal of joy. And saw Aubrey racing over the lawn, her eyes bright as sunbeams. And saw Grace, standing by the porch steps, her smile warm and just a little shy.

You've got no right, the nasty little voice in his head hissed. *No right to touch something so fine and bright.*

But, oh, he had a need, one that swamped him like a storm surge and left him floundering. When Aubrey launched herself at him, his arms reached down, swung her up and around as she shrieked in delight.

He wanted her to be his. With a bone-deep longing, he wanted this perfect, this innocent, this laughing child to belong to him.

Grace's knees wobbled as she walked to them. The picture they made flashed into her mind, into her heart, where she knew it would imprint itself. The lanky man with big hands and a serious smile and the golden-bright child with a pink bow in her hair.

The sun poured over them as full and rich as the love that poured from her heart.

"She's been ready to come over since she opened her eyes this morning," Grace began. "I thought we could come a little early and I'd give Anna a hand." He was watching her so intently, so quietly, her nerves did a rapid dance under her skin. "There's not much left to do, but—"

She broke off because his arm had snaked out, wrapped around her fast and hard to pull her against him. She had time to draw in one startled breath before his mouth came down on hers. Rough and needy, it shot bolts of heat into her blood, sent her startled brain into a dizzying spin. Dimly she heard Aubrey's happy squeal.

"Kiss, Mama!"

Oh, yes, Grace thought, sprinting to catch up to this frantic pace he'd set. Please. Kiss me, kiss me, kiss me.

She thought she heard some sound from him, a sigh perhaps, that came from someplace too deep inside to make a sound. His lips softened. The hand that had clutched the back of her shirt like a man gripping his own life opened, stroked. This gentler, sweeter emotion that shimmered from him was no calmer than that first whip of greed; it only gilded the edges of the yearning he'd stirred.

She could smell him, heat and man. She could smell her daughter, powder and child. Her arms circled them both, instinctively making them a unit, holding there when the kiss ended and she could press her face into his shoulder.

He'd never kissed her in front of anyone. She knew Cam had only been a few feet away when Ethan had taken hold of her. And Seth would have seen . . . and Anna.

What did it mean?

"Kiss me!" Aubrey demanded, patting her hand against Ethan's cheek and puckering up.

He obliged her, then nuzzled at her neck where it would tickle and make her laugh. Then he turned his head and brushed his lips over Grace's hair. "I didn't mean to grab you that way."

"I was hoping you did," she murmured. "It made me feel you've been thinking about me. Wanting me."

"I've been thinking about you, Grace. I've been wanting you."

Because Aubrey was wiggling, he set her down and let her run off toward Seth and the dogs. "I meant I didn't mean to be rough with you."

"You weren't. I'm not fragile, Ethan."

"Yes, you are." When he saw Aubrey fall on Foolish so they could wrestle in the grass, he looked back at Grace, into her eyes. "Delicate," he said softly, "like the white china with pink roses we only use on Thanksgiving."

It made her heart flutter pleasantly that he would think so, even if she knew better. "Ethan—"

"I was always afraid I'd pick it up wrong, break it in half from being clumsy. I never really got used to it."

He skimmed his thumb lightly across her cheekbone, where the skin was warm and soft and silky. Then he dropped his hand to his side. "We'd better pitch in before Anna drives Cam over the edge."

GRACE'S STOMACH CONTINUED to flutter with nervous delight even when she went about the chore of carting food from the kitchen out to the picnic table. She would catch herself stopping, a bowl or platter in hand, to watch Ethan drive the horseshoe stakes into the ground.

Look how his muscles ripple under his shirt. He's so strong. Look at the way he shows Seth how to hold the hammer. He's so patient. He's wearing the jeans I washed just the other day. The cuffs have gone white and they're starting to fray. There was sixty-three cents in the right front pocket.

See how Aubrey climbs up on his back. She knows she'll be welcome. Yes, he reaches back, gives her a little hitch to secure her there, then goes back to work. He doesn't mind when she steals his cap and tries to put it on her own head. His hair's gotten long, and the ends glint in the sun when he shakes it back out of his eyes.

I hope he keeps forgetting to go to the barber for a while yet.

I wish I could touch it, right now. Make those thick, sun-bleached ends curl around my finger.

"It's a nice picture," Anna murmured from behind her and made Grace jolt. With a quiet laugh, Anna set down the enormous bowl of pasta salad. "I do the same thing with Cam sometimes. Just stand and watch him. The Quinns are very watchable men."

"I think I'm just going to take a quick glance, then I can't stop looking." She grinned when Ethan rose, Aubrey still clinging to his back, and turned slow circles as if trying to find her.

"He has a wonderful, natural way with children," Anna commented. "He'll make a wonderful father."

Grace felt heat rise up into her cheeks. She'd been thinking the same thing. It was hard to believe that only a few weeks before she'd told her own mother she would never marry again. And now she was thinking, and wondering. And waiting.

It had been easy to put all thoughts of marriage aside when she hadn't believed she could ever have a life with Ethan. She made a poor job of marriage before because her heart had belonged to someone other than her husband. That was her fault, and she accepted the responsibility for the failure.

But she could make marriage shine with Ethan, couldn't she? They could build a home and a family and a future based on love and trust and honesty.

He wouldn't move quickly, she mused. It wasn't his way. But he loved her. She understood Ethan well enough to know that marriage would be the next step.

She was already poised to take it.

⚜

THE SMELL OF burgers smoking on the grill, the yeasty tang of beer pumped from a cold keg. The sounds of children laughing and adult voices lifted in bright conversation or lowered in juicy gossip. The low roar of a boat zipping over the water, with the thrilled shouts of its teenage occupants, the metallic clang of a horseshoe striking home.

There were scents and sounds and sights. There was the snappy red, white, and blue of the cloths covering the tables that were crowded with bowls and plates and platters and casseroles.

Mrs. Cutter's cherry pie. The Wilsons' shrimp salad. What was left of the bushel of corn the Crawfords had brought along. Jell-O molds and fruit salad, fried chicken and early vine tomatoes. People were spread out and gathered. On chairs, on the lawn, down at the dock, and on the porch.

Several men stood with hands on hips, watching the horseshoe match, their faces sober in the way men had when they kibitzed a sporting event. Babies napped in carriers or willing arms while others wailed for attention. The young splashed and swam in the cool water, and the old fanned themselves in the shade.

The sky was clear, the heat immense.

Grace watched Foolish nosing along the ground in search of dropped food. He'd found plenty, and she imagined he'd be sick as a—well, a dog—before the day was over.

She hoped it was never over.

She waded into the water, gripping Aubrey firmly despite the colorful floats wrapped around her arms. She dipped her daughter down, laughing when Aubrey's little legs began to kick with delight.

"In, in, in!" Aubrey demanded.

"Honey, I didn't bring my bathing suit." But she eased out a little more, until the water lapped at her knees, so she could let Aubrey splash.

"Grace! Grace! Watch this!"

Obliging, Grace squinted against the sun and watched Seth take a running leap off the dock, tucking knees, wrapping arms, and hitting the water like a bomb so that it shot it up in a glittering fountain. And all over her.

"Cannonball," he announced proudly when he surfaced. Then he grinned. "Gee, you got all wet."

"Seth, take me." Straining, Aubrey held out her arms. "Take me."

"Can't, Aub. Got bombs to blow." When he swam off to join the other boys, Aubrey began to sniffle.

"He'll come back and play later," Grace assured her.

"Now!"

"Soon." To ward off what Grace knew could turn into a fine temper, she tossed Aubrey up, catching her as she hit the water. She let her paddle and splash, then let her go, biting her lip as Aubrey reveled in the freedom.

"Swimming, Mama."

"I see that, baby. You're a good swimmer. But you stay close."

As Grace expected, the sun and water and excitement combined to tire the child out. When Aubrey blinked and widened her eyes as she did when she fought sleep, Grace drew her in. "Let's get a drink, Aubrey."

"Swimming."

"We'll swim some more. I'm thirsty." Grace lifted her, braced for the minor battle that was bound to come.

"What you got there, Grace, a mermaid?"

Mother and daughter looked up onto the wet slope and saw Ethan.

"She sure is pretty," he said, smiling into Aubrey's mutinous face. "Can I have her?"

"I don't know. Maybe." She leaned close to Aubrey's ear. "He thinks you're a mermaid."

Aubrey's lip trembled, but she'd nearly forgotten why she'd wanted to cry. "Like Ariel?"

"Yes, like Ariel in the movie." She started to climb out, then Ethan's hand was there, clasping hers firmly. And when she gained her balance, he plucked Aubrey out of her arms.

"Swimming," she told him, rather pitifully, then buried her face in the curve of his throat.

"I saw you swimming." She was cool and wet and curled against him. He reached out, took Grace's hand again and pulled her to level ground. This time, his fingers twined with hers and held. "Looks like I've got two mermaids now."

"She's tired," Grace said quietly. "It makes her cross sometimes. She's wet," she added and started to take Aubrey from him.

"She's fine." He released her hand only because he wanted to skim his over Grace's damp and shining hair. "You're wet, too." Then he slipped an arm around her shoulders. "Let's walk in the sun for a while."

"All right."

"Maybe around the front of the house," he suggested, smiling a little as Aubrey's breath fluttered against his skin, evening out into sleep. "Where there aren't so many people."

With surprise and a low surge of pleasure, Carol Monroe watched Ethan take her daughter and granddaughter walking. With a woman's eyes she saw more than a neighbor and friend strolling with a neighbor and friend. Impulsively, she tugged on her husband's arm, distracting him from his absorption in the current round of horseshoes.

"Hold on, Carol. Junior and I are playing the winners of this round."

"Look, Pete. Look at that. Grace is with Ethan."

Vaguely annoyed, he flicked a glance around, shrugged. "So what?"

"*With* him, Pete, you knothead." It was said with exasperation and affection. "Like a boyfriend."

"Boyfriend?" He snorted, started to dismiss it—Christ knew, Carol had the screwiest ideas from time to time. Like when she was all het up to take a cruise down to the Bahamas. As if he couldn't take a sail any damn time of the day or night right in his own backyard. But then he caught—something—in the way Ethan leaned his body toward Grace, the way she tilted her head up.

It made Pete shift his feet, scowl, look away. "Boyfriend," he muttered, and didn't know how the hell he was supposed to feel about that. He didn't poke his nose in his daughter's life, he reminded himself. She'd already gone her own way.

He scowled hard into the sun because he remembered what it had been like to have his little girl rest her head on his shoulder the way Aubrey was doing right then and there with Ethan Quinn.

When they were little like that, he thought, they trusted you and looked up to you and believed what you told them even if you told them thunder was just angels clapping.

When they got older they started to tug away. And to want things that didn't make a damn bit of sense. Like money to live in New York City, and your blessing to marry some sneaky bastard who wasn't half good enough for them.

They stopped thinking you were the man with the answers, and they broke your damn heart. So you had to put it back together as best you could, with a lock on it so it couldn't happen again.

"Ethan's just what Grace needs," Carol was saying in a low voice—just in case any of the fuddy-duddies, who thought tossing a horseshoe at an iron peg was an exciting way to spend the day, had sharp ears. "That's a steady man, and he's got gentleness in him. He's a man she could lean on."

"Won't."

"What?"

"She won't lean on nobody. She's too proud for her own good, and always has been."

Carol merely sighed. If it was true, Grace had gotten every stubborn ounce of that pride from her father. "You've never even tried to meet her halfway."

"Don't you start on me, Carol. I've got nothing to say." He shifted away from her, ignoring the guilt because he knew the gesture would hurt her. "I want a beer," he muttered and stalked away.

Phillip Quinn and some of the others were gathered around the keg. Pete noted with an amused snort that Phillip was flirting with the Barrow girl, Celia. He couldn't blame the boy—she was built like a Playboy pinup and not afraid to show it off. It wasn't something a man stopped noticing even if he was old enough to be her father.

"Want me to pull you one, Mr. Monroe?"

" 'Preciate it." Pete nodded toward the celebrants in the backyard. "Got you a crowd here, today, Phil. Fine spread, too. I remember how your folks'd throw a picnic most every summer. It's nice you're keeping up the tradition."

"Anna thought of it," Phillip told him, handing Pete a foaming beer in a tall plastic cup.

"Women do, more'n men, I suppose. If I don't get the chance, you tell her I appreciate the invite. I gotta get back to the waterfront in an hour or so, set up for the display."

"You always put on a good one. Best fireworks on the Shore."

"Tradition," Pete said again. It was a word that mattered.

⁂

CAROL MONROE HADN'T been the only one to notice the way Ethan and Grace had walked off together. Speculation and sly grins started to spread over the potato salad and steamed crabs.

Mother Crawford wagged her fork at her good friend Lucy Wilson. "You ask me, Grace is going to have to put her foot down if she wants Ethan Quinn to come up to snuff before that baby's old enough for college. Never seen a man moved so slow."

"He's thoughtful," Lucy said loyally.

"Not saying different. Just saying slow. Seen them moony-eyed over each other since before that boy got his own workboat. Has to be nearly ten years passed. Stella and I—bless her soul—had a conversation over it a time or two."

Lucy sighed over her fruit salad, and not just because she was watching her calories. "Stella knew her boys inside and out."

"That she did. I said to her one day, 'Stella, your Ethan's got cow's eyes for the young Monroe girl.' And she laughed, said how he had himself a hard case of puppy love, but that sometimes it was the best way to start the real thing. Never could figure why Ethan didn't step forward a bit before Grace got herself tangled up with that Jack Casey. Never did like him much."

"He wasn't a bad sort, just weak. Look there, Mother," Lucy said, lowering her voice like a conspirator. She nodded toward Ethan and Grace, as they walked back around the side of the house, hands linked, the baby sleeping on his shoulder.

"Nothing weak about that one." Mother wiggled her brows and leered at her friend. "And slow can be a fine thing in bed, can't it, Lucy?"

Lucy hooted. "It can, Mother. That it can."

Blissfully unaware of the speculation buzzing about a quiet walk around the house on a hot summer afternoon, Grace stopped to pour some iced tea. Before she'd half filled the first glass, her mother was bustling over, beaming smiles.

"Oh, let me hold that precious girl. Nothing so soothing as sitting with a sleeping baby." She'd slipped Aubrey out of Ethan's arms while she talked, her voice low and quick. "It'll give me a fine excuse to sit in the shade awhile and be quiet. I swear, Nancy Claremont's been talking both my ears off. You young people should be off enjoying yourself."

"I was going to lay her down," Grace began, but her mother just waved it away.

"No need, no need. I don't get nearly enough chances to hold her when she's still. Go on and finish your walk. Ought to get out of the sun, though. It's brutal."

"It's a good idea," Ethan mused as Carol hurried off, cooing to the sleeping Aubrey. "A little shade and a little quiet wouldn't hurt."

"Well . . . all right, but I've only got another hour or so before I have to leave."

He'd been tugging her gently toward the trees, thinking that he could find a sheltered spot, a private spot, and kiss her again. He stopped at the verge and frowned at her. "Leave for what?"

"For work. I'm on at the pub tonight."

"It's your night off."

"It was—that is, it usually is, but I'm putting on some more hours."

"You work too many hours already."

She smiled, distracted—then relieved when the shade she walked into cut the intense heat in half. "It's just a few more. Shiney was good about helping me out so I can make up what I had to pay for the car. Oh, this is nice." She closed her eyes, breathed deep of the moist, cool air. "Anna said you and your brothers were going to play later. I'll be sorry to miss that."

"Grace, I told you if money was a problem, I'd help you out."

She opened her eyes again. "I don't need you to help me out, Ethan. I know how to work."

"Yeah, you know how. It's damn near all you do." He paced away from her, paced back as if trying to shake off what was biting at his gut. "I hate you working down there."

Her spine stiffened—she could feel it go hard and straight, vertebra by vertebra. "I don't want to fight with you about that again. It's a good job, honest work."

"I'm not fighting with you, I'm saying it." He stalked toward her, the swirling temper in his eyes surprising enough that she backed up against a tree.

"I've heard you say it before," she said evenly. "And it doesn't change the facts. I work there, and I'm going to go on working there."

"You need looking after." It scraped him raw that he couldn't be the one to do it.

"I don't."

Hell she didn't. There were already tired smudges under those changeable green eyes, and now she was telling him she'd be carting trays until two in the morning. "Did you pay Dave for the car yet?"

"Half." It was humiliating. "He was good enough to give me until next month to pay him the rest."

"You won't pay him." That, at least, was something he could do. Would do, by Christ. "I will."

She forgot about humiliation. Her chin came up, sharp and fast as a bullet. "You will not."

Another time he would have persuaded, cajoled. Or simply done the deed on the quiet. But something was bubbling up in him— something that had been there, simmering, since he'd turned that morning and seen her. It wouldn't let him think, only feel and act. With his eyes on hers he slipped a hand up, over her throat.

"Be quiet."

"I'm not a child, Ethan. You can't—"

"I'm not thinking about you like a child." Her eyes were bright and sharp. They were heating the something that was inside him to a boil. "I stopped being able to do that, and I can't go back to it. Do what I want this time."

She didn't know when her breath had started to back up or her skin to shiver. Dimly she felt the rough bark of the tree bite into her hands as she pressed them against it. She didn't think he was talking about her accepting a few hundred dollars for a car any longer.

"Ethan—"

His other hand was on her breast. He hadn't meant to put it there, but it covered her and his fingers began to flex and knead. Her shirt was still damp, just a little damp. He could feel her skin go hot under it. "Do what I want this time," he repeated.

Her eyes were huge. He was falling into them, drowning in them. Her heart was pounding against his hand, as if he held it beating in his palm. His mouth crushed down on hers with a violent greed that he was for once helpless to stem. He heard her shocked cry muffled against his assaulting mouth. And it only thrilled him darkly.

The heat swarmed from him, stunning her. His teeth nipped roughly into her lip, making her gasp, opening herself to the swift and skillful invasion of his tongue.

Sensations flew too quickly to separate one from the other, but all were dark and keen and compelling. His hands were everywhere, tugging up her shirt, claiming her breasts, scraping those deliciously rough palms over her. She felt him quiver, gripped his shoulders to balance them both.

Then he was yanking at her shorts.

No! Part of her mind drew back in shock, all but screamed it. He couldn't mean to take her, here, like this, only yards away from where people sat and children played. But another part of her simply moaned in shocked excitement and whispered yes.

Here. Now. Like this. Exactly like this.

When he drove into her, her scream would have carried some of both, but it was swallowed by his mouth, lost in his ragged breaths.

He thrust hard, fast, deep, his body surging into hers, his hands biting into her tight, round bottom as he plunged. His mind was wiped clean of everything but this one desperate need. When she came, exploding over him, around him, in him, his thrill was dark and primal and coated his skin with sweat.

His own climax had claws, hot-tipped, razor-sharp, that ripped through him brutally, so that his vision went red.

Even when it cleared he continued to shudder, to pant. Gradually he became aware of what was. He heard the wild drumming of a woodpecker deeper in the woods, the tinkle of laughter from beyond the trees. And Grace's sobbing breaths.

He felt the breeze cooling his skin. And her trembles.

"Oh, God. Goddamn it." His curse was quiet, vicious.

"Ethan?" She hadn't known, would never have believed anyone could have such a need inside them. For her. "Ethan," she said again and would have lifted her weak arms around him if he hadn't stepped back.

"I'm sorry. I—" There weren't words. Nothing he could say would be right, would be enough. He bent, slipped her shorts back up, fastened them. With the same deliberate care, he straightened her shirt. "I can't offer you an excuse for that. There isn't any."

"I don't want an excuse. I don't ever need one for what we do together, Ethan."

He stared at the ground while a sick pounding began in his head. "I didn't give you a choice." He knew what it was not to have a choice.

"I've already made my choice. I love you."

He looked at her then, everything that lived inside him swirling into his eyes. Her mouth was swollen where he'd ravished it. Her eyes were enormous. Her body would carry bruises from his hands. "You deserve better."

"I like to think I deserve you. You made me feel . . . desired. That's not even the word." She pressed a hand to her still speeding heart. "Craved," she realized. "Craved. And now I'm sorry . . ." Her gaze flicked away from his. "I'm sorry for any woman who's never known what it is to be craved."

"I scared you."

"For a minute." Mortified, she blew out a breath. "Damn it, Ethan, do I have to tell you that I liked it? I felt helpless and overpowered and it was so exciting. You lost control, and you have this incredibly unshakable control most of the time. I liked knowing that something I did, or something I am, snapped it."

He pulled his hand through his hair. "You confuse me, Grace."

"I don't mean to. But I don't think that's such a bad thing, either."

He let out a sigh, then stepped forward just enough that he could smooth her tousled hair into place. "Maybe the trouble is we've been thinking we know each other so well. But we don't have all the pieces." He picked up her hand, studied it with that thoughtful frown she loved. Then he kissed her fingers in a way that made her lashes flutter.

"I don't ever want to hurt you. In any way." But he had, and he would.

He kept his hand in hers as he walked her back toward the sunlight. He would have to tell her about those pieces of himself soon. So she would understand why he couldn't give her more.

S O, I don't know if I'm going to go out with him anymore because he's getting way too possessive, you know? I don't want to hurt his feelings, but you gotta live, right?"

Julie Cutter crunched into the shiny green apple she'd plucked out of the fruit bowl in Grace's kitchen. She felt every bit as much at home there as she did next door. Comfortable, she hitched herself up to sit on the counter while Grace folded laundry on the table.

"Plus," Julie went on, gesturing with her apple, "I met this incredibly cute guy. He works at the computer store at the mall? He wears these little metal-frame glasses and has the sweetest smile." She grinned, lighting up her pretty heart-shaped face. "I asked him for his phone number, and he blushed."

"You asked him for his phone number?" Grace was listening with only half an ear. She loved it when Julie came over just to visit. She was always so full of fun and talk and energy. But today it was hard to concentrate. Her mind was so full of what had happened between her and Ethan in those shady woods. What had leapt out of him to devour her—and why had it left him so distant afterward?

"Sure." Julie cocked her head, her brown eyes full of humor. "Didn't you ever ask a guy out? Come on, Grace, we're at the dawn of the next millennium here. Most of them really like it when the woman takes the initiative. Anyway . . ." She shook back her long fall of straight-as-a-pin brown hair. "Jeff did—the sexy computer nerd? He got all flustered at first, but then he gave it to me, and when I called him I could tell he was happy about it. So we're going out Saturday, but I have to break up with Don first."

"Poor Don," Grace murmured, and glanced over absently as Aubrey knocked over the block tower she'd been building, then applauded its destruction.

"Oh, he'll get over it." Julie shrugged. "It's not like he's in love with me or anything. He's just used to having a chick."

Grace had to smile. A few months earlier, Julie had been wild about Don, rushing over to tell Grace every detail of their dates. Or, Grace suspected, at least an edited version of their dates. "You told me Don was the one."

"He was." Julie laughed. "For a while. I'm not ready for the *only* one yet."

Grace went to the refrigerator to pour the three of them a drink. At Julie's age—nineteen—she'd been pregnant, married, and worried about paying bills. She was only three years older than Julie, but it might as well have been three hundred. "You're right to look around, to be sure." She handed Julie a glass, held her gaze for a moment. "To be careful."

"I'm careful, Grace," Julie assured her, touched. "I'd like to be married one day. Especially if it means having a baby as beautiful as Aubrey. But I want to finish college, then see some of the world. Do . . . things," she added, gesturing widely. "I don't want to find myself tied down, changing diapers and working at some dead-end job because I let some guy talk me into . . ."

She trailed off, suddenly and sincerely appalled at herself. Eyes huge and apologetic, she slid off the counter. "God, I'm sorry. I can be so thick sometimes. I didn't mean that you—"

"It's all right." She gave Julie's arm a quick squeeze. "That's exactly what I did, exactly what I let happen to me. I'm glad you're smarter."

"I'm a moron," Julie murmured, very close to tears. "I'm an insensitive clod. I'm hateful."

"No, you're not." Grace gave a light laugh and picked up a pair of Aubrey's rompers from the basket. "You didn't hurt my feelings. I'd hate to think we weren't friends enough for you to be able to say what you think."

"You're one of my best friends. And I've got a big mouth."

"Well, you do." Grace chuckled at Julie's wince. "But I like it."

"I love you and Aubrey, Grace."

"I know you do. Now stop worrying about it, and tell me where you're going with Jeff the cute computer guy?"

"Safe date. Movies and pizza." Julie let out a soft sigh of relief. She'd have . . . shaved her head and dyed it purple, she decided, before she'd do anything to hurt Grace. Hoping to make up, just a little, for her insensitivity, she beamed a smile.

"You know, I'd be happy to keep Aubrey on your next night off if you and Ethan want to go out."

Grace had finished folding the rompers and started on socks. She stopped, staring, with a tiny white sock trimmed in yellow in each hand. "What?"

"You know—catch a movie, go to a restaurant, whatever." She wiggled her brows on the "whatever," then fought to bite back a grin at Grace's expression. "You're not going to stand there and tell me you're not seeing Ethan Quinn."

"Well, he's . . . I'm . . ." She looked helplessly down at Aubrey.

"If it was supposed to be a secret, he should be parking his truck somewhere other than your driveway on the nights he sleeps over."

"Oh, God."

"What's the problem? It's not like you're having this illicit affair— like Mr. Wiggins has been having with Mrs. Lowen on Monday afternoons at the motel on Route 13." At Grace's strangled sound, Julie just shrugged. "My friend Robin's working there and taking night classes at the college, and she says how he checks in every Thursday morning at ten-thirty while she waits in her car. Anyway—"

"What must your mother think?" Grace whispered.

"Mom? About Mr. Wiggins? Well—"

"No, no." Grace didn't want to think about the portly Mr. Wiggins's weekly motel romp. "About . . ."

"Oh, you and Ethan. I think she said something about 'high time.' Mom's not an idiot. He's such a *hunk*," Julie said with feeling. "I mean, the way he fills out a T-shirt is awesome. And that smile. It takes, like, ten minutes for it to finish moving over his face, and by then, man, you are *drooling*. Robin and I went down to the waterfront every day for a month last summer just to watch him offload his catch."

"You did?" Grace said weakly.

"We both built a real case on him." She reached into the white stoneware cookie jar and found two oatmeal raisins. "I flirted with him, big time, whenever I got the chance."

"You . . . flirted with Ethan."

"Mmm." She nodded, swallowing cookie. "Really put some effort into it, too. Mostly I think it embarrassed him, but I got a couple of great smiles out of him." She smiled sunnily when Grace kept staring. "Oh, I'm way over it now, so don't worry."

"Good." Grace picked up the drink she'd neglected and drank deeply. "That's good."

"Still, he's got a terrific butt."

"Oh, Julie." Grace bit her lip to keep from giggling and sent a meaningful look toward her daughter.

"She's not listening. So, anyway, how'd I get started on this? Oh, yeah, I'll keep Aubrey for you if you want to go out."

"I, well, thanks." She was trying to decide if she wanted to get well off the subject of Ethan Quinn, or linger on it, when she heard a knock and saw him standing at her front door.

"Like magic," Julie murmured, and romance bloomed in her heart. "You know, why don't I take Aubrey over to see Mom for a while? I'll just keep her and feed her dinner."

"But I don't have to leave for work for nearly an hour yet."

Julie rolled her eyes. "So make good use of the time, pal." Then she scooped Aubrey up. "Want to come to my house, Aubrey? See my kitty cat?"

"Oooh, kitty. Bye, Mama."

"Oh, but—" They were already sailing out her back door, with Aubrey calling for the kitty and waving madly. She looked at Ethan again, staring at his face through the screen, then lifted her hands.

He decided to take it as an invitation and stepped inside. "Was that Julie who ran off with Aubrey?"

"Yes. She's going to let Aubrey play with her kitten and have dinner over there."

"It's nice you have someone like Julie to look after her."

"I'd be lost without Julie." Puzzled, Grace angled her head. He was standing awkwardly, a hand tucked behind his back. "Is something wrong? Did you hurt your hand?"

"No." What an idiot he was, Ethan thought, offering her the flowers he had held behind him. "I thought you might like some." He wanted, desperately, to find ways to make up to her for the way he'd treated her in the woods.

"You brought me flowers."

"I stole some here and there. You may not want to mention it to Anna. I got the tiger lilies off the side of the road. They're blooming thick this year."

He'd picked her flowers. Not store-bought flowers but ones he'd stopped and selected and plucked with his own hands. On a long, trembling sigh, she buried her face in them. "They're beautiful."

"They made me think of you. Almost everything does." And when she lifted her head, when he saw that her eyes were stunned and soft, he wished he had more words, better ones, smoother ones. "I know you only have the one night off now. I'd like to take you to dinner if you don't have any plans."

"To dinner?"

"There's a place Anna and Cam like up in Princess Anne. Suit-and-tie place, but they claim the food's worth it. Would you like to?"

She realized she was nodding her head like a fool and made herself stop. "I'd like that."

"I'll come by for you. About six-thirty?"

There went her head, bobbing again like a spring robin drunk on worms. "Fine. That'd be fine."

"I can't stay now because they're expecting me at the boatyard."

"That's all right." She wondered if her eyes were as huge as they felt. She could have devoured him with them. "Thanks for the flowers. They're lovely."

"You're welcome." And with his eyes open, he leaned over, laid his lips on hers very gently, very softly. He watched her lashes flutter, watched the green of her irises go misty under those tiny flecks of gold. "I'll see you tomorrow night, then."

Her muscles had turned to putty. "Tomorrow," she managed and breathed out a long, long sigh as he walked away and out her front door.

He'd brought her flowers. She clasped the stems in both hands, held them out and waltzed through the house with them. Beautiful, fragrant, soft-petaled flowers. And if some of those petals drifted to the floor as she danced, it only made the scene more romantic.

They made her feel like a princess, like a woman. She sniffed them lavishly as she circled back into the kitchen for a vase. Like a bride.

She stopped abruptly, staring at them. *Like a bride.*

Her head went light, her skin hot, her hands trembly. When she realized she was holding her breath, she let it out with a whoosh, but it caught and stumbled as she tried to pull air in again.

He'd brought her flowers, she thought again. He'd asked her to dinner. Slowly, she pressed a hand to her heart, found that it was pumping light and fast, very fast.

He was going to ask her to marry him. *To marry him.*

"Oh, my. Oh." Her legs wanted to fold, so she sat down, right on the floor of the kitchen with the flowers cradled in her arms like a child. Flowers, tender kisses, a romantic dinner for two. He was courting her.

No, no. She was jumping to conclusions. He would never move that quickly to the next step. She shook her head, picked herself up, and found an old wide-mouthed bottle for a vase. He was just being sweet. He was just being considerate. He was just being Ethan.

She turned on the faucet and filled the bottle. Just being Ethan, she thought again, and found her breath gone a second time.

Being Ethan, he would think and he would do things in a certain manner. Struggling for calm, for logic, she began to arrange the precious flowers, stem by stem.

They'd known each other for . . . she could hardly remember not knowing him. Now they were lovers. They were in love. Being Ethan, he would consider marriage the next step. Honorable, traditional. Right. He would believe it right.

She understood that but had expected it to be months yet before he drifted in that direction. Yet why would he wait, she asked herself, when they'd already waited for years?

But . . . She had promised herself she would never marry again. She made that vow as she signed her name on the divorce papers. She couldn't fail so miserably at something ever again, or risk putting Aubrey through the misery and trauma. She'd made the decision that she would raise Aubrey alone, raise her well, raise her with love. That she herself would provide, would build the home, tend it, where her daughter could grow up happy and safe.

But that was before she had let herself believe Ethan would ever want them, would ever love her the way she loved him. Because it had always been Ethan. Always Ethan, she thought, closing her eyes. In her heart, in her dreams. Did she dare break her promise, one she had made so solemnly? Could she risk being a wife again, pinning her hopes and her heart on another man?

Oh, yes. Yes, she could risk anything if the man was Ethan. It was so right, so perfect, she thought, laughing to herself as her head and heart went light with joy. It was the happy-ever-after that she'd stopped letting herself yearn for.

How would he ask? She pressed her fingers to her lips, and those lips trembled and curved. Quietly, she thought, with his eyes so serious, so intent on hers. He would take her hand, in that careful way of his. They'd be outside with moonlight and breezes, with the scents of night all around them and the musical lap of water close by.

Simply, she thought, without poetry or fuss. He would look down at her, saying nothing for a long moment, then he would speak, without hurry.

I love you, Grace. I always will. Will you marry me?

Yes, yes, yes! She spun herself in giddy circles. She would be his bride, his wife, his partner, his lover. Now. Forever. She could give her child to him knowing, without hesitation, that he would love and cherish, would protect and tend. She would have more children with him.

Oh, God—Ethan's child growing inside her. Overwhelmed by the image, she pressed her hands to her stomach. And this time, this time, the life that fluttered inside her would be wanted and welcomed by both who'd made it.

They would make a life together, a wonderfully, thrillingly simple life.

She couldn't wait to begin it.

Tomorrow night, she remembered, and in a sudden panic, pushed at her hair. Dropped her hands to look at them in utter despair. Oh, she was a mess. She needed to look beautiful.

What would she wear?

She caught herself laughing, the laughter full of joy and nerves. For once she forgot work and schedules and responsibility and raced to her closet.

ANNA DIDN'T NOTICE the stolen flowers until the next day. Then she noticed them with a shout.

"Seth! Seth, you come out here right now." She had her hands on her hips, her sassy straw hat askew, her eyes snapping and dangerous.

"Yeah?" He came out, munching on a handful of pretzels, though dinner was simmering on the stove.

"Have you been messing with my flowers?" she demanded.

He slid a glance down to the mixed bed of annuals and perennials. And snorted. "What would I be messing with stupid flowers for?"

She tapped her foot. "That's what I'm asking you."

"I never touched them. Hey, you don't even want us to pull up weeds."

"That's because you don't know the difference between a weed and a daisy," she snapped. "Well, somebody's been in my flower beds."

"Wasn't me." He shrugged, then rolled his eyes in glee as she stormed past him into the house.

Somebody, Seth thought, was in for it big time.

"Cameron!" She stomped upstairs and into the bathroom where he was washing up from work. He glanced over, lifting a brow as water dripped from his face into the sink. She scowled for a moment, then shook her head. "Never mind," she muttered, slamming the door.

Cam would no more fiddle with her gardens than Seth, she decided. And if he was picking flowers for anyone, it damn well better be his loving wife, or she'd just murder him and be done with it.

Her eyes narrowed on the door to Ethan's room. And she made a low, threatening sound in her throat.

She did stop to knock, though it was only three staccato raps before she simply pushed open the door.

"Christ, Anna." Mortified, Ethan snatched up the slacks that lay on his bed and held them in front of him. He was wearing nothing but his briefs and a pained expression.

"Just save the modesty, I'm not interested. Have you been into my flowers?"

"Into your flowers?" Oh, he'd known this was coming. The woman had eyes like a cat when it came to her posies. But he hadn't expected the moment to come when he was half naked. Half, hell, he thought and clutched the slacks more firmly.

"Somebody's snapped off more than a dozen blooms. Snapped them right off." She advanced on him, her eyes scanning the room for evidence.

"Oh, well . . ."

"Problem?" Cam leaned on the doorjamb, tongue in his cheek. It was an amusing sight after a hard day's work, he decided. His well-riled wife stalking around his all-but-bare-assed brother.

"Somebody's been in my garden and they stole my flowers."

"No kidding? Want me to call the cops?"

"Oh, shut up." She whirled back to Ethan, who took a cautious and cowardly step in retreat. She looked fit to murder. "Well?"

"Well, I . . ." He'd intended to confess, throw himself on her mercy. But the woman glaring at him out of dark, furious eyes looked several quarts low on mercy. "Rabbits," he said slowly. "Probably."

"Rabbits?"

"Yeah." He shifted uncomfortably, wishing to Christ he'd at least gotten his pants on before she burst in. "Rabbits can be a problem with gardens. They just hop up and help themselves."

"Rabbits," she said again.

"Could be deer," he added, just a little desperately. "They'd graze over and eat every damn thing down to stubs." Counting on pity, he shot a look at Cam. "Right?"

Cam weighed the situation, knew Anna was city girl enough to buy it. Oh, Ethan would owe him for this, he decided and smiled. "Oh, yeah, deer and rabbits, big problem." Which having two dogs running tame pretty much eliminated, he mused.

"Why didn't anybody tell me!" She whipped off her hat, rapped it against her thigh. "What do we do about it? How do we make them stop?"

"Couple ways." Guilt stung, just a little, but Ethan rationalized that deer and rabbits *could* be a problem, so she should take precautions anyway. "Dried blood."

"Dried *blood*? Whose?"

"You can buy it at the garden store, and you just dump it around. It'll keep them away."

"Dried blood." Her lips pursed as she made a mental note to buy some.

"Or urine."

"Dried urine?"

"No." Ethan cleared his throat. "You just go out and . . . you know, around so they smell it and know there's a meat eater in the vicinity."

"I see." She nodded, satisfied, then whirled on her husband. "Well, get out there then and pee on my marigolds."

"Could use a beer first," Cam said and winked at his brother. "Don't worry, darling, we'll take care of it."

"All right." Calmer, she huffed out a breath. "Sorry, Ethan."

"Yeah, well, hmmm." He waited until she'd hurried out, then lowered himself to the edge of the bed. He slanted a look at Cam, who continued to lean against the door. "That wife of yours has a streak of mean in her."

"Yeah. I love it. Why'd you steal her flowers?"

"I just needed a few of them," Ethan muttered and pulled on his pants. "What the hell are they out there for if you get your head cut off for picking them?"

"Rabbits? And deer?" Cam began to hoot with laughter.

"They're garden pests right enough."

"Pretty brave rabbits who hop between two dogs and right up

to the house to select a few flowers. If they got that far, they'd mow the whole garden down to the ground."

"She doesn't have to know that. For a while. I appreciate you backing me up. I thought she was going to punch me."

"She might have. Since I saved your pretty face, I figure you owe me."

"Nothing comes free," Ethan grumbled and stalked to the closet for a shirt.

"You got that right. Seth needs a haircut, and he's already outgrown his last pair of shoes."

Ethan turned, shirt dangling from his fingertips. "You want me to take him to the mall?"

"Right again."

"I'd rather have the punch in the face."

"Too late." Cam hooked a thumb in his front pocket and grinned. "So, why'd you need the flowers?"

"Just thought Grace would like them." Muttering, Ethan shrugged into his shirt.

"Ethan Quinn stealing flowers, going out—voluntarily—to a jacket-and-tie restaurant." Cam's grin widened, his eyebrows wiggled. "Serious business."

"It's a usual thing for a man to take a woman out to dinner, bring her flowers now and then."

"Not for you it isn't." Cam straightened, patted his flat belly. "Well, I guess I'll go choke down that beer so I can be a hero."

"Man's got no privacy around here," Ethan complained when Cam sauntered away. "Women come right on into your bedroom, don't even have the courtesy to leave when they see you don't have your pants on."

Scowling, he dragged one of his two ties out of the closet. "People ready to skin you alive over a few flowers. And the next thing you know, you're at the goddamn mall fighting crowds and buying shoes."

He wrestled the tie under his collar and began to deal with the knot. "Never had to worry when I was in my own place. I could walk around buck-ass naked if I wanted to." He hissed at the tie that refused to cooperate. "I hate these fuckers."

"That's because you're happier tying a sheepshank."

"Who the hell wouldn't be?"

Then he stopped, his fingers freezing on the tie. His gaze stayed on the mirror, where he could see his father behind him.

"You're just a little nervous, that's all," Ray said with a smile and a wink. "Hot date."

Taking a careful breath, Ethan turned. Ray stood at the foot of the bed, his bright blue eyes merry, the way Ethan remembered they would sparkle when he was particularly tickled about something.

He was wearing a squash-yellow T-shirt that sported a boat under full sail, faded jeans, and scuffed sandals. His hair was long, past his collar, and shining silver. Ethan could see the sun glint on it.

He looked exactly like what he was—had been. A robust and handsome man who appreciated comfortable clothes and a good laugh.

"I'm not dreaming," Ethan murmured.

"It was easier for you to think so at first. Hello, Ethan."

"Dad."

"I remember the first time you called me that. Took you a while to come to it. You'd been with us almost a year. Christ, you were a spooky kid, Ethan. Quiet as a shadow, deep as a lake. One evening when I was grading papers, you knocked on the door. You just stood there for a minute, thinking. God, it was a marvel to watch your mind work. Then you said, 'Dad, the phone's for you.'" Ray's smile went bright as sunlight. "You slipped right out again, or you'd have seen me make a fool of myself. Sniffled like a baby and had to tell whoever the hell it was on the phone I was having an allergy attack."

"I never knew why you wanted me."

"You needed us. We needed you. You *were* ours, Ethan, even before we found each other. Fate takes its own sweet time, but it always finds a way. You were so . . . fragile," Ray said after a moment, and Ethan blinked in surprise. "Stella and I were worried we'd do something wrong and break you."

"I wasn't fragile."

"Oh, Ethan, you were. Your heart was delicate as glass and waiting to be shattered. Your body was tough. We never worried about you and Cam pounding on each other those first months. Thought it did both of you good."

Ethan's lips twitched. "He usually started the pounding."

"But you never were one to back off once your blood was up. Took some doing to get it up," he added. "Still does. We watched you watch and settle and think and consider."

"You gave me . . . time. Time to watch and settle, to think and consider. Everything I've got that's decent came from the two of you."

"No, Ethan, we just gave you love. And that time, and the place."

He wandered over to the window, to look out on the water and the boats that swayed gently at the dock. He watched an egret sail across a sky hazed with heat and plumped by clouds.

"You were meant to be ours. Meant to be here. Took to the water like you'd been born in it. Cam, he always just wanted to go fast, and Phillip preferred to sit back and enjoy the ride. But you . . ."

He turned back again, his gaze thoughtful. "You studied every inch of the boat, every wave, every turn of a river. You'd practice tying knots for hours, and nobody had to nag you into swabbing the decks."

"It came easy for me, right from the start. You wanted me to get a college degree."

"For me." Ray shook his head. "For me, Ethan. Fathers are human, after all, and I went through a time when I thought my sons needed to love schooling as much as I did. But you did what was right for you. You made me proud of you. I should have told you that more often."

"You always let me know it."

"Words count, though. Who would know that better than a man who spent his life trying to teach the young the love of them?" He sighed now. "Words count, Ethan, and I know some of them come hard for you. But I want you to remember that. You and Grace have a lot to say to each other yet."

"I don't want to hurt her."

"You will," Ray said quietly. "By trying not to. I wish you could see yourself as I do. As she does." He shook his head again. "Well, fate takes its time. Think of the boy, Ethan, think of Seth—and what pieces of yourself you see there."

"His mother—" Ethan began.

"Think of the boy for now," Ray said simply, and he was gone.

CHAPTER

16

THERE wasn't a hint of rain on the breezy summer air. The sky was a hot, staggering blue, an unbroken bowl that held a faint haze and fragile clouds. A single bird sang manically, as if mad to complete the song before the long day was over.

She was as nervous as a teenager on prom night. The thought of that made Grace laugh. No teenager had ever dreamed of nerves like these.

She fussed with her hair, wishing she had long, glossy curls like Anna's—exotic, Gypsy-like. Sexy.

But she didn't, she reminded herself firmly. And never would. At least the short, simple crop showed off the pretty gold drop earrings Julie had loaned her.

Julie had been so sweet and excited about what she'd termed the Big Date. She'd launched straight into a what-to-wear-and-what-to-wear-with-it routine—and naturally had deemed the contents of Grace's closet a total loss.

Of course, letting Julie drag her off to the mall had been sheer foolishness. Not that Julie had to yank very hard, Grace admitted. It had been so long since she'd shopped simply for the simple pleasure of shopping. For the couple of hours they'd spent swarming through the shops, she'd felt so young and carefree. As if nothing was really more important than finding the right outfit.

Still, she'd had no business buying a new dress, even if she did get it on sale. But she couldn't seem to talk herself out of it. Just this one little indulgence, this one little luxury. She so desperately wanted something new and fresh for this special night.

She'd yearned for the sexy, sophisticated black with its shoestring straps and snug skirt. Or the boldly sensuous red with the daringly plunging neckline. But they hadn't suited her, as she'd known they wouldn't.

It had been no surprise that the simple powder-blue linen had been discounted. It had looked so plain, so ordinary, hanging on the rack. But Julie had pressed it on her, and Julie had an eye for such things.

She'd been right, of course, Grace thought now. It was simple, almost virginal, with its unadorned bodice and graceful lines. But it looked pretty on, with the color cool against her skin, and the skirt floating around her legs.

Grace traced a finger over the square neckline, faintly amazed that the bra Julie had nagged her into buying actually did gift her with a hint of cleavage. A miracle indeed, Grace thought with a little laugh.

Concentrating, she leaned close to the mirror. She'd done everything Julie had instructed with the borrowed makeup. And her eyes did look bigger and deeper, she decided. She'd done her best to blot away the signs of fatigue and thought she had succeeded. Maybe she hadn't managed more than a wink of sleep the night before, but she didn't feel in the least tired.

She felt energized.

She reached out, and her hand hovered over the samples of perfumes they'd been given at the cosmetics counter. Then she remembered that Anna had told her to wear her own scent for Ethan before. That it would say something to him.

Choosing that instead, she closed her eyes and dabbed it on. With her eyes closed, imagining that his lips might brush here, brush there, linger and taste where her pulse beat that fragrance into life.

Still dreaming, she picked up a little ivory evening bag—another loan—and checked its contents. She hadn't carried such a small purse since . . . well, before Aubrey was born, she thought. It was so odd to look inside and see none of the dozens of mother things she was used to carrying. Only women things now, she mused. The little compact she'd splurged on, a tube of lipstick she rarely thought to use, her house key, a few carefully folded bills, and a tissue that wasn't thin and ragged from wiping a sticky face.

It made her feel feminine just to look at it, to slip her feet into impractical heeled sandals—oh, she'd be scrambling to pay off her charge card when the bill came—to turn in front of the mirror and watch her skirt follow the movement.

When she heard his truck pull up outside, she dashed across the room. Made herself stop. No, she wasn't going to race to the door like an eager puppy. She would wait right here until he knocked. And give her heart a chance to beat normally again.

When he did knock, it was still thundering in her ears. But she stepped out, smiled at him through the screen, and moved toward the door.

He remembered watching her walk to the door like this before, on the night they'd made love the first time. She'd looked so lovely, so lonely with the candlelight flickering around her.

But tonight she looked . . . he didn't think he had words for it. Everything about her seemed to glow—skin, hair, eyes. It made him feel awkward, humble, reverent. He wanted to kiss her to be certain she was real, and yet was afraid to touch.

He stepped back as she opened the screen, then took the hand she held out carefully. "You look different."

No, it wasn't poetry. And it made her smile. "I wanted to." She pulled the door closed behind her and let him lead her to his truck.

He wished immediately that he'd borrowed the 'Vette.

"The truck doesn't suit that dress," he said as she climbed in.

"It suits me." She swept her skirts in to be certain they didn't catch in the door. "I may look different, Ethan, but I'm still the same."

She settled back and prepared for the most beautiful evening of her life.

✤

THE SUN WAS still up and bright when they arrived in Princess Anne. The restaurant he'd chosen was in one of the old, refurbished houses where the ceilings were high and the windows tall and narrow. Candles yet to be lighted stood on tables draped in white linen, and the waiters wore jackets and formal black ties. Conversations from other diners were muted, as in church. She could hear her heels click on the polished floor as they were led to their table.

She wanted to remember every detail. The way the little table sat snug by the window, the painting of the Bay that hung on the wall behind Ethan. The friendly twinkle in the waiter's eyes when he offered them menus and asked if they'd like a cocktail.

But most of all she wanted to remember Ethan. The quiet smile in his eyes when he looked across the table at her, the way his fingertips continued to brush hers on the white linen.

"Would you like to have some wine?" he asked her.

Wine, candles, flowers. "Yes, that would be nice."

He opened the wine list, studied it thoughtfully. He knew she preferred white, and one or two of the types were familiar. Phillip always kept a couple of bottles chilling. Though God knew why any reasonable man would pay that much money on a regular basis for a drink.

Grateful that the selections were numbered and he wouldn't have to attempt to pronounce any French, he gave the waiter the order, privately pleased when he saw his choice met with approval.

"Hungry?"

"A little." She wondered if she'd be able to swallow a crumb around the delight in her throat. "It's just so nice to be here like this, with you."

"I should've taken you out before."

"This is perfect. There hasn't been much time for this."

"We can juggle some time." And it wasn't so bad, he discovered, wearing a tie, eating in a place surrounded by other people. Not when he got to look at her across the table. "You look rested, Grace."

"Rested?" The laugh bubbled out, making him smile uncertainly. Then her fingers squeezed his affectionately. "Oh, Ethan. I do love you."

⚜

THE SUN DIPPED lower, and the candles were lighted as they sipped wine and enjoyed a perfectly prepared meal served with flair. He told her about the progress of the boat, and of the new contract Phillip had finessed.

"That's wonderful. It's hard to believe you only started the business this spring."

"I'd thought about it for a long time," he told her. "Had a lot of the details worked out in my head."

He would have, of course, she thought. Thinking things through was innate with Ethan. "Even so, you're making it work. Really making it work. I've thought about coming by dozens of times."

"Why haven't you?"

"Before . . . If I saw you too often or in too many different places, it worried me." She loved being able to tell him, to watch his eyes change when she did. "I was sure you'd be able to see the way I felt about you—how I wanted to touch you, and have you touch me."

The blood hummed in his fingertips as they grazed hers. And his eyes did change, just as she'd wanted, deepening as they stared into hers. "I'd talked myself out of you," he said carefully.

"I'm glad it didn't stick."

"So am I." He brought her fingers over, touched his lips to them. "Maybe you'll come by the boatyard one of these days, and I'll look at you . . . and I'll see."

She angled her head. "Maybe I will."

"You could drop in some hot afternoon and . . ." His thumb cruised lazily over her knuckles. "Bring fried chicken."

Her laugh was quick and easy. "I should've figured that's what really attracted you to me."

"Yeah, it tipped the scales. A pretty face, sea-goddess eyes, long legs, a warm laugh—they don't mean much to a man. But you add a nice batch of southern fried chicken, and you've got something."

Delightfully flattered, she shook her head. "And here I was thinking I wouldn't get any poetry out of you."

His gaze skimmed over her face, and for the first time in his life he wished he had a talent for composing odes. "Do you want poetry, Grace?"

"I want you, Ethan. Just the way you are." With a long, contented sigh, she looked around the restaurant. "And you add an evening like this now and then . . ." She shifted her gaze back to him and grinned. "And you've got something."

"Sounds like a deal, since I like being out with you, like this. I like being anywhere with you."

She curled her fingers into his. "A long time ago. It seems like a long time, I used to dream about romance. The way I hoped it would be one day. This is better, Ethan. Real turned out to be better than the dream."

"I want you to be happy."

"If I was any happier, I'd have to be two people for it all to fit." Her eyes sparkled with the laugh as she leaned toward him. "And then you'd have to figure out what to do with two of me."

"One's all I need. Do you want to take a walk?"

Her heart soared. Would it be now? "Yes. I think a walk would be perfect."

The sun was nearly gone as they strolled along the pretty streets, casting shadows lovely and deep. In a sky dazzled by hot color, the moon was starting its rise. It wouldn't be full, Grace noted, but it didn't matter. Her heart was.

When he turned her into his arms just at the edge of the splash of light from a streetlamp, she melted into the long, slow kiss.

Different, Ethan thought again as he let himself take the kiss just a shade deeper. She felt softer, warmer, yielding against him, though he could feel faint tremors rippling through her.

"I love you, Grace." He said it to soothe both of them.

Her heart bounded straight into her throat, making her voice shaky. Stars were blinking to life overhead, brilliantly white points of light. "I love you, Ethan." She closed her eyes, held her breath in anticipation of the words.

"We'd better start back."

She blinked her eyes open. "Oh. Yes." Let out her breath. "Yes, you're right."

Foolish of her, she decided as they walked back to his truck. A man as careful and thorough as Ethan wouldn't propose to her on a street corner in Princess Anne. He would wait until they got back, until Julie had gone home and Aubrey had been checked on.

He'd wait until they were alone, private, in familiar surroundings. Of course, that was it. So she beamed a smile at him as he started the engine. "It was a wonderful dinner, Ethan."

THERE WAS MOONLIGHT, just as she'd imagined. It slanted through the window and slipped gently over Aubrey in her crib. Her baby dreamed happy dreams, she thought. And how much happier they would all be in the morning when they'd taken the next step toward becoming a family.

Aubrey already loved him, Grace thought as she stroked her daughter's hair. Just a short time ago, she had resolved to raise her child alone, to make certain that she was enough. All that was changing now. Ethan would be a father to her daughter, a loving parent who would watch over her.

One day they'd tuck Aubrey in together. One day they would stand over a crib watching another child sleep. With Ethan she could share the joy of a simple moment like that—that quiet moment in the moon-washed dark when you looked in and saw your child asleep and safe.

There was so much he could give them, she thought. And that she could give to him.

A man like Ethan, she knew, would feel that first flutter of life in his heart just as she would feel it in her womb. They could share that, and a lifetime of simple moments.

She moved quietly into the living room and saw Ethan standing, gazing through the screen door. She had an instant of panic. He wasn't going? He couldn't be leaving. Not now. Not before . . .

"Do you want some coffee?" She said it quickly, her voice rising before she could control it.

"No, thanks." He turned. "She sleeping all right?"

"Oh, yes, she's fine."

"She looks so much like you."

"Do you think?"

"Especially when she smiles. Grace . . ."

He watched her eyes fix on his, glow in the low light of the lamp. For a moment it seemed to him that nothing had come before, nothing would come after. It could be the three of them, there together on quiet nights just like this, in the little dollhouse. It could be his future. He wanted to believe it could be his life.

"I'd like to stay. I'd like to be with you tonight, if you want."

"I want. Of course I want." She thought she understood. He needed to show her love first. More than willing, she held out a hand. "Come to bed, Ethan."

He took care to be tender, to stroke her gently to peak. Holding her there, holding until her body bowed up, a trembling bridge of sensations. To make her float and sigh. He watched the moonlight dapple her skin, followed its shifting shadows with his fingertips, with his lips. Pleasured her.

Love surrounded her. It cradled her. It rocked her with a rhythm as gentle as a quiet sea. Gliding on it, she offered it back to him, a shimmering reflection.

His tenderness moved her to tears. She knew now that his needs could be ripe and raw and reckless. And that thrilled her. Yet this part of him, this compassionate, sensitive, and most generous part of him touched her heart at the core. She fell fathoms deeper into that wide well of love.

When he slipped into her, when they were joined, his mouth moved over hers to capture each sigh. She glided up, trembled on that silk-covered peak, holding, holding until he was trembling with her and they could catch each other on the slow tumble down.

After, he shifted her so that she curled into the curve of his arm. And stroked her. Her eyes grew heavy. Now, she thought as she began to drift. He would ask her now while they were both still glowing.

Waiting, she slid into sleep.

HE WAS TEN, and the last beating she'd given him had left his back a maze of purpling bruises and scarlet pain. She never hit him in the face. She'd learned quickly that most clients didn't care to see black eyes and bloody lips on the merchandise.

She'd stopped using her fists, mostly. She found a belt or a hairbrush more effective. She liked the thin, circular brushes that were all hard bristles. The first time she'd used one on him, the shock and pain had been so unspeakable that he'd fought back and it had been her lip that had been bloody. She'd used her fists then until he'd found escape in unconsciousness.

He was no match for her, and he knew it. She was a big woman and strong with it. When she was drunk, she was stronger yet and more ruthless. It didn't help to plead, it didn't help to cry, so he'd stopped doing both. And the beatings weren't as bad as the other. Nothing was.

She'd gotten twenty dollars for him the first time she'd sold him. He knew because she told him, and promised to give him two dollars for himself if he didn't make a fuss about it. He hadn't known what she was talking about. Not then. He hadn't known, not until she left him in the dark bedroom with the man.

Even then he didn't know, didn't understand. When those big, damp hands were on him, the fear was so blinding bright, the shame so dark, the terror so loud, as loud as his screams.

He'd screamed until nothing could crawl through his throat but a guttural whimper. Even the pain of being raped couldn't push more out of him.

She even gave him the two dollars. He burned it, there in the dirty sink in the horrible bathroom that stank of his own vomit, he watched the money curl up black. And his hate for her was just as black.

He promised himself, staring at his own hollow eyes in the spotty mirror, that if she ever whored him again, he would kill her.

"Ethan." Her heart tripping in her throat, Grace scrambled onto her knees to shake his shoulders. The skin under her hands was like ice. His body was rigid as stone, but trembling. It made her think wildly of earthquakes, volcanos. Boiling violence under a hard layer of rock.

The sounds he made had wakened her. They'd made her dream of an animal caught in a trap.

His eyes flew open. She could see only the glint of them in the dark, but they looked blind and wild. For a moment she was afraid that the boiling violence she sensed would break through and batter her.

"You were having a dream." She said it firmly, certain that that was what was needed to put Ethan back into those staring eyes. "It's all right now. It was a dream."

He could hear his breath rasping. More than a dream, he knew. It had been the cold-sweated flashback he hadn't had in years. But the result was the same. Nausea curled sickly in his stomach, his head pounded and swam with the pathetic echo of a young boy's scream. He shuddered once, violently, under the gentle hands on his shoulders.

"I'm okay."

But his voice was rough, and she knew he lied. "I'll get you some water."

"No, I'm okay." Not even water would settle on his jumping stomach. "Go back to sleep."

"Ethan, you're shaking."

He would stop it. He could stop it. It would only take a little time and concentration. He saw that her eyes were huge, more than a little frightened. He was both sick and furious that he had brought even the memory of that horror to her bed.

Dear God, had he let himself believe, for even an instant, that it could be different for him? For them?

He forced himself to smile. "Just spooked me, that's all. Sorry I woke you."

Reassured because she saw a shadow of the man she loved come back into his eyes, she stroked his hair. "It must have been awful. Scared both of us."

"Must've been. Don't remember." The next lie, he thought, abominably weary. "Come on, lie back down. Everything's all right now."

She snuggled up beside him, hoping to comfort, and laid a hand over his heart. It was still racing. "Just close your eyes," she murmured as she would have to Aubrey. "Close your eyes and rest now. Hold on to me, Ethan. Dream of me."

Praying for peace, he did both.

WHEN SHE WOKE to find him gone, Grace tried to tell herself that the weight of her disappointment was out of proportion. He hadn't wanted to disturb her so early, so he hadn't said good-bye.

Now that the sun was up, he would already be out on the water.

She rose, slipped on a robe, and padded in to make coffee and to grab those few minutes of alone time before Aubrey roused.

Then she sighed and stepped out on her little back porch. She knew her disappointment didn't stem from finding him up and gone when she woke. She'd been sure, so sure he was going to ask her to marry him. All the signs had been there, the scene set, the moment perfect. But the words hadn't come.

She'd all but written the script, she thought with a grimace, and he hadn't followed it. This morning was supposed to begin the next phase of their lives. She'd imagined running over to Julie's and sharing the joy of it, of calling Anna and babbling, begging for wedding advice.

Of telling her mother.

Of explaining it all to Aubrey.

Instead, it was a quiet morning.

After a beautiful night, she scolded herself. A lovely night. She had no business complaining about it. Annoyed with herself, she went back inside to pour the first cup of freshly brewed coffee.

Then she began to chuckle. What had she been thinking of? This was Ethan Quinn she was dealing with. Wasn't this the same man who'd waited—by his own admission—nearly a decade to so much as kiss her? At the rate he took things, it could be another one before he brought up the subject of marriage.

The only reason they'd moved from that first kiss to where they stood now was because she . . . well, she'd thrown herself at him, Grace admitted. Plain and simple. And she wouldn't have had the guts to do that if Anna hadn't shoved her along.

Flowers, she thought, turning so that she could smile at them, bright and pretty on her kitchen counter. Candlelight dinner, moonlit walks, and long, tender lovemaking. Yes, he was courting her—

and would likely continue to do so until she went mad waiting for him to take the next step.

But that was Ethan, she admitted, and just one of the things she adored about him.

She sipped coffee, bit her lip. Why did he have to take the step? Why shouldn't she be the one to move things along? Julie had told her men liked it when a woman took the initiative. And hadn't Ethan liked it when she finally worked up the courage to ask him to make love with her?

She could do some courting herself, couldn't she? And she could move it along at a faster pace. God knew she was an expert at getting things done on schedule.

It would only take the courage to ask him. She blew out a breath. She'd have to find that, but she would dig inside herself until she did.

TEMPERATURES SOARED, AND the humidity thickened in a syrupy morass that Cam not so cheerfully dubbed "fumidity." He worked belowdecks, trimming out the cabin until the heat sent him topside desperate for fluids and one stingy breeze.

Though he rarely complained about the working conditions, Ethan was—like Cam—stripped to the waist. Sweat poured as he patiently varnished.

"That's going to take a week to dry, it's so goddamn damp."

"Decent storm might blow some of it out."

"Then I wish to Christ we'd have one." Cam grabbed up the jug and glugged water straight from the lip.

"Close weather makes some people edgy."

"I'm not edgy, I'm hot. Where's the kid?"

"Sent him for some ice."

"Good idea. I could take a bath in it. There's no fucking air down there."

Ethan nodded. Varnishing was a miserable enough job in this weather, but working below in the little cabin where even the big fans couldn't reach was probably kin to working in hell. "Want to switch off for a while?"

"I can do my own goddamn job."

Ethan merely lifted a sweaty shoulder. "Suit yourself."

Cam gritted his teeth, then hissed. "Okay, I am edgy. The heat's frying my brain, and I keep wondering if that alley cat's gotten Anna's letter yet."

"Ought to. It went out Tuesday as soon as the post office broke the holiday. It's Friday now."

"I know what day it is, Ethan." Disgusted, Cam swiped sweat off his face and scowled at his brother. "Aren't you worried a damn bit about it?"

"It won't make any difference if I am or not. She'll do what she's going to do." His gaze flicked up to Cam's and was hard as a bunched fist. "Then we'll handle it."

Cam paced the deck, caught a whiff of air from the fans, paced back. "I never could understand how you can stay so calm when things go to hell."

"Practice," Ethan murmured and kept on varnishing.

Cam rolled his aching shoulders, drummed his fingers on his thigh. He had to think of something else or he'd go crazy. "How'd the big date go the other night?"

"Well enough."

"Jesus, Ethan, do I have to get the pliers?"

A smile moved over Ethan's mouth. "Had a nice dinner. Drank some of that Pouilly-Fuissé Phil's so wild about. Tastes fine enough, but I don't see what the big fuss is about."

"So, you get laid?"

Ethan flicked up another glance, took in Cam's wide grin, and decided to take the question in the spirit it was asked. "Yeah—did you?"

Entertained, if no cooler, Cam threw back his head and laughed. "Damn, she's the best thing that ever happened to you. I don't just mean the sex, though that's got to be part of what's perked you up around here lately. The woman fits you like the proverbial glove."

Ethan paused, scratched his belly where sweat dribbled and itched. "Why?"

"Because she's rock-steady, pretty as a picture, patient as Job, and she's got enough humor about life to tickle out yours. I guess we'll be sprucing up the yard for another wedding before long."

Ethan's fingers tightened on his brush. "I'm not going to marry her, Cam."

It was the tone as much as the statement that made Cam's eyes narrow. Quiet despair. "I guess I could be reading you wrong," Cam said slowly. "I figured, the way things were moving, you were serious about her."

"I am serious about Grace. About a lot of things." He dipped his brush again, watched the clean gold varnish drip. "Marriage isn't something I'm looking for."

Ordinarily Cam would have let a subject such as this drop. He'd have walked away from it with a shrug. Your business, brother. But he knew Ethan too well, had loved him too long to walk away from the pain. He crouched by the rail so their faces were closer.

"I wasn't looking for it either," he murmured. "Scared the hell out me. But when the woman comes into your life, *the* woman, it's scarier to let her go."

"I know what I'm doing."

The dug-in-at-the-heels look didn't stop Cam. "You always figure you do. I hope you're right this time. I sure as hell hope this isn't some shit that goes back to that ghost-eyed kid Mom and Dad brought home one day. The one who used to wake up screaming at night."

"Don't go there, Cam."

"Don't you go there, either. Mom and Dad did better by us than that."

"It has nothing to do with them."

"It all has everything to do with them. Listen—" He broke off with a mild oath as Seth came running in.

"Hey, this shit's already melting."

Cam straightened, scowled over at Seth out of habit rather than heat. "Didn't I tell you to find an alternate word for 'shit'?"

"You say it," Seth pointed out, shifting the bag of ice.

"That's beside the point."

Knowing the routine, Seth dumped the ice into the cooler. "Why?"

"Because Anna's going to have my ass if you keep it up. And if she has mine, pal, I'll have yours."

"Oh, now I'm scared."

"You oughta be."

They continued to bicker, Ethan continued the varnish. Tuning them out, concentrating on the job at hand, he locked his unhappiness away.

CHAPTER
17

IT was going to be perfect. It was so obviously right, Grace wondered that she hadn't thought of it before. A sunset sail on calm seas with skies going pink and gold in the west was a custom-made backdrop for both of them. The Bay was part of their lives, what it offered and what it took.

She knew it was more than a place where Ethan worked. It was a place he loved.

It had been easy to arrange. All she'd had to do was ask. He looked surprised, then he smiled. "I'd forgotten you love to sail," he said.

She was touched when he'd simply expected that Aubrey would come with them. There would be other times, she thought. A lifetime for the three of them. But this warm and breezy evening would be for the two of them only.

Giddy laughter continued to rise up in her as she imagined his reaction when she asked him to marry her. She could see it so clearly, the way he would stop, stare at her with surprise in those wonderful blue eyes. She would smile, hold out her hand to him as they glided along with soft wind and dark water. And she would tell him everything that was in her heart.

I love you so much, Ethan. I always have and always will. Will you marry me? I want us to be a family. I want to live my life with you. To give you children. To make you happy. Haven't we waited long enough?

Then, she knew, that would be the moment his smile would begin. That slow, beautiful smile that moved degree by degree over the planes and shadows of his face, into his eyes. He would probably say something about how he'd intended to ask her. That he'd been getting to it.

They would both laugh, and they would hold each other as the sun dropped red beyond the shore. And their lives together would really begin.

"Where are you sailing off to, Grace?"

She blinked, saw Ethan smiling back at her from the wheel. "Daydreaming," she told him, chuckling at herself. "Sunset's the best time for daydreams. It's so peaceful."

She rose, nestled herself under his arm. "I'm so glad you can take a few hours off so we can do this."

"We're going to have the boat trimmed out within the month." He nuzzled his face in her hair. "Couple weeks ahead of schedule."

"You've all worked so hard."

"It's going to be worth it. The owner was here today."

"Oh?" This was part of it, too, she mused. The easy talk about their days. "What did he say?"

"Hardly shut up, so it's hard to know what he said half the time. Spouted off the latest this and that he'd read in his boating magazines, asked enough questions to make your head ring."

"But did he like it?"

"I figure he was pleased with her, since he grinned like a kid on Christmas morning the whole afternoon. After he left, Cam wanted to bet me that he would run her aground first time out on the Bay."

"Did you take the bet?"

"Hell, no. He likely will. But you haven't really sailed the Bay until you've run aground."

Ethan wouldn't, she mused, watching his big, competent hands on the wheel. He sailed clean.

"I remember when you and your family were building this sloop." She trailed her fingers over the wheel. "I was helping out at the waterfront the first time y'all took her out. Professor Quinn was at the wheel and you were working the lines. You waved at me." Chuckling, she angled her head to look up at him. "I was thrilled that you noticed me."

"I was always noticing you."

She leaned up and kissed his chin. "But you were careful not to let me notice you noticing." On impulse she gave his jaw a teasing nip. "Until lately."

"I guess I lost my knack for it." He turned his head until his mouth found hers. "Just lately."

"Good." With a quiet laugh, she laid her head on his shoulder. "Because I like noticing you notice me."

They weren't alone on the Bay, but he stayed well clear of the zipping motorboats out for a summer-evening cruise. A flock of gulls frantically swooped and swirled around the stern of a skiff where a young girl tossed out bread. Her laugh carried, high and bright, to mix with the greedy calls of the birds.

The breeze rose up, filling the sails and whisking away the wet heat of the day. The few clouds drifting in the west were going pink around the edges.

Almost time.

Odd, she realized, she wasn't a bit nervous. A little giddy perhaps, because her head felt so light, her heart so free. Hope, so long buried, was golden bright once freed.

She wondered if he would slip into one of the narrow channels where the shade would be thick and the water the color of tobacco. He could thread past the bobbing buoy markers to a quiet place, one without even the gulls for company.

He was so content with her beside him, Ethan let the wind choose the course. He should make adjustments, he thought. The sails would reef before long if he didn't. But he didn't want to let her go—not quite yet.

She smelled of her lemon soap, and her hair was soft against his cheek. This could be their lives, he thought. Quiet moments, evening sails. Standing together. Building little dreams into big ones.

"She's having the time of her life," Grace murmured.

"Hmmm?"

"The little girl there, feeding the gulls." She nodded in the direction of the skiff, smiling as she imagined Aubrey, a few years from now, laughing and calling to the gulls from the stern of Ethan's boat. "Uh-oh, here comes her little brother to demand his share." She laughed, charmed by the children. "They're nice together," she murmured, watching as the two of them heaved bread high into the air for eager beaks to snatch. "Company for each other. There're more lonely times for an only child."

Ethan closed his eyes a moment as his own half-formed daydream shattered. She would want more children. Deserve them. Life wasn't all pretty sails on the Bay.

"I need to trim the sails," he told her. "Do you want to take the wheel?"

"I'll trim them." She grinned at him as she ducked under his arm to move to port. "I haven't forgotten how to handle lines, Cap'n."

No, he thought, she hadn't forgotten. She was a good sailor, as at home on deck as she was in her own kitchen. She ran the rigging with the same skill that she showed when she served drinks to a crowd at the pub.

"There's not much you can't do, Grace."

"What?" She glanced up, then laughed. "It's not hard to know how to use the wind when you grow up with it."

"You're a natural sailor," he corrected. "A wonderful mother, a fine cook. You know how to make people easy around you."

Her pulse went from calm to frantic. Would he ask her now, after all, before she had the chance to ask him? "Those are all things I enjoy," she said, watching him watch her. "Making a home here in St. Chris contents me. You do the same, Ethan, because it contents you."

"I've got a need for this place," he said softly. "It's what saved me," he added, but he'd turned away and she didn't hear.

Grace waited another moment, willing him to speak, to tell her, to ask her. Then with a shake of her head, she crossed the deck again.

The sun was sinking, coming close, so close to that long nightly kiss of the shore. The water was calm, little wavelets waltzing against the hull. The sails were full and white.

The moment, she thought with a leap of heart, was now.

"Ethan, I love you so much."

He lifted an arm to bring her against his side. "I love you, Grace."

"I've always loved you. I always will."

He looked down at her then, and she saw the emotion come into his eyes, deepening the blue. She lifted a hand to his cheek, held it there as she drew in the next breath.

"Will you marry me?" She saw the surprise, as she'd expected, but she didn't notice the way his body went stiff as she rushed on.

"I want us to be a family. I want to live my life with you. To give you children. To make you happy. Haven't we waited long enough?"

And she waited now, but she didn't see the slow smile slip across his face, into his eyes. He only continued to stare at her, with something she thought might be horror. Bony wings of panic fluttered in her stomach.

"I know you might have planned to do this differently, Ethan, and me asking you is a surprise. But I want us to be together, really together."

Why didn't he say something? her mind screamed. Anything. Why did he just stare at her as if she'd slapped him?

"I don't need courting." Her voice hitched and she stopped to try to steady it. "Not that I don't love things like flowers and candle-light dinners, but all I really need is for you to be there. I want to be your wife."

Afraid he would shatter if he looked into those hurt and baffled eyes another instant, he turned away. His hands white-knuckled on the wheel. "We have to come about."

"What?" She jerked back, staring at his set face, at the muscle that worked in his jaw. Her heart was still pounding, but no longer in anticipation. Now it was with dread. "You have nothing to say to me except that we have to come about?"

"No, I've things to say to you, Grace." His voice was as controlled as his heart was wild. "We have to go back so I can."

She wanted to shout at him to say them now, right now. But she nodded. "All right, Ethan. Come about."

THE SUN WAS gone when they docked. Crickets and peepers sent up their nightly chorus, filling the air with shrill, too-bright music.

Overhead a few stars blinked through the haze and a three-quarter moon shimmered.

The air had cooled quickly, but she knew that wasn't the reason she was cold. So cold.

He secured the lines himself, silently. Just as he'd sailed home, silently. He stepped back into the boat, sat across from her. The moon was still low, just riding the tops of the trees, but the early stars sprinkled down enough light for her to see his face.

There was no joy in it.

"I can't marry you, Grace." He spoke the words carefully, knowing they would hurt. "I'm sorry. I can't give you what you want."

She gripped her hands together tightly. She didn't know whether they wanted to ball into fists and pound or hang limp and shaking like an old woman's. "Then you lied when you said you loved me?"

It might be kinder to tell her so, he thought, then shook his head. No, it would only be cowardly. She deserved the truth. All of the truth. "I didn't lie. I do love you."

There were degrees of love. She wasn't fool enough to think differently. "But not the way you need to love a woman you'd marry."

"I couldn't love any woman more than I love you. But I'm—"

She held up a hand. Something had just occurred to her. If it was his reason for turning her away, she didn't think she could ever forgive him. "Is it because of Aubrey? Because I had a child with another man?"

He moved fast so rarely, it took her by surprise when he snatched her hand out of the air and squeezed it hard enough to rub bone against bone. "I love her, Grace. I'd be proud for her to think of me as her father. You have to know that."

"I don't have to know anything. You say you love me, and you love her, but you won't have us. You're hurting me, Ethan."

"I'm sorry. I'm sorry." He released her hand as if it had burned his palm. "I know I'm hurting you. I knew I would. I had no business letting things come to this."

"But you did," she said evenly. "You had to know I'd feel this way, that I'd expect you would feel the same."

"Yeah, I knew. I should have been honest with you. I've got no excuse for it." *Except I needed you. I needed you, Grace.* "Marriage isn't something I'm looking for."

"Oh, don't treat me like a fool, Ethan." She sighed now, too battered to be angry. "People like us don't have relationships, we don't have affairs. We get married and raise families. We're simple and basic, and as amusing as that might be to some, that's just who we are."

He stared down at his hands. She was right, of course. Or would have been. But she didn't know he wasn't simple or basic. "It's not you, Grace."

"No?" Hurt and humiliation tangled inside her. She imagined Jack Casey would have said the same thing, if he'd taken the time to say anything before he left her. "If it's not me, who is it? I'm the only one here."

"It's me. I can't raise a family because of what I come from."

"What you come from? You come from St. Christopher's on the southern Eastern Shore. You come from Raymond and Stella Quinn."

"No." He lifted his gaze. "I come from the stinking slums of D.C. and Baltimore and too many other places to count. I come from a whore who sold herself, and me, for a bottle or a fix. You don't know what I come from. Or what I've been."

"I know you came from a terrible place, Ethan." She spoke gently now, wanting to soothe the brutal pain in his eyes. "I know your mother—your biological mother—was a prostitute."

"She was a whore," Ethan corrected. " 'Prostitute' is too clean a word."

"All right." Cautious now, for she saw more than pain, she nodded slowly. There was fury as well, just as brutal. "You lived through what no child should ever have to live through before you came here. Before the Quinns gave you hope and love and a home. And you became theirs. You became Ethan Quinn."

"It doesn't change the blood."

"I don't know what you mean."

"How the hell would you?" He shot it at her like a bullet, hot and dangerously sharp. How would she know? he thought furiously. She'd grown up knowing her parents, and their parents, never once having to question what they had passed on to her, what she'd taken from them.

But she would, before he was done, she'd know. And that would end it. "She was a big woman. I get my hands from her. My feet, the length of my arms."

He looked down at those arms now, at those hands that had bunched into fists without his being aware of it. "I don't know where I get the rest from because I don't think she knew who my father was any more than I did. Just another john she had bad luck with. She didn't get rid of me because she'd already had three abortions and was afraid to risk another. That's what she told me."

"That was cruel of her."

"Jesus Christ." Unable to sit any longer, he rose, leaped onto the dock to pace.

Grace followed more slowly. He was right about one thing, she realized. She didn't know this man, the one who moved in fast, jerky steps with his fists clenched as if he would use them viciously on anything that moved into his path.

So she stayed out of it.

"She was a monster. A fucking monster. She beat me senseless for the hell of it as often as when she figured she had a reason."

"Oh, Ethan." Helpless to do otherwise, she reached out for him.

"Don't touch me now." He wasn't sure what he might do if he put his hands on her just then. And it frightened him. "Don't touch me now," he repeated.

She let her empty arms fall to her sides, battled back the tears that wanted to come.

"She had to take me to the hospital once," he continued. "I guess she was afraid I was going to die on her. That's when we moved from D.C. to Baltimore. The doctor asked too many questions about how I fell down the steps and gave myself a concussion and a couple cracked ribs. I used to wonder why she didn't just leave me behind. But then, she got some welfare money because of me and had a live-in punching bag, so I guess that was reason enough. Until I was eight."

He stopped pacing and stood still, stood facing her. There was so much rage inside him he could all but feel it searing his pores. And the bitter rise of it stung his throat. "That was when she figured I'd better start earning my keep. She'd been in the life long enough to know where to go to find men who didn't much care for women. Men who would pay for children."

She couldn't speak, even when she pressed a hand to her throat as if to push words, any words, out. She could only stand there, her face bone-white in the light of the rising moon and her eyes huge and horrified.

"The first time, you fight. You fight like your life depends on it, and part of you doesn't believe it's really going to happen. It just can't happen. Doesn't matter that you know what sex is because you've been around the ugly edge of it all your life. You don't know what this is, can't believe it's possible. Until it's happening. Until you can't stop it from happening."

"Oh, Ethan. Oh, God. Oh, God." She began to weep, for him, for the little boy, for a world where such horrors could exist.

"She made twenty dollars, gave me two. And made a whore of me."

"No," Grace said, helpless and sobbing. "No."

"I burned the money, but that didn't change anything. She gave me a couple of weeks, then she sold me again. You fight the second time, too. Harder even than the first, because now you know, and now you believe. And you keep fighting, every time, over and over through the same nightmare until you just give up. You take the money and you hide it because one day you'll have enough. Then you'll kill her and get out. God knows you want to kill her maybe even more than you want to get out."

She closed her eyes. "Did you?"

He heard the raspiness in her voice, took it for disgust rather than the sick fury it was. A fury for him, underscored with a vicious hope that he had. Oh, that he had.

"No. After a while it's just your life. That's all. Nothing more, nothing less. You just live it."

He turned away now to stare toward the house, where the lights glowed in the windows. Where music—Cam on guitar—carried by the breeze played a pretty tune.

"I lived it until I was twelve and one of the men she'd sold me to went a little crazy. He knocked me around pretty hard, but that wasn't so unusual. But he was flying on something and he went after her. They tore the place apart, made enough trouble that a couple neighbors who'd made it their business to mind their own got riled enough to beat on the door.

"He had his hands around her throat," Ethan remembered. "And I was sprawled on the floor, looking up, watching her eyes bulge, and I was thinking, Maybe he'll do it. Maybe he'll do it for me. She got her hand on a knife, and she jammed it into him. She jammed it into his back just as the people beating on the door busted it in. People were shouting and screaming. She pulled the son of a bitch's wallet out of his pocket while he was bleeding on the floor. And she ran. She never even looked at me."

He shrugged, turned back. "Somebody called the cops and they got me to a hospital. I'm not clear on it, but that's where I ended up. Doctors and cops and social workers," he said quietly. "Asking questions, writing things down. I guess they went looking for her, but they never found her."

He lapsed into silence so that there was only the lap of water, the call of insects, the echoing notes of a guitar. But she said nothing, knowing he wasn't finished. Not yet finished.

"Stella Quinn was at some medical conference in Baltimore, and she was doing guest rounds. She stopped by my bed. I guess she'd looked at my chart, I don't remember. I just remember her being there, putting her hands on the bed guard and looking down at me. She had kind eyes, not soft but kind. She talked to me. I didn't pay any attention to what she said, just her voice. She kept coming back. Sometimes Ray would be with her. One day she told me I could come home with them if I wanted."

He fell silent again, as if that was the end. But all Grace could think was that the moment when the Quinns had offered him a home had been the beginning.

"Ethan, my heart breaks for you. And I know now that as much as I loved and admired the Quinns all these years, it wasn't enough. They saved you."

"They saved me," he agreed. "And after I decided to live, I did everything I could to be something that honored that, and them."

"You are, and always have been, the most honorable man I know."

She went to him, wrapped her arms around him, and held tight despite the fact that his arms didn't enfold her in return. "Let me help," she murmured. "Let me be with you. Ethan." She lifted her face, pressed her mouth to his. "Let me love you."

He shuddered, broke. His arms came round her now, fiercely. His mouth took the comfort she offered. He swayed there, holding on to her, a lifeline in a thrashing sea. "I can't do this, Grace. It's not right for you."

"You're right for me." She clung when he would have eased her away. "Nothing you've said changes what I feel. Nothing could. I only love you more for it."

"Listen to me." His hands were steady, but they were firm as they gripped her shoulders and pushed her back. "I can't give you what you need, what you want, what you should have. Marriage, children, family."

"I don't—"

"Don't tell me you don't need them. I know you do."

She drew in air, let it out slowly. "I need them with you. I need a life with you."

"I can't marry you. I can't give you children. I promised myself I'd never risk passing on to a child whatever pieces of her are in me."

"There's nothing of her in you."

"There is." His fingers tightened briefly. "You saw it that day in the woods when I took you against a tree like an animal. You saw it when I yelled at you over working in a bar. And I've seen it too many times to count when someone pushes me the wrong way once too often. Holding it back doesn't mean it's not there. I can't take vows with you or make a child with you. I love you too much to let you believe it's ever going to happen."

"She scarred more than your body," Grace murmured. "It's your heart she really abused. I can help you heal it the rest of the way."

He gave her a quick, gentle shake. "You're not listening to me. You're not hearing me. If you can't accept the way things have to be between us, I'll understand. I'll never blame you for stepping back and looking for what you want with someone else. The best thing for you is for me to let you go. And that's what I'm doing."

"Letting me go?"

"I want you to go home." He released her and stepped back. Felt as if he'd entered a huge, dark void. "Once you think this all through, you'll see it my way. Then you can decide if we should go on seeing each other the way we have been or if you want me to leave you be."

"I want—"

"No," he interrupted. "You don't know what you want right now. You need time, and so do I. I'd rather you went on. I don't want you here right now, Grace."

She lifted a hand to her temple. "You don't want me here?"

"Not now." He set his jaw when he saw the hurt swim into her eyes. For her own good, he reminded himself. "Go home and leave me be for a while."

She took a step back, then another. Then turned and ran. Around the house rather than through it. She couldn't bear having anyone see her with tears on her cheeks and this awful tearing pain in her heart. He wouldn't have her, was all she could think. He wouldn't let her be what he needed.

"Hey, Grace! Hey." Seth abandoned his pursuit of the lightning bugs that flickered and flashed through the dark and raced after her. "I've got about a million of these suckers." He started to hold up a jar.

Then he saw the tears, heard them in her ragged breathing as she fumbled with the door handle on her car. "What's wrong? Why are you crying? Did you get hurt?"

She sobbed out a breath, pressed a hand to her heart. Oh, yes, oh, yes, I'm hurt. "It's nothing. I have to go home. I can't—I can't stay."

She tore open the car door, stumbled inside.

Seth's eyes went from puzzled to grim as he watched her drive away. Hot with fury, he stormed around the side of the house, slapping the bright jar on the edge of the porch. He saw the shadow on the dock and strode toward it with fists clenched for battle.

"You bastard. You son of a bitch." He waited until Ethan turned, then rammed his fist as hard as he could into his gut. "You made her cry."

"I know I did." The fresh and physical pain jolted through him, and joined the rest. "This isn't your business, Seth. Go on in the house."

"Fuck you. You hurt her. Go on, try to hurt me. It won't be so easy." Teeth bared, Seth swung again, and again, until Ethan picked him up by collar and seat and held him dangling over the end of the dock.

"Cool off, you hear, or I'll toss you in." He added a hard, threatening shake, but his heart wasn't in it. "You think I wanted to hurt her? You think I got any pleasure out of it?"

"Then why did you?" Seth shouted, struggling like a baited fish.

"There wasn't any choice." Suddenly abominably weary, Ethan dropped Seth to his feet on the dock. "Leave me alone," he murmured and sat on the edge. Giving in, he put his head in his hands, pressed his fingers to his eyes. "Just leave me alone."

Seth shifted his feet. It wasn't just Grace who was hurt. He hadn't really understood that a grown man could be, not this way. But Ethan was. Tentatively, he stepped forward. He stuck his hands in his pockets, pulled them out. Shuffled. Sighed. Then sat.

"Women," Seth said in a level and considering voice, "make a man want to shoot himself in the head and be done with it." It was something he'd heard Phillip say to Cam, and he thought it might be appropriate. He was rewarded when Ethan let out a short laugh, even if it wasn't a happy one.

"Yeah, I guess they can." Ethan draped an arm around Seth's shoulders, pulled the boy close to his side. And took a little comfort.

CHAPTER

18

ANNA weighed her priorities—and took the day off. She couldn't be sure what time Grace would be by to tend the house, and she couldn't risk missing her.

She didn't give a good damn what Ethan said—or didn't say. There was a crisis.

If she'd believed they'd simply had a spat or misunderstanding, she would have been sympathetic or amused, whichever was most called for. It wasn't a misunderstanding that had put misery into Ethan's eyes. Oh, he had a way of hiding it, she mused as she slowly and ruthlessly tugged out weeds that threatened her begonias in the front-yard bed. And he hid his more personal feelings very well. It just so happened she was a professional at filtering through to emotion.

Too bad for him that he'd inherited a social worker for a sister-in-law.

She'd poked at Seth a bit. There was no doubt in her mind the boy knew something. But she'd run straight into unwavering male loyalty. All she got out of him was a Quinn shrug and a zipped lip.

She could have wheedled it out nonetheless. But she hadn't had the heart to put a chip in that lovely bond. Seth could keep his loyalty to Ethan.

Anna would work on Grace.

She was positive they hadn't seen each other for days. It was pathetically easy to keep tabs on Ethan. He was out on the water every morning, in the boatyard every afternoon and through the evening. He poked at his dinner, then retreated to his room. Where she'd seen the light slanting under his door well into the night on several occasions.

Brooding, she thought with an impatient shake of her head. And if he wasn't brooding, he was looking for a fight.

She had broken up what would certainly have been bloodshed over the weekend when she walked in on the three brothers going nose to nose in the boatyard, Seth looking on with avid interest.

Whatever had caused it remained a mystery as she'd bounced straight off that same united male wall. Shrugs and snarls were all she got for her trouble.

Well, it was going to stop, she decided, and attacked some chickweed with enthusiasm. Women knew how to share and discuss. And if she had to bang Grace Monroe over the head with her garden spade, Grace was damn well going to share and discuss.

It was with pleasure that she heard Grace's car pull in. Anna tipped back her hat, rose, and offered a welcoming smile. "Hi, there."

"Hello, Anna. I thought you'd be at work."

"Took a mental health day." Oh, yes, misery here as well, she mused. And not quite as well coated as Ethan's. "You didn't bring Aubrey with you."

"No. My mother wanted her today." Grace ran a hand up and

down the strap of the oversized bag over her shoulder. "Well, I'll get started and let you get back to your gardening."

"I was just looking for an excuse to take a break. Why don't we sit down on the porch a minute?"

"I really should get the first load of laundry in."

"Grace." Anna laid a gentle hand on her arm. "Sit down. Talk to me. I count you as one of my friends. I hope you count me as one of yours."

"I do." Grace's voice wavered. She had to take three breaths to steady it. "I do, Anna."

"Then let's sit down. Tell me what's happened to make you and Ethan so unhappy."

"I don't know if I can." But she was tired, bone-tired, so she sat down on the steps. "I guess I made a mess of everything."

"How?"

She'd cried herself dry, Grace thought. Not that it had helped. Maybe it would help to talk things over with another woman, one she was beginning to feel close to. "I let myself assume," she began. "I let myself plan. He picked me flowers," she said with a helpless lift of her hands.

"Picked you flowers?" Anna's eyes narrowed fractionally. Rabbits, my butt, she thought, but filed it away for later retribution.

"And he took me to dinner. Candles and wine. I thought he was going to ask me to marry him. Ethan does things stage by stage, and I thought he was leading up to proposing."

"Of course you did. You're in love with each other. He's devoted to Aubrey and she adores him. You're both nesters. Why wouldn't you think it?"

Grace stared for a moment, then let out a long breath. "I can't tell you what it means to hear you say that. I felt like such a fool."

"Well, stop. You're not a fool. I'm not, and I certainly thought it."

"We were both wrong. He didn't ask me. But he loved me that night, Anna. So tenderly. I never believed anyone would feel so much for me. He had a nightmare later."

"A nightmare."

"Yes." And she understood it now. "It was bad, very bad, but he pretended it wasn't. He told me not to worry and brushed it off. So I didn't think any more about it. Then." Thoughtfully, she rubbed a faint bruise on her thigh that she'd given herself bumping into a table at Shiney's.

"The next day I decided if I sat around waiting for Ethan to do the asking, I'd have gray hair on my wedding day. Ethan doesn't exactly rush through life."

"No, he doesn't. He gets things done in his own time, and gets them done well. But he could sure use a poke now and then."

"He does, doesn't he?" She couldn't stop the warm, wistful smile. "Sometimes he just thinks things to death. And I thought this was going to be one of those times, so I made up my mind to do the asking myself."

"You asked Ethan to marry you?" Anna chuckled, leaned back on the steps. "Atta girl, Grace."

"I had it all worked out. Everything I wanted to say and how to say it. I thought, on the water where he's most content, so I asked him to take me out for an evening sail. It was so lovely, with the sun setting and the sails bright and full of wind. And I asked him."

Anna slipped a hand over Grace's. "I gather he turned you down. But—"

"It was more than that. If you'd seen his face . . . He went so cold. He said he'd explain things to me when we got back. And he did. I don't feel right telling you, Anna, because it's Ethan's business. But he said he can't marry me, won't marry me or anyone. Ever."

Anna didn't speak for a moment. She was Seth's caseworker,

which meant she'd had full access to the files on the three men who would stand as his guardians. She knew their pasts nearly as well as they did. "Is it because of what happened to him as a child?"

Grace's gaze flickered, then she stared straight ahead. "He told you?"

"No, but I know about it, most of it. It's part of my job."

"You know . . . what his mother—that woman—did to him, let other people do to him? He was only a little boy."

"I know that she forced him to have sex with clients for several years before she abandoned him. There are still copies of the medical reports in his file. I know that he was raped and beaten before Stella Quinn found him in the hospital. And I know what that kind of trauma, that kind of consistent abuse can do. Ethan could very well have become an abuser himself. It's a miserably common cycle."

"But he didn't."

"No, he became a thoughtful, considerate man with nearly unflappable control. The scars are there, under it. It's likely that his relationship with you has brought some of them closer to the surface."

"He won't let me help. Anna, he's got it into his head that he can't risk having children because he's got her blood in him. Bad blood that he would pass on. He won't marry because marriage means family to him."

"He's wrong, and he has the best example of how wrong in his own mirror. He not only has her blood but he spent the first twelve years—the most impressionable years—with her in an environment that could warp any young mind. Instead, he's Ethan Quinn. Why should his children—children that come from the two of you—be any less than he is?"

"I wish I had thought to say that," Grace murmured. "I was so shocked and sad and shaken." She closed her eyes. "I don't think it would have mattered if I had. He wasn't going to listen. Not to me," she said slowly. "He doesn't think I'm strong enough to live with what he's lived with."

"He's wrong."

"Yes, he's wrong. But his mind's made up. He won't want me now. He says the choice is mine, but I know him. If I say I can accept this and we go on as we are, it'll eat at him until he pulls away."

"Can you accept it?"

"I've asked myself that, thought about that for days now. I love him enough to want to, maybe to settle for it, at least for a while. But it would eat at me, too." She shook her head. "No, I can't accept it. I can't accept only one part of him. And I won't ask Aubrey to accept anything less than a father."

"Good for you. Now, what are you going to do about it?"

"I don't know that there's anything I can do. Not when we both need different things."

Anna let out a huff of breath. "Grace, you're the only one who can decide. But let me tell you, Cam and I didn't just float to the altar on gossamer wings. We wanted different things—or thought we did. And to find out what we wanted together, we hurt each other, we got in each other's faces and we dealt with it."

"It's hard to get in Ethan's face about anything."

"But it's not impossible."

"No, it's not impossible, but . . . He wasn't honest with me, Anna. Underneath it all, I can't forget that. He let me spin my daydreams, all the time knowing he was going to cut the threads of them and let me fall. He's sorry for it, I know, but still . . ."

"You're angry."

"Yes, I guess I am. I had another man do that to me. My father," she added, coolly now. "I wanted to be a dancer, and he knew I was pinning my hopes on it. I can't say he ever encouraged me, but he let me go on taking lessons and wishing. And when I needed him to stand up and help me try for that dream . . . he cut the threads. I forgave him for it, or tried to, but things were never the same. Then I got pregnant and married Jack. I guess you could say that cut his threads, and he's never forgiven me."

"Have you tried to resolve things there?"

"No, I haven't. He gave me a choice, too, just like Ethan did. Or what they seem to think of as a choice. Do this their way. Accept it, or do without them. So I'll do without."

"I understand that. But while it may buffer your pride, what does it do to your heart?"

"When people break your heart, pride's all you've got left."

And pride, Anna thought, could turn cold and bitter without heart. "Let me talk to Ethan."

"I'll talk to him, as soon as I can work out what needs to be said." She blew out a breath. "I feel better," she realized. "It helps to say it all out loud. And there was no one else I could say it to."

"I care about both of you."

"I know. We'll be all right." She gave Anna's hand a squeeze before she rose. "You helped me stop feeling weepy. I hate feeling weepy. Now I'm going to work off some of this mad I didn't realize was in there." She managed to smile. "You're going to have a damn clean house when I'm done. I clean like a maniac when I'm working off a mad."

Don't work it all off, Anna thought, as Grace went inside. Save some of it for that idiot Ethan.

⌇⌇⌇

IT TOOK TWO and a half hours for Grace to scrub, rinse, dust, and polish her way through the second floor. She had a bad moment in Ethan's room, where the scent of him, of the sea, clung to the air, and the small, careless pieces of his daily life were scattered about.

But she drew herself in, calling on the same core of steel that had gotten her through a divorce and a painful family rift.

Work helped, as it always had. Good, strenuous manual labor kept both her hands and her mind busy. Life went on. She knew it firsthand. And you got through from one day to the next.

She had her child. She had her pride. And she still had dreams—though she'd come to the point that she preferred to think of them as plans.

She could live without Ethan. Not as fully perhaps, not as joyfully, certainly. But she could live and be productive and find contentment in the path she forged for herself and her daughter.

She was finished with tears and self-pity.

She started on the main floor with the same single-minded fervor. Furniture was polished until it gleamed. Glass was scrubbed until it sparkled. She hung out wash, swept porches, and battled dirt as if it were an enemy threatening to take over the earth.

By the time she got to the kitchen her back ached, but it was a small and satisfying pain. Her skin wore a light coat of sweat, her hands were pruny from wash water, and she felt as accomplished as a corporate president after a major business coup.

She checked the clock, measured time. She wanted to be finished and gone before Ethan came in from work. Despite the purging wrought by labor, there was a small, simmering ember of anger still burning in her heart. She knew herself well enough to understand that it would take very little to fan it to full flame.

If she fought with him, if she said even a portion of the things that had careened through her head over the last few days, they would never be able to be civil again, much less friends.

She wouldn't force the Quinns to take sides. And she wouldn't risk putting her precious and vital relationship with Seth at risk because two adults in his life couldn't mind their tempers.

"I won't lose my job over it, either," she muttered as she went to work on the countertops. "Just because he can't see what he's throwing out of his life."

She hissed out a breath, scooped her fingers through her hair, which the heat and her exertion had dampened at the temples. And calmed herself by giving the drip pans on the ancient range a good scouring.

When the phone rang, she snatched it up without thinking. "Hello?"

"Anna Quinn?"

Grace glanced out the window, saw Anna puttering happily among the back garden. "No, I'll—"

"I got something to say to you, bitch."

Grace stopped, two steps from the screen door. "What?"

"This is Gloria DeLauter. Who the hell do you think you are, threatening me?"

"I'm not—"

"I got rights. Do you hear me? I got fucking rights. The old man made a deal with me, and if you and your bastard husband and his bastard brothers don't live up to it, you're the ones who'll be sorry."

The voice wasn't just hard and harsh, Grace realized. It was manic, the words shooting out so fast that one ran into the back of the other. This was Seth's mother, she thought as more abuse rang in her ear. The woman who'd hurt him, who frightened him. Who'd taken money for him.

Sold him.

She wasn't aware that she had twisted the phone cord around her hand, that it was so tightly wrapped it bit into the flesh. Struggling for calm, she took a deep breath. "Miss DeLauter, you're making a mistake."

"You're the one who made the goddamn mistake, sending me

that fucking letter instead of the money you owe me. You fucking *owe* me. You think I'm scared 'cause you're some asshole social worker. I don't give a shit if you're the goddamn Queen of goddamn England. The old man's dead, and if you want things to stay like they are you're going to deal with me. You think you can hold me off with words on paper? You're not going to stop me if I decide to come back and take that boy."

"You're wrong," Grace heard herself say, but her voice sounded far away, echoing in her head.

"He's my flesh and blood and I got a right to take what's mine."

"Try it." Rage tore through her like a storm surge. "You'll never put your hands on him again."

"I can do what I like with what's mine."

"He's not yours. You sold him. Now he's ours, and you're never going to get near him."

"He'll do what the hell I tell him to do. He knows he'll pay for it otherwise."

"You make one move toward him, I'll take you apart myself. Nothing you've done to him, however monstrous, is close to what I'll do to you. When I'm finished, they'll barely have enough left to scrape up and toss in a cell. That's just where you'll go for child abuse, neglect, assault, prostitution, and whatever it is they call a mother who sells her child to men for sex."

"What kind of lies has that brat been telling? I never laid a finger on him."

"Shut up. You shut the hell up." She'd lost track, mixed Seth's mother and Ethan's into one woman. One monster. "I know what you did to him, and there isn't a cage dark enough to lock you in to suit me. But I'll find one, and I'll shove you in it myself if you come near him again."

"I just want money." There was a wheedle in the voice now, both sly and a little scared. "Just some money to help me through. You've got plenty."

"I don't have anything for you but contempt. You stay away from here, and you stay away from that child, or you'll be the one who pays."

"You better think again. You just better think again." There was a muffled sound, then the clink of ice against glass. "You're no better than me. I'm not afraid of you."

"You should be afraid. You should be terrified."

"I'm . . . I'm not finished with this. I'm not done."

The click of the disconnect was loud. "Maybe not," Grace said in a soft and dangerous voice. "But neither am I."

"Gloria DeLauter," Anna murmured. She stood just on the other side of the screen door, where she'd been for the last two minutes.

"I don't think she's human. If she'd been here, if she'd been in this room, I'd have had my hands around her throat. I'd have choked her like an animal." She began to shake now, fury and reaction crashing against each other inside her. "I'd have killed her. Or tried."

"I know how it feels. It's hard to think about someone like her as a person and not a thing." Anna pushed the door open, her eyes on Grace. She would never have expected to see that white-hot rage in such a mild-tempered woman. "I see it all too often in my work, but I never get used to it."

"She was foul." Grace shuddered. "She thought I was you when I answered the phone. I tried to tell her at first, but she wouldn't listen. She just shouted and threatened and swore. I couldn't let her get away with it. I couldn't stand it. I'm sorry."

"It's all right. From the end of the conversation I could hear, I'd say you handled it. You want to sit down?"

"No, I can't. I can't sit." She shut her eyes, but still only saw that blinding red haze. "Anna, she said she'd come back and get Seth if you didn't give her money."

"That's not going to happen." Anna moved to the refrigerator, pulled out a bottle of wine. "I'm going to pour you a glass of this. You're going to drink it, slowly, while I get my notebook. Then I want you to try to tell me what she said, as close as possible to exactly what she said. Can you do that?"

"I can. I can remember."

"Good." Anna glanced at the clock. "We're going to want to document everything. If she does come back, we're going to be ready."

"Anna." Grace stared down into the wine Anna had given her. "He can't be hurt anymore. He shouldn't have to be afraid anymore."

"I know it. We'll make sure he's not. I'll only be a minute."

ANNA TOOK HER through the conversation twice. As she went through it the second time, Grace found herself unable to sit. She rose, leaving her glass of wine half full, and got a broom.

"The way she said things was every bit as vile as what she said," she told Anna as she began to sweep. "She must use that same tone on Seth. I don't know how anyone can speak to a child that way." Then she shook her head. "But she doesn't think of him as a child. He's a thing to her."

"If you were called on to testify, you'd be able to swear under oath that she demanded money."

"More than once," Grace agreed. "Will it come to that, Anna? Will you have to take Seth into court?"

"I don't know. If it heads in that direction, we should be able to add extortion to the list of charges you reeled off. You must have scared her," she added with a small, satisfied smile. "You'd have scared me."

"Things just come flying out of my mouth when I get worked up."

"I know what you mean. There are things I'd like to say to her, but in my position, I can't. Or I shouldn't," she said with a long sigh. "I'll type this up for Seth's file, then I suppose I'll have to compose another letter to her."

"Why?" Grace's fingers tightened on the handle of the broom. "Why do you have to have any contact with her?"

"Cam and his brothers need to know, Grace. They need to know exactly what Gloria DeLauter and Seth were to Ray."

"It's not what some people are saying." Grace's eyes flashed as she yanked a dustpan out of the broom closet. She couldn't seem to sweep away the simmering anger inside her. "Professor Quinn wouldn't have cheated on his wife. He was devoted to her."

"They need to have all the facts, and so does Seth."

"I'll give you a fact. Professor Quinn had taste. He wouldn't have looked twice at a woman like Gloria DeLauter—unless it was with pity, or disgust."

"Cam certainly feels the same way. But another thing people say is that when they look at Seth they see Ray Quinn's eyes."

"Well, there's another explanation for it, that's all." Her own eyes were hot as she shoved the broom and dustpan away, yanked out a bucket and a mop.

"Perhaps. But it may have to be faced and dealt with that the Quinns hit a rocky patch in their marriage, as people often do. Extramarital affairs are distressingly common."

"I don't give a damn about all the statistics you hear on television or read in magazines about how three out of five men—or whatever it is—cheat on their wives." Grace dumped cleanser in the bucket, dropped it into the sink, and turned the water on full blast. "The Quinns loved each other, and they liked each other. And they had an admiration for each other. You couldn't be around them and not see it. They were tied only tighter together because of their sons. When you saw the five of them together, you were seeing family. Just the way the five of you are family."

Touched, Anna smiled. "Well, we're working on it."

"You just haven't had as many years as the Quinns did." Grace hauled the bucket out of the sink. "They were a unit."

Units, Anna thought, often broke down. "If something had happened between Ray and Gloria, would Stella have forgiven him?"

Grace thrust the mop into the bucket and gave Anna a cool, decisive look. "Would you forgive Cam?"

"I don't know," Anna said after a moment. "It would be hard to because I'd have killed him. But I might, eventually, put flowers on his grave."

"Exactly." Satisfied, Grace nodded. "That kind of betrayal doesn't swallow down easily. And it follows that if the Quinns had that kind of tension between them, their sons would have known it. Children aren't fools, no matter how many adults might think so."

"No, they're not," Anna murmured. "Whatever the truth is, they need to find it. I'm going to type up my notes," she said as she rose. "Will you take a look at them, see if there's anything you want to add or change before they go into the file?"

"All right. I've still got some wash to hang out, then I'll be . . ."

They heard it at the same time, the wildly happy barking of dogs. Grace's reaction was pure distress. She'd lost track of the time, and Ethan was home.

Going on instinct, Anna slipped her notebook into a kitchen drawer. "I want to talk to Cam about this before we tell Seth about the phone call."

"Yes, that's best. I . . ."

"You can go out the back, Grace," Anna said quietly. "Nobody could blame you for not wanting another emotional hit today."

"I have wash to hang out."

"You've done more than enough for one afternoon."

Grace straightened her shoulders. "I finish what I start." She turned into the laundry room and the lid of the washer clanged as she tossed it up. "Which is more than can be said of some people."

Anna lifted a brow. Ethan was in for a surprise, she decided. And wasn't it handy that she was around to see him get it?

WHEN he saw her car in the driveway, Ethan had to force himself not to rush into the house just for a look at her. A quick glimpse, just one. He could take all of her into his mind with just one look.

He hadn't known it was possible to miss a woman—to miss anything—the way he was missing Grace.

The way, he thought, that left him empty and achy and edgy every hour of every day until he was desperate to fill the void. Until he laid awake at night listening to the air breathe.

Until he thought he was losing his mind.

The control he'd kept in place for so many years where she was concerned seemed constantly shaky these days. The walls of that control had already been breached, were tumbled at his feet so that he could swear he was choking on their dust.

He supposed once a man let it go, it was hard to build it back up again.

But he'd left the choice in her hands, he reminded himself. Since she hadn't made a move in his direction in days, he was afraid he knew which choice she'd made.

He couldn't blame her for it.

She would find someone else—someone she could make a life with. The thought burned in his gut as he loitered by his truck, but he refused to let it pass. She deserved to have what she wanted out of life. That was marriage and children and a pretty home. A father for Aubrey, a man who would appreciate both of them for the treasures they were.

Another man.

Another man who would slip his arms around her waist, rub his mouth over hers. Hear her breath quicken, feel her bones go soft.

Some faceless son of a bitch who wasn't good enough for her would turn to her in the night, sink inside her. And smile every goddamn morning because he knew he could do it again.

Christ, Ethan thought, it was making him crazy.

Foolish bumped into his legs, a ratty tennis ball clamped hopefully in his mouth, his tail wagging persuasively. In a habitual move, Ethan tugged the ball free and tossed it. Foolish bounded after it, yapping furiously when Simon darted like a bullet from the left and intercepted.

Ethan only sighed when Simon pranced back, sat, and waited for the game to continue.

It was as good an excuse as any to stay outside, Ethan decided. He would fool with the dogs, go fiddle with his boat, stay out of Grace's way. If she had wanted to see him, she could have found him.

The dogs worked him around the side yard, and taking pity on the slower, less skilled Foolish, Ethan found a stick to toss along with the ball. It lightened his mood a little to watch them bash into each other, wrestle, fetch, and retrieve.

You could depend on a dog, he thought, giving the ball a higher, harder toss that sent Simon bounding in pursuit. They never asked for more than you could give them.

He didn't see Grace until he was well around the house. Then he simply stood.

No, one look, one quick glimpse, wasn't enough. Would never be enough.

The sheet she lifted to the line flapped wetly in the breeze as she pegged it. The sun was on her hair. As he watched, she bent to the basket, took out a pillowcase, gave it a quick snap, then clipped it beside the sheet.

Love flooded into him, swamped him, left him weak and needy. Small details hammered him—the curve of her cheek in profile. Had he ever noticed how elegant her profile was? The way her hair sat on her head, feathered at the back of her neck. Was she letting it grow? The way the trim cuff of her shorts skimmed her thigh. She had such long, smooth thighs.

Foolish rapped his head against Ethan's leg and snapped him back.

Abruptly nervous, he wiped his hands on his work pants, shifted his feet. It was probably best, he decided, if he just slipped back around the front, went into the house and upstairs. He took the first step back, then pulled up short when she turned. She gave him a long look, one he couldn't read, then bent to take out another pillowcase.

"Hello, Ethan."

"Grace." He tucked his hands in his pockets. It wasn't often he heard her voice quite so cool.

"It's foolish to go all the way back around to the front of the house just to avoid me."

"I was . . . going to check something on the boat."

"That's fine. You can do that after I talk to you."

"I wasn't sure you'd want to talk to me." He approached her cautiously. Her tone of voice took the blistering heat right out of the day.

"I tried to talk to you the other night, but you weren't inclined to listen." She reached into the basket, apparently unperturbed that she was now hanging his underwear. "Then I needed a little time to myself, to settle everything in my head."

"And have you?"

"Oh, I think so. First, I should tell you that what you told me about what you went through before you came here shocked me, and it hurt me, and I have nothing but pity for that little boy and rage about what happened to him." She glanced at him as she secured the next clothespin. "You don't want to hear that. You don't want to think that I have feelings about it, that it touched me."

"No," he said evenly. "No, I didn't want it to touch you."

"Because I'm so fragile. Because I'm so delicate of nature."

His brows drew together. "Partly. And—"

"So you hoarded that nasty little seed all for yourself," she went on, calmly working her way down the clothesline. "Even though there's nothing in or of my life that you don't know. It's the way it should be, in your opinion, that I'm an open book and you're a closed one."

"No, it wasn't that. Exactly."

"What could it have been exactly?" she wondered, but he didn't think it was a question and wisely formed no answer. "I've been thinking about that, Ethan. I've been thinking about a number of things. Why don't we go back a ways first? You like to do things in neat, logical steps. And since you like things to be done your way, we'll just be neat and logical."

The dogs, sensing trouble, retreated to the water. Ethan found himself envying them.

"You told me you've loved me for years. Years," she said with such quick fury that he nearly stumbled back. "But you don't do anything about it. You don't once, not once, come up to me and ask me if I'd like to spend some time with you. One word from you, one look from you, would have thrilled me. But oh, no, not Ethan Quinn, not with his broody mind and incredible control. You just kept your distance and let me pine over you."

"I didn't know you had those kind of feelings for me."

"Then you're blind as well as stupid," she snapped.

His brows drew together. "Stupid?"

"That's what I said." Seeing the outrage cross his face was balm to her battered ego. "I would never have looked twice at Jack Casey if you'd given me anything to hope for. But I needed someone to want me, and it sure as hell didn't appear it was ever going to be you."

"Now just a damn minute. I'm not to blame for you marrying Jack."

"No, I take the blame. I take the responsibility, and I don't regret it because it gave me Aubrey. But I blame you, Ethan." And those gold-flecked green eyes blazed with it. "I blame you for being too pigheaded to take what you wanted. And you haven't changed a damn bit."

"You were too young—"

She used both hands, and all the force of her temper went into the shove. "Oh, shut up. You had your say. Now I'm having mine."

⁂

IN THE KITCHEN, Seth's eyes went hot. He made a dash for the door, only to be brought up short by Anna, who was eavesdropping as hard as she could.

"No, you don't."

"He yelled at her."

"She's yelling, too."

"He's fighting with her. I'm going to stop him."

Anna cocked her head. "Does she look like she needs any help?"

His mouth set, Seth glared through the screen. Then reconsidered when he saw Grace shove Ethan back a full step. "I guess not."

"She can handle him." Amused, she gave Seth a scrubbing pat on the top of the head. "How come you don't leap to my defense when Cam and I argue?"

"Because he's afraid of you."

Anna rolled her tongue into her cheek, enjoying the idea. "Oh, really?"

"Half afraid, anyway," Seth said with a grin. "He never knows what you'll do. And besides, you guys like to argue."

"Observant little brat, aren't you?"

He shrugged, cheerful now. "I see what I see."

"And know what you know." Laughing, she edged closer to the door with him, hoping for a better view.

"LET'S MOVE TO the next step, Ethan." Grace shoved the empty basket out of her way with her foot. "Fast-forward a few years. Think you can keep up?"

He took a long breath because he didn't want to yell at her again. "You're pissing me off, Grace."

"Good. I mean to, and I hate to fail at something I'm working on."

He wasn't sure which emotion came out on top, annoyance or bafflement. "What's gotten into you?"

"Oh, I don't know, Ethan. Let's see—could it be the fact that you think I'm some brainless, helpless female? Yes, you know . . ." She jabbed her index finger into his chest like a drill into wood. "I bet that's just what's gotten into me."

"I don't think you're brainless."

"Oh, just helpless, then." Even as he opened his mouth she was rolling over him. "Do you think a helpless woman can do what I've been doing the last few years? Do you think— What was it you called me once—delicate, like your mama's good china? I'm not china!" she exploded. "I'm good solid stoneware, the kind you can drop and it rattles around on the floor. It doesn't shatter. You have to *work* to break good stoneware, Ethan, and I'm not broken yet."

She punched a finger into his chest again, darkly pleased when his eyes flashed a warning. "I wasn't so helpless when I got you into my bed, was I? Which is just where I wanted you."

"You didn't get me anywhere."

"Hell, I didn't. And *you're* brainless if you think differently. I reeled you in like a goddamn rockfish."

It gave her pleasure, oh, such vivid pleasure, to see both fury and frustration race over his face. "If you think a statement like that flatters either of us—"

"I'm not trying to flatter you. I'm telling you straight out, I wanted you and I went after you. If I'd left the matter up to you, we'd have been pinching each other's butts in a nursing home."

"Jesus, Grace."

"Just be quiet." There was no stopping now, whatever the consequences, not with this roaring sea crashing in her head. "You just think about that, Ethan Quinn. You give that some good long thought and don't you *dare* call me fragile again."

He gave her a slow nod. "It's not the word that's coming to mind at the moment."

"Good. I haven't needed you or anyone to help me build a decent life for my baby. I used muscle, and I used guts to do what needed to be done, so don't you tell me I'm china."

"You wouldn't have had to do it all alone if you weren't too damn proud to settle things with your father."

The truth of that put a hitch in her step. But she balled her fists and rushed on. "We're talking about you and me. You say you love me, Ethan, but you don't for one minute understand me."

"I'm starting to agree with that," he muttered.

"You've got some ego-ridden male idea in your head that I need to be taken care of, protected, coddled—when what I need is to be needed and respected and loved. And you'd know that if you paid attention. You ask yourself this, Ethan, who seduced whom? Who said 'I love you' first. Who proposed marriage? Are you so near-sighted you can't see I've had to take every step first with you?"

"You make it sound like you've been leading me by the nose, Grace. I don't care for that."

"I couldn't lead you by the nose if I jabbed a fish hook in it. You go exactly where you want to go, Ethan, but you can be so infuriatingly slow. I love that about you, and I admire it, and now I understand it more. You had a terrible period in your life when you had no control, now you take care not to lose it. But you can slip from control into stubbornness in one short step, and that's just what you've done."

"I'm not being stubborn. I'm being right."

"Right? It's right for two people to love each other and not build a life out of it? It's right to pay all your life for what someone else did to you when you were too young to defend yourself against it? Is it right for you to say you can't and won't marry me because you're . . . stained and you made some ridiculous promise to yourself never to have a family of your own?"

It sounded off when she said it like that. It sounded . . . stupid. "It's the way it is."

"Because you say so."

"I told you how it is, Grace. I gave you the choice."

Her jaw hurt from clenching it. "People like to say they've given somebody a choice when what they're really saying is 'do this my way.' I don't like your way, Ethan. Your way only takes into account what was and doesn't add what is, or what could be. You think I don't know what you expected? You'd take your stand and sweet, delicate Grace would just fall in line."

"I didn't expect you to fall in line."

"Then crawl off, wounded, and pine after you for the rest of my life. You're getting neither. I'll give you a choice this time, Ethan. You straighten yourself out, you go on and think things through for the next eon or two, then you let me know what conclusions you've come to. Because my stand is this. It's marriage or it's nothing. I'll be damned if I'll spend the rest of my life pining over you. I can live without you." She tossed back her head. "Let's see if you're man enough to live without me."

She whirled around and stalked off, leaving him fuming.

⁘

"UPSTAIRS," ANNA HISSED at Seth. "He's coming inside. Now it's my turn."

"Are you going to yell at him, too?"

"Maybe."

"I want to watch."

"Not this time." She all but shoved him out of the room. "Upstairs. I mean it."

"Hell." He stomped to the stairs, waited a moment, then slipped back down the hallway.

Anna was pouring herself a homey cup of coffee when Ethan slammed the back door. Part of her wanted to go over and give him a big, sympathetic hug. He looked so miserably unhappy and confused. But the way she figured it, there were times when it was best all around to kick a good man when he was down.

"Want some?"

He flicked a glance at her and kept walking. "No, thanks."

"Hold it." She smiled sweetly when he stopped, when she all but saw the jittery waves of impatience shimmering around him. "I need to talk to you for a minute."

"I'm about talked out for the day."

"That's all right." Deliberately she pulled a chair out from the table. "You sit down and I'll talk."

Women, Ethan decided as he dropped into the chair, were the bane of his existence. "I guess I'll take the coffee, then."

"All right." She poured him a mug, brought him a spoon so he could dump his customary heaps of sugar into it. She sat, folded her hands neatly, and continued to smile.

"You stupid jerk."

"Oh, Jesus." He rubbed his hands over his face, left them there. "Not another one."

"I'm going to make it easy on you at first. I'll ask a question, you answer. Are you in love with Grace?"

"Yes, but—"

"No qualifications." Anna cut him off. "The answer is yes. Is Grace in love with you?"

"Hard to say just now." He shifted his hand to nurse the point on his chest where she'd all but bored a hole in him.

"The answer is yes," Anna said coolly. "Are you both single, otherwise unattached adults?"

He could feel himself sinking into a sulk, and detested it. "Yeah—so?"

"Just laying the groundwork, gathering the facts. Grace has a child, correct?"

"You know damn well—"

"Correct." Anna lifted her cup, took a sip of coffee. "Do you have feelings of affection for Aubrey?"

"Of course I do. I love her. Who wouldn't?"

"And does she have feelings of affection for you?"

"Sure. What—"

"Wonderful. We've established the emotions of the parties involved. Now let's move on to stability. You have a profession, and a new business. You appear to be a man with skill, who's willing to work and has the capability of earning a good living. Have you incurred any large, outstanding debts you believe you'll have difficulty meeting?"

"For God's sake!"

"No offense intended," she said brightly. "I'm simply approaching this matter the way I assume you would, calmly, patiently, step by tedious step."

He narrowed his eyes at her. "Seems to me people are having major problems with how I do things lately."

"I love the way you do things." She reached across the table and gave his tense hand an affectionate squeeze. "I love you, Ethan. It's wonderful for me to have a big brother at this stage of my life."

He shifted in his chair. He was touched by the obvious sincerity in her eyes, but he had a feeling she was tenderizing him in preparation for the roasting to come. "I don't know what's going on around here."

"I think you'll figure it out. So, we'll say you're financially sound. Grace, as we know, is well capable of earning a living. You own your own home, and a one-third share in this one. Shelter certainly isn't an issue. So, we'll move on. Do you believe in the institution of marriage?"

He knew a trick question when he heard one. "It works for some people. Doesn't work for others."

"No, no, do you believe in the institution itself? Yes or no."

"Yes, but—"

"Then why the hell aren't you down on one knee with a ring in your big, clumsy hand, begging the woman you love to give your fat head another chance?"

"I'm a patient man," Ethan said slowly, "but I'm getting tired of insults."

"Don't you dare get out of that chair," she warned when he started to scrape it back. "I swear I'll belt you. God knows I want to."

"That's another thing that's going around." He subsided only because it seemed easier to get it all over with at once. "Go ahead then, say what you have to say."

"You think I don't understand. You think I can't relate to what's eating you up inside. You're wrong. I was raped when I was ten years old."

Shock jolted his heart, pain squeezed his soul. "Jesus, Anna! Jesus, I'm sorry. I didn't know."

"Now you do. Does it change me, Ethan? Aren't I the same person I was thirty seconds ago?" She reached for his hand again, held it this time. "I know what it is to be helpless and terrified and want to die. And I know what it is to make something of your life, despite that. And I know what it is to have that horror in you always. No matter how much you've learned, no matter how much you've come to accept it and know it was never, ever your fault."

"It's not the same."

"It's never the same, not for any two people. We have something more in common as well. I never knew who my father was. Was he a good man or a bad one? Tall or short? Did he love my mother, or did he use her? I don't know what parts of him were passed to me."

"But you knew your mother."

"Yes, and she was wonderful. Beautiful. And yours wasn't. She beat you, physically and emotionally. She made you a victim. Why are you letting her keep you one? Why are you letting her win even now?"

"It's me now, Anna. There has to be something twisted, something sour inside a person to make them the way she was. I came from that."

"Sins of the fathers, Ethan?"

"I'm not taking on her sins, I'm talking about heredity. You can pass on the color of your eyes, your build. Weak hearts, alcoholism, longevity. Those things can run in families."

"You've given this a lot of thought."

"Yeah, I have. I had to make a decision, and I made it."

"So you decided you could never marry or have children."

"It wouldn't be fair."

"Well, then, you'd better talk to Seth before too long."

"Seth?"

"Someone has to tell him he's never going to be able to have a wife and children. It's best if he knows that early, so he can try to protect himself from becoming emotionally involved with a woman."

For a trio of heartbeats he could only gape at her. "What the hell are you talking about?"

"Heredity. We can't be sure what bad traits Gloria DeLauter passed down to him. God knows she's got something twisted inside her, just as you said. A whore, a drunk, a junkie, from all accounts."

"There's nothing wrong with that boy."

"What difference does that make?" She met Ethan's furious stare blandly. "He shouldn't be allowed to take chances."

"You can't mix him in with me this way."

"I don't see why. You both come from similar situations. In fact, there are far too many cases that come through social services nationally that slip into parallel categories. I wonder if we can pass a law to prevent children of abusers from marrying and having children of their own. Think of the risks we'd avoid."

"Why don't you just geld them?" he said viciously.

"That's an interesting concept." She leaned forward. "Since you're so determined not to pass on any unhealthy genes, Ethan, have you considered a vasectomy?"

The instinctive and purely male cringe nearly made her laugh. "That's enough, Anna."

"Is that what you would recommend to Seth?"

"I said that's enough."

"Oh, it's more than enough," she agreed. "But answer this last question. Do you think that bright, troubled child should be denied a full and normal life as an adult because he had the bad luck to be conceived by a heartless, perhaps even evil woman?"

"No." His breath shuddered out. "No, that's not what I think."

"No buts this time? No qualifications? Then I'll tell you that in my professional opinion, I couldn't agree with you more. He deserves everything he can grab, everything he can make, and everything we can give him to show him that he's his own person and not the damaged product of one vile woman. And neither are you, Ethan, anything but your own man. Stupid, maybe," she said with a smile as she rose. "But admirable, honorable, and incredibly kind."

She went to him, put an arm around his shoulders. When he sighed, turned his face to press it against her midriff, tears stung her eyes.

"I don't know what to do."

"Yes, you do," she murmured. "Being you, you'll have to think about it for a while. But do yourself a favor this time, and think fast."

"I guess I'll go down to the boatyard and work until I get it clear in my head."

Because she was feeling suddenly maternal toward him, she bent and kissed the top of his head. "Do you want me to pack you some food?"

"No." He gave her a squeeze before he rose. When he saw that her eyes were damp, he patted her shoulder. "Don't cry. Cam'll have my head if he finds out I made you cry."

"I won't."

"Well, then." He started out, hesitated, then turned back briefly to study her as she stood in the kitchen, her lashes wet, her hair tangled from being out in the breeze. "Anna, my mother—my real mother," he added, because Stella Quinn was in his mind all that was real—"would have loved you."

Hell, Anna thought as he walked away, she was going to cry after all.

Ethan kept going, particularly when he heard Anna's sniffle. He needed to be alone, to clear out his head and let the thoughts gather again.

"Hey."

With his hand on the door, he looked over his shoulder and saw Seth on the stairs—where the boy had dashed like a skillful rabbit seconds before Ethan had started out of the kitchen.

"Hey what?"

Seth started down, slowly. He'd heard everything, every word. Even when his stomach had begun to pitch, he had stayed and listened. As he studied Ethan now, owlishly, he thought he understood. And he felt safe.

"Where you going?"

"Back to the boatyard. I got some things I want to finish up."
Ethan let the door ease closed again. There was something in the
boy's eyes, he thought. "You okay?"

"Yeah. Can I go out on the workboat with you tomorrow?"

"If you want."

"If I went with you, we'd finish sooner and be able to work on
the boat with Cam. When Phil comes down on the weekend, we
can all work on her together."

"That's how it goes," Ethan said, puzzled.

"Yeah. That's how it goes." All of them, Seth thought with a flash
of pure joy, together. "It's hard work because it's hot as a bitch in
heat."

Ethan bit back a chuckle. "Watch the mouth. Anna's in the
kitchen."

Seth shrugged, but aimed a wary glance behind him. "She's cool."

"Yeah." Ethan's smile spread. "She's cool. Don't stay up half the
night drawing or bugging your eyes out at the TV if you're working
with me in the morning."

"Yeah, yeah." Seth waited until Ethan was outside, then snatched
up the bag sitting beside the chair. "Hey!"

"Christ, boy, are you going to let me out of here before tomorrow?"

"Grace forgot her purse." Seth pushed it into Ethan's hand and
kept his face bland and innocent. "I guess she had something on her
mind when she left."

"I guess." Brows knit, Ethan stared down at it. Damn thing
weighed ten pounds if it weighed an ounce, he thought.

"You ought to take it over to her. Women go nuts if they don't
have their purses. See you."

He raced back inside, pounded up the stairs and straight to the first window that faced the front of the house. From there he could watch Ethan scratch his head, shove the purse under his arm like a football, and walk slowly to the truck.

His brothers sure could be weird, he thought. Then he grinned to himself. His brothers. Letting out a whoop, he raced down the steps to head for the kitchen and nag Anna for something to eat.

chapter 20

G RACE intended to cool off and calm down before she stopped
by her parents' house to pick up Aubrey. When she was this
emotionally churned up, there was no hiding it from anyone, much
less from a mother or a very perceptive child.

The last thing she wanted was questions. The last thing she felt
capable of giving was explanations.

She'd said what needed to be said and done what needed to be
done. And she refused to feel sorry for it. If it meant losing a
long-standing friendship, one that she had always treasured, it
couldn't be helped. Somehow she and Ethan would manage to be
adult enough to be polite when in public and not to drag anyone else
into their battles.

It certainly wouldn't be an easy or happy situation, but it could
work. The same arrangement had worked for three years with her
father, hadn't it?

She drove around for twenty minutes, until her fingers were no

longed gripping the wheel like a vise and the reflection of her face
in the rearview mirror was no longer capable of frightening children
and small dogs.

She assured herself that she was now perfectly under control. So
under control that she thought she'd take Aubrey out to McDonald's
for a treat. And on her very next evening off, she was taking them
both to Oxford for the Firemen's Carnival. She certainly wasn't
going to stay around the house moping.

She didn't slam the door of her car, which she felt was an excellent
sign of her now placid mood. Nor did she stomp up the steps of her
parents' tidy Colonial. She even paused for a moment to admire the
pale purple petunias spilling out of a hanging planter near the picture
window.

It was just bad luck and bad timing that her gaze shifted a few
inches past the blooms and that she spotted her father through that
picture window, lounging in his recliner like a king on his throne.

Temper geysered and blasted her through the door like a
sharp-edged pebble from a well-aimed slingshot.

"I have a few things to say to you." She let the door slam at her
back and marched up to where Pete rested his feet. "I've been saving
them up."

He goggled at her for the five seconds it took for him to arrange
his face. "If you want to speak to me, you'll do it in a civilized tone
of voice."

"I'm through being civilized. I've had civilized up to here." She
made a sharp slashing motion with her hand.

"Grace! Grace!" Cheeks flushed, eyes huge, Carol hustled in from
the kitchen with Aubrey on her hip. "What's gotten into you? You'll
upset the baby."

"Take Aubrey back to the kitchen, Mama. And it won't trauma-
tize her for life to hear her mother raise her voice."

As if to prove arguments were inevitable, Aubrey threw back her head and sent up a wail. Grace stifled the urge to grab her, run out of the house with her, and smother her face with kisses until the tears stopped. Instead she stood firm. "Aubrey, stop that now. I'm not mad at you. You go on in the kitchen with Grandma and have some juice."

"Juice!" Aubrey sobbed it at the top of her lungs, straining away from Carol with her arms held out to Grace and fat tears trembling on her cheeks.

"Carol, take the child in the kitchen and calm her down." Pete clamped down the exact urge as Grace's and waved a hand at his wife impatiently.

"Child hasn't shed a tear all day," he muttered, with an accusing look at Grace.

"Well, she's shedding them now," Grace snapped back, adding layers of guilt onto frustration as Aubrey's sobs echoed back from the kitchen. "And she'll forget them five minutes after they're dry. That's the beauty of being two. You get older, you don't forget tears as easily. You made me cry plenty of them."

"You don't get through parenthood without causing some tears."

"But some people can get through it without ever knowing the child they raised. You never looked at me and saw what I was."

Pete wished he was standing. He wished he had shoes on his feet. A man was at a distinct disadvantage when he was kicked back in a recliner without his damn shoes on. "I don't know what you're talking about."

"Or maybe you did—maybe I'm wrong about that. You looked, you saw, and you put it aside because it didn't fit in with what you wanted. You knew," she continued in a low voice that nonetheless snapped with fury. "You knew I wanted to be a dancer. You knew I dreamed of it, and you let me go right on. Oh, taking the lessons was fine with you. Maybe you grumbled about the cost of them from time to time, but you paid for them."

"And a pretty penny it came to over all those years."

"For what, Daddy?"

He blinked. No one had called him Daddy in nearly three years and it pinched at his heart. "Because you were set on having them."

"What was the point if you were never going to believe in me, never going to let go enough or stand by enough to let me try to take the next step?"

"This is old business, Grace. You were too young to go to New York, and it was just foolishness."

"I was young, but not too young. And if it was foolishness, it was my foolishness. I'll never know if I was good enough. I'll never know if I could have made that dream real, because when I asked you to help me reach for it, you told me I was too old for nonsense. Too old for nonsense," she repeated, "but too young to be trusted."

"I did trust you." He jerked his chair up. "And look what happened."

"Yes, look what happened. I got myself pregnant. Isn't that how you put it at the time? Like it was something I managed all by myself just to annoy you."

"Jack Casey was no damn good. I knew it the first time I laid eyes on him."

"So you said, over and over again until he took on the gleam of forbidden fruit and I couldn't resist sampling it."

Now Pete's eyes flashed and he rose out of the chair. "You're blaming me for getting yourself in trouble?"

"No, I'm to blame if there has to be blame. And I won't make excuses. But I'll tell you this—he wasn't nearly as bad as you made him out to be."

"Left you high and dry, didn't he?"

"So did you, Daddy."

His hand shot up, shocking both of them. It didn't connect, and it trembled as he lowered it. He'd never done more than paddle her bottom when she was a toddler, and even then he'd suffered more than she had because of it.

"If you'd hit me," she said, struggling to keep her voice low and even, "it would be the first real feeling you've shown me since I came to you and Mama and told you I was pregnant. I knew you'd be angry and hurt and disappointed. I was so scared. But as bad as I thought it would be, it was worse. Because you didn't stand by me. The second time, Daddy, and the most important of all, and you weren't there for me."

"A man's daughter comes in and tells him she's pregnant, that she's gone on and been with a man he took trouble to warn her away from, it takes him time to deal with it."

"You were ashamed of me, and you were angry thinking of what the neighbors were going to say. And instead of looking at me and seeing that I was scared, all you saw was that I'd made a mistake you were going to have to live with."

She turned away until she was sure, absolutely sure, there wouldn't be tears. "Aubrey is not a mistake. She's a gift."

"I couldn't love her any more than I do."

"Or me any less."

"That's not true." He began to feel sick inside and more than a little scared himself. "That's just not true."

"You stepped back when I married Jack. Stepped back from me."

"You did some stepping back yourself."

"Maybe." She turned around again. "I tried to make it once without you, putting my money away for New York. I couldn't do it on my own. I was going to make my marriage work without any help. But I couldn't do that, either. All I had left was the baby inside me, and I wasn't going to fail there, too. You never even came to the hospital when I had her."

"I did." Groping, he picked up a magazine from the table, rolled it into a tube. "I went up and looked at her through the glass. She looked just like you did. Long legs and long fingers and nothing but yellow fuzz on her head. I went and looked in your room. You were asleep. I couldn't go in. I didn't know what to say to you."

He unrolled the magazine, frowned at the fresh-faced model on the cover, then dropped it back on the table. "I guess it made me mad all over again. You'd had a baby, and you didn't have a husband, and I didn't know what to do about it. I've got strong beliefs about that kind of thing. It's hard to bend."

"I didn't need you to bend very much."

"I kept waiting for you to give me the chance to. I thought when that son of a bitch ran out on you, you'd figure out you needed some help and come home."

"So you could have told me how right you were about everything."

Something flickered in his eyes that might have been sorrow. "I guess I deserve that, I guess that's what I would've done." He sat down again. "And damn it, I was right."

She gave a half laugh, weary around the edges. "Funny how the men I love are always so damn right where I'm concerned. Am I what you'd call a delicate woman, Daddy?"

For the first time in too long to remember she saw his eyes laugh. "Hell, girl, about as delicate as a steel rod."

"That's something, anyway."

"I always wished you had a little more give in you. Instead of coming once, just once, and asking for help, you're out there cleaning other people's houses, working until all hours in a bar."

"Not you, too," she murmured and moved to the window.

"Half the time if I see you down on the waterfront you've got shadows under your eyes. 'Course, the way your mother's jabbering, that'll change before long."

She glanced over her shoulder. "Change?"

"Ethan Quinn's not a man who'll let his wife wear herself to the bone working two jobs. That's the kind of man you should have been looking at all along. Honest, dependable."

She laughed again, pushed a hand through her hair. "Mama's mistaken. I won't be marrying Ethan."

Pete started to speak again, closed his mouth. He was smart enough to learn by his mistakes. If he'd pushed her toward one man by pointing out his flaws, he might also push her away from another by listing his virtues.

"Well, you know your mother." He let it go at that. Trying to fit the words in his head, he plucked at the knee of his khakis. "I was afraid to let you go to New York," he blurted out, then shifted when she turned from the window to stare at him. "I was afraid you wouldn't come back. I was afraid, too, that you'd get yourself hurt up there. Hell, Gracie, you were only eighteen, and so damn green. I knew you were good at dancing. Everybody said so, and you always looked pretty to me. I figured if you got yourself up there and didn't get your head bashed in by some mugger, you'd find you wanted to stay. I knew you couldn't manage it unless I gave you the money to start you out, so I didn't. I thought you'd either stop wanting to go so damn bad, or if you didn't, it'd take you a year or two to put by enough."

When she said nothing, he sighed and leaned back. "A man works hard all his life building something, and while he's doing it he thinks that someday he'll pass it on to his child. My daddy passed the business on to me, and I always figured I'd pass it on to my son. Had a daughter instead, and that was fine. I never wanted to change that. But you never wanted what I was planning on giving you. Oh, you'd work. You were always a good worker, but anybody could see you were only doing a job. It wasn't going to be a life. Not your life."

"I didn't know you felt that way."

"Didn't matter how I felt. It wasn't for you, that's all. I started to think that you'd get married one day and maybe your husband would come into the business. That way I'd still be passing it on to you, and to your children."

"Then I married Jack, and you didn't get your dream, either."

His hands rested on his knees, and he lifted his fingers, let them fall. "Maybe Aubrey'll have an interest in it. I'm not planning on retiring anytime soon."

"Maybe she will."

"She's a good girl," he said, still looking down at his hands. "Happy. You . . . you're a fine mother, Grace. You're doing a better job than most under hard circumstance. You've made a good life for both of you, and done it on your own."

Her heart trembled and ached. "Thank you. Thank you for that."

"Ah . . . your mother would like it if you'd stay for dinner." Finally he looked up, and the eyes that met hers weren't cool, weren't distant. In them was both plea and apology. "I'd like it, too."

"So would I." Then she simply walked over, climbed into his lap and buried her face in his shoulder. "Oh, Daddy. I missed you."

"I missed you, Gracie." He began to rock and to weep. "I missed you, too."

❧❧❧

ETHAN SAT ON the top step of Grace's front porch and put her purse down beside him. He had to admit he'd been tempted several times to open it and poke inside to see just what a woman carted around with her that was so damned heavy and so indispensable.

But so far he'd managed to resist.

Now he wondered where she could be. He'd driven by her house nearly two hours earlier before going to the boatyard. Since her car wasn't in the drive, he didn't stop. Odds were, her door was unlocked and he could have set her purse inside the living room. But that wouldn't have accomplished anything.

He'd done some hard thinking while he worked. Some of that thinking centered on how long it was going to take her to cool off from snarling mad to mildly irritated.

He figured he could deal with mildly irritated.

He decided it was probably best that she wasn't home quite yet. It gave them both more time to settle down.

"Got it all figured out yet?"

Ethan sighed. He'd smelled his father before he heard him, before he saw him sitting comfortably on the steps, feet crossed at the ankles. It was the salted peanuts in the bag Ray had in his lap. He had always had a fondness for salted peanuts.

"Not exactly. I can't seem to think it through so it gets clear."

"Sometimes you have to go with the gut instead of the head. You've got good instincts, Ethan."

"Following instinct's what got me into this. If I hadn't touched her in the first place . . ."

"If you hadn't touched her in the first place, you'd have denied both of you something a lot of people look for all their lives and never find." Ray rattled into the bag and pulled out a handful of nuts. "Why regret something that rare and that precious?"

"I hurt her. I knew I would."

"That's where you went wrong. Not in taking love when it was offered but in not trusting it for the long haul. You disappoint me, Ethan."

It was a slap. The kind that both knew would sting the most.

Because it did, Ethan stared hard at the thirsty little pansies going leggy beside the steps. "I tried to do what I thought was right."

"For whom? For a woman who wanted to share your life, wherever that would take you? For the children you may or may not have. You're on dangerous ground when you second-guess God."

Annoyed, Ethan slanted a narrow look at his father's face. "Is there?"

"Is there what?"

"Is there a God? I figure you ought to know, seeing as you've been dead the last few months."

Ray threw back his big head, let out his wonderful rolling laugh. "Ethan, I've always appreciated your understated wit, and I wish I could discuss the mysteries of the universe with you, but time's passing."

Munching on nuts, he studied Ethan's face, and as he did, Ray's wickedly amused grin softened, warmed. "Watching you grow into a man was one of the greatest pleasures of my life. You've got a heart as big as your Bay. I hope you'll trust it. I want you to be happy. There'll be trouble coming for all of you."

"Seth?"

"He'll need his family. All his family," Ray added in a murmur, then shook his head. "There's too much misery in the short time we spend living, Ethan, to turn away happiness. You remember to value your joys." Then his eyes twinkled. "I'd brace myself, son. Your thinking time's over."

Ethan heard Grace's car, glanced toward the road. He knew without looking that his father was no longer beside him.

When Grace saw Ethan sitting on her front porch steps she wanted to lay her head on the steering wheel. She wasn't sure her heart could handle yet another trip through an emotional wringer.

Instead, she climbed out of the car and went around to unstrap the sleeping Aubrey from her car seat. With Aubrey's head heavy on her shoulder, she walked to the house and watched Ethan unfold his long legs and rise.

"I'm not willing to go through another round with you, Ethan."

"I brought your purse by. You left it at the house."

Startled, she frowned when he held it out to her. It showed just how jumbled her mind had been that she hadn't even realized she'd been without it. "Thank you."

"I need to talk to you, Grace."

"I'm sorry. I have to put Aubrey to bed."

"I'll wait."

"I said I'm not willing to talk about this again."

"I said I need to talk to you. I'll wait."

"Then you can just wait until I'm good and ready," she told him and sailed into the house.

It appeared she hadn't quite gotten down to mildly irritated, he decided. But he sat again. And he waited.

SHE TOOK HER time, stripping Aubrey down to her training pants, covering her with a soft sheet, tidying the bedroom. She went into the kitchen and poured herself a glass of lemonade she didn't want. But she drank every drop of it.

She could see him through the screen door, sitting on the steps. For a moment, she considered simply going to the door, closing it, and tossing the bolt to make her point. But she discovered she didn't have quite enough mad left to be that petty.

She opened the screen, let it close quietly.

"Is she down for the night?"

"Yes, she's had a long day. So have I. I hope this won't take long."

"I guess it doesn't have to. I want to tell you I'm sorry for hurting you, for making you unhappy." Since she didn't come down and join him on the steps, he stood and turned to her. "I went about it wrong, and I wasn't honest with you. I should have been."

"I don't doubt you're sorry, Ethan." She walked to the rail, leaned out, looked over her little patch of yard. "I don't know if we can be friends the way we were before. I know it's hard to be at odds with someone you care about. I made up with my father tonight."

"Did you?" He stepped forward, then stopped because she'd shifted away. Just a little, just enough to tell him he no longer had the right to touch. "I'm glad."

"I suppose I have you to thank for it. If I hadn't been so mad at you, I wouldn't have let myself be mad at him and get everything out. I'm grateful for that, and I appreciate your apology. Now I'm tired, so—"

"You said a lot of things to me today." She wasn't going to brush him off until he'd finished.

"Yes, I did." She shifted again, met his gaze straight on.

"Some of it was right, but not all. Not acting on how I felt about you before . . . it's the way it had to be."

"Because you say so."

"Because you couldn't have been more than fourteen when I started loving you, and wanting you. I was close to eight years older. I was a man when you were still a girl. It would have been wrong to touch you then. Maybe I waited too long." He stopped, shook his head. "I did wait too long. But I'd had time to think it through and I'd promised myself I wouldn't get you tangled up with me. You were the only one who I wanted enough that it mattered. Part of it was for me because I knew if I ever had you I wouldn't want to let you go."

"And you'd already decided that you would."

"I'd decided that I was going to live my life pretty much alone. I was managing that well enough until recently."

"You see it as a noble sacrifice. I see it as ignorance." She lifted her hands, knowing she was heating up again. "I guess we'd better leave it at that."

"You know damn well that if we were to get married you'd want more children."

"Yes, I would. And while I'll never agree with your reasoning for not making them together, there are other ways to make a family. You of all people should know. We could have adopted children."

He stared at her. "You . . . I figured you'd want to get pregnant."

"You figured right. I would want it because I would treasure your child living inside me, and knowing you were there with us. But that doesn't mean I couldn't find another way. What if I couldn't have children, Ethan? What if we were in love and planning to be married, and we found out I couldn't have babies? Would you stop loving me because of it? Would you tell me you couldn't marry me?"

"No, of course not. That's—"

"That's not love," she finished. "But it's not a matter of can't. It's a matter of won't. And I could have tried to understand your feelings if you hadn't kept them from me. If you hadn't turned me away when all I wanted was to help you. And I won't compromise on everything. I won't be with a man who doesn't respect my feelings and who won't share his problems with me. I won't be with a man who doesn't love me enough to stay. To make a promise to me to grow old with me and to be a father to my child. And I won't spend my life having an affair with you and then having to explain to my daughter why you didn't love and respect me enough to marry me."

She stepped toward the door.

"Don't." He shut his eyes, fought down panic. "Don't turn away from me, Grace."

"I'm not doing the turning away. Don't you see, Ethan? You've been doing the turning away all along."

"I've ended up right back where I started. Looking at you. Needing you. I'm never going to be able to stop now. I made so many promises to myself about you. I keep breaking them. I let her put her hands on this, too," he said slowly. "I let her put her mark on what we have. I want to clear that mark away, if you give me the chance."

He lifted his shoulders. "I've been doing some thinking."

She nearly smiled. "Well, there's news."

"Do you want to hear what I'm thinking now?" Following instinct, listening to his heart, he started up the stairs. "I'm thinking it's always been you, Grace, and only you. It's always going to be you, and only you. I can't help it if I want to take care of you. It doesn't mean I think you're weak. It's only because you're precious to me."

"Ethan." He would make her give in. She knew it. "Don't."

"And I'm thinking I'm not going to be able to give you the chance to live without me after all."

He took her hands, holding them when she tried to tug them free. And keeping his eyes on hers, he drew her out and down the steps to catch the last gilded light of the setting sun.

"I'll never let you down," he told her. "I'll never stop needing you to stand beside me. You make me happy, Grace. I haven't valued that enough, but I will from now on. I love you."

He touched his lips to her brow when she trembled. "The sun's setting. You said that was the best time for daydreams. Maybe it's the best time to pick the dream you want to hold on to. I want to hold on to this one. I need you to look at me," he said softly and lifted her face to his. "Will you marry me?"

Joy and hope blossomed within her. "Ethan—"

"Don't answer yet." But he'd seen the answer, and overcome with gratitude, he brought her hands to his lips. "Will you give Aubrey to me, let me give her my name? Let me be her father?"

Tears began to swim in her eyes. She willed them back. She wanted to see him clearly as he stood watching her with his face so serious, lit by the last quiet light of the day. "You know—"

"Not yet," he murmured and this time touched his lips to hers. "There's one more. Will you have my children, Grace?"

He saw the tears she'd been struggling to hold back spill over and wondered that he could ever have thought to deny them both that joy, that right, that promise.

"Make a life with me, one that comes from love, one that I can watch grow in you. Only a fool would believe that what comes from what we have together would be anything but beautiful."

She framed his face with her hands, took that picture into her heart. "Before I answer, I need to know that this is what you want, not just for me but for yourself."

"I want a family. I want to build what my parents built, and I need to build it with you."

Her lips curved slowly. "I'll marry you, Ethan. I'll give you my daughter. I'll make children with you. And we'll take care of each other."

He drew her close, just to hold, while the sun slipped away and the light shimmered into evening. Her heart beat quick and light against his. Her single quiet sigh echoed seconds before the whip-poorwill began to sing in the plum tree next door.

"I was afraid you weren't going to be able to forgive me."

"So was I."

"Then I figured, hell, she loves me too much. I can get around her." The laugh rumbled out as he nuzzled her throat. "You're not the only one who can reel somebody in like a damn rockfish."

"Took you long enough to bait the hook."

"If you take your time about things, you end up with the best at the end of the day." He buried his face in her hair, wanting the scent and the texture. "Now, I've got the best. Good, solid stone-ware."

Laughing, she leaned back so she could see his eyes. The humor there, she thought, was aimed at both of them. "You're a smart man, Ethan."

"Few hours ago you said I was stupid."

"You were." She pressed a noisy kiss on his cheek. "Now you're smart."

"I missed you, Grace."

She closed her eyes and held tight, thinking it was a day for forgiveness. And hope. And beginnings. "I missed you, Ethan." She sighed, then gave the air a puzzled sniff. "Peanuts," she said and snuggled against him. "That's funny. I could swear I smell peanuts."

"I'll explain it to you." He tilted her head up for one soft kiss. "In a little while."

Keep reading for an excerpt from the third book
in the Chesapeake Bay Saga by Nora Roberts

INNER HARBOR

Now available from Jove Books

P HILLIP loosened the Windsor knot in his Fendi tie. It was a
long commute from Baltimore to Maryland's Eastern Shore,
and he'd programmed his CD player with that in mind. He started
out mellow with a little Tom Petty and the Heartbreakers.

Thursday-evening traffic was as bad as predicted, made worse
by the sluggish rain and the rubberneckers who couldn't resist a
long, fascinated goggle at the three-car accident on the Baltimore
Beltway.

By the time he was heading south on Route 50, even the hot
licks of vintage Stones couldn't completely lift his mood.

He'd brought work with him and somehow had to eke out time
for the Myerstone Tire account over the weekend. They wanted a
whole new look for this advertising campaign. Happy tires make
happy drivers, Phillip thought, drumming his fingers on the wheel
to the rhythm of Keith Richards's outlaw guitar.

Which was a crock, he decided. Nobody was happy driving in rainy rush-hour traffic, no matter what rubber covered their wheels.

But he'd come up with something that would make the consumers think that riding on Myerstones would make them happy, safe, and sexy. It was his job, and he was good at it.

Good enough to juggle four major accounts, supervise the status of six lesser ones, and never appear to break a sweat within the slick corridors of Innovations, the well-heeled advertising firm where he worked. The firm that demanded style, exuberance, and creativity from its executives.

They didn't pay to see him sweat.

Alone, however, was a different matter.

He knew he'd been burning not a candle but a torch at both ends for months. With one hard slap of fate he'd gone from living for Phillip Quinn to wondering what had happened to his cheerfully upwardly mobile urban lifestyle.

His father's death six months before had turned his life upside down. The life that Ray and Stella Quinn had righted seventeen years ago. They'd walked into that dreary hospital room and offered him a chance and a choice. He'd taken the chance because he'd been smart enough to understand that he had no choice.

Going back on the streets wasn't as appealing as it had been before his chest had been ripped open by bullets. Living with his mother was no longer an option, not even if she changed her mind and let him buy his way back into the cramped apartment on Baltimore's Block. Social Services was taking a hard look at the situation, and he knew he'd be dumped into the system the minute he was back on his feet.

He had no intention of going back into the system, or back with his mother, or back to the gutter, for that matter. He'd already decided that. He felt that all he needed was a little time to work out a plan.

At the moment that time was buffered by some very fine drugs that he hadn't had to buy or steal. But he didn't figure that little benefit was going to last forever.

With the Demerol sliding through his system, he gave the Quinns a canny once-over and dismissed them as a couple of weirdo do-gooders. That was fine with him. They wanted to be Samaritans, give him a place to hang out until he was back to a hundred percent, good for them. Good for him.

They told him they had a house on the Eastern Shore, which for an inner-city kid was the other end of the world. But he figured a change of scene couldn't hurt. They had two sons about his age. Phillip decided he wouldn't have to worry about a couple of wimps that the do-gooders had raised.

They told him they had rules, and education was a priority. School didn't bother him any. He breezed his way through when he decided to go.

No drugs. Stella said that in a cool voice that made Phillip re-evaluate her as he put on his most angelic expression and said a polite *No, ma'am.* He had no doubt that when he wanted a hit, he'd be able to find a source, even in some bumfuck town on the Bay.

Then Stella leaned over the bed, her eyes shrewd, her mouth smiling thinly.

You have a face that belongs on a Renaissance painting. But that doesn't make you less of a thief, a hoodlum, and a liar. We'll help you if you want to be helped. But don't treat us like imbeciles.

And Ray laughed his big, booming laugh. He squeezed Stella's shoulder and Phillip's at the same time. It would be, Phillip remembered he'd said, a rare treat to watch the two of them butt heads for the next little while.

They came back several times over the next two weeks. Phillip talked with them and with the social worker, who'd been much easier to con than the Quinns.

In the end they took him home from the hospital, to the pretty white house by the water. He met their sons, assessed the situation. When he learned that the other boys, Cameron and Ethan, had been taken in much as he had been, he was certain they were all lunatics.

He figured on biding his time. For a doctor and a college professor they hadn't collected an abundance of easily stolen or fenced valuables. But he scoped out what there was.

Instead of stealing from them, he fell in love with them. He took their name and spent the next ten years in the house by the water.

Then Stella had died, and part of his world dropped away. She had become the mother he'd never believed existed. Steady, strong, loving, and shrewd. He grieved for her, that first true loss of his life. He buried part of that grief in work, pushing his way through college, toward a goal of success and a sheen of sophistication—and an entry-level position at Innovations.

He didn't intend to remain on the bottom rung for long.

Taking the position at Innovations in Baltimore was a small personal triumph. He was going back to the city of his misery, but he was going back as a man of taste. No one seeing the man in the tailored suit would suspect that he'd once been a petty thief, a sometime drug dealer, and an occasional prostitute.

Everything he'd gained over the last seventeen years could be traced back to that moment when Ray and Stella Quinn had walked into his hospital room.

Then Ray had died suddenly, leaving shadows that had yet to be washed with the light. The man Phillip had loved as completely as a son could love a father had lost his life on a quiet stretch of road in the middle of the day when his car had met a telephone pole at high speed.

There was another hospital room. This time it was the Mighty Quinn lying broken in the bed with machines gasping. Phillip, along with his brothers, had made a promise to watch out for and to keep the last of Ray Quinn's strays, another lost boy.

But this boy had secrets, and he looked at you with Ray's eyes.

The talk around the waterfront and the neighborhoods of the little town of St. Christopher's on Maryland's Eastern Shore hinted of adultery, of suicide, of scandal. In the six months since the whispers had started, Phillip felt that he and his brothers had gotten no closer to finding the truth. Who was Seth DeLauter and what had he been to Raymond Quinn?

Another stray? Another half-grown boy drowning in a vicious sea of neglect and violence who so desperately needed a lifeline? Or was he more? A Quinn by blood as well as by circumstance?

All Phillip could be sure of was that ten-year-old Seth was his brother as much as Cam and Ethan were his brothers. Each of them had been snatched out of a nightmare and given a chance to change their lives.

With Seth, Ray and Stella weren't there to keep that choice open.

There was a part of Phillip, a part that had lived inside a young, careless thief, that resented even the possibility that Seth could be Ray's son by blood, a son conceived in adultery and abandoned in shame. It would be a betrayal of everything the Quinns had taught him, everything they had shown him by living their lives as they had.

He detested himself for considering it, for knowing that now and then he studied Seth with cool, appraising eyes and wondered if the boy's existence was the reason Ray Quinn was dead.

Whenever that nasty thought crept into his mind, Phillip shifted his concentration to Gloria DeLauter. Seth's mother was the woman who had accused Professor Raymond Quinn of sexual harassment. She claimed it had happened years before, while she was a student at the university. But there was no record of her ever attending classes there.

The same woman had sold her ten-year-old son to Ray as if he'd been a package of meat. The same woman, Phillip was certain, that Ray had been to Baltimore to see before he had driven home—and driven himself to his death.

She'd taken off. Women like Gloria were skilled in skipping out of harm's way. Weeks ago, she'd sent the Quinns a not-so-subtle blackmail letter: If you want to keep the kid, I need more. Phillip's jaw clenched when he remembered the naked fear on Seth's face when he'd learned of it.

She wasn't going to get her hands on the boy, he told himself. She was going to discover that the Quinn brothers were a tougher mark than one softhearted old man.

Not just the Quinn brothers now, either, he thought as he turned off onto the rural county road that would lead him home. He thought of family as he drove fast down a road flanked by fields of soybeans, of peas, of corn grown taller than a man. Now that Cam and Ethan were married, Seth had two determined women to stand with him as well.

Married. Phillip shook his head in amused wonder. Who would have thought it? Cam had hitched himself to the sexy social worker, and Ethan was married to sweet-eyed Grace. And had become an instant father, Phillip mused, to angel-faced Aubrey.

Well, good for them. In fact, he had to admit that Anna Spinelli and Grace Monroe were tailor-made for his brothers. It would only add to their strength as a family when it came time for the hearing on permanent guardianship of Seth. And marriage certainly appeared to suit them. Even if the word itself gave him the willies.

For himself, Phillip much preferred the single life and all its benefits. Not that he'd had much time to avail himself of all those benefits in the past few months. Weekends in St. Chris, supervising homework assignments, pounding a hull together for the fledgling Boats by Quinn, dealing with the books for the new business, hauling groceries—all of which had somehow become his domain— cramped a man's style.

He'd promised his father on his deathbed that he would take care of Seth. With his brothers he'd made a pact to move back to the Shore, to share the guardianship and the responsibilities. For Phillip that pact meant splitting his time between Baltimore and St. Chris, and his energies between maintaining his career—and his income—and tending to a new and often problematic brother and a new business.

It was all a risk. Raising a ten-year-old wasn't without headaches and fumbling mistakes under the best of circumstances, he imagined. Seth DeLauter, raised by a part-time hooker, full-time junkie, and amateur extortionist, had hardly come through the best of circumstances.

Getting a boatbuilding enterprise off the ground was a series of irksome details and backbreaking labor. Yet somehow it was working, and if he discounted the ridiculous demands on his time and energy, it was working fairly well.

Not so long ago his weekends had been spent in the company of any number of attractive, interesting women, having dinner at some new hot spot, an evening at the theater or a concert, and if the chemistry was right, a quiet Sunday brunch in bed.

He'd get back to that, Phillip promised himself. Once all the details were in place, he would have his life back again. But, as his father would have said, for the next little while . . .

He turned into the drive. The rain had stopped, leaving a light sheen of wet on the leaves and grass. Twilight was creeping in. He could see the light in the living room window glowing in a soft and steady welcome. Some of the summer flowers that Anna had babied along were hanging on, and early fall blooms shimmered in the shadows. He could hear the puppy barking, though at nine months Foolish had grown too big and sleek to be considered a puppy anymore.

It was Anna's night to cook, he remembered. Thank God. It meant a real meal would be served at the Quinns'. He rolled his shoulders, thought about pouring himself a glass of wine, then watched Foolish dash around the side of the house in pursuit of a mangy yellow tennis ball.

The sight of Phillip getting out of his car obviously distracted the dog from the game. He skidded to a halt and set up a din of wild, terrified barking.

"Idiot." But he grinned as he pulled his briefcase out of the Jeep.

At the familiar voice, the barking turned into mad joy. Foolish bounded up with a delighted look in his eyes and wet, muddy paws. "No jumping!" Phillip yelled, using his briefcase like a shield. "I mean it. Sit!"

Foolish quivered, but dropped his rump on the ground and lifted a paw. His tongue lolled, his eyes gleamed. "That's a good dog." Gingerly Phillip shook the filthy paw and scratched the dog's silky ears.

"Hey." Seth wandered into the front yard. His jeans were grubby from wrestling with the dog, his baseball cap was askew so that straw-straight blond hair spiked out of it. The smile, Phillip noted, came much more quickly and easily than it had a few months before. But there was a gap in it.

"Hey." Phillip butted a finger on the bill of the cap. "Lose something?"

"Huh?"

Phillip tapped a finger against his own straight, white teeth.

"Oh, yeah." With a typical Quinn shrug, Seth grinned, pushing his tongue into the gap. His face was fuller than it had been six months before, and his eyes less wary. "It was loose. Had to give it a yank a couple of days ago. Bled like a son of a bitch."

Phillip didn't bother to sigh over Seth's language. Some things, he determined, weren't going to be his problem. "So, did the Tooth Fairy bring you anything?"

"Get real."

"Hey, if you didn't squeeze a buck out of Cam, you're no brother of mine."

"I got two bucks out of it. One from Cam and one from Ethan."

Laughing, Phillip swung an arm over Seth's shoulders and headed toward the house. "Well, you're not getting one out of me, pal. I'm on to you. How was the first full week of school?"

"Boring." Though it hadn't been, Seth admitted silently. It had been exciting. All the new junk Anna had taken him shopping for. Sharp pencils, blank notebooks, pens full of ink. He'd refused the *X-Files* lunch box she'd wanted to get him. Only a dork carried a lunch box in middle school. But it had been really cool and tough to sneer at.

He had cool clothes and bitching sneakers. And best of all, for the first time in his life, he was in the same place, the same school, with the same people he'd left behind in June.

"Homework?" Phillip asked, raising his eyebrows as he opened the front door.

Seth rolled his eyes. "Man, don't you ever think about anything else?"

"Kid, I live for homework. Especially when it's yours." Foolish burst through the door ahead of Phillip, nearly knocking him down with enthusiasm. "You've still got some work to do on that dog." But the mild annoyance faded instantly. He could smell Anna's red sauce simmering, like ambrosia on the air. "God bless us, every one," he murmured.

"Manicotti," Seth informed him.

"Yeah? I've got a Chianti I've been saving just for this moment." He tossed his briefcase aside. "We'll hit the books after dinner."

He found his sister-in-law in the kitchen, filling pasta tubes with cheese. The sleeves of the crisp white shirt she'd worn to the office were rolled up, and a white butcher's apron covered her navy skirt. She'd taken off her heels and tapped a bare foot to the beat of the aria she was humming. *Carmen*, Phillip recognized. Her wonderful mass of curling black hair was still pinned up.

With a wink at Seth, Phillip came up behind her, caught her around the waist, and pressed a noisy kiss onto the top of her head. "Run away with me. We'll change our names. You can be Sophia and I'll be Carlo. Let me take you to paradise where you can cook for me and me alone. None of these peasants appreciate you like I do."

"Let me just finish this tube, Carlo, and I'll go pack." She turned her head, her dark Italian eyes laughing. "Dinner in thirty minutes."

"I'll open the wine."

"Don't we have anything to eat now?" Seth wanted to know.

"There's antipasto in the fridge," she told him. "Go ahead and get it out."

"It's just vegetables and junk," Seth complained when he pulled out the platter.

"Yep."

"Jeez."

"Wash the dog off your hands before you start on that."

"Dog spit's cleaner than people spit," Seth informed her. "I read how if you get bit by another guy it's worse than getting bit by a dog."

"I'm thrilled to have that fascinating tidbit of information. Wash the dog spit off your hands anyway."

"Man." Disgusted, Seth clomped out, with Foolish slinking after him.

Phillip chose the wine from the small supply he kept in the pantry. Fine wines were one of his passions, and his palate was extremely discriminating. His apartment in Baltimore boasted an extensive and carefully chosen selection, which he kept in a closet he'd remodeled specifically for that purpose.

At the Shore, his beloved bottles of Bordeaux and Burgundy kept company with Rice Krispies and boxes of Jell-O Instant Pudding.

He'd learned to live with it.

"So how was your week?" he asked Anna.

"Busy. Whoever said women can have everything should be shot. Handling a career and a family is grueling." Then she looked up with a brilliant smile. "I'm loving it."

"It shows." He drew the cork expertly, sniffed it and approved, then set the bottle on the counter to breathe. "Where's Cam?"

"Should be on his way home from the boatyard. He and Ethan wanted to put in an extra hour. The first boat by Quinn is finished. The owner's coming in tomorrow. It's finished, Phillip." Her smile flashed, brilliant and glowing with pride. "At dock, seaworthy and just gorgeous."

He felt a little tug of disappointment that he hadn't been in on the last day. "We should be having champagne."

Anna lifted a brow as she studied the label on the wine. "A bottle of Folonari, Ruffino?"

He considered one of Anna's finest traits to be her appreciation for good wine. "Seventy-five," he said with a broad grin.

"You won't hear any complaints from me. Congratulations, Mr. Quinn, on your first boat."

"It's not my deal. I just handle the details and pass for slave labor."

"Of course it's your deal. Details are necessary, and neither Cam nor Ethan could handle them with the finesse you do."

"I think the word they use, is 'nagging.' "

"They need to be nagged. You should be proud of what the three of you have accomplished in the last few months. Not just the new business, but the family. Each one of you has given up something that's important to you for Seth. And each one of you has gotten something important back."

"I never expected the kid to matter so much." While Anna smothered the filled tubes with sauce, Phillip opened a cupboard for wineglasses. "I still have moments when the whole thing pisses me off."

"That's only natural, Phillip."

"Doesn't make me feel any better about it." He shrugged his shoulders in dismissal, then poured two glasses. "But most of the time, I look at him and think he's a pretty good deal for a kid brother."

Anna grated cheese over the casserole. Out of the corner of her eye she watched Phillip lift his glass, appreciate the bouquet. He was beautiful to look at, she mused. Physically, he was as close to male perfection as she could imagine. Bronze hair, thick and full, eyes more gold than brown. His face was long, narrow, thoughtful. Both sensual and angelic. His tall, trim build seemed to have been fashioned for Italian suits. But since she'd seen him stripped to the waist in faded Levi's she knew there was nothing soft about him.

Sophisticated, tough, erudite, shrewd. An interesting man, she mused.

She slipped the casserole into the oven, then turned to pick up her wine. Smiling at him, she tapped her glass on his. "You're a pretty good deal too, Phillip, for a big brother."

She leaned in to kiss him lightly as Cam walked in.

"Get your mouth off my wife."

Phillip merely smiled and slid an arm around Anna's waist. "She put hers on me. She likes me."

"She likes me better." To prove it, Cam hooked a hand in the tie of Anna's apron, spun her around, and pulled her into his arms to kiss her brainless. He grinned, nipped her bottom lip and patted her butt companionably. "Don'cha, sugar?"

Her head was still spinning. "Probably." She blew out a breath. "All things considered." But she wiggled free. "You're filthy."

"Just came in to grab a beer to take into the shower." Long and lean, dark and dangerous, he prowled over to the fridge. "And kiss my wife," he added with a smug look at Phillip. "Go get your own woman."

"Who has time?" Phillip said mournfully.

⬙⬙⬙

AFTER DINNER, AND an hour spent slaving over long division, battles of the Revolutionary War, and sixth-grade vocabulary, Phillip settled down in his room with his laptop and his files.

It was the same room he'd been given when Ray and Stella Quinn had brought him home. The walls had been a pale green then. Sometime during his sixteenth year he'd gotten a wild hair and painted them magenta. God knew why. He remembered that his mother—for Stella had become his mother by then—had taken one look and warned him he'd have terminal indigestion.

He thought it was sexy. For about three months. Then he'd gone with a stark white for a while, accented with moody black-framed, black-and-white photographs.

Always looking for ambience, Phillip thought now, amused at himself. He'd circled back to that soft green right before he moved to Baltimore.

They'd been right all along, he supposed. His parents had usually been right.

They'd given him this room, in this house, in this place. He hadn't made it easy for them. The first three months were a battle of wills. He smuggled in drugs, picked fights, stole liquor, and stumbled in drunk at dawn.

It was clear to him now that he'd been testing them, daring them to kick him out. Toss him back. Go ahead, he'd thought. You can't handle me.

But they did. They had not only handled him, they had made him.

I wonder, Phillip, his father had said, *why you want to waste a good mind and a good body. Why you want to let the bastards win.*

Phillip, who was suffering from the raw gut and bursting head of a drug and alcohol hangover, didn't give a good damn.

Ray took him out on the boat, telling him that a good sail would clear his head. Sick as a dog, Phillip leaned over the rail, throwing up the remnants of the poisons he'd pumped into his system the night before.

He'd just turned fourteen.

Ray anchored the boat in a narrow gut. He held Phillip's head, wiped his face, then offered him a cold can of ginger ale.

"Sit down."

He didn't so much sit as collapse. His hands shook, his stomach shuddered at the first sip from the can. Ray sat across from him, his big hands on his knees, his silvering hair flowing in the light breeze. And those eyes, those brilliant blue eyes, level and considering.

"You've had a couple of months now to get your bearings around here. Stella says you've come around physically. You're strong, and healthy enough—though you aren't going to stay that way if you keep this up."

He pursed his lips, said nothing for a long moment. There was a heron in the tall grass, still as a painting. The air was bright and chill with late fall, the trees bare of leaves so that the hard blue sky spread overhead. Wind ruffled the grass and skimmed fingers over the water.

The man sat, apparently content with the silence and the scene. The boy slouched, pale of face and hard of eye.

"We can play this a lot of ways, Phil," Ray said at length. "We can be hard-asses. We can put you on a short leash, watch you every minute and bust your balls every time you screw up. Which is most of the time."

Considering, Ray picked up a fishing rod, absently baited it with a marshmallow. "Or we could all just say that this little experiment's a bust and you can go back into the system."

Phillip's stomach churned, making him swallow to hold down what he didn't quite recognize as fear. "I don't need you. I don't need anybody."

"Yeah, you do." Ray said it mildly as he dropped the line into the water. Ripples spread, endlessly. "You go back into the system, you'll stay there. Couple of years down the road, it won't be juvie anymore. You'll end up in a cell with the bad guys, the kind of guys who are going to take a real liking to that pretty face of yours. Some seven-foot con with hands like smoked hams is going to grab you in the showers one fine day and make you his bride."

Phillip yearned desperately for a cigarette. The image conjured by Ray's words made fresh sweat pop out on his forehead. "I can take care of myself."

"Son, they'll pass you around like canapés, and you know it. You talk a good game and you fight a good fight, but some things are inevitable. Up to this point your life has pretty much sucked. You're not responsible for that. But you are responsible for what happens from here on."

He fell into silence again, clamping the pole between his knees before reaching for a cold can of Pepsi. Taking his time, Ray popped the top, tipped the can back, and guzzled.

"Stella and I thought we saw something in you," he continued. "We still do," he added, looking at Phillip again. "But until you do, we're not going to get anywhere."

"What do you care?" Phillip tossed back miserably.

"Hard to say at the moment. Maybe you're not worth it. Maybe you'll just end up back on the streets hustling marks and turning tricks anyway."

For three months he'd had a decent bed, regular meals, and all the books he could read—one of his secret loves—at his disposal. At the thought of losing it his throat filled again, but he only shrugged. "I'll get by."

"If all you want to do is get by, that's your choice. Here you can have a home, a family. You can have a life and make something out of it. Or you can go on the way you are."

Ray reached over to Phillip quickly, and the boy braced himself for the blow, clenched his fists to return it. But Ray only pulled Phillip's shirt up to expose the livid scars on his chest. "You can go back to that," he said quietly.

Phillip looked into Ray's eyes. He saw compassion and hope. And he saw himself mirrored back, bleeding in a dirty gutter on a street where life was worth less than a dime bag.

Sick, tired, terrified, Phillip dropped his head into his hands. "What's the point?"

"You're the point, son." Ray ran his hand over Phillip's hair. "You're the point."

Things hadn't changed overnight, Phillip thought now. But they had begun to change. His parents had made him believe in himself, despite himself. It had become a point of pride for him to do well in school, to learn, to remake himself into Phillip Quinn.

He figured he'd done a good job of it. He'd coated that street kid with a sheen of class. He had a slick career, a well-appointed condo with a killer view of the Inner Harbor, and a wardrobe that suited both.

It seemed that he'd come full circle, spending his weekends back in this room with its green walls and sturdy furniture, with its windows that overlooked the trees and the marsh.

But this time, Seth was the point.